Also by Arunava Sinha in Aleph

The Greatest Bengali Stories Ever Told
Tagore for the 21st Century Reader

THE MOVING SHADOW

ELECTRIFYING BENGALI PULP FICTION

Selected & Translated by

ARUNAVA SINHA

ALEPH

ALEPH

ALEPH BOOK COMPANY
An independent publishing firm
promoted by *Rupa Publications India*

First published in India in 2018
by Aleph Book Company
7/16 Ansari Road, Daryaganj
New Delhi 110 002

ISBN: 978-93-87561-43-4

1 3 5 7 9 10 8 6 4 2

Contents

Arunava Sinha translates classic, modern and contemporary Bengali fiction and non-fiction into English. Over forty of his translations have been published so far. He has selected and translated the bestselling *The Greatest Bengali Stories Ever Told*. He has won the Crossword Translation Award for Sankar's *Chowringhee* (2007) and Anita Agnihotri's *Seventeen* (2001). He has also won the Muse India Award for his translation of *When the Time is Right* (2012). His translation of *Chowringhee* was shortlisted for *The Independent* Foreign Fiction Prize (2009). His translations have also been published in the UK, US, Europe and Asia through further translation.

He grew up in Kolkata and lives in New Delhi.

Introduction

'Ding-dong ding-dong! The clock struck one.'

And with these two lines begins the pulp fantasy of the dutiful Bengali reader brought up on a diet of Rabindranath Tagore and Bibhutibhushan Bandyopadhyay (or of Manik Bandyopadhyay and Mahasweta Devi in the case of the revolutionary). Pulp fiction is the guilty secret of Bengali literature, for both readers and writers. And considering that it effectively predates Tagore and Bankim Chandra Chattopadhyay—in the form of salacious accounts in energetic prose of the lives of sex workers and their clients, among others—it is fitting and proper that Bengali literature should have had a long and virtually uninterrupted lineage of books depicting the, shall we say, seamier side of life.

As with the impossibility of a clock striking one with four bells, there is a large dose of epic impossibility in the storylines of this form. All the gritty naturalism, poverty-powered anguish, socialist idealism, existentialist dilemmas and even postmodern anti-narratives of over a century of fine Bengali fiction are crushed by the desperate, delicious and dubious stories featuring spies, detectives, criminals, ghosts, black magic practitioners and, of course, femme fatales. Every clichéd character lives, loves and loathes in exaggerated measure, but oh, how impossible it is to put down these extraordinary tales, ranging from the murderous to the macabre.

What began as malicious anthropology—a patriarchal, but admittedly wickedly witty, detailing of lives lived in debauchery—soon turned into the Bengali equivalent of the penny dreadful, sensational stories published at low cost for the secret sensual satisfaction of the literate in a repressed society where only the rich had the luxury of licentiousness. A prime example of this was *Haridaser Guptokatha* (*Haridas's Scandals*) by Bhubanchandra Mukhopadhyay, published serially from 1870 to 1873 as a precursor to what went on to become a genre: household scandals. (Just to put those dates in perspective, Bankim Chandra Chattopadhyay's *Durgeshnandini* or *The Castellan's Daughter*, arguably the first 'novel' in the Western sense written in an Indian language, was published in 1865.) It was also one of the first of what has been known for a long time as 'Bottolar Boi'—literally referring to books sold beneath the 'bot' or banyan tree. Admittedly, not all of these books were scandalous accounts, for they also attempted to paint pictures of society, often in colours of morality, the lack of which was decried (some things never change).

Here are some examples of the titles published in this genre in the nineteenth century, all of them—with numerous other such works— republished recently with scholarly notes in two volumes commemorating the colourful form of cheap publishing: *Narcotics are Painful, Earthquake in Benaras!, How are Women So Arrogant?, The Agony of a Wife Who Stings, Secret Affairs are Humiliating, Whores, Clowns, Lies: What Calcutta is Made Of.*

However, as orthodox urban middle-class morals caught up with people, the literature lost its bodice-ripping quality and moved towards sensational crime, with former police inspector Priyanath Mukhopadhyay leading the charge, delving into his case files to create his true crime stories. At the same time, detective fiction from the Victorian era, most notably Arthur Conan Doyle's Sherlock Holmes stories, found readers in Calcutta, and some of them turned into writers. The outcome of this, around and soon after the turn of the nineteenth century into the twentieth, were stories with titles such as: *The Two Inspectors, Murder by Kisses, Murder or Unmurder, Terrible Vengeance, The Severed Arm* etc.

These works also set off what turned into a parallel movement of fiction writing that was just as free-flowing as the more 'literary' stream. It began as early as in 1932, with the publication of Mrityunjoy Chattopadhyay's weekly *Romancho (Thrills)*, featuring the first part of a story titled 'The Incident in the Yangtse Hotel', written by Pranab Roy. With this began a succession of pulp magazines that went on publishing till the 1980s, with contributors forming a distinct community of their own. Inspired greatly by American pulp, these stories then spawned novels as well, weaving improbable webs of espionage, deceit, crime and stunts on the one hand, and branching off into horror and some forms of science fiction on the other.

Not that there were no crossover writers, with the erudite and often incomprehensible Kamal Kumar Majumdar, a true literary writer if there was one, starting the short-lived *Detective Weekly* in 1952. It lasted only three issues. What Majumdar did, however, was to show that blood, gore and spirits were far from being off the menu for Bengal's literary writers.

So, antithesis though it was to the thesis of bhodrolok literature, pulp fiction soon went on to be adopted by mainstream Bengali writers over the years to forge a Hegelian synthesis. In any case, most Bengali novelists considered themselves all-rounders, and everyone from Rabindranath Tagore to Buddhadeva Bose, from Premendra Mitra to Satyajit Ray, from Shirshendu Mukhopadhyay to Sunil Gangopadhyay, from Humayun Ahmed to Muhammed Zafar Iqbal, tried their hand—often successfully— at a more genteel version of pulp fiction in the form of detective, horror and supernatural, and science-fiction stories and novels. This is not to be confused with the literary depiction of sexual desire, fantasies and conflicts that has informed much of Bengali literature, more implicitly than explicitly. These works were more in the genre of noir as a literary form, an excuse to tell a riveting story without being bound by the plausible, attempts to capture the underbelly or urban life without actually having much first-hand experience of it.

Not surprisingly, given the literary strain of Bengal, many of these stories are not only plotted intricately—if improbably at times—but they also create a grainy milieu of light and darkness. Whether it moves closer to or further from the real world in the process is beside the point. The fact is that this stream of imaginative fiction from Bengal—and imaginative is the operative word here—was widely written and consumed, becoming something of a cult amongst aficionados, and a substitute for the real thing for readers ranging from hormonal students to thwarted middle-aged men, from homemakers to unemployed frequenters of addas—Bengalis of virtually every stripe, in other words.

The writing, publishing and consumption of Bengali noir continued to thrive until television, multiplex cinema and, eventually, the Internet took over the entire experience. The world of make-believe no longer needed the participation of the reader's imagination. This book is an invitation to return to—or have a first taste of—that world of words that could create 'romancho' sharp enough to thrill, or, sometimes, to just pander to your wish for things that will never take place in your life or in mine. Pro tip: switch off all the lights except one when you read this. For reasons you will (soon) find out.

Arunava Sinha
Indira Gandhi International Airport, New Delhi,
and St James's Park, London,
June 2018

Crime Stories

Parashar Barma Makes a Bid

PREMENDRA MITRA

1

'Ten rupees!'

'Twelve rupees!'

'Fifteen rupees!'

'Twenty-five rupees!'

Suddenly, startling everyone: 'Fifty rupees!'

'Fifty rupees going once, fifty rupees going twice…'

'Seventy-five rupees.'

No need to explain that these were bids at an auction.

I had no inkling when I left home that day that I'd find myself in that particular world.

But I should have known, because when Parashar Barma is your companion you must be prepared for odd, unexpected incidents.

Parashar came to my house in the morning. He left the taxi waiting in the street.

'Come along, come along, we have to go to Park Street.'

'Park Street! Why Park Street?' I asked in surprise. 'And that too, at the crack of dawn. If it were afternoon or evening, I'd have assumed you wanted to sample the food there. Park Street has turned into a heaven for gourmets. But who eats lunch or dinner at this hour?'

'Let me inform you that Park Street holds a great many more attractions. Can I bother you to get dressed?'

There was no escaping Parashar. I had no choice but to accompany him. All I had found out on the way was that he wanted to buy a refrigerator. He had yet to decide on the brand or model. The trip to Park Street was to survey the options.

'But why do you need me to buy a fridge?' I couldn't help but protest. 'It's not as though I know anything about them.'

'You don't need to,' Parashar interrupted me, 'All you have to do is keep me on a leash.'

'Keep you on a leash!' I was bewildered. 'You're going to buy a fridge, what do you mean keep you on a leash? And why, for that matter?'

'So that I don't buy the first thing I see,' Parashar interrupted me. 'That's my tragic flaw, you see. I cannot control myself when it comes to purchasing things. I might blindly buy the first fridge I see. That's why you're coming along. Tug my sleeve if you see me about to buy in haste so I stop and look at other models.'

I doubt if anyone has ever been saddled with such a peculiar responsibility. But why was Parashar suddenly keen on buying a fridge? I wanted to tease him by asking if he was planning to freeze his poetry. However, it was dangerous to bring up poetry with Parashar. So I decided not to.

But what sort of fridge-buying expedition was this!

As soon as we entered Park Street, Parashar instructed the driver to turn into a side road.

'Where are we going?' I objected. 'All the big shops and showrooms are on Park Street.'

'Actually,' Parashar justified himself, 'I suddenly remembered all the auction marts on this road. They sell all kinds of things. Sometimes you get good bargains. Why not take a look?'

The taxi stopped in front of an auction mart.

Parashar paid the fare. As we entered the shop, Parashar asked, 'Have you ever been to these places?'

It wasn't as though I had never visited an auction house. But they weren't the kind of places I'd visit out of choice. I found the atmosphere intolerable. But I didn't tell Parashar any of this. Instead, I said, 'It's true you can get bargains, but you can also be cheated into buying worthless stuff. And how do you know they have a fridge on auction anyway?'

'Let's take a look around the place, we'll found out soon enough.' Parashar began inspecting the wares.

I couldn't for the life of me tell what there was to inspect.

The usual things were put up for auction. Cupboards and desks, sofas and couches here, china and crystal there, typewriters, radios, gramophones and cycles against the wall—all the things one would expect to find.

There was certainly no refrigerator anywhere. Nor did I spot anything

I wanted to take home.

I was about to tell Parashar as much and lead him out when I found to my surprise he was nowhere around.

⌒

The auction was about to begin. There was quite a crowd already. I pushed my way through the crowd from one end of the room to the other looking for Parashar.

Finally I found him in a corner. He seemed to be mesmerized by some junk arranged on a small table. I had to nudge him to shake him out of his reverie. I smiled at him and asked, 'I thought you wanted to buy a fridge, but you seem to be stuck. What's so exciting?'

'Have you seen that small bowl there?' Parashar looked as though he was still under a spell.

I'd noticed the bowl. It was made of metal, inlaid with silver in the Bidri style. Flamboyant but old-fashioned. Nothing to write home about. I told Parashar as much. 'Doesn't look particularly unique to me. You get far better samples of Bidriware everywhere these days.'

Parashar didn't reply.

The bidding had begun. Everyone was gathered around the auctioneer. Parashar joined the crowd, so I had no choice but to follow.

I had never been in doubt that Parashar was eccentric. I was even more certain now. He placed one or two bids for everything that was being placed on the auction block.

A broken three-legged table. The auctioneer sang its praises and set the floor, 'Two rupees.'

Parashar was the first to bid. 'Three rupees.'

Three rupees!

'Three rupees—going once! Three rupees—going twice!' The auctioneer announced loudly.

'Four rupees!' Fortunately someone else made a higher bid from the other side of the room, whereupon I breathed a sigh of relief. Or else, Parashar would have been saddled with the broken table.

But it wasn't just that table. Parashar seemed to have his eyes on everything that was up for bidding.

A worthless old tennis racket, a stained china teaset, a set of Jaipuri flower vases—Parashar didn't let any of them go by without a bid.

But when it came to the fancy Bidri bowl, Parashar went berserk.

The auctioneer had begun at ten rupees.

'Twelve rupees,' said Parashar.

'Fifteen,' someone upped the bid.

'Twenty-five,' responded Parashar.

'Fifty!' The other bidder startled us.

The pleased auctioneer had begun striking the gavel. 'Fifty rupees! A bowl with the famous Bidri design. Exquisite patterns. Made by a master craftsman of yore! Only fifty rupees!'

I couldn't help but observe the man who had bid fifty. Judging from his clothes at least, he was not exactly a member of the leisured class interested in the arts. He looked quite the plebeian. The trousers and shirt had probably been purchased at the Dharmatallah Market. They didn't even look clean. The man himself appeared skinny and down on his luck. It was doubtful whether he had ever left home with fifty rupees in his pocket. It was equally hard to believe that he was willing to go bankrupt for a bowl.

✓

The auctioneer was shouting, 'Fifty rupees—going once! Fifty rupees—going once!'

'Seventy-five rupees!'

Parashar had moved directly to seventy-five.

I had no choice now but to push through the crowd and tug at his sleeve. Parashar had told me to adopt this technique to restrain him if he lost his head. I hadn't imagined I'd have to use it in the auction house. He didn't seem to realize that you could get three Bidri bowls, like the one he was bidding for, for seventy-five rupees.

But whom was I trying to restrain! Parashar was oblivious to his surroundings. He didn't pay the slightest attention to me. He probably wouldn't have noticed if I'd torn the shirt off his back, never mind tugging at his sleeve.

The auctioneer too was flabbergasted.

He was announcing in bewilderment, 'Seventy-five, seventy-five! This Bidri design bowl for seventy-five rupees going once...'

He didn't have to go as far as going twice. 'Hundred!' croaked Parashar's opponent.

The auctioneer opened his mouth to speak, but before that Parashar announced, 'Two hundred!'

His adversary was truly defeated now. Such absurd drama can't have been a common sight at auction houses. A crowd had gathered around us. Everyone was staring at Parashar and his competitor.

The opponent looked around helplessly. He wanted to say something but all he could do was gulp.

The auctioneer was closing the bid. 'Bidri bowl two hundred—going once! Two hundred going twice! Two hundred—sold!'

He brought his gavel down on the table.

Everyone else had forgotten about the auction. They could only gape at Parashar.

But Parashar was unmoved. He had already taken two hundred-rupee notes out of his pocket. 'Should I make the payment to you?' he asked the auctioneer.

'No.' The auctioneer looked at him respectfully. 'You can deposit the payment at the counter over there and collect your bowl.'

⌣

Parashar had to submit his name and address along with the payment. I had expected him to give fictitious details, but he wrote down his name and address.

You should have seen the pride on his face as he emerged from the auction hall with his bowl wrapped in a newspaper. He looked quite pleased with himself, as though he had got the Crown Jewels at a discount.

I was mad with anger. Outside the shop I said, 'Do you know why they asked for your name and address?'

'Must be the rule,' Parashar answered naively.

'No, it's not,' I taunted him. 'They don't see such idiots every day, so they kept a record.'

'I see.' Parashar did not seem to mind that I had insulted him.

'Are you still interested in buying a fridge?' I asked him.

'Fridge!' Parashar seemed astounded. When he remembered why we had set out on an expedition this morning, he seemed embarrassed. 'Oh yes, I do have to buy a fridge. But you know what, I've already spent a lot a money so let's not buy the fridge now.'

'When you do plan to buy your fridge,' I warned him, 'please don't ask me to come along with you.'

'Of course not, how can I trouble you again?' Parashar tried to mollify me.

I had mentioned that the auction house had asked Parashar for his name and address because he was an idiot. But I hadn't imagined the outcome.

The next afternoon, Parashar turned up at the newspaper office where I worked.

I am always on my guard when Parashar comes to my office. I'm constantly worried that he will produce a sheaf of poetry from his pocket. I cannot wriggle out by refusing to print the poems—I have to listen to them regardless.

Today, however, it wasn't a manuscript but a letter that Parashar produced. It had arrived by the morning post.

He handed me the letter saying, 'You threw such a fit over my buying that bowl yesterday. Now read this.'

I took the letter from him and asked him teasingly, 'Do I really need to read it? I can tell who it's from.'

'What can you tell?' Parashar sound a little surprised.

'It must be the auction house trying to fob off some more of their useless things on you.'

'Just read the letter.' Parashar sounded impatient now.

So I had to read it. I was genuinely surprised when I did. Someone, not a Bengali, had written to Parashar that he was ready to pay up to three hundred rupees for the bowl he had purchased at the auction yesterday, if Parashar would be so kind as to sell it. The writer had not given his address, but only included a phone number. He had requested Parashar to ring him at this number between two and three in the afternoon if he was willing to sell the bowl.

'This is so strange,' I couldn't help saying. 'The bowl is made of ordinary metal with inlaid designs in silver. Simple Bidriware. Not gold or platinum, just an alloy and silver. Why is it so precious? It was very strange that the man bidding against you yesterday bid so high. And now someone wants to pay twice the amount to buy it off you.'

'That's exactly what I'm saying.' Glancing at the clock on the wall, an elated Parashar said, 'It's past two. Shall we ring him?'

'Go ahead.' I agreed.

Someone seemed to have been waiting for the phone call. He answered at once.

I pieced the conversation together from Parashar's responses.

'Yes, this is Parashar Barma.'

'No, I didn't buy it to make a profit. Even if you offer four hundred instead of three. I'm not interested.'

'I see, five hundred. And an identical bowl as well. Very well, I'll think about it. Tell me your address.'

'No, don't send anyone tonight, with or without the payment. Tomorrow morning at ten would be better. Can you ring me before coming? My number is…'

Parashar put the phone down after giving his number.

He looked at me triumphantly and said, 'What do you think?'

'Just that it's got to be a cock and bull story,' I replied. 'It might be a good idea to have the bowl evaluated in a laboratory. It's possible to hide anything between those thin silver plates, but maybe the material isn't what we think it is.'

'You think I haven't done that already?' Parashar smiled. 'The chemical tests didn't reveal anything but the usual alloy used by Bidri artisans.'

'What is it then?' I looked at Parashar with some concern. Reminding him of chemical analysis was a mistake; I'd forgotten that he's an amateur scientist himself.

What he asked next surprised me. 'Do you know anyone who knows Arabic and Persian?'

'Someone who knows Arabic and Persian?' I asked in bewilderment. 'What do you need someone like that for? Are you planning to use Arabic and Parsi forms in Bengali poetry? Mohitlal and Nazrul have already…'

Parashar practically shouted at me, 'I'm not asking you for a history of poetry. Just tell me whether you know someone or not.'

I remembered my friend Sobhan. We went to school together and I remembered he had studied Arabic and Persian. He had even translated some poetry from those languages and had them published in newspapers. So I mentioned him to Parashar.

Parashar left immediately, but not before expressing the wish that I should bring Sobhan to his home at nine the next morning.

2

Parashar's request was equivalent to an order. I managed to track Sobhan down and we went to Parashar's house at eight in the morning.

Sobhan had come along reluctantly. He belonged to the world of academia and didn't pay any attention to anything outside it. He hadn't even heard of Parashar Barma; nor had I succeeded in explaining why I was taking him to Parashar's house. How could I, when I myself didn't know? There was no doubt that Sobhan had agreed to spare the time because I was his friend.

Even after we arrived, it wasn't clear why Parashar had summoned Sobhan. Not that he wasn't gracious—after all, he did keep track of Urdu, Persian and Arabic poetry. For about half an hour that's what they talked about over breakfast and endless cups of tea.

But surely he hadn't wanted to meet someone who knew Arabic and Persian just to have this conversation? It soon became evident that Parashar had something else in mind. After breakfast, he set the bowl from the auction on the table in front of Sobhan.

'What do you make of this bowl, Sobhan saab?' Parashar asked with great enthusiasm.

Sobhan seemed to be taken with the bowl. Expressing his appreciation, he said, 'This is exquisite! Bidriware, I notice. Very high quality traditional craftsmanship. You don't see such fine finishing these days.'

'Yes, the commercial aspect has taken over now,' Parashar agreed. 'Wealthy connoisseurs in Europe and America have turned their attention to these things. The craftsmen just concentrate on pleasing them.'

Just as I was beginning to think that the discussion wouldn't go beyond art, Parashar asked, 'Do you think there's anything written in these minute silver designs?'

Sobhan had probably been trying to check just that even before Parashar had asked. He held the bowl close to his eyes and examined it with rapt attention.

'Do you have a magnifying glass?' he asked excitedly.

'No, not a magnifying glass,' Parashar seemed prepared for the question, 'but I do have this.' Pulling a loupe out of his pocket, the kind used by watch-repairers and jewellers, he said, 'Will this do?'

'It will do very well.' Sobhan fixed the loupe in one eye, closed the other, and carefully examined the patterns on the bowl.

We looked at him anxiously.

But the initial excitement that lit his face dimmed a bit.

Sobhan removed the loupe and set the bowl on the table. Glumly, he said, 'I don't see anything.'

'Nothing?' Parashar seemed rather disappointed. 'No hidden letters or words in those loops and curls?'

'It looks like a script all right,' Sobhan told him gravely, 'but it isn't Urdu or Persian or Arabic or anything like that. There's a superficial similarity, but that's about all…'

'I troubled you for nothing, then,' Parashar said in embarrassment. 'It looked like Arabic to me. That's why I requested your help. Please do not mind.'

'Of course not, why should I mind?' Sobhan said in all sincerity. 'I'm fortunate that I got the chance to meet you.'

᠎

There was no point asking Sobhan to stay any longer. I helped him find a taxi and returned to discover Parashar examining the bowl closely through the loupe.

'Did you think this person who's desperate for the bowl thinks that the bowl has some secret inscription?' I asked with a smile and sat next to him.

Parashar removed the loupe and admitted reluctantly, 'Yes, I did. There has to be a reason for setting such a high price on an ordinary bowl.'

'But Sobhan himself told you there's no inscription. You could, of course, consult an expert.' I tried to lift Parashar out of his gloomy mood.

'No need,' said Parashar, admitting defeat. 'It had seemed to me that the inscription was Arabic, in which case your friend Sobhan would have immediately identified it. So I guess the solution to the mystery lies elsewhere.'

᠎

The solution was revealed about five minutes later.

Whoever it was did not bother to ring the bell. He banged on the door and in a slurred voice called out, 'Mr Verma? Is there a bastard named Verma living here?'

Parashar had rigged up some smart devices that automatically opened his front door. But he didn't use them all the time. He had once surprised me with a demonstration soon after we met.

Instead of using any of the devices today, he rang the bell for his servant and asked him to open the door and lead the stranger into the drawing room.

'Must be your telephone client,' I said. 'He must have become impatient and arrived early. It's nowhere near ten.'

We were more than a little surprised by the appearance of the man Parashar's servant ushered in. He was frightfully young, and not only well-dressed but also someone who could be said to be handsome, had it not been for the signs of a dissolute life evident on his appearance despite his youth.

It was obvious from his gait and his talk that he was drunk even at this early hour.

He tottered to the middle of the room and looked at Parashar and me in turn before asking in English, 'May I know which of you is Parashar Verma?'

Suddenly, Parashar pointed at me. 'This is Parashar Barma.'

'I see, it's you. Allow me to introduce myself in that case. I am Jaysukh Advani. Pleased to meet you.'

Jaysukh Advani probably meant to come up to me to shake hands, but he changed his mind after taking a step and sat down on a sofa nearby. 'I'm sure I have your permission to take a seat.'

'But of course.' That was all I could say as I recovered from Parashar's unexpected sense of humour.

Once seated, however, Jaysukh was a different man. He looked at me with blazing eyes and said, 'On whose advice did you plan to get the better of me? Who has been instigating you? Out with it.'

'I really don't know what you're talking about.' I did not have to pretend. I was telling nothing but the truth.

'You don't know!' Jaysukh flew into a rage and rose to his feet. 'Do you mean to tell me your exorbitant bids for an ordinary Bidri bowl were made on a whim?'

'Excuse me,' Parashar intervened from the other side of the room, 'When you rang yesterday…'

Parashar was instantly rebuked for his joke.

'Be quiet. I'm not talking to you.' Jaysukh practically screamed at

Parashar, cutting him off. He turned back to me and glared, 'There's no point in prolonging a meaningless conversation. I want that bowl. You have to give it to me. That's what I'm here for.'

I'd read the signal in Parashar's eyes. I continued pretending to be him and replied, 'If that's what you're here for, do you think you can intimidate me into parting with it? At least, judging from what you said on the phone yesterday…'

Jaysukh flared up again at the mention of the phone call. 'What's this phone call you keep mentioning? I didn't ring you or anything. I got hold of your address from the auction house and came here directly. I would have been here last evening, but I was detained elsewhere. Where's the bowl? Let me see it.'

Parashar and I exchanged uncomprehending glances. Suppressing my astonishment, I said, 'Just a moment, please be patient. If you're not the one who rang, then there's someone else who wrote a letter asking for the bowl and then spoke to me on the phone. Do you know how much he's offering? Five hundred rupees and an identical bowl.'

Jaysukh seemed taken aback. He looked at me perplexed and said, 'So much money! I knew it, I knew it.'

Exchanging glances with Parashar again, I asked, 'What is it that you know?'

Without answering, Jaysukh asked in a fury, his voice loaded with suspicion, 'Are you sure he'll pay such a high amount? Or are you trying to take advantage of me?'

'Where's the question of taking advantage of you!' I feigned annoyance.

'What makes you think I am willing to take advantage even if you are ready to pay a high price for it? I did not buy the bowl to sell it. I won't sell it.'

Jaysukh went from bewilderment to hopelessness and then despair. He collapsed on the sofa next to mine and said pitifully, 'But I simply have to have that bowl. And I cannot afford five or six hundred rupees.'

'And yet, you expect me to give it to you!'

Parashar asked Jaysukh, 'Why do you so desperately want that bowl?'

Jaysukh was now in the throes of despondency. He no longer had the nerve to ignore Parashar. 'I'll be ruined if I don't get the bowl back,' he appealed to Parashar. 'If I cannot produce it before my father in the next three days, he'll disown me.'

'If that's the case why did you sell it to the auction house?' Parashar asked sternly.

'I sold it! I? Who told you that?' Jaysukh protested, sounding injured and surprised, but soon he broke down and confessed.

'No, there's no point hiding anything any more. I did make a hundred rupees selling all those items to the auction mart. Do you suppose I had any idea that I would get into so much trouble because of that bowl? I hadn't imagined Pitaji would remember that junk and demand that it be brought to him.'

'Your father's name is Mangaldas Advani, isn't that right?' Parashar looked sharply at Jaysukh. 'How long have you been pilfering art objects from your family home in Bombay and selling them?'

Jaysukh was speechless.

'How did your father find out that the bowl was no longer at home?' Parashar continued.

'How do you suppose? Someone must have complained behind my back,' replied an agitated Jaysukh. 'Otherwise, he wouldn't have enquired about the bowl of all things.'

'Where was the bowl usually kept?' Parashar asked.

'There are some old trunks in one of the rooms in our Bombay house. It must have been in one of those, or perhaps in a glass cabinet in my room. I don't remember.'

'And you have been selling the things stored in those trunks and cabinets for quite some time on the assumption that no one would look for them.' Parashar no longer sounded as stern as before. 'When did your father ask you about the bowl?'

'About a week ago,' Jaysukh replied. 'I had just returned to Bombay after several days in Calcutta. When I went back, I was told Pitaji had been combing the trunks and safes and drawers and cabinets all over the house in search of that bowl. He had discovered that I'd made off with a lot of things. But none of that would have mattered; it's just that he was furious that the bowl was among them. He gave me seven days to get it back. I have three days left.'

'Why didn't you arrange to retrieve it from the auction mart earlier?' I asked.

'How could I?' Jaysukh said miserably. 'I sold different things in different places. It took time to make enquiries about whom I'd sold the bowl to. By the time I found out it was at the auction mart, it was already too late. The auction was scheduled the next day. They didn't agree to sell it to me in advance.'

'So you sent someone to the auction the next day to bid for it?' Parashar asked.

Jaysukh seemed puzzled by this question. He looked at Parashar in surprise, 'What do you mean, send someone to bid for it? You think I have anyone to bid on my behalf? I hadn't thought these small items would come up for auction right at the beginning. I got a little late getting there. And by the time I arrived, it was already gone. I had to bribe them for your address. I should have come yesterday, it's just that…'

Jaysukh stopped, clearly uncomfortable.

Parashar didn't insist that Jaysukh complete his sentence. 'May I ask where you're staying in Calcutta?' he said instead.

The hotel that Jaysukh mentioned was, while not exactly shabby, not exactly luxurious. An average place that was always crowded because of its relatively low rates.

Now, Parashar got to the point. 'So you need the bowl badly. How much are you ready to pay for it?'

'I told you already,' Jaysukh said helplessly. 'I cannot afford to pay five or six hundred. To tell you the truth I haven't even been able to get hold of what you bid for it. I…I've a hundred rupees on me today. If you give it to me I promise I'll pay you the rest, I'll write you an IOU.'

'Is your IOU worth anything, Mr Advani?' Parashar smiled. 'In Calcutta alone, your IOUs worth a lakh or so are floating around, not even worth the paper they're written on. It's because the IOUs are useless that you've taken to stealing precious objects from your home and selling them.'

The blood seemed to have been drained from Jaysukh's face. He stared at the floor for a few moments and said feebly, 'I have nothing more to say. But whatever little chance I might have of honouring the IOUs will be gone if I don't get the bowl. Pitaji is bound to cut me out of his will. Very well, I'll go now, namaste.'

Parashar stopped Jaysukh as he was about to leave. 'Are you planning to go without taking your bowl?'

'How can I take it?' Jaysukh asked piteously. 'All I have is a hundred rupees.'

Parashar surprised both Jaysukh and me. 'All right, give me the hundred for now,' he said to Jaysukh. 'You owe me another hundred. Pay me when it's convenient.'

Jaysukh seemed so overwhelmed with gratitude that he could not speak.

After seeing Jaysukh off with the bowl, I pounced on Parashar.

'You gave it to him. But the people who promised you five hundred will be here soon.'

'I don't think they'll come any more,' said Parashar.

I didn't care for the mysterious smile on Parashar's face. 'Then what was the point of the phone call?' I asked, a trifle brusquely, it must be admitted. 'Jaysukh Advani denied ringing you or sending someone to bid on his behalf. Was he lying, then?'

'I wouldn't say that.' I didn't know whether Parashar was deliberately deepening the mystery.

'You must remember the phone number they gave you yesterday.' I tried a different tack. 'Surely it can be traced.'

'I did that already,' answered Parashar, lost in thought. 'It's the number of the phone in the lobby of the hotel where Jaysukh is staying. It's like a public booth anyone can use.'

'So it's all going to remain a mystery,' I said in disappointment.

'Yes, not all mysteries can be solved, can they!' Parashar sighed philosophically.

3

Whether the mystery was solved or not, I hadn't imagined we would get entangled in it all over again.

It all began in Bombay, where Parashar was on another mission.

Parashar had gone to Bombay on an insignificant assignment. He had to be a witness in a case of a forged passport. Although the case lasted for only a couple of days, we stayed on for a few days at the invitation of Nanabhai, Parashar's friend and admirer. We were invited to stay in a flat on the top floor of his palatial home in Malabar Hill.

It was called a flat but it was, in fact, like a royal residence. There was a self-service lift. The top floor had five large rooms with all modern amenities; the bedrooms, drawing room and living room were air-conditioned. And the most pleasing feature of the flat was a magnificent balcony that offered a panoramic view of Bombay.

Of course, the balcony was as dangerous as it was beautiful. It awakened Parashar's poetic sensibilities.

But, I couldn't say why, in spite of such an idyllic environment, the fount of Parashar's poetry had run dry. He sat in the balcony for hours every morning and evening to make his verses flow but all he had managed to write were these paltry lines:

Bombay
Without any effort rhyming words come to play.
Eat meat greet seat feet and so many more
I expect to see a festival of poetry lying in store.
Yet when I sit down with a pen to write
The nib wears out but not a line appears in sight
The more ardently I implore the glorious muse
The more vehemently she seem to refuse
Chains of gold bind my fingers into disuse.

While Parashar worshipped at the altar of poetry, I wandered around Bombay to my heart's content.

⌣

Mangaldas Advani's letter arrived after two or three days had passed this way. There was a strange coincidence about the arrival of the letter.

I went to Vile Parle in the morning to meet an old friend. He saw me off at the station. As we were walking towards the first-class compartment, he stopped suddenly.

'Who are you staring at in the third-class compartment?' I asked. 'Anyone you know?'

He smiled and replied, 'Not exactly someone I know, but certainly someone who's worth knowing. Do you know who that man in the tattered clothes is? That's Mangaldas Advani.'

The name rang a bell. I found myself gazing in amazement at a scrawny, shrivelled, ageing man whose face was covered with grey stubble. I asked my friend, 'The millionaire Mangaldas Advani! No, you must be mistaken, that old man there looks like a beggar on the street.'

'Yes, that's Mangaldas's peculiarity. Despite his millions, he likes to dress like a vagabond. I had the chance to meet him once. There are many people in business circles who have only heard of him but never actually set eyes on him.'

Since I was taking a local train, there was no time for a prolonged conversation. So I didn't have a chance to get more details.

When I returned to the flat, I was astonished to hear that a letter had arrived from the very same Mangaldas. I recounted the incident on the platform to Parashar.

The contents of the letter was strange, too. It had been hand delivered. Mangaldas's secretary had written that his employer wished to consult Parashar Barma on a special matter and would be pleased if Parashar could call on him at his residence at seven this evening. Parashar should take the letter along with him.

'What do you suppose the special matter might be?' I asked Parashar over the sumptuous lunch Nanabhai had arranged for us from a famous restaurant. 'Could it be a continuation of the Bidri bowl saga?'

'No idea,' answered Parashar absently, 'I'm just wondering how Mangaldas got my address.'

I decided to stroke Parashar's ego. 'It is easy for word to get around business circles that someone as famous as you is in Bombay as Nanabhai's guest,' I told him.

Parashar might have been pleased had he not been so distracted. But, he was still immersed in his own thoughts. 'Can you describe Mangaldas Advani to me?'

I described Mangaldas as accurately as I could.

'In that case you must come with me,' Parashar said at once.

'Me!' I felt not a little apprehensive about this. 'It's you he wants to meet. What should I go along for? And to do what?'

'But why should you let go of the chance to meet such a strange man?'

It was evident from his voice that he wasn't going to entertain my objections.

⌐

The letter had the address. We left around 6.30 in the evening. It would have been simpler to take the car Nanabhai had given Parashar to use, but for some reason he called for a taxi.

Meanwhile, I had learnt more about Mangaldas Advani from Parashar. It was obvious from his name that he was from Sindh. His family was renowned, influential and wealthy at one time. They had owned a part of

Sindh, the size of a kingdom, for nearly four hundred years. But at the time of independence, Mangaldas lost his family wealth. He left Sindh with his wife and child with nothing but the clothes on their backs. The early days were hard as he struggled to make a living. His wife died, leaving behind an infant. As his wife lay dying, Mangaldas vowed to rebuild his wealth. He had miraculously succeeded. In honour of the memory of his wife, Mangaldas had not given up his frugal ways. There were rumours that he had developed a quirk in his old age. No, it wasn't anything scandalous like marrying someone young—he was collecting all possible information about one of his ancestors.

The name of his ancestor was Jugalram. He had lived around 1818, when the English had defeated the Marathas and were developing Bombay. After a falling out with his brother, Jugalram moved to Bombay with his meagre resources and made a fortune exporting cotton to America. He built an enormous building near Bandra, designed like the palace his forefathers had lived in for many generations, in Sindh. The building was now in ruins. Mangaldas Advani had located and purchased the dilapidated building at an absurd price. The strange thing was that despite the money he had spent on it, Mangaldas had not tried to restore it. He had left it as it was. For all these reasons, people considered him an eccentric and bad-tempered old man. Just as businessmen in general avoided him unless they had no choice, he too did not seek out anyone. He was obsessed with his passion. Jaysukh, the child his wife had left behind, was the only annoyance in his life. Mangaldas had given up after several efforts to have his son join his business. Besides a small monthly allowance, all means to a degenerate, prodigal life were closed to Jaysukh now. Many were convinced that Mangaldas was the kind of disciplinarian who would not hesitate to cut his son out of his will unless the young man reformed.

∫

Mangaldas's residence was as peculiar as the man himself. It was located in an unappealing neighbourhood of Bombay, housed with mills and labourers' quarters.

We checked the address and got out of the taxi in front of a large building. It was difficult to say whether it was a home or part of a factory. It was hard to believe that a millionaire like Mangaldas would not live in Marine Drive or Malabar Hill, and hide away in this run-down part of the city. His attempt to conceal himself was obvious in many ways.

The thought of entering this ugly, prison-like building made me choke.

The front entrance was a hinged four-panelled gate, much like an entrance of a warehouse. It was locked. I looked around for the doorbell and found it on the side of the gate. When we rang the bell, a panel in the gate was slid open. Evidently someone was watching us.

Then we heard a key being turned in a padlock, after which the gate was opened.

But no warm welcome awaited us. A burly man who was both the guard and doorman stood there, blocking our way.

'Whom do you want?' he asked harshly in Marathi.

He did not allow us to enter even after Parashar had told him the purpose of our visit.

'What proof did we have that Advani senior had sent for us?'

Parashar showed him the letter from Mangaldas. I don't know what the doorman made of it, but, he handed it back, locked the gate and asked us to follow him.

It was seven o'clock on a Bombay evening. There was still some light outdoors but it was almost pitch dark inside. The only source of light came from a dim electric bulb hanging on the wall.

The spiral staircase was made of wood. The building must have been ancient. Several of the steps groaned in protest under our feet.

The doorman stopped at the landing. The door that led out was closed.

'Is this Mr Advani's room?' asked Parashar.

'No, are you looking for him?'

A sweet, feminine voice startled us. We turned around to find a pretty young woman standing on the landing of the stairs that led to the upper floor.

When she heard Mr Advani had invited us, she frowned, and walked up to us. 'He called you personally? He can't have called you on the phone. Do you have any proof?'

Her aggressive final sentence would have sounded much more unpleasant had she not been so pretty and her voice so sweet.

'Yes, I do.' Parashar was forced to produce his letter once more.

The landing was not as dimly lit as downstairs. The young woman read the letter and appeared slightly embarrassed. With an awkward smile, she returned the letter to Parashar. 'Forgive me,' she said, 'I was surprised because Mr Advani never sends for anyone.'

Turning to the doorman, she asked him sternly, 'If they have come to meet Mr Advani, why have you brought them to his secretary's room?'

The doorman told her sullenly that he was only following orders.

The young woman smiled wryly and shrugged. It seemed like she found it difficult to keep track of Mr Advani's whims.

She was about to leave them when Parashar stopped her.

'If you don't mind, Ms Sambrani...'

She turned towards us and interrupted Parashar, 'Do you know me?'

'Is it possible that those who are familiar with Bombay,' Parashar said ingratiatingly, 'will not know the women's table-tennis champion Sonia Sambrani?'

'Your flattery is making me uncomfortable.' This time Sonia spoke with a pleasant, amused smile. 'I'm not the champion, only the runner-up. Thank you for thinking so highly of me. Now, ask your question quickly. Mangaldas Advani is not the kind of man who likes to be kept waiting.'

'I was asking whether his son Jaysukh is at home now,' Parashar asked hesitantly.

'It would be quite natural if he were not.' Sonia smiled in chagrin. 'When is he ever home? But you could easily have asked the doorman.'

'I could have, but wouldn't it be appropriate to ask someone from the family?'

'That is true.' The smile on Sonia's face was both mischievous and sarcastic. 'But then, I'm not part of the family. One of my uncles is a close friend of Mr Advani's. He lives here, and I visit him sometimes. I trust this satisfies your curiosity. Isn't this what you wanted to know?'

Without waiting for an answer, Sonia drifted downstairs, leaving in her wake a radiance of youth and high spirits.

It was probably her presence that had kept the doorman from expressing his impatience and anxiety all this while.

Muttering indignantly, 'It's me whom sir will be angry with,' he knocked softly on the closed door.

What his tentative, fearful knocking led us to expect was borne out by the harsh shout it elicited from within.

I'd been told that Mangaldas was bad-tempered at the best of times. At this moment, he seemed furious. It was true that his belligerent response was to give permission to enter, but it sounded like the roar of a wild animal.

Gesturing at us to go in, the doorman departed in a hurry.

When we pushed open the door we were dazzled by the bright lights in the room. In contrast to the dim lights in the rest of the house, this room was dazzlingly lit up.

We stopped at the threshold, waiting for our eyes to adjust to the brightness. Mr Advani was sitting behind a high secretariat desk at the back of the room. Not only was there a light hanging from the ceiling, there was also a table lamp pointing at the door, which was what had blinded us when we entered.

Mr Advani's greeting was a stern reprimand, 'You were supposed to have been here at seven.'

Before Parashar could explain, there was a muted snarl. 'Who's that with you? Did I ask you to bring your friends here for a chat?'

These outbursts made me angry with Parashar, and uncomfortable too. Why had he brought me along to be humiliated?

Parashar's response calmed me down. Sounding as belligerent as Advani, he said, 'I have no idea why you have asked me here, but I am not your paid servant. My friend will remain here. If that does not meet with your approval, I will leave.'

An angry Parashar made to leave.

'What's this, are you leaving in a huff?' Advani still sounded harsh, but his tone had softened. 'If you trust him, so can I, probably. I hope he will not repeat our conversation. Take a seat.'

The last sentence was virtually an order. We stepped up to the wide desk to take a couple of chairs facing Advani. His first question was unexpected.

'What is your fee for giving advice?'

'That depends on what advice is being sought.' Parashar sounded distinctly grim.

'Not just advice, I want to ask you some questions too,' Advani said brusquely. 'I don't take anything from anyone without paying a fair price. Here's five hundred.'

Mangaldas slid five crisp one-hundred-rupee notes across the desk.

But Parashar didn't touch them. 'Just as you pay a fair price for everything, I too do not accept an advance without knowing what the assignment is.'

'Why should it be an advance?' Mangaldas said impatiently. 'Think of it as fee for your time here. I trust the amount is not too low.'

'Whether it's too low or too high will be clear only after I've heard what you have to say. Let the money be for now. Come to the point.'

Mangaldas was not accustomed to such talk. With great effort, he controlled his temper and said, 'Very well. Give me answers keeping in mind the fact that I have eyes and ears everywhere. I am aware that my son Jaysukh has purchased a certain object from you. How much did he pay?'

I would never have imagined Parashar pretending he knew nothing.

Feigning surprise, he said, 'How can I answer this question unless you tell me who your son is and what object he has purchased from me?'

'You don't know who my son is?' Mangaldas was enraged. 'You mean you don't know Jaysukh!'

'Jaysukh…Jaysukh…' Parashar seemed to be trying to place the name. 'Oh yes, Jaysukh Advani. I remember now. But we have met only once, in Calcutta. A Bidri bowl I bought at an auction…'

Cutting Parashar short, Mangaldas said, 'Yes, that bowl. How much did you sell it to him for? When?'

'I don't exactly remember when.' Parashar seemed to probe his memory again. 'Ah yes, I think it was a Saturday about a month ago.'

Mangaldas interrupted him again. 'All right, never mind when. I'm sure you remember how much Jaysukh paid for it.'

'Of course, why wouldn't I?' Parashar smiled. 'I asked Jaysukh the same price that I had paid at the auction. Two hundred rupees.'

'Two hundred! Only two hundred!' Mangaldas was outraged.

'That was it—two hundred rupees. Should I have asked for more?' Parashar seemed to rue his own foolishness. 'But I had no idea how much it was worth. It looked like an ordinary bowl with Bidri designs. It caught my eye at the auction, which is why I bid for it. Your son Jaysukh came looking for it and when I saw that he was interested, I gave it to him at cost price. He said family memories are associated with it.'

'Yes, a hundred and fifty years of memories,' Mangaldas exclaimed in outrage, 'which that worthless fellow had sold somewhere for a few paise.'

'At least you've got it back.' Parashar tried to gauge the expression on Mangaldas's face.

I observed Mangaldas silently. Although the table lamp was no longer pointed directly at us, his face was not clearly visible behind it. But his restlessness was evident. He might have looked like a gaunt, shrivelled old man, but it wasn't hard to miss his boundless energy.

Mangaldas did not respond directly to Parashar's last statement. Changing the subject, he said, 'Did anyone else propose to buy the bowl off you?'

This time Parashar astounded me entirely. Nonchalantly he said, 'Anyone else? No. You mean someone else had his eye on that trifle thing?'

'Just answer my question.' Mangaldas sounded impatient again. 'So no one else made you an offer?'

'As I said, no one.' Parashar pretended to be surprised. 'Not that I would have sold it even if they did want to buy it. It was only because your son Jaysukh mentioned family history that I let him have it.'

After a pause, Parashar continued, 'I've answered all your questions. Now may I get an answer to one of mine?'

'What question?' Mangaldas was irked.

'You said that bowl is linked to a hundred and fifty years of family memories. What memories, if I may ask?' Mangaldas was silent initially. Then he said, in spite of himself, 'It's too long a history to recount in detail. What's enough for you to know is that nearly a hundred and fifty years ago, Jugalram, one of my forefathers, had made a fortune here in Bombay. Even in that age, collecting art from all over the world was his passion. He took a small part of his collection to the family home in Sindh and deposited it there. Apparently he had wanted to go back and live there in his old age. But that wish was unfulfilled because he died right here. No one in the family in Sindh knew how much property he had amassed. Their kingdom was so large that no one cared to find out. After all these years, I'm trying to retrieve the details from the past. I cannot put a monetary value to his collection of art. And it was a treasure from this collection that my good-for-nothing greedy son sold.'

'Still, you've got it back, haven't you?' Parashar repeated his question.

'No, I haven't,' answered Mangaldas sourly, leaving us surprised. 'The wretch said it was stolen on his way from Calcutta to Bombay. I don't believe him.'

'Is there any reason not to?' Parashar's query seemed innocent. 'It's Jaysukh who will pay if he cannot return it to you.'

'Perhaps the rascal does not understand this yet. Or he has another motive.'

'What motive could he possibly have?' Parashar pleaded on Jaysukh's behalf. 'It holds some value only for you. Someone else might pay four or five hundred for it at most, as I did on a whim. But surely Jaysukh is not foolish enough not to be aware that he might lose a priceless inheritance for four or five hundred rupees.'

Mangaldas was listening closely, his eyes boring into Parashar's. He shrugged impatiently when Parashar finished, saying, 'You cannot even begin to imagine what's going on in Jaysukh's head. He thinks I am about to die. He's hoping that I don't change my will before I die.'

'What are you saying?' Parashar was as bewildered as I was. 'Why should Jaysukh harbour such an idea?'

'There's reason for him to,' said Mangaldas firmly. 'And it is to get your opinion on this matter that I have sent for you. Tell me, do you believe in the supernatural?'

Had Mangaldas really gone mad? None of this sounded like it was coming from a sound mind.

Parashar appeared as mystified as I was. 'Why this sudden question?' he asked worriedly.

'You'll know in a moment.' Mangaldas deepened the mystery. 'But first, tell me whether you believe in supernatural events.'

'I do and I don't.' Parashar tried to sidestep the question. 'What appears to be supernatural and miraculous often turns out on investigation to have rational explanations.'

'Then try to find this rational explanation you speak of after you hear what I have to say. This is specifically what I've called you here for.'

Mangaldas paused to gather his thoughts and began to speak slowly and calmly. 'Over the past three months, two strange things have been happening repeatedly. They seem to be related. Both incidents happened on the same day. The first incident was the entrance of a bat into my room at night.'

Mangaldas flared up in rage at the hint of a smile on Parashar's face. 'Don't smile. It's nothing to smile at. Listen to the whole story. Don't assume it was a small nocturnal insect or something, it was a distinctly large bat. Everyone knows of the insects, but no one has heard of such a large bat entering a house in the city. Still, although it was unusual, I had assumed it was a coincidence. Perhaps the bat had lost its way and somehow wandered into my room. It didn't stay indoors for long. It flapped its wings frantically, colliding into the wall and cupboard before flying out. And then…'

'Do you remember what time it was?' Parashar interrupted him.

'Very clearly,' said Mangaldas. 'I usually go to bed late. I'm usually up until midnight sitting at a small desk next to my bed, looking over my business papers by the light of a table lamp. I go to bed around quarter past twelve. That night as I was about to put out the light before going to bed I was startled by a flapping sound overhead. At the same time, a shadow fell on the table. When I looked up I saw the bat, flying from one wall to the other, colliding with things, and then sailing out through the window.

'Although it was an odd incident I didn't worry about it, but that was also the first night I had a strange dream. I sleep very little, but even at this age I sleep very deeply. I never have dreams. But that night I had one. It was so vivid that it seemed real at the time. It was evening and I was working at my desk in my bedroom, when the clock struck seven. Although there was still light outside, the room was quite dark. I was about to switch on the table lamp when I sensed someone in my room. The staircase to the second floor leads to a long hall, where I usually meet people. Sometimes, the directors' meetings of my various companies are held there. Beyond the hall lies a row of three rooms. The one in the middle is mine. Jaysukh occupies a room on one side, while the other one is a guestroom. But never mind all that. I explained the layout just to convey what's special about my room. Each of the rooms on either side of mine can be entered through a corridor. But the only door to my room is from the hall. The servants are not even allowed to enter the hall, leave alone my room, without my permission. But it seemed to me that someone had entered my room from the hall. The lights had not been switched on yet in there. The hall is quite dark because it gets no sunlight from either the east or the west. I saw an indistinct form at my door in the darkness. Annoyed at this audacious intrusion, I asked angrily who it was. The figure approached me without answering. The room seemed to have grown darker. The closer it came, the more I felt a grip of cold fear. 'Who is it?' I screamed twice. The figure kept coming closer silently as though it was my fate confronting me. I have a pistol in my desk drawer. It's only for show, I have never considered using it. Now, almost numb with terror, I managed to open the drawer and pick it up with frozen fingers. At once, I discovered a pistol glinting in the stranger's hand. As soon as I raised my pistol he, too, raised his pistol. I pointed my pistol at him with my right hand and switched on the table lamp with my left. I trembled fearfully at what I saw. The figure was no one but myself, like a reflection in a mirror. The figure and I fired at each other simultaneously. Then I woke up screaming, soaked in sweat.'

Mangaldas paused and asked, 'Can you explain this dream?'

'How can I?' Parashar admitted humbly. 'Maybe a psychiatrist can.'

'I tried that,' Mangaldas said dismissively, 'but not after the first time I had that dream. I told myself that dreams can be strange. But I kept having the same dream, and always on the night a bat enters my room. The bat is like an omen—just as it has a fixed time to appear, so too is the striking of the clock in my dream. The bat enters soon after midnight, and the scene in the dream begins as soon as the clock strikes seven. Can you make a connection?'

'Not yet,' said Parashar, shaking his head. 'You must have told the psychiatrists everything. What did they have to say?'

'Each of them had a different view,' Mangaldas said. 'They don't want to believe the business of the bat. They consider it a hallucination. Some of them even interpreted the dream as my secret desire to kill myself. A plan to commit suicide.'

Mangaldas laughed derisively. He stopped abruptly, 'There is no question of my harbouring any desire for suicide, covert or otherwise. I have not developed an aversion to life. My health is sound for my age. I will happily live for another twenty years at least. My sole regret is that my only son has not proved himself worthy—but to tell the truth, I don't care about that either. Everyone is bound to pay for their karma. No one's going to be absolved just because he's my son.'

'Have you told anyone other than the psychiatrists about the bat and the dream?' Parashar asked.

'Yes, I've told Jaysukh. That is why he thinks all these are portents of my imminent death. He believes that even if I intend to change my will, I will die before that can happen. I guess he has sold the bowl to someone after he retrieved it from you. He's always running short of cash, and will always be. I may not change my will so easily, but what he is expecting will not happen either. I'll live for a long time yet. I cut his monthly allowance as punishment for wasting money—I'm not going to raise it.'

Mangaldas appeared to be warning us as if we were representatives of his son.

'So, your son is the only one you've told,' said Parashar. 'Was it to get his advice?'

'Advice! From that imbecile!' Mangaldas snorted. 'All I wanted to know was whether a bat had entered his room too. Since there are three rooms in a row, I wanted to understand whether it was only my room that the bat had chosen.'

'What did Jaysukh say?' Both Parashar and I looked expectantly at Mangaldas.

'He said that although it hadn't entered his room, he had indeed seen a bat flying past his window. Not that I believed him. It's not often that he is in his senses when he returns home. He may have seen something while in drunken state.

'Still, I asked him whether anything had happened to frighten him the night he saw the bat. He looked at me strangely, as though I was mad. Maybe it was because I was in a foul mood, or perhaps there was some other reason, but I told him my dream. Do you know what he said?'

'What?' Parashar seemed eager to know.

'He told me to give him the pistol in my drawer.' An odd, harsh laugh emerged from Mangaldas. Suddenly he looked at his watch and seemed eager to get rid of us. 'You must leave now. You couldn't solve either of my two mysteries, but take the money as compensation for wasting your time.'

'No, Mr Advani,' said Parashar as both of us rose to our feet. 'I don't accept a fee without working for it. I've heard you out. If I can solve the mysteries, I demand a larger fee. But I have two last questions.'

'What are they?' Mangaldas was clearly impatient now.

Even I was astonished at Parashar's unexpected question. 'Do you know anyone who studies ancient history, especially Egyptology?'

Although he seemed startled, Mangaldas answered instantly. 'I don't know whether it was Egyptology,' he said, 'but my forefather Jugalram Advani's interest in ancient history was obvious from his art collection. He had visited Egypt in connection with his cotton business. And besides, my friend Mahendra Sambrani is himself an expert in ancient history.'

'My second question is, has a marriage between your friend Mahendra Sambrani's niece, Sonia, and your son, Jaysukh, ever even discussed?'

I hadn't expected Mangaldas to fly into a temper at this question. His choleric temperament rose to a new high. 'Of course it has been discussed,' he said in a voice dripping with venom. 'But what use are such discussions? Jaysukh marry Sonia? That's like casting pearls before swine. I can't be blinded by love just because he's my son.'

'By the way, your secretary…'

Parashar had barely begun when Mangaldas cut him off unceremoniously. 'My secretary is supremely inefficient,' he said testily. 'He chose the wrong time to take off for a couple of hours. He should have been back by now to remind me of the time. I have answered both your questions. Namaste.'

Realizing that this 'namaste' meant 'get out', we were about to leave without further ado. But we had to stop—because Mangaldas was calling us back.

'Wait,' he practically ordered Parashar. 'Return the letter I sent you.'

Although he was surprised, Parashar couldn't resist quipping as he returned it, 'Obviously you don't want to keep any proof of this meeting.'

Mangaldas didn't deem it necessary to reply.

4

I was plagued by questions. But before I could ask Parashar any of them during dinner, he said, 'What did you make of Mangaldas Advani?'

'To tell the truth, I couldn't make him out,' I admitted to Parashar. 'He can't be just a crotchety, bad-tempered, eccentric but formidable businessman. There's more to him.'

'Yes, but what? Think about it and tell me.' I didn't know whether Parashar was casually trying to instigate me.

'The more I think, the more confused I get,' I said with a smile. 'Something about him doesn't add up, but I can't put my finger on it.'

Parashar looked at me in wonder. 'You surprise me, Krittibash.'

Suspecting that he was joking, I tried to gauge his expression. 'Surprise you? How?'

'To put it simply, with the penetrating nature of your investigative gaze.' Although the smile on Parashar's face suggested amusement, the praise appeared genuine. 'Mangaldas told us an improbable mystery, but he himself is no less of an enigma. He seems to be a tangle of several characters from different plays.'

'I don't understand the literary metaphors,' I laughed, 'but some of the things he said and did are indeed bizarre.'

'Such as?' Parashar encouraged me to speak up.

'For instance, offering to pay you right at the beginning.'

'No,' said Parashar after some thought, 'I can't call it either bizarre or inexplicable. It's not unusual for a self-made man to do things this way. Next?'

'Next, didn't you find him far too detached concerning his son?'

'Even if that were the case, it's not impossible,' said Parashar. 'Not everyone is equally well disposed towards their children. It's entirely natural not to feel affection for a wastrel.'

Aggrieved, I said, 'You're dismissing all my arguments. But flying into a temper when you brought up the question of his son's marriage to Sonia—wasn't that unusual?'

Parashar frowned and said after a pause, 'I agree you can't call it natural, but it may not be difficult to explain either.'

'Really? How do you explain it?'

'The explanation is partly a matter of psychology,' Parashar said with a note of amusement in his voice. 'A complex and slightly twisted psychology, however.'

'Stop talking in riddles,' I said sharply.

'In simple terms, it's a case of Mangaldas's weakness for the young woman.' Parashar further explained. 'Though Mangaldas himself may not be aware of it. Such instances are not unknown. There are many cases of the father marrying the woman he had selected as his son's bride.'

'What you're saying suggests something quite disturbing,' I said in surprise. 'This is not merely unnatural, this is a symptom of a severe perversion.'

'Which is why I cannot be certain that the explanation is correct. But there is no doubt that perversions have appeared in Mangaldas's mind.'

'Is that how you're interpreting the strange dream and the sighting of the bat?'

'There doesn't appear to be any other logical explanation,' Parashar said with a worried expression.

'But don't forget Jaysukh saw the bat too.'

'I cannot reconcile that to any explanation at all,' Parashar admitted.

'All right, let's put this particular mystery aside for now.' I went back to my earlier question. 'Now that you've dismissed all my arguments, let me hear why you consider Mangaldas an enigma.'

'You want to know why?' Parashar said with great seriousness. 'Because he sent for me to talk about the dream and the bat.'

'What's so strange about that?' It was my turn to refute his argument.

'You're a renowned detective. Instead of accepting the psychologists' explanations, he sent for you to find out whether someone might be up to some mischief. Besides, his real objective might have been to find out how Jaysukh retrieved the bowl from you.'

'Hmm.' Without protesting, Parashar said, 'That's the other thing. It's a little unusual for him to be so interested in finding out how Jaysukh persuaded me to part with the bowl. Or how much he paid for it.'

He paused for a moment, but continued immediately afterwards without allowing me to get a word in edgeways, 'The third reason was his annoyance with his secretary.'

I was flabbergasted by Parashar's reasoning, and I told him as much. 'It makes no sense to consider someone an enigma because of these reasons.'

'Then I must be mistaken.' Parashar appeared to accept defeat far too easily.

But I wasn't about to let him off the hook. 'Will you explain your own riddle now?' I asked.

'What do you mean by my riddle?' Parashar seemed disappointed.

'Why did you ask the question on ancient history and Egyptology? How are those subjects relevant in this case?'

Parashar appeared to be taken aback for a moment. Then he smiled. 'It must have been something I saw in that room. Didn't you notice some samples of Egyptian art in there?'

I tried, but I couldn't remember. Accepting Parashar's explanation, I said, 'One more question. It's one thing for you to have known that Sonia Sambrani is a table-tennis player, but how did you know that a marriage with Jaysukh was being discussed?'

'How could I have known?' Parashar answered smoothly. 'It was a guess. If a young woman and a young man of that age have the chance to meet each other freely, doesn't the possibility of marriage arise at once?'

'Maybe it does,' I couldn't help opposing his assumption, 'but for one thing Mangaldas is not in favour of the marriage, and for another it's hard to believe that a woman like Sonia will be willing to marry a useless degenerate like Jaysukh.'

'How can you forget that worthiness or the lack of it is irrelevant when it comes to love?' Parashar smiled. 'I doubt,' he continued, 'that Miss Sambrani visits that house so often only to meet her uncle.'

The next day I had the opportunity to find out the source of Sonia Sambrani's attraction in Mangaldas's house.

I had woken up a little late that day. I was surprised when I went out to the balcony. Parashar was not there.

He normally wakes up before I do. I would usually find him on the balcony with paper and pen, gazing at the sprawling city of Bombay.

But he wasn't there today. Where had he disappeared to so early in the day, abandoning his poetry?

I waited for him until it was time for breakfast. He did not turn up so I went out on my own. I had a plan.

I'd read in the papers that there would be an exhibition table-tennis match between Sonia Sambrani and someone from Delhi at Marina Club in Chowpatty. I knew Hardikar, the secretary of Marina Club. I went with the hope that he would help me get a seat to watch the game.

I didn't know why I was suddenly struck by the thought of watching the match, but if I hadn't, I would certainly not have learnt what I did, something that enabled me to surprise Parashar.

By the time my taxi reached Marina Club, the match had already begun. Although the hall was filled with spectators, I had no trouble getting a seat with Hardikar's help. He made me sit next to him on one of the chairs set aside for the club officials.

Sonia's game was truly spectacular. She had that rare skill that the best players possess—a combination of swift aggression with unbreakable patience. Her stroke play was unique too. Sonia's opponent was no match for her. She had at least tried to put up a fight in the first game, but she lost the second to love.

Although I was no expert in table tennis, I could tell a good player when I saw one. During the second set, I was very impressed by Sonia's game. 'Judging from her game, Sonia Sambrani should be the Indian champion,' I said to Hardikar.

'Of course, she should be,' replied an annoyed Hardikar, 'and all of us had assumed as much. But it's difficult to tell what's wrong with her these days. One day she plays like a champion, the next day she is distracted and hits shots like a novice. Sometimes, she completely loses her concentration. You can't become a champion that way.'

'Why?' I asked. 'Is she in love or something? But it's others who must be head over heels in love with her. She can't be the one suffering. What's going on?'

'I don't know anything,' said Hardikar with a smile. 'And even if I did, I wouldn't be telling a newspaperman like you. Who knows what story you'll make up and get me into trouble?'

Hardikar didn't have to reveal anything, after all.

The match had ended. Sonia was surrounded by fans who congratulated her. But she looked around nervously, as though she was searching for someone.

I spotted the young man she must have been looking for. He was standing apart from the crowd at a distance—a simply dressed, tall and thin fellow amidst a gaggle of fashionable youngsters.

He went up to Sonia once the wave of congratulations had died down. She might be a modern sportswoman, but that didn't mean she lacked any of the traditional tricks of her sex. Since the person she had been looking for was standing right in front of her, she pretended not to see him. Later, of course, I saw her leaving with him and getting into a taxi.

Hardikar had come out with me.

'Now you'll probably tell me you have no idea who that young man with Sonia is,' I told him with a smile.

'Why would I say any such thing?' Hardikar chuckled. 'How can I not know the person who's almost a constant companion of Sonia Sambrani's? But he's not anyone well known.'

'Who is he, tell me anyway.'

'His name is Rajinder Nigam. He works as a mere slave for a powerful Bombay businessman.'

'Who's this businessman? What sort of slavery are you talking of?' I asked.

'The official designation is secretary, but he does everything he's asked to,' said Hardikar sympathetically. 'And even though the businessman is a powerful one, the name may not be familiar to you. Not many people in Bombay have heard of Mangaldas Advani.'

I was startled, but I didn't let it show. 'I have another question,' I said. 'How long have this Nigam and Sonia been in love?'

'What's going on?' Hardikar frowned at me suspiciously. 'Have you developed a weakness for Sonia Sambrani? Coming all this way to watch her play, and now this barrage of questions. I'm beginning to smell a rat.'

'And what's wrong with developing a weakness?' I replied lightly. 'A girl like that can easily conquer your heart. I'm trying to find out how far back my competitor's claim goes.'

'About a year,' laughed Hardikar. 'At least, I've seen Rajinder Nigam hovering around her since last year's championships. That was probably when Sonia's dilemma began.'

'Dilemma?' I looked at Hardikar in surprise.

'Yes. On the one hand there's Rajinder—despite some sort of distant relationship with Seth Mangaldas, he's nothing more than an employee...' Hardikar paused to look across the road, 'and on the other is the prince who has now arrived in person. His quest is for Sonia, of course.'

By then, I'd noticed the sports car parked across the road. I was surprised to see the person who got out and crossed the road to come up to us. It was none other than Jaysukh.

'Is the match over?' he asked anxiously.

'Of course it is. Matches are held on time.' Hardikar clearly sounded hostile.

However, this didn't bother Jaysukh. 'Has Sonia left?' he asked worriedly.

'So I saw.' Hardikar's response was dry and brief.

'This is going to be a problem.' As he looked up at sky in dismay, Jaysukh noticed me.

'What are you doing here?' He had recognized me.

'I came to watch the match,' I said with a polite smile.

'I wasn't fortunate enough to have caught it. I couldn't make it here on time even after borrowing someone's car.' Jaysukh muttered to himself. As he was leaving, he suddenly towards me and said, 'Where do you stay? I can give you a lift if you like.'

'Thank you,' I said to avoid him, 'but that won't be necessary. I have to discuss some things with Mr Hardikar here.'

'I see.' Jaysukh seemed disappointed. Then, as though he had just remembered, he said before leaving, 'You can trust me to keep my promise to you.'

⏝

'So you know Jaysukh Advani!' said Hardikar with some surprise after he had left. 'You never told me.'

'Because it didn't seem relevant,' I reassured him with a smile. 'In any case it wouldn't be right to say I know him. We met just once in Calcutta. So Jaysukh is the other half of Sonia's dilemma.'

'The attraction is not on Sonia's part, that's for sure,' Hardikar said. 'But whether Jaysukh's interest in her is sincere or not, that doesn't stop him from pursuing her. I think Sonia is in trouble because of this. She cannot reject the son of Rajinder Nigam's employer outright on account of Rajinder's job. She's worried and I suspect this is why her performance has been inconsistent this year.'

'Now you have told me everything,' I told Hardikar, laughing. 'But I promise, none of this will be published in any newspaper or magazine, not even as an insinuation.'

I wasn't going to give up on the opportunity of gaining an upper hand on Parashar when I returned, but it was he who surprised me instead.

He was sitting in the drawing room, copying something from two pieces of paper into a notebook.

The two sheets were laid on the table, held in place by paperweights. When I glanced at them, I was astonished.

'What's all this? Have you begun learning Urdu and Persian at this age?'

'You're never too old to learn.' Putting the sheets away in a drawer, he looked at me strangely and said, 'Where did you go? Was it to watch Sonia Sambrani play?'

I stared at him in bewilderment.

'Are you wondering how I knew?' Parashar smiled. 'Not by using Sherlock Holmes's methods of deduction. I found out through a trusted reporter. And the reporter's name is Mr Jaysukh Advani. You met him at Marina Club, didn't you?'

'I did.' I was still perplexed. 'But did Jaysukh come here? How did he get our address?'

'Our address is not particularly difficult to discover,' said Parashar with a laugh. 'But he didn't come here. I visited him.'

'Was it to meet him that you left so early in the morning?'

'No, I had other things to do before that. I met Jaysukh afterwards. He had just returned from Marina Club.'

'Why did you meet him? Was it to do with that bowl?' My questions were sharp because I suspected him of hiding something.'

'No, it had nothing to do with bowl.' Parashar sounded grim now. 'I went to warn him.'

'Warn Jaysukh?' I asked hotly, wondering if Parashar was deliberately talking in riddles. 'Warn him about what?'

'There is something he has to be careful about,' Parashar said grumpily, 'But do you suppose I got the chance to tell him? Jaysukh seemed quite worked up about something that had happened at Marina Club. "I've told your friend whatever I had to," he said in a foul mood. "He had been to Marina Club to watch Sonia play." He left without giving me a chance to talk. I wouldn't have minded so much if this humiliation hadn't taken place in the presence of Mangaldas's secretary, Rajinder or whatever his name is. Of course, Rajinder did apologize on behalf of his employer's son.'

'This must have been the first time that you met Rajinder, wasn't it?' I asked.

'First time?' Parashar thought for a moment. 'Yes, first time, of course. He was on leave that evening when we went to meet Mangaldas.'

'Let me tell you then.' I broke the news at last. 'The real attraction that draws Sonia Sambrani there is not Jaysukh but Rajinder Nigam. It's Rajinder she's in love with, and your Jaysukh is the hurdle to their romance. It was because Mangaldas knows his son well that he was so enraged when you brought up the marriage.'

'Really!' Parashar looked at me in astonishment. 'Where did you hear this news? Was it at Marina Club?'

'I not only heard it, I also saw it for myself.'

'Hmm.' Parashar looked at me gravely. After a pause he said, almost to himself, 'I should have realized that the problem would become more serious and complex.'

'What problem are you talking about?' I asked impatiently. 'Is it the one concerning the Bidri bowl, or Mangaldas's strange dream, or the rivalry between Rajinder and Jaysukh over Sonia?'

'All of them,' replied Parashar worriedly. 'All the problems are related. Something dreadful will happen any moment unless a quick solution is found. That's what I'd gone to warn Jaysukh about.'

'But why Jaysukh?'

'Who else should I warn?' Parashar seemed agitated. 'He's at the centre of it all.'

5

I was shocked the next morning to discover how well founded Parashar's fear was.

The news was in the papers. Prominently displayed.

The three-column headline read: 'Business magnate commits suicide.'

An extended account of the suicide was given below the headline. It was particularly detailed because Mangaldas Advani was an important figure in Bombay's business world. But still, the event would not have been given so much coverage had it not been for the presence of several journalists in his house yesterday. Even if they weren't exactly witnesses, the incident could be said to have taken place under their noses.

The time of death was between six-thirty and seven-thirty in the evening. A group of journalists had been interviewing wealthy businessmen and industrialists on a particular topic over the past few days. The topic was how to bring all the hidden black money into the open. The journalists had made an appointment with Mangaldas yesterday to find out whether he supported or opposed the government's recent move on black money.

Mangaldas had invited them home at six-thirty in the evening. His secretary, Rajinder Nigam, had asked them to wait in the hall outside Mangaldas's room.

But Mangaldas hadn't kept his word. When it was nearly seven, his son Jaysukh had pushed his father's door open and entered the room. Before that he had assured the waiting journalists that he would remind his father of the interview.

But Jaysukh probably hadn't got the opportunity. The door had shut behind him automatically, and the journalists had not heard his conversation with Mangaldas. However, they had realized from his angry exit that there had probably been a serious altercation between father and son. What Jaysukh had told his father loudly on his way out had made it easy for the journalists to draw their own conclusions. An agitated Jaysukh had practically been screaming, 'I will certainly be ruined, but I'm telling you that it won't be long before you are as well.' Jaysukh had slammed the door shut behind him and stomped off, his face red with anger, ignoring everyone. He was so angry that the journalists had not dared to ask him any questions. It was ten past seven. They were considering leaving in vexation after their long and fruitless wait when Mangaldas's secretary Rajinder appeared before them. He had seemed both surprised and embarrassed at the fact that they were still waiting. Apologizing on behalf of his employer and promising to remind him at once, he had entered Mangaldas's room, only to rush out in a state of panic. Overcome with fear, he had requested the journalists to accompany him to Mangaldas's room. Not knowing what was going on, they had followed him in, but they had observed nothing unusual at first. But then, they had noticed the carpet behind a large table, on which Mangaldas Advani was lying, covered in blood. A pistol was lying nearby on the floor.

The journalists ensured that nothing was touched and called the police. They had also made enquiries of Jaysukh's whereabouts. He had left home after the quarrel with his father earlier. One more person had rushed in on hearing the news. It was Mahinder Sambrani, Mangaldas's childhood friend, who was originally from Sindh. He lived largely at Mangaldas's house now, occupying the room next to his as a guest. He had gone out for his evening walk a short while ago, and had come running frantically after he heard the news.

The police weren't tardy in arriving. The journalists had left after the police had taken control of the situation. They were convinced that it was suicide, even though the matter was still under investigation.

This was roughly the account of events that I managed to piece together from several newspapers.

✧

Although there was no reason to have developed any respect or fondness for Mangaldas Advani, I was saddened by this unexpected tragic end to his life. I was also surprised and puzzled.

I told Parashar as much.

So Mangaldas's nightmare had indeed come true. The time of his suicide was 7 p.m., give or take a few minutes. This was what I was astonished by. Was it true then that people can intuitively sense the outcome of their actions?

A distracted Parashar was restlessly pacing up and down. He seemed to be castigating himself.

He stopped and said, 'It was entirely my mistake.'

'What mistake have you committed?' I asked uncomprehendingly. 'Are you talking of trying to warn Jaysukh, or of assuming that Sonia was in love with him?'

'No, none of these.' He snapped, shaking his head so vehemently that it seemed wise not to ask him any further question.

6

We were no longer enjoying our stay in Bombay. Even the paradise that was Nanabhai's flat was losing its charm.

To leave Bombay in a week proved impossible. Although Parashar spent all his time in his room, absorbed in his own thoughts, he showed no inclination to return to Calcutta. And then came the summons from the police, which made it impossible to leave.

For a couple of days, I followed the results of the investigation of Mangaldas's suicide in the papers. The evidence that the police had gathered supported the suicide theory. There was no doubt from the journalists' testimonies that no one could have entered the room under their noses and committed a murder. And the pistol had yielded Mangaldas's own fingerprints, although they were faint.

A few days later, the police suddenly summoned us.

The reason was the letter Mangaldas had written to Parashar. It had been found among the documents in his room. The police wanted to know why Mangaldas had sent for Parashar. The deputy commissioner took our depositions.

I discovered that Parashar knew Deputy Commissioner Hindelkar very well. He needed Parashar's assistance. He had been forced to summon me because I had visited Mangaldas too.

Hindelkar warmly welcomed us to his private office. He began by apologizing to Parashar, 'I had to trouble you only because of protocol, Mr Barma. Please don't mind. It was necessary to find out the details of your conversation with the deceased...'

'There's no need to explain, Hindelkar,' said Parashar with a smile. 'Far from being offended, I was eagerly waiting for your summons.'

'Eagerly waiting!' Hindelkar was astonished. 'So you knew we were going to send for you?'

'Of course, I did,' smiled Parashar. 'It's not very difficult to conclude that the police are unlikely to ignore a letter to me lying in Mangaldas's desk drawer.'

Parashar hadn't said anything particularly remarkable. I could not understand why Hindelkar cast a sharp glance at him. After a few moments of stiff silence, he relaxed and said, 'If you could tell us about your conversation with Mangaldas that evening? Whatever you remember, that is.'

'I remember the entire conversation,' said Parashar a trifle pompously, 'and I would like to tell you everything.'

Parashar's memory is truly extraordinary. I was astounded by his detailed recounting of the conversation with Mangaldas. Hindelkar looked worried when he had heard everything. Confessing as much to Parashar, he said, 'All that you've told me only strengthens the evidence that Mangaldas Advani indeed committed suicide. But can we rationally believe in this business of a bat entering the room repeatedly and having the same dream constantly?'

'All this lies beyond the realm of reason.' Parashar appeared to be arguing for the other side. 'And no matter how unreal it all sounds, Mangaldas's suicide proves its dreadful significance.'

'That's true.' Hindelkar couldn't seem to shake off his doubts. 'Still, I find it hard to believe this is the only factor behind the suicide.'

After a pause, Hindelkar said with a guileless smile, 'My official work is done, Mr Barma. I'm now asking you as a friend and fellow traveller for your personal opinion. You were in touch with Mangaldas at least once. You must have drawn your own conclusions about this suicide. I would be obliged if you would share them with me.'

Parashar was silent for some time. Then, looking intently at Hindelkar, he said with a touch of harshness in his voice, 'Do you really want to hear what I think, Hindelkar? It might upset all your calculations and cause more trouble for you.'

'So be it,' said Hindelkar hesitantly. 'Please don't consider us so incompetent that we would prefer an incorrect solution for the sake of convenience.'

'No, that's not what I think,' said Parashar with a smile. 'My conclusions are in a completely different direction from yours,' he continued.

'Completely different direction! What do you mean?' Hindelkar's bewilderment was palpable.

'I mean that in my opinion Mangaldas did not commit suicide. In fact, why call it an opinion? I am certain.'

Not just Hindelkar, even I was speechless on hearing this.

It was Hindelkar who recovered first to ask, 'Are you saying someone murdered Mangaldas? But how is that possible? I presume you also know when and how it happened.'

'Of course, I do,' said Parashar determinedly. 'Still, I'd like to get some more information from you. You must have taken down everyone's testimonies.'

'Naturally,' said Hindelkar, sounding offended. 'The police do not make mistakes on such routine matters. I can give you a copy if you like.'

Hindelkar gave instructions to someone over the phone.

'I'll get my answers in the transcripts. But let me first ask you something,' said Parashar. 'Jaysukh must have been asked why he had quarrelled with his father that day.'

'Yes, he was,' said Hindelkar grimly.

'If you could tell me what his answer was.'

'Jaysukh said Mangaldas had sent for him with a false accusation. Mangaldas gave his son a monthly allowance that was usually paid by cheque. Mangaldas alleged that Jaysukh had forged the amount on the cheque that month and taken extra money. He was enraged when he saw the bank returns that day and sent for Jaysukh. This was what they had argued about.'

'What does Jaysukh have to say about the allegation?' asked a mildly amused Parashar. 'Has he confessed to the fraud?'

'No,' Hindelkar shook his head. 'Jaysukh said he hadn't even received the cheque for the month. He had been thinking of reminding Mangaldas. Which was why he had flown into a temper when he was wrongly accused and had given his father a piece of his mind.'

'Hmm.' There was an inscrutable smile on Parashar's face. 'What do you make of such an explanation from someone who has debts of a lakh or two?'

'What I make of it is the obvious,' said Hindelkar. 'But I still don't see anything in there to change my mind about Mangaldas's suicide.'

A constable entered, saluted Hindelkar and deposited a pile of documents on his desk. Pushing them towards Parashar, Hindelkar said, 'Here you are. All the testimonies are in there. Of course, you have drawn your conclusions already, which will probably not change on reading these.'

'No, I won't change them,' said Parashar firmly.

'May I know where you drew those conclusions from?' Hindelkar's voice was frosty.

'Primarily   from   Mangaldas's   strange   nightmares.'   Parashar's pronouncement shocked us.

'From the nightmares!' Hindelkar made no attempt to hide his astonishment. 'You're talking in riddles, Mr Barma.'

'I'll unravel the riddle, Hindelkar,' Parashar said eagerly, 'if you give me a chance. I will also prove my hypothesis. Will you give me the opportunity?'

Hindelkar had probably not been expecting such a proposal. Despite some initial misgivings, he said after a pause, 'Tell me what sort of opportunity do you want.'

Parashar had pulled out of his pocket a large sheet of paper, folded in half. 'I've written everything down here,' he said. 'Including one or two minor things that I need the police to help me with. If you're willing, call me by this evening.'

It did not appear from the way Hindelkar took the paper that he would readily agree to Parashar's proposal.

7

However, that afternoon Hindelkar called.

And the opportunity that Parashar had asked for materialized three days later.

All of us were gathered on the second-floor hall of Mangaldas's house at 6.30 that evening.

Parashar had not divulged his plan to me. My pride did not allow me to ask him, so I remained a silent companion.

When we arrived at Mangaldas's house shortly before 6.30, the rest had already arrived—Jaysukh, Mahinder Sambrani and Rajinder Nigam and Sonia Sambrani, too. The three journalists who had been present during the incident had also been invited. Parashar, I and Hindelkar in plain clothes made up the rest of the gathering.

The seating arrangement had been altered for the meeting. Parashar and Hindelkar were seated behind a low table with their backs to the door to Mangaldas's room. I had been given a single-seater sofa next to them. The others were seated in a circle on either side of us.

We took our seats at exactly 6.30. Hindelkar conveyed the objective of the meeting with a short introductory statement. 'We have gathered here to examine whether some more light can be cast on the tragic incident that took place the other day. My friend Parashar Barma will conduct whatever interrogation is necessary.'

Parashar's fat folio bag was lying on the table in front of him. Extracting a sheaf of documents with everyone's testimonies, Parashar began speaking.

Looking around the room, he launched into a preamble with pretence of embarrassment and reluctance, apologizing for having troubled everyone by asking them to attend this redundant meeting. All of them had already said all they had to; there was nothing new to be learnt over and above the findings of the police; Mangaldas Advani's suicide, no matter how unexpected, had to be accepted considering the evidence, etc., etc.

And then his eyes suddenly settled on Rajinder Nigam. 'How long have you been working for Mangaldas, Mr Nigam?' he asked, his voice oozing empathy.

'Not very long,' answered Rajinder, flustered at having been picked out. 'Just two years.'

'What sort of boss was Mangaldas Advani?' Parashar seemed to be asking out of natural curiosity. 'The formidable kind?'

'No, not very formidable,' Rajinder stammered. 'But...he meant business. If he spotted a mistake in my work...'

Since he was hesitating, Parashar completed the sentence for him, '...he erupted like a volcano.'

'Yes, I mean no, not exactly a volcano...' Rajinder was floundering.

'Why are you hiding the truth, Mr Nigam?' Parashar sounded stern now. 'Mangaldas was a garrulous man, and when he flew into a rage his words turned into a burning stream of lava, isn't that right?'

Before a discomfited Rajinder could reply, Mahinder Sambrani, seated next to his niece Sonia, could be heard protesting.

'No, Mr Barma, I'm forced to protest. It's true my friend Mangaldas had a temper that flared up like wildfire, but his anger never lasted beyond a few moments. Besides, whether in his regular frame of mind or in the grip of anger, he was never garrulous. He was a man of few words. He was even more reluctant to waste words than to waste money.'

'Thank you, Mr Sambrani.' Parashar replied sarcastically. 'But kindly allow the person I am questioning to answer. You can say whatever you have to say when your turn comes.'

Mahinder Sambrani's face turned red with anger. But without paying the slightest attention to this, Parashar turned to Nigam and asked, softening his voice at once, 'Do you agree with Mr Sambrani then, Mr Nigam? Would you say that even if Mangaldas was a bit short-tempered, he wasn't the kind of man to bully someone into submission?'

Nigam nodded his agreement, hoping for release. But he didn't get it.

Parashar continued without a pause, 'Irrespective of how harshly he scolded others, when was the last time he scolded you?'

'The last time?' Nigam stammered with a helpless, pitiful expression.

Parashar appeared exasperated by Nigam's mumbling. He said, 'You cannot remember? Do you mean he didn't scold you in the past few days?'

'No. No, he did,' Nigam admitted shamefacedly. 'He was angry with me on the morning of the very day he died.'

'Why?' Parashar was terse.

'It wasn't exactly my fault,' Nigam interjected quickly.

'Then whose fault was it? Why should you have been scolded for someone else's fault?' Parashar was positively acerbic by now.

Nigam was unable to answer. Throwing frightened looks around the room, he was about to say something, but stopped himself.

'Why are you silent? Answer the question.' It was Hindelkar's turn now to bark at Nigam. 'Don't forget that the questions are coming from the police, even if Mr Barma is the one asking them.'

Looking crestfallen, Nigam finally said, 'He was angry because I had delayed giving him a bank statement. The statement had arrived a few days earlier, but I didn't give it to him. That day I had no choice but to hand it over because he had been asking for it repeatedly.'

'You tried to hide the statement? Why?' Parashar's eyes were boring into Nigam.

'If he saw the statement,' Nigam said after some hesitation, 'he would have been furious.'

'What did the statement say?' Parashar answered his question. 'That a cheque had been encashed for a much larger sum than Mangaldas had written out for, right? And it had been made out to Jaysukh Advani. Was he the one who encashed it?'

While Nigam had no choice but to admit this, Jaysukh roared angrily, 'Lies. I never even saw the cheque.'

'Silence,' Hindelkar ordered Jaysukh. 'We will listen to what you have to say in due course.'

Parashar turned to Nigam. 'Mangaldas realized what had happened as soon as he saw the statement, right? And he scolded you because he knew

The Moving Shadow

why you had delayed handing it over. All the same, it appears Mangaldas trusted you a great deal.'

Nigam offered a gratified silence.

'Aren't you related to Mangaldas Advani in some way?' Parashar continued.

'Yes, but distantly,' said Nigam. 'Although it was on the strength of the connection that I got the job.'

'After which you were expecting to get something bigger, weren't you?' Parashar's question stunned not just Nigam but the rest of us as well.

'Expecting something bigger!' Nigam looked at Parashar, dumbfounded.

'Yes, much bigger,' said Parashar mockingly. 'In fact, why not all of Mangaldas Advani's property and assets?'

'What are you saying!' Nigam was overcome with fear.

'Am I completely off the mark?' Parashar continued to taunt him. 'You are his nearest relative after his only son, Jaysukh. Moreover, you're loyal and trustworthy. Considering how his loathing for his son was rising by the day, he probably would have changed his will and left everything to you, had he not died suddenly. But he never got the opportunity. So whoever might benefit from his unexpected death, it's not you.'

Everyone breathed a sigh of relief along with Nigam at the change of course from accusation to praise.

'So who would benefit from this death in that case?' Surveying everyone in the room in turn, Parashar stopped at Mahinder Sambrani. 'You're Mangaldas's childhood friend, Mr Sambrani. You devoted your life to scholarship, while he chose business. But your friendship was unbroken till the end. It was you who encouraged him to buy his ancestor Jugalram's collection and ruined mansion. You were the first to discover that some items in Jugalram's collection were priceless. One of these is a square bowl of traditional Bidri design that resembles a modern bowl. The bowl would not have been particularly valuable despite its age and design, but it's priceless for a different reason. The reason is a coded message included in the silver patterns on it. But it's not a code that can be deciphered easily. Your knowledge helped you to read it accurately, Mr Sambrani. But out of greed, you did not pass on the message to your friend Mangaldas. Your plan was to retrieve the treasure from the location encoded in the bowl, all by yourself. You intended to deprive Mangaldas of what was rightfully his. Can you hold your hands out, Mr Sambrani? I'd like to examine your nails.'

Not just me, but everyone seemed bewildered by Parashar's preposterous and meaningless request. Had he gone mad?

'This is no time for absurd jokes, Mr Barma,' Hindelkar said in annoyance.

'I never joke when I am working, Mr Hindelkar, least of all in the presence of a top police officer,' said Parashar, and jumped to his feet to examine Mahinder Sambrani's nails.

Then, to our consternation, he said, 'You shouldn't have been too lazy to clip your nails, Mr Sambrani.'

'Can you explain, Mr Barma?' asked Hindelkar impatiently.

Returning to his chair, Parashar said, 'Certainly. I'll also prove that I'm not just making wild, unsubstantiated accusations. Mahinder Sambrani's nails prove that he's been making use of the information he has decoded from the Bidri bowl. The priceless bowl did slip out of his grasp once. He had not been able to tell his friend Mangaldas its real value. It used to be kept in Mangaldas's room among the many everyday objects. Mahinder Sambrani had not yet succeeded in deciphering the code. Then, it suddenly disappeared. Mangaldas was particularly agitated about its loss on Sambrani's instigation. Sambrani was losing his mind over the loss of the bowl. He knew that Jaysukh sometimes sold family heirlooms for quick cash. But asking Jaysukh about the bowl would have made his intention obvious. So Mahinder incited his friend to anger by informing him of Jaysukh's pilferage. He stressed on the need to recover the bowl as a sample of rare, traditional design. Mangaldas was already incensed with his reckless, spendthrift son. Realizing that he might lose his inheritance if he did not get back the bowl, Jaysukh tried his best to retrieve it. He usually sold these things to auctioneers in Calcutta, for fear of being found out in Bombay. He had to knock on several doors to locate the bowl in Calcutta. This was his punishment for not remembering which auctioneer he had sold it to. I learnt from an employee at one of the auctioneers that a young man from a wealthy family in Bombay was doing the rounds of auction houses to buy certain objets d'art. It made me suspicious. So, I attended several of the auctions. My suspicions deepened when I was told by one of the auctioneers that someone had been trying to buy the Bidri bowl the day before the auction. Masquerading as an ordinary customer, I deliberately raised the bids for the bowl. Someone did match my bids up to a point. I assumed he was the rich man's son, but that was not the case. He was Sambrani's man. Mahinder was in a hurry to recover the bowl. It was he who followed Jaysukh to Calcutta and set a man on his tail to locate the bowl. He had thought of acquiring it quietly himself before Jaysukh could get his hands on it. Whether Jaysukh was bold enough to go back to Mangladas empty-handed or not, Mahinder Sambrani would accomplish his purpose in secret. But I came in his way, bidding a higher amount than what he had provided his representative with. Then, he tried his best to buy it off me at any price. Jaysukh didn't know any of this. True to his lackadaisical nature, he had not made it to the auction on time. The next morning, he came to my residence looking for the bowl. Although I had not fathomed the entire mystery yet, I let him have the bowl at whatever price he could afford, so that I could keep an eye on things. Of course, I had suspected a hidden code so I had made paper copies of the design before I let him have the bowl.'

The journalists had been listening to this long speech with rapt attention. One of them asked Parashar sceptically as soon as he paused, 'But what is this mysterious message that leads to a treasure, and why does it need special knowledge to decipher it?'

'All this is either the ravings of a mad man or a hoax to claim that he's a great detective!' Mahinder Sambrani snarled before Parashar could speak. 'I know that bowl quite well. Its only value is in its traditional design. There's not even a trace of a code in it.'

'If that's the case why did you steal it from Jaysukh?'

Parashar's eyes were like searchlights.

'I stole it from Jaysukh?' Mahinder was raging now.

'Yes. You were disappointed when you couldn't get hold of the bowl even after offering me five hundred. But because you were watching my house, you saw Jaysukh enter and leave happily, which gave you a fresh lease of life. You had no trouble at all relieving a careless and irresponsible fellow like Jaysukh of the bowl soon after he returned to Bombay. You could decipher the code peacefully and start work according to its instructions.'

'What exactly was this work?' asked Hindelkar.

'The work was to look for the hidden treasure here in this ruined mansion that once belonged to Jugalram. Jugalram not only possessed the intelligence and industriousness needed to amass a fortune, but also a passion for knowledge and a romantic heart. Although he was a cotton trader, he actually visited Egypt even in that era and probably returned with a working knowledge of a lost script. It's now called the Demotic script. Similar to the

Arabic script, and also written from right to left. But the similarity ends there. Even today's experts cannot decipher it properly. It's said that the oldest Christian community of Egypt, the Copts, still use it to send secret messages. Jugalram decided to encode in the designs of these bowls, the locations where he had hidden his treasures. One of them had reached the family home in Sindh. Mahinder Sahib is an Egyptologist himself, and the Demotic script is not unknown to him. As soon as he saw the bowl in the family collection, he got a hint of a code written in the Demotic script. The little that he could decipher immediately made him greedy for Jugalram's hidden riches. He was the one who made Mangaldas buy this dilapidated mansion in the guise of preserving his forefather's memory. And for some time now, he has been secretly digging in here. The soil beneath his nails proves this. I do not know whether Mahinder has unearthed anything yet, but he could no longer continue searching in peace. Despite Mangaldas's pressure, Jaysukh had said nothing more than the fact that the bowl had been stolen. Mangaldas was an extremely intelligent man. Perhaps it had not been difficult for him to conclude that Jaysukh was telling the truth. He would have discovered his friend's betrayal soon. If he got to know that Mahinder was secretly visiting the ruined portions of the building, he would have put two and two together at once. This would have destroyed Mahinder's chances. So, Sambrani had a great deal to gain by getting rid of Mangaldas before he made the discovery. There would be no obstacle in his path after Mangaldas's death. It wouldn't occur to anyone that Jugalram's ruined mansion could be a goldmine. Mahinder Sambrani knew a great deal about his friend. Such as where he kept his pistol, for instance. He may have heard about Mangaldas's nightmares too.'

'No, no, no!' Mahinder Sambrani protested plaintively. 'I didn't know any of this. I didn't kill Mangaldas.'

After a few moments of silence, as though to allow everyone to compose themselves, Parashar said grimly, 'But you did want to keep the treasure for yourself. You did decipher the coded message in the bowl and try to buy it through a frontman from the auction house in Calcutta. You did steal the bowl from Jaysukh. And now you are digging amidst the ruins every day to find that treasure. I saw you myself.'

'Yes.' Mahinder Sambrani was a broken man now. Lowering his eyes, he said, 'I betrayed my friend. I did it for the chance to be rich at last. We had grown up together, and most of us were exiled from our homes because of the Partition. Mangaldas got out of extreme poverty with hard work and became enormously wealthy, while I gave my life to acquiring knowledge and remained a beggar. Although Mangaldas took care of my needs like a brother, I couldn't help envying him. It was when I saw the bowl that I felt the desire to match his wealth. Mangaldas was already a rich man. Why did his wealth have to increase? I decided to keep the treasure to myself. But I never ever dreamt of killing Mangaldas, you must believe me.'

'I believe you, Mr Sambrani.' Parashar's tone turned sympathetic. 'You may be greedy and envious, but we accept that you're no murderer.'

Parashar was about to continue when a journalist interrupted him. 'How did you know there was a secret code in the bowl, Mr Barma? And how did you manage to read the Demotic script, for that matter?'

'I didn't read it myself,' Parashar admitted with a humble smile. 'I referred it to an expert on Egyptology. Not that he could decipher it entirely either—he could only provide some indicators. The intensity of the bidding for the bowl made me suspect it was more valuable then it appeared to be. It could not have fetched such a high price just by being a rare example of traditional craftsmanship. When I examined it closely, I suspected that the patterns could actually be a secret code. Because of its similarity with the Arabic script, I had it examined by a maulvi. I didn't give up when he failed. I copied the patterns before handing the bowl over to Jaysukh. Talking to experts on ancient scripts revealed that the Demotic script was similar to the Arabic. Fortunately, I managed to track down an Egyptologist, who helped me in partially deciphering the code. The mystery became clearer when I learnt that Mahinder Sambrani is the only Egyptologist here.'

After a pause Parashar continued, 'But our investigation doesn't end there. Who wanted Mangaldas to die? Who would benefit the most?'

Suddenly turning to Jaysukh, Parashar said, 'As Mangaldas's only child and heir, doesn't Jaysukh have the greatest stake in his father's death? The extent of his stake needs to be explained. Of course, Jaysukh expected to inherit his father's wealth in any case, but it was doubtful whether his expectations would be met if Mangaldas lived longer. He was gradually losing all hope in his undisciplined and profligate son. He had run up huge debts, relying on his father's assets to pay them back. He had stolen and sold many valuable objets d'art to fund his reckless spending. When Mangaldas learnt all of this, he reduced Jaysukh's monthly allowance to a pittance. Realizing that his son would squander his hard-earned wealth, he decided that he might as well soon change his will. He may have threatened Jaysukh with this. Wouldn't Mangaldas's sudden death solve Jaysukh's problems? Especially since Mangaldas had himself paved the way for his murder to be passed off as suicide by talking of the bat and the nightmare of being shot by a figure resembling himself? Jaysukh probably decided to take advantage of the opportunity that presented itself when his father told him of the bat and the nightmare…'

'Rubbish! Raving lunatic!' Grinding his teeth violently, Jaysukh was screaming at Parashar. 'All these are your devilish twisted lies. My father was not a mad man who would have such ludicrous nightmares and then go telling people about it. His suicide itself is unbelievable.'

'So you accept that it's hard to believe your father committed suicide.' Seizing on Jaysukh's admission, Parashar ran his eyes across the room before continuing. 'If it was not suicide, then someone must have killed Mangaldas. Now, no matter how many people might have benefited from his death, who were the ones who had access to him? The journalists were present in this room at the time. Jaysukh entered Mangaldas's room in their presence and emerged shortly afterwards.'

One of the journalists was about to speak up but Parashar interrupted him. 'I know what you were going to say. All of you heard Jaysukh threatening Mangaldas as he came out of his father's room. But none of you could see Mangaldas. How do you know whether he was alive or dead at the time? What if I said Jaysukh had shot Mangaldas with his own pistol and then pretended to threaten him from the doorway…'

'No, this is impossible. I don't believe it.'

Startling us with her desperate, ardent protestations, Sonia jumped up from her chair and ran to Jaysukh, falling to her knees beside him and saying, 'Tell me you didn't do this, tell me you can't do this. Tell me it's a lie.'

However, not even Sonia's fervent appeal could hide a faint note of suspicion.

But an agitated Jaysukh said, taking her hands in his, 'These are lies, Sonia. Utter lies. It's true that addiction made me depraved. After you went away from me in revulsion I have been trying to reform. Believe me, Sonia, Pitaji never told me about these nightmares. I never saw the cheque they're accusing me of forging. I didn't know there was a pistol in Pitaji's room.'

'I know, Jaysukh, I believe you.'

'Let's end the drama right there, Miss Sambrani,' cut in Parashar harshly, as though unwilling to indulge them any longer. 'Don't you think you've left it too late to say what's in your heart? But let me finish first.'

Almost as if to stoke our curiosity, Parashar paused again. Then he said, 'I began these discussions with a consideration of who might have the most to gain from Mangaldas's sudden death. We saw straightaway that Rajinder stood to gain nothing at all. But would things not change if it could be proven that Jaysukh Advani had murdered his father? Rajinder was Mangaldas's nearest relative after Jaysukh and the only other heir. So, Mr Nigam, all your wishes could be fulfilled this way.'

'I don't understand,' said Rajinder in dismay.

'Then let me make it clearer.' Parashar was at his sarcastic best. 'It was you who thought of killing two birds with one stone, Rajinder Nigam. Mangaldas would appear to have suddenly committed suicide. On the face of it, you had nothing to gain from his death. The benefit would go entirely to Jaysukh. The police would make a strange discovery at first, supporting the possibility of suicide. To ensure that the police asked me about it, the letter that had been sent to me would have to be taken back and placed among Mangaldas's papers. I am a detective, after all, even if not a professional one. So my account of that meeting would be taken seriously. And I would mention not only the peculiar dream but also the fact that Jaysukh considered his father's death imminent. The police would also come to know from my statement that Jaysukh was aware of his father's pistol. You were not wrong in assuming that the police are not blind, and would start suspecting Jaysukh. All the suspicion had to be centred on one individual. The strategy for getting Jaysukh to present himself to Mangaldas at that hour was an ingenious one. The amount on the cheque issued to Jaysukh had been forged and the extra money withdrawn shortly before the date on which the statement arrived. The statement was suppressed not out of pity for Jaysukh but to ensure that it was shown to Mangaldas at the opportune moment. Mangaldas followed strict rules, and never deviated from routine. Between six and eight, he examined the accounts related to his business and the house in his room. The statement was made available to him in a way that led him to summon Jaysukh to his room that evening. That particular day and time were chosen to coincide with the arrival of the journalists. Obviously, Jaysukh protested vehemently when his father accused him of forging the cheque. He quarrelled with Mangaldas about this. Even if he hadn't issued a threat from the doorway, the journalists would have confirmed that he had gone into his father's room and then came out some time later. Jaysukh's proclivities, the accusation of the forged cheque and his standing to gain in the event of his father's death all worked against him, just as Rajinder Nigam had calculated. Jaysukh would have been in handcuffs by now, had Rajinder not made two fatal errors.'

'What were these two errors?' It was Rajinder who asked this question, a transformed figure now, his voice dripping contempt.

'The first mistake was using a silencer,' said Parashar with a smile. 'We know that Jaysukh went into Mangaldas's room that day. But let's not forget that so did Rajinder Nigam. Not even the best doctor can identify the time of death without an error margin of thirty minutes either way. Mangaldas was hale and hearty when Jaysukh left. After this Rajinder appeared on the scene, ostensibly to help the journalists. I can surmise what he did. Going up to Mangaldas, he fired at him using a pistol whose butt was wrapped in a handkerchief. The bullet immediately killed Mangaldas. Now, Rajinder held the pistol by its barrel after covering it with the handkerchief and pressed Mangaldas's right hand to the butt to get his fingerprints on it. Then he tossed the pistol on the floor at a short distance away from the body. He chose the right hand deliberately. At first it would appear to support the suicide theory, but even a cursory investigation would reveal just the opposite. For Mangaldas was left-handed. It didn't take long for the police to discover this, whereupon they were sure that it wasn't suicide—just as Rajinder had intended. After this he came out of the room in a disturbed state and ushered the journalists inside. But using the silencer was a fatal error. The door to the room is so thick and fits so tightly that no sound would have escaped anyway. And even if a sound was heard, there would have been no reason to consider it a gunshot. This neighbourhood is full of factories, and vehicles drive by all the time. Even a tyre bursting on the road would make a louder sound than a pistol being fired. But Rajinder made his first mistake by being extra careful and using a silencer. Mangaldas bought his pistol a long time ago. Rajinder was right in assuming that the police would use the number and trademark to identify the shop from which it had been bought. The trail would have gone cold had Rajinder not used the silencer. But the possibility of a silencer occurred to me as soon as I realized it was not a case of suicide. I asked Mr Hindelkar to enquire about the sale of a silencer for this make of pistol. That was how the police discovered that such a silencer had indeed been purchased recently, with Mangaldas recorded as the buyer. This was particularly suspicious. Even if Mangaldas had a pistol for self-defence, why would he suddenly need a silencer? Documents were needed to buy one, and Mangaldas was unlikely to give them to Mahinder Sambrani or Jaysukh or Rajinder Nigam without a good reason. However, as his secretary, Rajinder had access to all his papers and could easily remove the necessary document. That's why I said it would have been a little more difficult to figure out Rajinder's role had he not used a silencer.

'His second fatal error was to meet me disguised as Mangaldas and behave in a way inconsistent with his employer.'

'What! You mean it was Rajinder who disguised himself as Mangaldas to meet you that evening?' asked Sonia Sambrani, her eyes wide with astonishment.

'Yes, Miss Sambrani. Think about it. The only person who can pass himself off as Mangaldas is Rajinder. Jaysukh is taller and bigger than his father. Your uncle is short and thickset. Rajinder, who is tall and thin, was the only one who could have disguised himself as Mangaldas. It was his misfortune that we met you on the stairs that evening. Perhaps it was to meet Jaysukh that you had gone to the second floor on the pretext of meeting your uncle. Your surprise on seeing us wait to meet Mangaldas outside the secretary's room on the first floor tipped me off that something was wrong. My enquiries revealed that Mangaldas was always alone in his room at that hour and, moreover, he never met anyone in his secretary's room. It was Rajinder who had sent the letter purportedly from Mangaldas, and had made all the arrangements. This wouldn't have done any harm, but although Rajinder used flawless make-up to make himself look like Mangaldas, he didn't keep the character in mind. As all of you and Rajinder himself have revealed, Mangaldas was a man of few words. But Rajinder talked so much while telling us about the nightmare that it did not match Mangaldas's nature at all. Once I had found out more about Mangaldas, it was this discrepancy rather than the contents of the nightmare that bothered me more. And it was also this that yielded the first clue to unravelling the mystery of his death. Rajinder Nigam had set a fine trap to grab Mangaldas's property and win Sonia Sambrani at the same time. But his two mistakes snared him in his own trap.'

Two police sergeants had silently appeared behind Rajinder Nigam. As soon as Parashar finished his speech, one of them slipped a pair of handcuffs onto his wrists at Hindelkar's signal.

I had only a few questions for Parashar on our way back to the flat in Malabar Hill that evening.

My first question: 'You kept saying "my mistake" after learning of Mangaldas's death. What was this mistake?'

'The mistake was linking the mystery of the bowl to Mangaldas's death. That's why it took me so long to solve the mystery.'

My second question was, 'You said you went to warn Jaysukh. About what, considering that Mangaldas wasn't dead yet?'

'I went to warn him about the hour of visiting his father,' said Parashar. 'I wanted to tell him not to visit him at seven in the evening at any cost. But Jaysukh didn't give me the chance. Because of the way Rajinder, disguised as Mangaldas, kept harping about seven o'clock, I suspected that hour could be dangerous for Jaysukh.'

My third question was meant to be a barb. 'You solved the mystery adequately, but was all this drama necessary?'

'Of course, it was,' said Parashar with a smug smile. 'It was to get the real-life drama end on a happy note that I had to make a theatrical presentation of the mystery. Sonia and Jaysukh would never have given themselves to each other without this performance.'

The Moving Shadow

SWAPAN KUMAR

THE CORPSE VANISHES

Calcutta Police Morgue. 5 p.m.

The corpse of a man who had died mysteriously lay on a table—the dissection table. Dr Birupakasha Mitra was running his scalpel across the body.

He was deep in concentration, silent, still…

He extracted the entrails, liver, spleen and other organs and placed them on a tray. They would have to be examined carefully.

Suddenly the phone rang in the next room.

Dr Mitra rushed to answer it.

'Hello, who is it?'

'You don't know me. There's a reason I'm ringing you.'

'What reason?'

'Nothing special. It was necessary for you to come into this room to answer the phone.'

'Why?'

'That's what I'm about to tell you. Look, I will not tell you who I am. For now, assume I'm a stranger. I need the corpse on your dissection table.'

'What! Why?'

'I need it urgently.'

'Impossible.'

'Meaning?'

'It is illegal to hand over a dead body to an unknown person.'

'I see. But I need it for a specific reason which will benefit everyone. So I shall have to take it whether you agree or not. I have made arrangements.'

'What do you mean?'

'Very simple. I shall take it without your knowledge. That is how I have planned it. I knew you wouldn't agree to handing it over. So I lured you away from the room and am accepting the body now.'

'What!'

'Yes, when you go back the corpse will no longer be there.'

'You're lying. Let me check.'

Dr Mitra put down the receiver and rushed back to the dissection room. A huge surprise awaited him. The corpse and the organs on the tray had all vanished.

Only a few scattered drops of blood remained, bearing witness to the theft of the corpse.

Once he had recovered from the shock, an unarticulated rage took hold of him.

Who was this stranger? Such audacity! Drawing him away to the phone and making off with the corpse meanwhile! But to what purpose? Waves of thoughts swarmed over Dr Mitra. He didn't even know when he assaulted the bell on his desk.

Tring tring tring...

The bearer came running.

'Salaam, sahib.'

'Where were you all this time?'

'Just outside, huzoor.'

'What! Then who took the corpse away?'

'But you ordered for it to be taken away, sahib.'

'Me?'

'Yes, two men took it away. I assumed you had ordered them.'

Dr Mitra felt himself burn with fury from head to toe. The sheer nerve of spiriting the corpse away right under his nose! He went outside.

'Ramdeen Chaubey!'

'Yes, sir!'

'Did you see two men carry something away?'

'Yes, sir. They took something away in a car a short while ago.'

'Why didn't you stop them?'

'Sir, they said you had told them to take it away.'

'I'm surrounded by idiots.'

He paced up and down impatiently. The lines of anxiety hardened on his face. How would it help them to take a corpse?

After some thought, he went back to the telephone. He dialled a number and said, 'Hello, connect me to police headquarters, Lalbazar.'

THE BLOOD BANK

The Medical College. 9 p.m.

The large room next to the emergency area was the cardiology department. The blood bank was located there. The blood stored here was transfused into patients as required.

A car stopped outside.

Monsoon. It was raining incessantly. The wind whistled. Occasional flashes of lightning.

Two men in raincoats got out of the car. They entered the blood bank.

Two students were on duty. One of them asked the strangers, 'Who are you looking for?'

'Dr Mukherjee...'

'Oh. He's in the emergency room.'

'We'd be very grateful if you could send for him.'

'What is it for?'

'We've brought an emergency patient. He's in bad shape. Please tell him Dr Majumdar is with the patient...'

'Oh, are you Dr Majumdar? Good evening.'

'Good evening.'

'Please have a seat, Dr Mukherjee will be here soon.'

One of the students put on his raincoat and went out to fetch Dr Mukherjee. The strangers remained standing. The other student said, 'Please sit down.'

'Yes.'

A mysterious smile appeared on the stranger's face for a moment. At once, his companion sprayed the student with a liquid chemical. A strange smell. Sweet, but not like the fragrance of flowers or perfume. A heavy sensation. Sleep...Sleep descended. Fatigue. Exhaustion. The student slumped into the arms of deep slumber.

The two strangers smiled. Triumphant smiles, signifying success.

Swiftly they ran towards the blood bank.

Fifteen minutes later.

The other student returned accompanied by Dr Mukherjee.

But where were the strangers? Where had they vanished suddenly? And what was the meaning of this abrupt disappearance? Why was the other student asleep?

'Moloy! Moloy!'

They tried to wake him up. But it was beyond them to rouse him. Then they turned to the blood bank. A shock awaited them. They had never imagined being confronted with such an extraordinary turn of events.

Dr Mukherjee rushed to the telephone. He dialled the local police station.

'Hello, who is it?'

'This is Dr Mukherjee. From the Medical College.'

'What's the matter, Dr Mukherjee? This is Inspector Tarafdar.'

'Something bizarre has happened, Mr Tarafdar. Please come at once. Someone has stolen 400 cubic centimetres of blood from our blood bank.'

'Stolen blood?'

'Yes.'

'How strange! This is extraordinary, Dr Mukherjee.'

'Yes, I am not aware of such a thing having happened ever before at the medical college.'

'It's truly unusual. I'm on my way, Dr Mukherjee.'

Tarafdar searched the place thoroughly but found no clue. All he found was a note.

It said:

We are forced to take away 400 cubic centimetres of blood for a crucial need, Dr Mukherjee. You can be assured that it will be used for the benefit of society. We have no evil intentions. Greetings.

Sincerely,
The Moving Shadow

Dr Mukherjee, Tarafdar and the student stared at the note in astonishment.

A NEW EXPLOIT OF THE MOVING SHADOW

Ballygunge Lake.

Eight o'clock the following evening.

A young man and woman were seen sitting by Ballygunge Lake. The man seemed to be about twenty-five. The woman, a year or two younger.

This area near the lake was usually deserted.

Moreover, the sky was dark. The moon was yet to rise. Everything was sunk in darkness.

It was obvious from the young woman's clothes that she was a rich man's daughter. The impression was reinforced not just by her polished appearance, but also her fine style and expensive jewellery.

The young man was dressed in simple clothes—but tastefully.

They were so absorbed in their conversation that it was difficult to say whether they had the slightest awareness of the outside world.

The young woman was speaking.

'I understand clearly what you're saying, but I cannot support it wholeheartedly.'

'Why not?' Anup questioned her.

'Since my father has immense wealth, he should not be attached to it anymore. You agree, don't you?'

'I have no choice but to agree.'

'I am his only child. Should he not in that case ensure that my life is successful in every way?'

'I don't deny it.'

'Then he should accept the person I want as my companion in life, shouldn't he? It will make me happy if he does. But if he forces me to marry a rich man, is that not injustice towards me? He has no need for money. There is no one to enjoy the wealth he has. Should his daughter's happiness not be more important to him than wealth?'

'Looked at this way, you are telling the truth, Bina.'

'Then why are you advising me to obey his wish?'

'Because, all said and done, he is your father. I cannot advise you to defy him.'

'Even if my father's unfairness goes against my conscience?'

'There's one more thing.'

'What is it?'

'If your father is trying to find a wealthy husband for you, it is for your happiness…'

'But he has enough money for any couple to be happy. He should not be coveting more wealth.'

'Maybe he thinks you will not be happy this way.'

'Then it would have been better not to have given his daughter an education. He should not have let me think independently. It would have been better to have married me off to a pile of money when I was younger. But since that did not happen, and since I have chosen someone from a middle-class family as my life's companion, is it right for him to stop me?'

'I cannot answer this question at the moment, Bina.'

'No one who examines my reasoning carefully will be able to find a flaw in it, Anup-da.'

Anup sighed.

He was lost in thought. What a strange world, and how peculiar its people and their games of joys and sorrows, their laughter and tears! And yet everything was so transient. Still they wanted to be happy.

What he wanted in his heart and soul was just what Bina desired too.

Their thoughts were one. That was why they were so close to each other. And yet, so distant from everything else in the world.

'You have chosen an unsuitable hour to be here. A very bad time, in fact.'

Someone nearby was speaking. Anup's thoughts were interrupted.

Bina too looked around.

A tall, middle-aged man was standing in front of them. There was no sign of anyone else nearby.

It was probably about 9 p.m. now. The still nocturnal hours throbbed with an unbroken silence. A mild breeze was blowing. The faint rustling of the leaves of coconut trees. The slight trembling of the water.

'We didn't realize it was so late. Come on, Bina, let's go.'

'Yes, let's go.'

The stranger emitted an odd laugh.

What a strange man!

Anup looked him up and down. Unkempt hair. French beard. Bushy moustache. Black suit. Strange glittering eyes. Anup was not pleased with the way he had intruded on them.

'There was no need to warn us. We would have left when it was time.' Anup said brusquely.

'That's right,' the man continued to smile, 'of course, you'd have left. But given how bad the times are, everyone should be careful, don't you think?'

'Thank you.'

Anup turned to Bina. 'Come on, Bina, let's go.'

They walked off towards the car parked nearby.

As they were getting inside the car, Anup noticed that the strange man had followed them. He could not comprehend what the stranger's intention was.

'Why are you...'

Anup could not complete his sentence. A strange smell. Sweet. Cold. Overpowering. Both of them slumped to the ground, unconscious. A mysterious smile appeared on the middle-aged man's face.

Much later, Anup recovered consciousness. An icy wind made him shiver. He felt as though he had woken up from a long sleep. He looked around carefully, trying to recollect what had happened. He remembered everything. Anup sat up with a start, looking around for Bina. But where was she?

Anup's probing eyes swept the place. But Bina was nowhere in sight. Only the tread of car tyres was visible in the soft earth.

They had wound their way into the distance. Was all this the strange man's doing then? But there was no evidence that he had a car. And why should he do something like this anyway?

But who was this strange man? No sooner had Anup taken a step or two than his eyes were drawn to a folded sheet of white paper on the ground. Picking it up, he unfolded it. In tiny handwriting, it said:

I'm taking her for some urgent business. Don't worry, she will come to no harm. I will return her safely.

Her father might suspect you have spirited her away. Hence, this letter. Show it to the police and explain everything.

Sincerely,

The Moving Shadow

Reading the letter breathlessly, Anup was bewildered. Who was this Moving Shadow? Was it the strange man? But how could that be possible? Anyway, he had to inform the police at once. Anup got into the car and started the engine.

He set off for the nearest police station leaving behind a cloud of smoke.

Private detective Dipak Chatterjee had long been used to drinking a cup of coffee on waking up in the morning. His assistant and friend, Ratanlal, had often warned him about his. 'Look, it's unhealthy to drink coffee on an empty stomach.' But Dipak had paid no attention. He needed his morning coffee to get going and concentrate on his work.

The four letters that had arrived in the mail lay on his desk. Dipak began to read them.

The first two were greetings from old clients. One was from a distant relative. Dipak picked up the last one.

It was in an envelope. He slit it open and found a small slip of paper inside. It was heavy for its size. Clearly torn out of an expensive writing pad.

Dipak concentrated on the letter.

Dear Dipak Chatterjee,

You may not know me, but I know you rather well. We have not met formally, but I have heard a lot about you.

I've been told you're a nationally famous detective. It does not take you long to solve the most complex of cases. Even if you had not known my name through this letter, you would have heard a great deal about me in a day or two. You may even have to devote a considerable part of your energies to capture me. For no one else in the police department has the mental faculties necessary to apprehend me.

And now, a request to you, Mr Chatterjee. All I have done or am about to do is not for my own benefit but for the welfare of society. These acts may be considered illegal, but I had no choice but to adopt this route. The person to whom I had opened my heart was the one who chose to ignore me, to slight me, to loathe me. So I was compelled to go my own way.

But if I am successful, my fame will spread around the world. The newspapers will publish my photographs. The government will be eager to withdraw all cases against me and give me a handsome reward.

But let that pass. What I wish to tell you is this: pray do not involve yourself too much with my case. You may be intelligent but you are not powerful. I am both intelligent and powerful.

Therefore, if you prove an impediment to me I shall have no choice but to eliminate you by force. India will lose a fine detective.

There is no need to write anything further. I trust that a discerning person like you will draw the right conclusions.

My affectionate regards,

Sincerely,
The Moving Shadow

Dipak looked up and found Ratanlal gazing at him. 'What are you reading with such great concentration?' He sounded curious.

'This letter,' Dipak handed it to him.

Ratanlal read it closely twice.

'It's a mystery from start to finish. But all said this letter does not augur well for you.'

'Why not?'

'I am certain that it will make you even keener to track down this Moving Shadow. Far from good, this letter will do harm.'

Dipak did not respond.

Ratanlal said to himself, 'Who is this Moving Shadow?'

⟡

ON THE INVESTIGATIVE TRAIL

Who was this Moving Shadow?

The newspaper editorial said:

Who is this person who can ignore both the police and the public to break the law all over Calcutta and still be at large with such arrogance?

We know the powers of the police are limited. But if the DD and the CID are unable to track down the criminal and apprehend him in time, the lives and property of the people will have no value any more. The city will be in a state of anarchy under the rule of bandits.

Sometimes it is not possible to capture the perpetrator after one or two crimes. But considering that the Moving Shadow has struck at three places in three days and successfully committed his illegal acts, it is difficult to predict how much more damage he will cause. We are not aware of such a succession of crimes in this metropolis.

Admittedly, the public suffered no damage in two of these cases. But after the mysterious disappearance of a young woman from the vicinity of the Ballygunge Lake in the evening, what words of consolation will the police offer her parents? Our reporter has apprised us that she is the only child of wealthy parents. We do not have the words to mitigate their agony at this difficult hour.

∿

Detective Dipak Chatterjee looked up from the newspaper and turned to Ratanlal.

'I can finally hazard a guess about the letter that came yesterday.'

'Say what you like, this Moving Shadow is an accomplished man. Striking at three places in three days is no mean feat!'

Dipak smiled. He did not respond.

'What are you smiling at?'

'I'm wondering why this man behaved like a criminal despite being highly educated and a scientist to boot.'

'What do you mean?'

'Can't you see how strong his predilection is for announcing his name and claiming notoriety?'

'But why do such things happen?'

'That's what I'm wondering. He knows his letter will fire my curiosity and that I will try to track him down. Still he wishes to stoke this instinct in me. Besides, leaving a letter at the scene of each of his crimes also speaks of the tendency of traditional criminals to announce their presence.'

'That's all very well, but what have you decided to do?'

'I am not willing to waste my mental energy on this without an invitation from the police. It does not matter how many letters the Moving Shadow writes to provoke me.'

'Why are you assuming that the Moving Shadow is trying to provoke you?'

'Are you saying there is no reason to assume as much? The letter makes it clear that the Moving Shadow deeply desires that I should set out on his trail. He wants a renowned and talented detective like me to be involved in this case. And he wants to derive his satisfaction by outwitting me. Hence the threat in the letter, that attempting to capture him will mean inevitable death. Which means, let me see if you dare to ignore the possibility of death to come after me, Dipak Chatterjee…'

Dipak couldn't finish what he was saying. There was rustle near the window.

Thok! A sharp dagger flew in and embedded itself in the desk.

'Who's that?'

Dipak raced to the window.

A figure ran across the garden and got into a car waiting outside. It drove off with a cloud of smoke.

Dipak smiled.

'You see how sharp the eyes in my back are? Anyway, let's see what the dagger has brought.'

A piece of paper was impaled on the tip of the blade. Folded over. Dipak unfolded it and read:

> Try as you might, you cannot stay away. I sense that you will receive an invitation to track me down. Fate will force you to follow me. But beware! This is my final warning.
>
> Sincerely,
> The Moving Shadow

'He has guessed that I will be asked to trace him. But is he right?'

Tring tring tring… The phone rang.

'Yes?'

'This is the deputy commissioner, DD [Detective Department] North…'

'Ah, Mr Morrison? How are you, sir?'

'Have you read the papers, Mr Chatterjee?'

'Yes, I paid close attention to the news of the Moving Shadow.'

'What should our course of action be now? It won't be long before the reputation of the police is besmirched. The newspapers are harassing us…'

'What steps are you considering?'

'That's what I was wondering, so I thought of consulting you. Would you please take on this case, Mr Chatterjee. I will help you in every possible way.'

'But there's something I need from you, Mr Morrison.'

'Yes, tell me.'

'You'll have to keep it a secret. You must not let anyone know I have taken on this case.'

'Very well.'

'I will come by Lalbazar in the evening to collect the case files.'

'Thank you.'

✧

Dipak disconnected the call and turned to Ratanlal.

'I just couldn't refuse it.'

'What is it?'

'Mr Morrison's orders. Therefore, I have to take on the Moving Shadow case.'

The phone rang loudly again.

'Hello, who is it?'

'This is the Moving Shadow.'

'Oh?'

'Yes, you know who I am. So the case has finally come to you. You may want to keep your involvement a secret, but nothing escapes my eyes.'

'But how did you find out that I have taken the case?'

'Very simple, Dipak-babu. I heard every word of your phone conversation. Anyway, what have you decided? Do you plan to honour my request?'

'No, not all. My fight against those who break the law will always continue. I will not have the slightest regret even if I have to give up my life for it.'

Dipak slammed down the phone without waiting for a response.

✧

NIRUPAMA, THE ACTRESS

Everyone desires a woman in the first flush of youth. More so, if she is beautiful. But the curse of God makes youth transient. And sadly, the longevity of a woman's beauty and grace is far shorter than that of a man's.

And so those women who earn respect, fame and wealth for their youth and beauty eventually attract humiliation, poverty and neglect, and much more when that youthfulness wanes. This was especially true of the actress Nirupama Debi.

Nirupama was born into a poor family. She was orphaned at a young age. Her uncle married her off to an older man. Three months later, her husband died. Nirupama Debi was no longer welcome at her husband's house. Her family too had shunned her.

One day, Nirupama met a friend who was an actress. Nirupama told her the story of her life—the agony of poverty, the mockery of fate, the game of dice life played on her.

Her friend replied, 'You are so young and beautiful—what are you worried about?'

'What do you mean?'

'You must join films. Unlimited money, unending happiness, eternal peace—whatever you want.'

Sweet water to tempt the parched traveller.

Nirupama joined films. A heroine's role on debut. She didn't have much talent for acting. Her performance in her first film was remembered as lacklustre.

But audiences did not care for acting skills; they wanted the glamour and allure of the beautiful young woman to fulfil their fantasies.

That was why Nirupama Debi still remembered that first day. She had watched her own performance from a box in the theatre when her film was released. As soon as she appeared on screen, there was a murmur, whispers, applause and more.

Nirupama had been elated. Her heart was filled with pleasure at the thought that it was not the glow of her performance but her appeal and youth that had made a mark on the audience.

After this, the years of her life had passed with the speed of the frames of a film. Everywhere she went, she had been met with love, praise and adulation. Producers wooed her with money. Those dreamlike days were still etched in her memory.

Exactly twelve years had passed this way.

And then?

And then one day, she found the number of her contracts dwindling to a point where only one producer was still offering her roles. And that too, as a mother or an aunt.

Meanwhile the heroines' roles had been given to newly-arrived beautiful actresses.

Nirupama had the chance to take a good look at herself in the mirror that day. The signs of nature's unchecked journey were evident in the corners of her eyes, the creases on her face, the lines on her forehead. She had lost her unparalleled appeal; she had lost, too, the immaculate and radiant perfection of her youth. What had she turned into? Who would give her a chance any more?

Nirupama could not sleep well at night. Her days passed in anxiety. But how long could she go on this way? She was not talented enough as an actress to secure serious roles. She would have to spend the rest of her life in a mess, unable to do anything useful. Forced to stay on the same wobbling, aimless meridian of life, with conversations and laughter banned from her existence.

How long would the money in her bank account last? Perhaps nine or ten years, at most. After which she would possibly have to look at unsavoury and unpalatable options to earn a living. And there was no guarantee that even those would succeed. She could see no ray of hope anywhere.

Nirupama's days passed, filled with these worries.

But the gods smiled on her suddenly. She found just the person she had been seeking with all her heart.

Every day and night she had been wondering whether modern science could offer a way to preserve her beauty. Was there nothing that could bend it to human will? Was eternal youth only to be found in poetry? Was it completely unreal, utterly impossible to achieve?

It was at this time that a discreet advertisement in the newspaper caught Nirupama's eye.

> Any man or woman who wishes to sustain their youth by choice may take my help. Free operation. Payment only on proven success. Older men and women will have their youth restored. Write to PO No…
>
> *World News* magazine

Nirupama sat up straight.

Yes, finally she had found the scientist she was seeking. No fraud here. First, the surgery. Payment only if successful.

Nirupama's face lit up with happiness.

Drawing her expensive writing pad to herself, she began to write.

⁓

The next evening.

A Cadillac drew up outside Nirupama's house. The doorbell rang. Nirupama opened the door.

'Who is it?'

'We have received your letter in response to our advertisement in *World News* magazine. Are you Nirupama Debi?'

'Yes.'

'Get into the car. We will operate on you tomorrow, provided of course you are fit for surgery.'

'And if I am not?'

'In that case, you will have to remain under our doctor's treatment for about ten days in our special hospital. You will be operated on as soon as your health permits it.'

'But…' Nirupama appeared a little worried.

'There's nothing to fear. You will be well looked after. When your operation is successful, you will give a written statement to the press.'

'But why are you doing this selflessly?'

'It is not selfless. We will experiment on you and another person. If the experiment is successful, word will spread through the newspapers. Our doctor will become world-famous. A scientific achievement of this proportion has not yet been achieved on earth.'

'Of course. But where is the doctor?'

'He does not leave his specially constructed laboratory.'

'Very well, let's go. At the very least I will have a chance to meet him.'

Nirupama got inside the car and the man followed suit. He left a note behind that said:

Do not fear, Nirupama Debi has not disappeared. She will be in our care. She is being taken away because she has agreed to be operated on. We hope the police will not involve themselves. We are certain that even if attempts are made to locate Nirupama Debi, there is no power on earth that can succeed.

She will return after the operation is completed successfully. And if it fails, she will die.

Sincerely,
The Moving Shadow

∿

Two days later, the news of Nirupama Debi's disappearance along with the contents of the letter from the Moving Shadow made a splash in the newspapers.

Dipak was deep in thought when he read the report. He turned to Ratanlal.

'Do you think an actress would willingly take part in a scientific experiment involving surgery?'

Ratanlal had no answer.

Dipak thought for a while.

'Although it's confusing I think I see a ray of light.'

'Did you find a clue in there?'

'The Moving Shadow is a scientist. He is far superior to the people who are maintaining surveillance and doing his work on his behalf. But I cannot tell what sort of scientific discovery needs him to commit all these crimes. I think I will seek some help from my friend, the well-known surgeon Premnath Sharma. He has performed intricate operations with great success and is involved in complex medical research. Let's see if new facts come to light.'

THE MESSENGER OF DEATH

With his pockmarked face, matted hair, dirty appearance, and crippled leg, the beggar outside police headquarters at Lalbazar elicited hatred and revulsion rather than compassion.

Still, Dipak threw a couple of coins at him absently as he was about to enter the station.

It wasn't clear what the man muttered in response. Paying no attention, Dipak walked off towards Deputy Police Commissioner Morrison's chamber.

Mr Morrison was delighted to see him, greeting him with a warm smile.

'Please come in, Mr Chatterjee. I'm very pleased to see you. You must have heard the news.'

'You mean Nirupama Debi's disappearance and the letter left by the Moving Shadow?'

'How should we proceed, Mr Chatterjee?'

'I see a ray of light, Mr Morrison.'

'Really?'

'Look, there has been no other incident besides the theft of a corpse, the blood that was stolen, Nirupama Debi's voluntary disappearance and the abduction of a young woman. These people are not interested in money or any other form of riches.'

'That's obvious.'

'And then the attempt to keep me at a distance. This holds some clues too. All told, everything points towards an imminent scientific experiment or something similar. And someone has taken on the pseudonym, the Moving Shadow, to get all this done. The actual acts may be the work of many people, but behind them all, there's one mastermind.'

'But what is the basis of your conclusions, Mr Chatterjee?'

'You could say I'm building castles in the air. All of this is guesswork. But it would probably be correct to say that some of my guesswork is accurate.'

'I'm sure that's true.'

Mr Morrison smiled.

'What strategy do you plan to adopt now?'

'I am taking the help of a friend of mine, a surgeon. I must first find out from him what sort of scientific experiment might need all these things, an experiment that Nirupama Debi is willing to participate in.'

'Why are you assuming she's participating willingly?'

'The Moving Shadow may not be a law-abiding person, but he has not lied yet. If it had not been voluntary, he would definitely have left a note saying he was abducting her forcibly. That is one of the things I am assuming.'

Mr Morrison was about to speak when the phone rang out loudly.

'Hello, who is it?'

'I'd like to speak to Mr Chatterjee.'

Mr Morrison looked at Dipak.

'It's for you, Mr Chatterjee.'

'How did he who's ringing know I'm here? Anyway, let me see what he wants.'

Dipak picked up the phone.

'Yes, Chatterjee speaking. Who's this?'

'I am the Moving Shadow. I'm ringing from a public phone. Now listen, Mr Chatterjee, you have shown great courage by ignoring my warnings. I genuinely admire brave people, Mr Chatterjee. So, I'm giving you one more chance. You still have time to back out from this case. Why do you want to go on a wild goose chase and lose your life in the process? Abandon the case, you will be suitably compensated.'

'I do not change my mind so easily.' Dipak sounded determined.

'Look, my people are tailing you round the clock. In fact, they even know the details of your conversation with Mr Morrison. I am aware of the strategy you are planning to adopt. I am sure you can understand how little time it will take me to snuff out your life.'

'Even so I'm not willing to change my mind.' Dipak spoke calmly.

'In that case I am warning you. Try to protect your life in every possible way as you leave Lalbazar and drive back home. You may consider taking help from Mr Morrison. Dipak Chatterjee's name will be obliterated from the face of the earth in a very short period of time.'

'Thank you.' Dipak replaced the receiver and turned to Mr Morrison.

'My friend has given me a last and final warning. Since I paid no attention, he has informed me that I will be made to depart from this earth this very day.'

'What will you do now, Mr Chatterjee?' Mr Morrison sounded worried.

'Cowards die many times before their death, Mr Morrison. But I intend to die only once,' Dipak laughed uproariously.

⁀

Dipak walked out of Lalbazar and climbed into his car, a tiny Morris Minor.

With Dipak's hands on the wheel, the car seemed to have acquired a new life. The car moved ahead like an arrow on the smooth, shining asphalt roads of the metropolis.

Past Dalhousie and turning right at Esplanade, the vehicle turned towards south….The evening had darkened. There were lights at every crossing. The silken surface of Chowringhee Road was glistening. Deepak accelerated, driving towards his home in Bhawanipore.

Ow! Something had pricked him in the back. Gripping the steering wheel firmly, Dipak looked over his shoulder. Behind him was the beggar from Lalbazar. But what was this! How had his clothes changed suddenly?

A revolver gleamed in his right hand. He was looking mockingly at Dipak with a smile on his face. In his left hand he held something like a needle.

'Stop the car,' he ordered sharply.

But he did not have to complete his order. Dipak had already started reeling under the effect of the poison. His head was spinning. Evidently the intruder had injected some sort of poisonous substance into his blood stream.

Dipak's senses began to swim.

He lost consciousness and slumped inside his car.

Twenty minutes later, Mr Morrison received another phone call.

'Dipak Chatterjee was proving to be a menace. Therefore, I have taken him into captivity. My work will continue without deterrence. My best wishes to you, Mr Morrison.'

The line went dead before Mr Morrison could reply.

Dismay and disappointment spread over Mr Morrison's face. The pallor of failure. He replaced the receiver and stood up.

IN THE HANDS OF THE ENEMY

Dipak Chatterjee woke up feeling like the genie from the *Arabian Nights* who had woken up after an entire age had passed. He looked around carefully as soon as he regained consciousness. It took him some time to recollect all that had happened, and how.

He was inside a closed room whose doors and windows were shut. It was unbearably hot. A musty smell permeated the whole room. He felt like he had been buried alive. All the sounds of the world were a long way from here. There was not the slightest sign of any human beings anywhere.

Except for a continuous sound—chak chak chak—like sounds emanating from a factory or a machine.

Dipak felt weak and hungry. But there was no route for escape from these criminals.

A faint beam of light was filtering in from a ventilator near the ceiling. It was probably the source of air too. There was no contact with the world outside. He would need an instrument to prise open the tiny ventilator. But he didn't have any. For now he had no option but to suppress his hunger and suffer in silence.

He heard footsteps outside, followed by the sound of a door being opened. Four people entered the room. One of them had a revolver in his hands. The other three had large, sharp knives.

'Do I have to go somewhere?' Dipak's tone was light.

'Yes, the boss has sent for you.'

'But I am starving.'

'You can tell that to the boss. Now stand up like a good boy.'

Dipak realized that resistance was futile. He walked up to the man with the revolver and stood next to him, while the three men with knives stood in front.

'Let's go.'

The five men left the room. A corridor ran past the room. It led to a veranda. And finally, a staircase that led upstairs.

When they got to the foot of the stairs, Dipak launched into an unexpected manoeuvre. None of the four men was prepared for this.

Dipak suddenly twisted the arm of the man with the revolver, who was not on his guard, and wrenched the gun from his grasp. The man had not expected this. The revolver was in Dipak's hand in no time.

The three men with the knives turned towards the sound, but it was too late. Dipak had the gun in his hands.

'Anyone who tries to stop me will be shot at once.'

A brief, unbroken silence. Suddenly one of the men with the knives raised his arm.

Dipak spun to one side and shot him. Then he leapt off the bottom step and began to run.

There was an uproar. A loud clamour. The sleeping palace of monsters had awakened.

Dipak ran as fast as he could. A car stood in one corner of the garden. Theirs, possibly. He jumped into the car. Bullets flew past him.

Several men were racing towards him, their feet thumping on the ground. Dipak started the car and raced away at great speed.

The building was situated somewhere near Barrackpore. There were no other buildings nearby. The nearest police station was a long distance away.

Dipak had driven a mile or so before enquiring about the location of the police station from a pedestrian. Then, he drove there directly.

Dipak did not know the officer in charge, Hariram Goenka. He introduced himself.

'You have to come with me at once to search the building.'

'I'd like to phone Lalbazar first and understand the situation thoroughly.'

'I'm taking the entire responsibility, Mr Goenka. You mustn't waste a moment. They must not be given any opportunity to escape.'

But Mr Goenka ignored Dipak and rang Mr Morrison.

An hour and a half had passed when they finally left with the police force after elaborate preparations.

It did not take them long to locate the building. But despite searching it with a toothcomb they found no one. The building was completely empty. All the criminals had got away.

After searching the entire building Dipak went to the attic on the second floor.

A few shattered pieces of glass were lying there, along with a folded note.

Dipak Chatterjee,

I admire your courage and intelligence, but still I must inform you that no one on earth has the power to catch me till my experiment is completed. I had thought of sparing your life this time, but not any more. Your death is inevitable.

Sincerely,
The Moving Shadow

DR PREMNATH SHARMA

The dim shadows of the evening had barely begun to descend. The darkness had not deepened yet.

Dipak's car was racing towards Ballygunge. Dr Premnath Sharma's house was situated at the far end of Old Ballygunge.

Dipak was alone in his car. His constant companion, his revolver, was attached to his waist. This one object had saved his life many times without fail.

Dipak's shampooed hair was blowing in the light breeze. There was a nip in the air. He drew his coat tightly around himself.

He stepped on the accelerator. As the car sped by, the lamp posts became a blur as they were left behind one after the other. There was Dr Premnath Sharma's house. This was the hour when he was home after a busy day at the hospital.

Dipak parked the car outside and walked the rest of the way. He crossed the lawn in front of the house. At the door, he gently pressed the bell.

Ding dong, ding dong…

The door opened.

'Who is it?'

An exquisitely beautiful young woman peeped out. Her age seemed to have stopped at eighteen. A shapely body, unmatched grace.

'I'd like to meet Dr Premnath Sharma to discuss an urgent matter.'

'I see.' The young woman smiled. A flash of beauty seemed to cut through the gathering darkness.

'But my father isn't home right now.'

'Really? Where is he?'

'He has been called away for a surgery. Who are you?'

'My name is Dipak Chatterjee. I have to discuss some things with him. We met in Rangoon.'

The woman smiled. 'My father mentions you often. Come in. He should be back soon.'

Dipak leaned back on a soft couch in the drawing room. He turned to the woman.

'So, you're his only daughter.'

'Yes. My name is Kaberi.'

'What a beautiful name.' Dipak's tone was flirtatious.

'Just a minute, let me get some tea for you.'

Kaberi disappeared. A pleasant breeze.

She was back in a few minutes.

'I have heard a great deal about you from my father. There's no greater detective than you in the country. Will you tell me some stories from your life?'

Dipak smiled. 'Not stories but incidents. True incidents.'

'I know.'

Her intelligent eyes brimmed with eagerness. Curiosity was written all over her unblemished features. 'Reading made-up stories doesn't provide even one per cent of the joy of listening to real life incidents.'

Dipak lit a cigarette.

Gazing at the bluish coils of smoke, he recounted a half-remembered incident from a long time ago.

Time flew by. Dipak paid no attention. The entire world seemed to have been obliterated from his senses. There were just the two of them.

Dipak and Kaberi. Her eyes, as restless as a fawn's, were fixed eagerly on him. Dipak was engrossed in telling his tale. His face radiated with the glory he had earned in the past.

A car was heard outside.

'My father is probably back, Dipak-babu.' The young woman leapt up and ran to the door.

Dr Premnath Sharma entered.

Dr Sharma was tall and lithe with salt-and-pepper hair. He was so fair that he could easily be mistaken for an Anglo-Indian. He was dressed in an expensive suit and wore crepe-sole shoes. A Havana cigar dangled from his lips.

'Good evening, Dipak-babu.'

'Good evening, Dr Sharma. And where did you rush off to suddenly?'

Dr Sharma hung his cap on a peg.

'An operation. Emergency. That's why it took some time. I hope you didn't mind waiting.'

'Not at all. Your daughter is extremely hospitable. I didn't mind waiting at all.'

'Dipak-babu was telling me wonderful stories, Baba.' Kaberi's lips curved in a smile.

'Did you enjoy them?' Dr Sharma mussed her hair affectionately.

'V-e-e-e-ry much…'

She paused and then continued. 'Just a minute, Baba, let me find out what's taking Bhojua so long with the tea. Would you like tea or coffee?'

'Tea will be fine.'

Kaberi disappeared.

'To what do I owe this unexpected honour? Did you get lost?'

'No, there's something important…'

'That's obvious. You haven't set foot in my home despite countless invitations. I knew you would never visit me except on urgent work.'

Dr Sharma burst into laughter. Dipak joined in.

⌣

Dr Sharma sighed in pleasure as he lit a fresh cigar after finishing his tea.

'Now tell me your story, Mr Chatterjee.'

'There's no story, just a couple of questions.'

'Why me of all people, Mr Chatterjee?'

Dipak smiled. 'I don't know many people in India who know as much about surgery as you do, Dr Sharma. Nor does anyone keep abreast of recent developments in the field like you do.'

Dr Sharma laughed. 'There's nothing to be gained from hearing praise for oneself, Mr Chatterjee. Now tell me what you wish to know. I will help you to the best of my abilities.'

'I've been told that surgery can achieve the impossible. Such as changing people's appearances, reversing ageing, reducing extra weight and so on. Do you know of the progress made in these fields in our country, Dr Sharma? Or how far one can go in these areas?'

Dr Sharma drew on his cigar. 'After my wife's death I have just two loves in the world, Mr Chatterjee. The first is my daughter and the second, surgery. And yet I do not know with certainty how successful plastic surgery has been. It is still a subject of research abroad. Those who claim that surgery can achieve the impossible are making a big mistake. Still, let me tell you.'

Dr Sharma had created an atmosphere of mystery. Everything he said sounded fascinating. Dipak listened closely.

'No expert capable of experimenting with plastic surgery has been born in India. As for reversing ageing—where questions of ionization and calcification are closely connected—our country is far, far behind.'

'But how successful have scientists abroad been, Dr Sharma?'

'Yes, experiments are underway. Scientists have established that the reason for ageing is the shower of cosmic rays from the sun. Calcium metabolism is responsible too. I do believe that these aspects can be controlled through specialized surgery so that youth can be prolonged in human beings. But who has the resources for this research? And so, surgery is still lagging a long way behind, Mr Chatterjee.'

Dr Sharma was about to say something more. But he was interrupted by a rattling of the window shutters.

A pebble with a piece of paper wrapped around it was hurled into the middle of the room.

Dipak drew his revolver and rushed to the window.

But the man had already leapt off the window-sill and dashed off like an arrow.

THE CHASE

Dipak unfolded the piece of paper to read it.

Dr Premnath Sharma,

Beware!
One more word from you and death will follow!

Sincerely,
The Moving Shadow

Dipak folded the sheet of paper and put it in his pocket.

'I'll take your leave, Dr Sharma. There's no point in exposing you to greater danger. I'll meet you again if I need to.'

Dipak bade him goodbye and got into his car. He drove away at terrifying speed. The speedometer crept to the right. Forty, fifty, sixty, seventy, eighty...

There could be an accident any moment.

In the distance, the red tail lights of the quarry became visible. It was in that car that the Moving Shadow's henchman had vanished.

Dipak gripped the steering wheel firmly. He mustn't let the car out of his sight.

Two cars raced along the roads of the metropolis, maintaining a safe distance between them.

Rash Behari Avenue...Russa Road...Ashutosh Mukherjee Road... Chowringhee...

The car in front turned into Bentinck Street. Dipak followed, maintaining a gap. No one in that car should have the slightest suspicion they were being followed.

Mission Row Extension. The car turned right and came to a stop in front of a small cafe.

Dipak stopped his car at a distance, at the kerb on Bentinck Street.

Then, he swiftly began to put on a disguise without getting out of the car. No one would believe that he could transform his appearance with the contents of the box stowed beneath the seat.

When Dipak emerged from his car after donning his disguise, it was impossible to think of him as anything but a Muslim from north India.

There was a public phone on Bentinck Street.

Dipak dialled a number and popped a coin in. Then he said into the receiver, 'Hello, connect me to South...'

'Who is this?' Ratanlal's voice.

'Ratanlal?'

'Yes.'

'Go to Lalbazar at once and tell Mr Morrison to be ready with his force.'

'Why? Have you traced the Moving Shadow?'

'Not exactly traced, but I have a clue. I'm hoping that following it will yield results. If I find something, I'll have to go to Lalbazar at once and go on a raid with the force.'

'Excellent, I hope you're successful.'

'Let's see. But every step is hazardous.'

'Should I join you?'

'No need, just do as I say. When I get there I don't want to have to wait a moment.'

'All right, I'm leaving at once.'

Dipak disconnected and walked up to the café to find the car still parked there. He smoothened his clothes and casually entered the café and took a seat.

It was a tiny café. There weren't many people inside.

An Anglo-Indian couple was sitting in a corner. A nondescript Bengali gentleman was sitting on the other side. Next to him two men in suits were smoking and drinking coffee.

Dipak's attention was drawn to them.

He could hear snatches of their conversation. He surmised that one of them was the man who had thrown the pebble at him in Dr Sharma's house.

Time went by. Seconds…minutes…an hour…

Exactly an hour later the two men paid their bill and went out.

One of them had dropped a piece of paper on the floor while taking the money out of his pocket. He had not noticed.

They got in their car.

The car disappeared within a few moments. But instead of following them, Dipak went to the table the two men had vacated. When the waiter was not looking, he picked up the piece of paper lying on the ground.

It was a slip with an address scrawled on it in red. House No. 3, 117 Russa Road South, Tollygunge.

Dipak put the piece of paper in his pocket and ordered another cup of tea.

It took him no more than fifteen minutes to empty his cup, settle the bill and return to his car.

He drove away in the direction of Lalbazar.

ELECTROTHERAPY

On arriving at Lalbazar, Dipak went directly to Deputy Commissioner's chamber. Mr Morrison was anxiously waiting for him. Ratanlal was sitting next to him.

'Hello Mr Chatterjee. What progress?'

'Some. Just an address. I don't know how useful it is.'

'Let's take a chance. But how did you get the address, Mr Chatterjee?'

Dipak explained everything.

'Let's hope we're successful. Tonight is a night of great sport for us, don't you agree, Mr Chatterjee? I don't know who the victor will be.'

Dipak laughed. 'Ratanlal must have asked you to keep your force ready.'

'Yes.'

'Not that I had expected to get an address. I thought following them would lead me to their den. But now we have an address in our hands. Of course, it's only thanks to luck that we do.'

Two police vehicles sped off southwards. A lorry and a jeep.

Both vehicles raced along furiously, as though every moment was valuable.

Dipak glanced at his watch. Nine-thirty. They have to arrive by ten. The longer they took, the lower the chances of success.

The speedometer crept to the right.

And the tension in the car grew thicker.

Finally, the car stopped on Russa Road South. It was not difficult to locate the address.

But what was this!

The building was sunk in darkness. It was impossible to imagine that the poisonous vapours of a criminal conspiracy could be bubbling in each of its invisible corners.

'Have we come to the wrong address, Mr Chatterjee?' Mr Morrison sounded anxious.

'Maybe, let's find out. You and I will enter first. The police force can attack as soon as we blow our whistles.'

'Yes, good idea. But all the doors and windows are closed.'

'That needn't stop us. There's a drainpipe over there. It won't be much trouble to climb up that pipe quietly.'

Mr Morrison protested mildly.

'Very well, I'll go in alone.'

'No, we'll go in together.'

They shimmied up the pipe. As soon as they came near the first floor, a window opened.

A tall man stood there. Dressed in black from head to toe. He had a mask on his face.

Mr Morrison tried to raise his gun. Dipak stopped him. He climbed up to the same level as the man in black.

'Good evening, Mr Morrison. Hello, Mr Chatterjee. Please come in. I never thought I would have the opportunity to welcome you here…'

The masked man ushered them in.

'But I will arrest everyone in this building.' Mr Morrison's voice rang out sharply.

'There's no need. By way of people here, there's just me. And two others in the laboratory. Come with me if you wish to see them. Don't worry, I won't stop you.'

Mr Morrison was astonished. Dipak, too.

The man continued speaking.

'I know the police force is waiting outside. I know they will storm the building at a signal from you. But there was no need for any of this.'

Mr Morrison and Dipak followed the man in bewilderment. They climbed down to the ground floor. At the end of the corridor, there was a large room lit by dim blue light. The room was filled with numerous instruments of all kinds.

'Do either of you know what these are?' The masked man asked them.

'No.' Their voices held curiosity.

'All the crimes I have committed till now, the enormous team I have coordinated for assistance, was all for these laboratories. But still you didn't leave me in peace. I had to escape from Barrackpore to Tollygunge.'

'But why did you commit all these crimes?' Dipak sounded accusatory.

'There was a very good reason. There was no one to help me with the work. I realized its immense possibilities. No living person would have willingly allowed his organs to be removed. I could not have procured a large quantity of blood at will. And who was going to supply me with fresh corpses?'

'But what is the subject of your research?'

'A combination of surgery and electrotherapy that I had pioneered in this country. I wanted to conquer age. To reverse the unstoppable verdict of nature. My surgery and electrotherapy could have achieved this.... But...'

'Where are the people you abducted?' Mr Morrison asked.

'Do you want to see them? They're in the room over there.'

As soon as he pressed a button, a section of the wall slid away slowly. Two women lay on two tables.

'Who are they?'

'One of them is Bina Debi, whom I abducted, and the other, Nirupama Debi, on whom I was conducting surgery.'

'But what did you need Bina Debi for?'

'Some of her organs have been transplanted into Nirupama Debi's body. But this has caused her no harm. I expect her to recover very soon.'

'Have you completed your surgery, then?' The question came from Mr Morrison.

'Yes, I have. And a small error has brought upon me the calumny of complete failure. Nirupama Debi would have regained eternal youth had my operation been successful, but I have not been so fortunate. Because of a severed vein, she has died of excessive bleeding. Perhaps an incompetent surgeon like me should not have tried to...'

He did not finish.

The masked man pulled out a long syringe from the folds of his garments. The liquid inside gleamed in the dim blue light.

Dipak lunged towards him to snatch away the syringe from his hand. But before he could succeed, the man plunged the needle into his arm and collapsed into a chair.

'You didn't have to take the trouble, Dipak-babu. I have atoned for my mistake. Goodbye to both of you.'

The masked man's body slumped to the floor.

Mr Morrison raised the whistle and blew hard.

✧

Tumult. Policemen flooded the house. Mr Morrison went up to the masked man. Dipak accompanied him. Ratanlal entered along with four or five police officers.

'Who was the masked man?'

'Who was the Moving Shadow?'

Everyone was bursting with curiosity. Mr Morrison removed the mask from his face. Dr Premnath Sharma's body lay on the floor.

The poison had turned his face blue. His eyes were closed. Death was imminent.

'Dr Sharma!'

Everyone looked at him questioningly.

'I had guessed as much. But I hadn't expected to be proven right.' Dipak's voice was heavy with emotion.

Ratanlal was nonplussed.

Mr Morrison was silent.

The shadows of the night had deepened outside by then.

The Secret Agent

VIKRAMADITYA

Ministry of Defence, New Delhi.

An important meeting was being held on how to capture the latest F-16s on the radar. The participants were Defence Secretary Shiv Charan Pandey, Chief Scientific Adviser Brij Mohan Iyengar, and Intelligence Department Director, Madhavan Shankar.

The American government had recently supplied Pakistan with forty F-16 planes. It was the most advanced modern day combat aircraft, flown electronically, with the capability to fly undetected by radar. It was able to do this by absorbing the electric 'beep' of the radar instead of reflecting it. Everyone knew the F-16 was unbelievably fast and capable of great strike power. It had the capacity to destroy every airport in north India within half an hour of taking off.

But the discussion was centred around the fact that even though the movement of these F-16 aircrafts could not be tracked by radar, scientists in the defence department had developed another technique for detecting these planes on their monitors. This was based on the fact that the F-16 generated a certain amount of heat when taking off. This heat, in turn, created air pressure of somewhere between 3 and 5 microns. Infrared ray sensors could capture this change in air pressure using television cameras. Indian scientists had been successful with their research. It was for this reason that eight special television cameras had been installed on the India-Pakistan border. Indian scientists had verified that whenever an F-16 aircraft took off from an airport in Pakistan, its movement could be monitored using the infrared ray sensors. The defence department had kept the news of this research and of the installation of the television cameras a closely-guarded secret. The only people who knew about this were the prime minister, defence minister, defence secretary, chief scientific adviser and the man who had developed the technique, Arindam Saxena. But yesterday two of Pakistan's major newspapers, *Dawn* and *Jung*, had published the news of this research with great prominence. Even the locations of the television cameras on the border had been disclosed. The prime minister and defence minister were extremely perturbed and had enquired how the news had reached Pakistan's newspapers. An explanation would have to be provided to the prime minister within thirty days. He had made a loaded comment in a note: 'There must be a Pakistani secret agent in the defence ministry. Who is it? Why has this person not been apprehended yet?'

That wasn't all. Scientists in the defence ministry had recently conducted research on the 'space bomb' with the help of their Russian counterparts. This space bomb was officially known as the FOBS (Fractional Orbital Bombarding System). This bomb could be sent into space targetted at a specific spot in a specific country with the help of computers. The publication of news about this secret project in Pakistani newspapers had stirred a hornets' nest in the defence ministry. The department of research and development in the ministry had adopted stringent secrecy measures. But with the information about tracking the movement of F-16s being leaked to Pakistani newspapers, the Indian government, the prime minister and defence minister were naturally perturbed.

The main agenda of today's secret meeting of the top brass was to discuss ways and means to arrest the secret agent.

It is necessary to state that the boss of the R&D department of the defence ministry, Arindam Saxena, was a skilled electronic, electrical and radar science specialist. Before being transferred to the ministry of defence in Delhi, he used to work as an electronics engineer and radar specialist at HAL (Hindustan Aeronautics Limited) in Bangalore. Later, he was appointed radar specialist and chief planning officer at the R&D department of the defence ministry. He had developed the special technique for tracking F-16 aircrafts. He had also been at the forefront of the collaboration with Russian scientists for the space bomb, and all his research had proved successful so far. So, he had quite the reputation both in the defence ministry and in the scientific community at large.

Arindam Saxena's office for scientific research was at Ramakrishna Puram in Delhi. Many Indian scientists were engaged in the research, all of them competent and industrious officers.

The head of the intelligence department, Madhavan Shankar, had been invited to join the meeting. After discussions, the defence secretary, the chief defence adviser and Madhavan Shankar had taken a joint and confidential decision. But, following the prime minister's instructions, they had determined that the secret agent would have to be identified within thirty days.

This is the background to the story that follows.

⌐

The Delhi Gymkhana Club.

During the British era, the Delhi Gymkhana Club was the watering hole for senior government officials and important businessmen. There used to be music and dancing every night. Members would start drinking before sunset and leave drunk after midnight with someone else's wife on their arms. Then again, the ICS (Indian Civil Services) officials of various government departments would also take important official decisions here.

But the atmosphere at the Gymkhana changed after India gained independence. The ICS officers were replaced by the new bosses of the country, the IAS (Indian Administrative Services) officers. New businessmen took over from the old ones—the Agarwals and Jhunjhunwallas and Bhallas and Chaubeys. Because of opposition from the public, alcohol was kept off the premises for quite a long time. Then, caving in to demands, made-in-India liquor was permitted, but foreign liquor was not. Senior officers no longer analysed government policy and decisions at the club. They mainly discussed how to keep the ministers happy, how to get promotions while the wives concentrated on finding suitable grooms for their daughters.

The barman at the Gymkhana was named Ratanlal, who went back to the British era. Who drank what and how much, which lady met her lover secretly at the bar—Ratanlal had all this information on his fingertips. The ladies and gentlemen used to be as generous with their tips as they were with their drinking. They were not miserly with their money.

But the times had changed. The IAS officers got drunk after just three drinks. And their wives drank rum in secret with their Coca-Cola. Ratanlal never made more than two or three rupees in tips, but he got much more by way of abuse. The members no longer addressed him as Ratanlal. They called him 'son of a bitch'. Of course, this form of address was used only when drunk.

Another major attraction at the Gymkhana Club was gambling. The ladies played rummy for high stakes. The gentlemen played flush. These card games could turn people into kings or beggars in a matter of days.

But despite all this, an air of lassitude hung over the club.

The biggest attraction at the Gymkhana now was Maqbool Peshwani. All the women at the club, married or unmarried, thronged around him like moths to a flame. Maqbool was impossibly handsome. The women called him Adonis for his perfect body and irresistible smile. Everyone was desperate to talk to him. Maqbool was an electronics engineer. He had worked for some time in that capacity in the R&D department of the defence ministry. But he had recently been fired, apparently because the ministry was overstaffed. But everyone knew this was not the real reason. His primary offence was drinking too much. Every time he drank, he felt an insatiable urge to flirt with women. Despite being a competent engineer, he was sacked because of this problem. Or so it was believed.

Ratanlal knew Maqbool very well. Every evening, Maqbool would be at his spot at the bar. One drink would turn to two, two to four, and Maqbool would end the night ten or twelve drinks down. Sometimes he would pay by cash, and at other times he would sign on his tab. Calculations showed that Maqbool had spent some five thousand rupees on alcohol in the past two months. Ratanlal had been forced to tell him, 'I can't put your drinks on your tab any more, sir. You'll have to pay cash from now on.' Maqbool had had no problems clearing his bills when he was employed, but he was hard up now.

Maqbool Peshwani was a bachelor. He did not lack for girlfriends. And besides, which woman could resist his charm!

Everyone knew that Maqbool would marry Arati Sharma, the only daughter of the famous business contractor, Sudarshan Sharma. She was not only beautiful but there was something alluring about her appearance that could only be called sex appeal. If the Delhi Gymkhana Club ever held a contest for sex appeal, Arati would undoubtedly be the winner. Although she did love Maqbool deeply, she had never been able to reconcile herself to his alcohol addiction. It wasn't just his drinking, it was his drunken and incorrigibly flirtatious behaviour that Arati found intolerable. 'I will marry you the day you give up drinking,' she had told him. Maqbool had been unable to give up drinking. So the marriage had not materialized. No one knew when or if it would.

After the Gymkhana Club, Maqbool usually went to the Defence Club that was owned by Brijlal Malkani. His son, Ratilal Malkani, used to be the administrative officer in the R&D department of the defence ministry.

Maqbool's former colleague, in other words. Many people from the defence ministry frequented the Defence Club to drink and socialize in the evening. Their wives often came to the club where they could freely drink and flirt. Of course, it was also rumoured that the real object of their visits was to feast their eyes on Maqbool. The barman here was called Shankar. But the club had also engaged a twenty-five-year-old woman to keep the accounts. Her name was Malia. She was another attraction at the Defence Club. Malia wore miniskirts to entice the male clientele at the club. Here too, rummy and flush were played for high stakes.

Maqbool had been drinking since late afternoon. According to Ratanlal he had already had seven drinks. But Maqbool was not drunk. He hadn't even said anything risqué to any women yet. Ratanlal calculated Maqbool's bill for the day at about four hundred rupees. As we know, he already owed the Gymkhana Club over five thousand rupees.

After seven drinks, Maqbool was slightly tipsy. He held out his empty glass, 'Another one, please, Ratan,' he shouted.

Ratanlal smiled. Everyone knew what this smile meant. It meant no more drinks on the tab.

'No, Ratanlal, not one, but two double shots of whisky. One for you and one for me.'

Drunk customers often requested Ratanlal to join them. He pulled out the register.

'Please don't mind, sir. You've run up a bill of four hundred rupees already today.'

'Only four hundred! Never mind, Ratanlal. Give me a double. I thought it would have been five or six hundred by now. Four hundred is small change. I'll pay it tomorrow.'

But Ratanlal stood firm. 'What can I do, sir?' he said, 'the secretary has given strict instructions. You owe the club five thousand rupees. I cannot put your drinks on your tab until you pay your bill.'

'Don't worry, Ratanlal. My friend Alok Bhatia will be here soon. I'll borrow some money from him.'

Maqbool tried to reassure Ratanlal, who was not to be convinced.

'No, sir, Bhatia sahib has not been to the club in the past three days,' Ratanlal replied.

Alok Bhatia was also a former colleague of Maqbool's.

Maqbool racked his brains. He was desperate for a drink. He had to drink some more tonight. His soul wouldn't take wing unless he did.

He unstrapped his expensive Rolex watch.

'Want to buy this watch, Ratanlal?'

Ratanlal had been involved in such deals before. Whenever British officers ran out of money while drinking, they pawned their watches or gold cigarette cases to Ratan. This had changed after the British left the country. People no longer pawned their possessions. So Ratanlal was a bit surprised, but he did not refuse the Rolex. He had had his eye on that watch for a long time. 'Where did you buy this watch, sir?' he had asked Maqbool many times.

Maqbool had not bought the watch with his own money. It was a birthday gift from Arati. But tonight he was so desperate for a drink that he sold it to Ratanlal for a mere seven hundred rupees. He gave four hundred to the barman. He put the remaining three hundred in his pocket, took a taxi and left the Gymkhana. 'Defence Club,' he instructed the driver. Most taxi drivers in Delhi knew where Defence Club was. Maqbool was already high. He began to hum a song. The taxi driver threw him a glance but said nothing.

Defence Club was situated at the entrance to Defence Colony. The clientele here was varied. Senior officers of the armed forces, diplomats, journalists, bureaucrats and businessmen all added up to an interesting mix. Maqbool knew almost everyone here. The clients and the authorities also knew who Maqbool was and what he did for a living.

It wasn't very late in the evening when Maqboo entered Defence Club. The crowd was still thin. People came here later in the night. Some brought their wives and some brought their girlfriends or other people's wives. But Maqbool usually frequented the club by himself. He had never brought Arati here.

As soon as he entered, he told Malia, 'A double Scotch, darling. Why are you looking so mournful tonight, sweetheart?'

Malia did not answer but smiled instead. It was hard to be angry with Maqbool for a very long time. Besides, she was used to such flirtatious advances from not just Maqbool but also from other men.

'I am mournful because I cannot give you drinks on credit any more.'

'But why?'

Maqbool was neither surprised nor angry at this response. These days, no one was willing to sell him drinks unless he paid for them upfront.

'Don't worry, I'll pay you cash tonight,' said Maqbool and smiled.

'Nothing doing,' said Malia firmly. You've already run up a huge bill. Pay the bill or I can't serve you a drink.'

Maqbool took three hundred rupees out of his pocket and handed it to Malia.

'Here's part payment. I'll pay the rest later…'

But Maqbool realized Malia wasn't going to give in easily. He wouldn't get a drink here until he has cleared all his dues.

While Maqbool was talking to Malia, a woman was staring at him covetously. Maqbool had never seen her at this club. She was worth a second look. He stared back at her.

'What's the name of that woman there staring at me, darling?' Maqbool asked Malia.

'Why, do you want to meet her? Her name is Sumita Chaudhuri. She's a friend of Alok Bhatia's.'

'In that case I'd certainly like to talk to her.'

'Of course, can't you see the look in her eyes? She wants to eat…talk to you too.'

Malia took Maqbool to Sumita's table and introduced them. 'Don't trust this man, Mrs Chaudhuri. Maqbool pretends to be in love with every woman he sees after he's had a few drinks…'

'No, it's Malia whom you mustn't believe,' interrupted Maqbool. 'I don't pretend to be in love. I try to actually be in love.'

'So all your talk of love with Malia all this while, was that pretence or real love?' asked Sumita.

'Oh but what can I do? Malia refuses to let me buy a drink on credit. I was just telling her it's not a large sum I owe the club, so why this unwillingness to get me a whisky?'

Like the other women, Sumita too was attracted by Maqbool's smile.

She was drinking a gimlet.

'Would you accept if I were to offer you a drink?'

'With pleasure,' said Maqbool with a smile. 'I never say no when women offer a drink or a kiss.'

'Excellent,' said Sumita, not the least bit embarrassed. 'Could you please get a double Scotch, Malia? And another gimlet for me.'

'Thank you ever so much for the drink.'

'Are you in love with Malia?' asked Sumita.

'Of course, I'm even ready to marry her if need be…'

'Don't trust Maqbool at all,' said Malia with a smile. 'Maqbool Peshwani has married me fifteen times so far, and given me talaq fifteen times too. Whenever he's in need of a drink it's Malia, I want to marry you. And if I don't give him one, "talaq talaq talaq".'

'So you can flirt effortlessly,' said Sumita, smiling. 'I'll remember that.'

'Tell me, where have I seen you before?' Maqbool asked suddenly. 'Maybe I haven't, maybe it's the whisky that's telling me I have.'

Maqbool had never seen Sumita before, but still he couldn't help asking. 'I don't know whether you've seen me or not, but I have certainly seen you,' he said.

Sumita replied, 'You were playing flush at Alok Bhatia's house. Can we have a quiet chat somewhere? You're always surrounded by women.'

'Oh yes, I remember now, that's where I saw you. Alok is my best friend. Are you his girlfriend?'

'I know Alok well. But don't call me his girlfriend. His wife, Suraiya, will be very angry if she hears.'

Maqbool saw reason in this. But if Alok knew her, she was certainly a girlfriend. Although Maqbool knew the subtle difference between an acquaintance and a girlfriend.

He downed his drink in a single gulp. 'Another one, Mr Peshwani?' asked Sumita with a smile.

'Please don't call me Mr Peshwani, call me Maqbool.'

'Call me Sumita. That's what Alok calls me. You must, too. Do you come to Defence Club every day?'

'Why do you ask?' Maqbool poured the last of his second drink down his throat.

'In that case, I'll see you every day. You are so handsome, any woman would go wild seeing you and talking to you.'

'Lovely! You're a friend of Alok's. We were colleagues for a long time. Now both of us are unemployed. You will find me wherever Alok goes. Sometimes we're at the Gymkhana, sometimes here. But we never get to spend much time together. Because I am addicted to alcohol. But I must admit Alok has better tastes than I do. He loves beauties, Suraiya can turn heads. There isn't a prettier woman in Delhi. And then look at you. You're a beauty queen. It's a matter of great fortune to have a girlfriend as pretty as you. Perhaps I've drunk too much today. That's why I'm babbling. Please don't mind. You know why I get into trouble? Women fall in love with me at first sight. You mustn't fall in love with a drunkard like me. You'll only be inviting danger. Goodbye…thanks for the drinks.'

Maqbool rose to his feet. Before leaving, he said, 'If you run into Alok, please tell him I'd like to see him. It's an important matter.'

'Where would you like to meet him?'

'Wherever he prefers. Could be the Gymkhana, could be right here. We frequent the same clubs and bars. Goodbye, darling.'

Maqbool left.

∽

A thousand questions crowded Arindam Saxena's mind on his way to the office. He had not found the answers to all of them. And there was another one in addition to these.

His wife Geeta had reminded him over and over again about drinks and dinner at Arati's house this evening. 'Please come home early,' she had said.

Arindam promised Geeta to be home on time every day. On time meant 8 p.m. but he could never keep his promise. By the time he got home after finishing his work at the office, it was usually midnight or sometimes 1 a.m. There were many research projects he had to look after. All of them top secret. Geeta had requested him several times to come home early. She had gone silent after getting no reply.

As soon as Arindam entered his office his secretary, Romola asked him, 'Have you read *Dawn* and *Jung*, sir?'

It was Romola who usually read both the local and the foreign newspapers. She passed on the important news to Arindam, who didn't want to waste his time on newspapers. And besides, Romola was his trusted private secretary. She used to work with him in Bangalore too. She had been transferred to Delhi on his recommendation. The intelligence bureau had investigated her past and found nothing suspicious.

'What have they published?' Arindam asked disinterestedly.

'Sir, both *Dawn* and *Jung* have published complete details of your research on infrared ray sensors. Not just that, they have even named the spots where we have installed our special television cameras. Mr Iyengar telephoned. He wants you to meet him at once. He wants to discuss the whole thing with you.'

'*Dawn* has published the details of my research? What are you saying, Romola?' Arindam was dumbfounded. He refused to believe that Pakistan knew about his top-secret project.

But then, the details of his space bomb had also been published in Pakistan's leading newspapers a couple of months ago. At that time Iyengar had managed to keep the news of this leak under wraps. Or else there would have been chaos in the Indian media and in parliament.

Romola handed him a copy of *Dawn*. He read the report thrice. No mistake. It was on the front page. 'Don't worry so much, sir,' Romola said. 'Mr Iyengar didn't seem perturbed. He said quite casually, "Arindam needn't worry about this. But he should meet me as soon as he comes in to work".'

Arindam knew Iyengar had only been trying to put Romola at ease. He knew the enormous significance of the report. He would have to go to South Block at once to meet Iyengar. It couldn't be delayed. 'Inform Mr Iyengar's secretary I'll be there in half an hour,' he told Romola.

Arindam left with the copy of *Dawn* tucked under his arm.

⌣

Brij Mohan Iyengar was waiting for Arindam in South Block. There was no trace of worry in his expression. On the contrary, he was smiling.

'Sit down, Arindam. I have some important things to discuss with you. You must have read *Dawn* by now.'

'Yes, sir. I cannot imagine how they got the information. It's just the four or five of us who have the details. Even my secretary Romola knew nothing about it. I hand-wrote everything in the file on the subject and handed it over to you.'

Iyengar thought for a few moments. Then he said, 'We're particularly worried about this secret information that has been published. The prime minister has instructed me and the defence secretary to find out who's been leaking secrets to Pakistani newspapers. We have just thirty days. As you know, Russia was very upset when the news about the space bomb was leaked.'

Arindam was silent. He recalled that the prime minister had been extremely annoyed the last time this had happened.

'The prime minister has faith in you. He is particularly pleased by your research and has recommended a promotion for you. You will be designated as joint chief scientific adviser and work as my assistant from next month onwards. This, of course, is good news. But before that, we must find out who the secret agent is in the ministry.'

Arindam was delighted to hear of his promotion. But all he said was, 'Thank you. Please inform the prime minister we shall definitely identify the secret agent.'

'This was the response I was expecting from you. Tell me, is your secretary Romola trustworthy? We appointed her on your recommendation. But I have a feeling it's not a good idea to have a woman in the R&D department. We'll transfer her as soon as this investigation is completed.'

'No, sir,' protested Arindam. 'Romola is trustworthy and she understands the scientific work that we do. Besides, the IB has investigated her personal life and her past and found nothing suspicious. I think it's someone else from the defence ministry who's passing on the information.'

'The prime minister and the defence minister had suggested that we seek the help of the IB. Secretary Shiv Charan Pandey and I opposed the idea of involving the IB in an intra-ministry investigation. The defence minister had accepted this. Meanwhile, we've received some other important news from the prime minister.'

'What news?' asked Arindam, sounding perturbed.

'There's no reason not to tell you. You remember the new research project we have started with Russian help?'

'You mean the TIROS project?' said Arindam. 'The television and infrared ray observation satellite. Our research into the images taken by the battery-operated vidicon cameras installed on the satellite was quite successful. It's just that we didn't have the funds to continue…'

'That's right, Arindam. But the IB has informed the PM that one of their agents in Pakistan has sent word. News of our TIROS project has also reached the Pakistani government. It's serious. We cannot afford any delays. This secret agent must be identified within thirty days. And since it's vital and confidential, we are entrusting you with the task of locating the secret agent.'

'Me? You're giving me this task? But you know I'm busy with research day and night, sir. I don't even get home before one or two in the morning these days.'

'I know just how good your work is. It was because I told the PM and the defence minister of your work that they agreed to give you the promotion. Don't worry. Although we're going to conduct the investigation ourselves, we'll have to consult the IB on the methodology. I will give you an assistant. He will work under your supervision. Do you remember we sacked three senior officers from the department two months ago on suspicions of spying? What were their names again?'

'Maqbool Peshwani, Alok Bhatia and Ratilal Malkani. But we didn't have any proof.'

'I know. You had opposed the move to sack them. But the IB's contention was that someone within the R&D department had been passing on state secrets to foreign powers. Now, we need to know who they are.'

Iyengar continued after a pause. 'We'd asked you to keep a close eye on these three, because we needed to know where they were going, whom they were meeting. Did you do that?'

'Yes, sir. I invited them home for lunch and dinner from time to time. Besides, my wife Geeta maintains close relationships with them. But I haven't learnt anything.'

'Let me conclude what I have to say. Then we will discuss how to find this secret agent. The IB is convinced that this Maqbool Peshwani is spying for a foreign government. But there's a big difference between suspecting someone and catching them in the act.'

Arindam couldn't believe that Maqbool, despite his drinking and womanizing, was a spy. 'No, sir, the IB's got it wrong when it comes to Maqbool,' he protested. 'He's got an Honours degrees in solid physics and electronics from Bristol University. He has helped me with my research. I don't think he's a spy. This is the IB's imagination, sir, you mustn't believe them.'

'But the thing is, we don't have any evidence to prove that they're wrong. Even Alok Bhatia is a brilliant scientist. And we'll never find an administrative officer as efficient as Ratilal Malkani. But it was the IB that proposed removing them. They said Alok had gambled away his father's wealth and needed money. But would they ever understand how competent he was with radar technology? The allegation against Ratilal was that his father owns the Defence Club. Many senior officers in our armed forces as well as diplomats go there for lunch and dinner. But the IB said that it wouldn't be right to have anyone connected with this club in important positions. So we had to ask Ratilal Malkani to leave.

'Anyway, let me get to the point. I agree with the IB in this instance. I had suspected Maqbool Peshwani from the beginning. He might be brilliant at his work, but can a man who cannot pass an hour without a drink and wants to flirt with any woman he sees be given important responsibilities? Besides, Maqbool himself doesn't know the creature he becomes when he's had a drink. He may well have parted with secret information and research findings while drunk. He knew about the space bomb, he was closely associated with it. He knew about our plans to track the F-16 too.'

After some thought, Arindam agreed. 'There's good reason for you and IB to suspect Maqbool. Not only did he have all this information, he often worked from home. He told me he worked better there. I didn't object, because what mattered to us was the work he did, not where he did it. I used to discuss our research with him, and he always came back the next day with his responses. It's true that he had access to the information and the opportunity to pass it on.'

'You know what I think? For all his drinking and debauchery, Maqbool is no fool. He sells secrets in the open market to get money for his alcohol. Now listen to the IB's innovative plan for nabbing the secret agent. They're saying that we have to use a spy to catch a spy. Since Maqbool is a spy, according to them, they want to use him to identify the secret agent. So, Maqbool will conduct the investigation and you will be his controlling officer. He will give you weekly reports. IB believes that he will make a blunder or disclose something when drunk that will enable us to catch him in flagrante. We will not be able to prove he is guilty without proof.'

Arindam didn't understand the plan. It seemed ridiculously unrealistic. How could you catch a spy with a spy?

'What are you saying, sir? Maqbool will protect himself if he's suspected of being a spy. Why would he allow himself to be caught?'

Iyengar smiled. 'I thought so too when the IB's proposal came. But later I found the plan logical. Sometimes spies don't understand they're making a mistake and end up making huge blunders. Anyway, there's no point arguing about it. Because we have to conduct our investigations according to the instructions laid down by the IB. Now let me explain what you have to do.

'First, you will meet Maqbool today and request him to take the responsibility for this investigation. Tell him defence ministry secrets are being published in Pakistani newspapers. Someone from the ministry is selling these secrets—we want to know who it is.

'You mustn't scrimp on expenses. We're ready to spend ten thousand, twenty, even a lakh. Maqbool won't be able to reject the lure of money. You can withdraw twenty thousand from the secret fund right away. No records of expenses have to be kept. Maqbool might ask why the police have not been asked to carry out the investigations. Tell him it's an internal investigation. If the Delhi newspapers get to know, they will publish the details with great relish. After which the whole thing will be discussed in parliament, and create a sensation across the country. The investigation has to be kept a secret. We don't want to invite danger. Both the PM and the defence minister have approved of the IB plan. "Splendid idea", the PM said. So, arguments are pointless. You'd better get going.'

Surprised at this explanation, Arindam protested again. 'Maqbool may well be a spy, sir, but a different strategy has to be found to arrest him. It isn't possible to get him to do anything useful. He's perpetually drunk. When he's tipsy he flirts with women. Where's the time for him to investigate anything? Don't put him in charge of this investigation.'

'We're merely following orders. We're obliged to follow IB instructions. Arguments are useless. Best to get a move on.'

Iyengar realized Arindam was not happy with the plan.

'Tell me, Arindam,' he continued, 'why are the women of Delhi crazy about Maqbool?'

Arindam smiled. He was curious too. Why was Maqbool such a darling of the women?

'Maqbool knows how to win women's hearts,' he said. 'Besides, he's handsome. But I'm warning you, sir, within half an hour of entrusting Maqbool with this task, every woman in Delhi will come to know that he's working on catching a spy. It will get around at lightning speed. And then the papers will publish the news.'

'There's nothing I can do, Arindam. I told Madhavan Shankar the same thing. Do you know what he said? "Don't worry, we know Maqbool is a ladies' man. That's why we're giving him the responsibility. He will be able to extract secrets from Delhi's women. And that will help identify the culprit. The wives always know what their husbands are up to, how much money they're earning on the side. So, Maqbool is the right choice." But you must be careful, Arindam. You must warn him if he tries to shirk his responsibilities.'

Arindam realized there was no point arguing. 'As you wish, sir,' he said with dismay. 'I will follow your instructions and brief you on the outcome.'

'Very well. Remember, money is not an issue. Make sure you meet Maqbool today and tell him his appointment is with immediate effect.'

Arindam returned to his office.

Arindam sent for Romola. Although she was his trusted secretary, he kept his secret files—the Not to Go to Office or NGO files and the Top Secret files—in his own drawer. The keys were always with him. He received government files about the purchase of weapons, planes, radar equipment and other defence requirements every day for his comments. Romola was not allowed to read them.

Arindam was not in the least inclined to discuss today's developments with Romola. But he would need her help to contact Maqbool. For he knew that she kept in touch with him—something he had never questioned her about.

'Romola,' he said, entering her cabin, 'do you remember a former assistant of mine named Maqbool Peshwani?'

Romola hadn't been expecting such a question from Arindam. She was flustered. Everyone in the department knew of her friendship with Maqbool. She didn't answer; instead, she said, 'Mrs Saxena rang. I told her you were at South Block. She will ring again soon. All she told me was that there is a cocktail dinner at Arati Sharma's house tonight to celebrate her birthday. Mrs Saxena wants you to be back home early.'

Arindam did not reply. Everyone in Delhi knew Arati's parties were lavish affairs. Arindam had often wondered why she spent so much money on these parties, and where she got the money from.

'Do you run into Maqbool at all?' asked Arindam. 'I want to know who he keeps in touch with in this department.'

The question made Romola uneasy. But she made no attempt to lie. She knew it was impossible for a defence ministry employee to lie. The police and IB were always watching them. 'Maqbool had invited me to dinner at the Gymkhana Club last Saturday,' she said.

Arindam did not press her any further. He knew he would learn nothing more from her. His private telephone rang at that moment. Geeta was ringing. Arindam entered his cabin. Geeta said urgently, 'Arati rang a little while ago, darling. She asked us repeatedly to attend her party.'

'I know, but it's impossible for me tonight. A lot of work has come up. Something terrible has happened.'

'What's the matter?' asked Geeta with a mixture of anxiety and curiosity.

'You know we've been working on a project to track Pakistan's F-16 aircraft. It was an extremely secret project, but, I don't know how, the details have been published in Pakistani newspapers. The bosses are very worried about how the news got out. Very few people knew of the project. I didn't even tell *you* the details. Now I've been instructed to find out who sold our secret to Pakistan.'

'Really?' Arindam didn't discern any interest in Geeta's brief reply. 'There's something else,' he continued. 'You'll be amazed to hear this. The IB suspects Maqbool Peshwani of being a Pakistani spy. They think he pretends to be drunk so that people blurt out state secrets to him, which he sells to other countries. The IB has also told the PM there's a spy in the defence ministry. And I've been told to use a spy to catch a spy. Meaning I have to recruit Maqbool for this task. He might lead us to the spy, or he might make a mistake under the influence of alcohol and give himself away. I will be supervising his work personally. You could say I'll be the controlling officer of the mission to catch the spy. I had refused at first, but Iyengar said this is a departmental enquiry, and as the head of the department I would have to lead the investigation. It'll take a lot of time to get all this sorted. So I can't go to Arati's party tonight. Oh yes, there's another thing, this will make you happy. I'm likely to get a promotion. The PM has approved my appointment as Iyengar's principal assistant.'

This time, too, Geeta sounded indifferent. 'All right, if you can't make it to the cocktail dinner, I'll go with Alok.'

'Alok Bhatia?' Arindam was silent for a few moments, thinking. Then he said, 'Of course, if Alok's willing you must go with him. One thing more. Everything I told you is top secret. Don't tell any of your friends about it.'

Calling out to Romola, Arindam said, 'I have to meet Maqbool, Roma. Ring him at home. If he's not home, he'll surely be at either Gymkhana Club or Defence Club. Those are his haunts. Tell him I'm inviting him to lunch. I have some urgent things to discuss with him. I'll be at the Gymkhana at one.'

A little later, Romola told Arindam, 'I managed to track Maqbool down. He was drinking at Defence Club. He has accepted your invitation with pleasure.'

'That's the problem. Once Maqbool starts drinking it's impossible to discuss anything serious with him.'

'It's true that Maqbool drinks, sir, but I've never seen him get drunk,' said Romola. Arindam considered this bit of information particularly significant. Maqbool drank but he never got drunk. Iyengar was right. Maqbool only pretended to be drunk. Arindam would have to size him up carefully at lunch.

Arindam arrived at the Gymkhana Club on the dot at 1 p.m. Maqbool was sitting at the bar with a double Scotch. A young woman next to him was sipping a Campari. Maqbool must have been telling funny stories, for his companion was rolling with laughter. Arindam realized that Maqbool was flirting with her.

He stopped when he saw Arindam. He turned to the woman and said, 'I'm sorry, madam, but I have to leave you now. My friend has arrived. We'll take up soon where we left off. I'll tell you many more stories.' Her smile disappeared. Arindam realized she was very disappointed. Maqbool could give Casanova a run for his money.

Maqbool left the bar and joined Arindam at his table.

'Who was that woman?' Arindam asked.

'Oh no, I forgot to ask her name. Anyway, why bother? One more pest to deal with. Now tell me what this important matter is. I prefer talking about important things before lunch. I forget things discussed after I've eaten and had a few drinks. By the way, may I make a request?'

'What request?' Arindam asked in surprise. He wasn't going to ask if the woman could join them for lunch, was he?

'I've had three whiskies and the woman two Camparis. If you don't mind, will you pay for them, please? I'm down to my last twenty rupees. The club secretary reminded me again today. Apparently I owe them a lot by way of membership fees and unpaid bills. I won't be allowed to use the bar until I've paid them.'

Arindam's first impulse was to laugh. How did Maqbool have the gall to treat women to Camparis and himself to three whiskies when he was broke? But then he felt sorry for the man. Maqbool was drinking both himself and his talent to death.

'Of course, don't worry. I will pay the bill. I didn't know you were so hard up.'

'You'd be aghast if I told you the entire story, my friend. Still, the long and the short of it is, that I am a poor man now. I've truly fallen on bad days after losing my job.'

They were interrupted. The woman who had been drinking Campari appeared at their table. Arindam finally had the chance to take a good look at her. She was quite ordinary looking, though well dressed. Arindam found no logical reason for Maqbool to be interested in someone like her. She looked exactly like the kind of person who loitered at the club, trying to cadge free drinks from members. She told Maqbool, 'Goodbye Mr Peshwani, we'll meet again. Thanks for the drinks.'

'Goodbye, my love,' Maqbool answered seductively. Arindam realized this was how Maqbool sweet-talked women into relationships. 'We'll meet again. At the Defence Club if not here.'

She left.

Arindam wanted to know all about the woman. But Maqbool had admitted a moment ago that he didn't know her at all.

'Look, Maqbool, this is very important…' Arindam began.

'But Arindam, my throat is parched, which leaves me in no condition for serious talk. May I have another double Scotch?'

'Of course.' Arindam ordered a double Scotch for Maqbool and a gimlet for himself. It was his favourite drink. He ordered lunch too.

Finally, the discussion began. 'Do you know anything about the F-16, Maqbool?' This was Arindam's first question.

Maqbool took a long sip of his drink and said, 'Why shouldn't I? I know every component of the F-16 like the back of my hand. Let me give you a list. Pratt and Whitney engine, very powerful. Weight, 24,000 pounds. Speed, 1,300 miles per hour, that's about 2,100 kilometres. Westinghouse radar. Delco computer. MK-82 cannons. Enemy radars cannot detect the presence of this aircraft.'

Arindam was surprised. Why was Maqbool keeping track of the F-16?

'I can see you know almost everything about it,' said Arindam. 'This plane is the subject of our discussion. The first thing I must tell you is that our government has been worried ever since Pakistan has got those F-16s. Because we know that they can destroy every airport in North India within half an hour of taking off. We tried to track them on the radar. It didn't work. I have been working on an infrared ray sensor…'

Arindam paused and continued to explain how the technology he had developed worked. Then, he said, 'But news of this research has been published in two newspapers in Pakistan. We do not know how Pakistan got the information…'

'There must be a secret agent in your department,' Maqbool interrupted him.

'That's right. And the PM has asked us to find out who it is. So he has ordered a departmental enquiry. It's not just this project, there are two other bits of secret information that have also been leaked. You remember, you and I were working on TIROS with the Russians…'

'But we couldn't complete the project,' Maqbool said.

'Yes, we ran out of money. The Russians were very upset when news of the project was published in Pakistani newspapers. It was the Russians who developed the TIROS satellite. In addition, Pakistan is also aware of our work on heavy water and space bombs. The bosses want to know who's been selling these secrets. You know most of the people in my department. That's why we've picked you to help me with the investigation. You could say you'll be my assistant…'

Maqbool finished his whisky in a gulp. 'Another one, please,' he said.

'Really, Maqbool you drink too much,' Arindam chided him. 'You should cut down…'

Maqbool was not the least bit concerned. 'What can I do?' he laughed. 'Drinking is my life. You could say alcohol has consumed me, I don't consume alcohol.'

Arindam ordered another drink for Maqbool without protesting further.

'Where was I?' he continued. 'Oh yes. You're a popular bachelor of Delhi. You're particularly popular among the women. You'll have to use your contacts among them, besides talking to the people in my department, to identify the spy. We're ready to spend money for this. Ten, fifteen, twenty thousand. You just have to ask. You will give me weekly reports. But I don't want anyone to know I'm your controlling officer. I will stay in the background. You will pass on all information to me through Geeta. She will give you whatever money you need. She will be our middleman. If you can meet our expectations on this assignment, we might reinstate you in your old job.'

Maqbool listened without interrupting. After a long pause, he said, 'Very interesting. I was a scientist, as you know. Now, I am being turned into an investigating officer. But I'm willing to take this assignment. You know why? The first and primary reason is that you're paying me a fat fee for it. As I told you, I'm neck-deep in debt. If I can make some money, I can think of going back to scientific research with a free mind. I don't enjoy being unemployed, you know. You remember the complex calculations I used to take home? It gave me such joy to solve those problems. My fiancé, Arati, has been very upset with me of late. She says no one in society cares for unemployed men, leave alone marry one of them. Arindam, I have no objection to conducting this secret investigation as your assistant. You can rely on me to help you in every possible way. You've chosen a unique way to conduct this investigation, using Geeta as a decoy. Brilliant idea. Geeta will know I'm engaged with important work, and she's bound to inform Arati about this. Arati will come to know I'm not unemployed any more. The timing couldn't have been better. I'm extremely grateful to you.'

Maqbool continued after taking a sip of his drink, 'You may be worried I won't be able to do this job. But I *will* do it. I know you'd prefer it if I did not drink, but my brain doesn't work without alcohol. No matter how much I drink, I'll do my job perfectly. You'd probably like me to stop womanizing too. But I can't help it, they flock to me. Let me ask you something. You must have discussed this whole thing with Geeta…'

'Don't worry about Geeta,' Arindam broke in to reassure Maqbool. 'I will tell her the details now that you're willing to take the assignment. One more thing, don't go telling people about this. It's a very important and secret mission. You can discuss it with her this evening. I'm very busy at work, I can't go to the party. Oh and one more thing, you don't have to account for the money I give you. It's a secret fund. Best not to keep accounts.'

'That's true,' Maqbool smiled. 'I agree with you there. I'll never forget what you've done for me today.'

Arindam ordered another drink for Maqbool at his request. He had objected at first, but gave in when Maqbool said it was one for the road. 'I'm depending on you,' he said. 'Don't mess it up.'

'Don't worry,' Maqbool told Arindam with a smile. 'Since I've taken the responsibility, I shall discharge it. I will identify your secret agent in the next fifteen days.'

It wasn't clear whether Arindam was reassured. He looked grave and did not respond before leaving the Gymkhana Club.

Back in his car, Arindam began to ponder over what had happened. His first thought was that it had not been right to entrust Maqbool with such a huge responsibility. He did not agree with his bosses' idea of catching a spy with a spy. His instinct said it was amateurish. He knew Maqbool very well. The man could not be trusted with anything. He had become even more wayward after losing his job. The bosses' strategy might work in the movies, but not in real life. Iyengar had said there was nothing to worry about, they already know who the spy was; they were only going through this charade to catch Maqbool Peshwani in the act.

But Arindam had not accepted this argument. The spy would destroy all evidence if he came to know the police was on his trail. There was one more thing. Arindam had realized that Maqbool knew a great deal about the F-16. However, what reassured Arindam was that he was the head of this investigation. And no one in Delhi would know he was connected to it.

Arindam remembered two other former colleagues, Alok Bhatia and Ratilal Malkani. Like Maqbool, they too had been sacked for reasons other than cost-cutting. Alok was a skilled radar specialist, an electrical engineer who had, like Arindam, graduated from Cambridge. But the real reason everyone in Delhi knew him was his beautiful wife, Suraiya. According to popular opinion, she was the prettiest woman in Delhi. Surayia was not just lovely but sexy too. No one who had seen her would say she was Indian. This was not entirely incorrect, for her mother was a foreigner, though no one knew for sure which country she belonged to. The other rumour was that her married life with Alok Bhatia was not a happy one. This wasn't untrue either.

As for Ratilal Malkani, the club he managed, the Defence Club, had an unsavoury reputation. Not only did senior officers of the armed forces and diplomats go there for lunch and dinner, they also played flash and poker for high stakes. These days there were secret sessions of roulette too. This was why the bosses in the defence ministry had dispensed with Ratilal's services. But he was from an affluent family, not hard up like Maqbool and Alok. In fact, he had a fat income from the club. Of late, he had been hiring pretty women known as hostesses to lure customers, especially senior officers in the armed forces.

There were many reasons for Ratilal and Maqbool to be at loggerheads. From the very beginning, Ratilal had not looked upon Maqbool favourably. For some unknown reason he had objected to Maqbool's appointment. There were constant clashes between the two of then. The administrative officer had negative comments to make on each and every file concerning Maqbool. The second reason for their enmity was Maqbool's fiancé, Arati. It was no secret that Ratilal had a soft spot for Arati. Everyone said he was jealous of Maqbool.

If Maqbool was unable to catch the spy, Arindam might not get his promotion. Although he hadn't said it in as many words, Iyengar had indicated that the promotion depended on the success of the mission. So Arindam would have to keep a close watch on Maqbool, ensuring that he made no mistake.

But something happened that night, utterly changing the course of Arindam's life.

٭

After his discussion with Arindam, Maqbool rang Arati. He had neither met her nor spoken to her for some time. So, she had reason to be unhappy. But Maqbool's excuse for not keeping in touch with her was that he had not been able to give up drinking; as she had wanted him to.

Arati expressed no surprise, curiosity or pleasure when Maqbool rang her. She was silent for some time. Then, she asked evenly, 'How are things with you, Maqbool? It's been a while since you rang or met me. I hear you're drinking a lot these days. And that you've acquired one or two young girlfriends too.'

Maqbool had long followed the policy of not responding to everything that women accused him of. It was wise to avoid all this. Today, however, he realized that Ratilal must have told her about Malia. So he changed the subject, saying, 'Pay no attention to rumours. You know my nature. But I'll give you some good news today. It'll please you. Are you alone?'

There was a reason for this question. Arati usually got together with her girlfriends at this hour.

'Suraiya is with me. You can speak freely.'

'I have no problem saying this in her presence. But tell her it's top secret, she mustn't discuss it with anyone. Listen, my unemployed days are over. I've got a job. I have to assist Arindam with a departmental enquiry.

The pay is good. And if I do it well, I'll get my old job back.'

Maqbool waited for Arati's reaction.

'You're going to conduct a departmental enquiry? Meaning a detective's job? It's doomed to fail. Couldn't Arindam find someone suitable in all of Delhi for this? Who's going to do all the drinking and flirting with those hussies if you get involved in serious work?' Arati's voice was dripping with sarcasm. 'What kind of investigation do they want you to do?'

'Arindam took me to lunch at the Gymkhana. He said there's a spy in his department. My job is to find the spy.'

Arati wouldn't believe that Maqbool could pull off something as important as this. She tried to dissuade him. 'You'll never be able to do it.'

'You'll see. I'll do it perfectly. Do you know Arindam has given me an advance of ten thousand rupees?'

'How could Arindam trust you with so much money?' Arati asked in astonishment. 'I'm surprised. Anyway, I'm not going to argue about it. You know it's my birthday, don't you? I'm throwing a party. You must come. But don't you dare touch a drop before you get here. And I don't want you to get here drunk and create a scene. I'll never see you again if you get drunk. Do you know what all my girlfriends ask me? How can you marry a drunkard? Everyone says you're a drunkard. So I'm warning you in advance. Also, please come well dressed.'

Maqbool tried to protest. 'Don't worry. I won't create a scene at your party. All right, see you tonight.'

Maqbool lost himself in thought. He decided to meet Malia at the Defence Club and ask her a few questions. Questions that he needed answers to. He knew he might have to flirt with her to extract the answers. He believed that women became vulnerable and revealed secrets when he feigned love for them. 'There's something about you that's pure sex appeal, Malia,' Maqbool said in his head. This was the quality that excited men. Malia had many suitors at the club.

When Maqbool arrived at the club, Malia was in the office, checking the accounts. It usually was occupied by the owners, but Malia made use of it in their absence.

She looked grim. Her eyes suggested she was in a bad mood. 'I was thinking of you,' she told Maqbool accusingly when he appeared.

'I am a lucky man,' Maqbool said with a smile. To please her, he added, 'You look ravishing today. Is there a reason?'

Malia didn't smile. 'There are several reasons to think of you. I was looking at your tab. You've run up a huge bill. The boss reminds me every day not to give you drinks on credit. He says I'm serving you drinks despite his instructions.' Malia had begun brusquely, but gradually her voice softened. Both her mind and her body relented when she saw Maqbool.

He smiled. 'You're worrying for no reason,' he said. 'I'm going to pay back every penny right now. And I have some good news for you too.'

'Good news!' Malia was keen to hear it.

'But answer a question first.'

'What question?'

'The word is that you are in love with me. I want to hear it from your own lips.' Malia was pleased with the question. She began to wonder how to answer it. She knew he had many other girlfriends. All of them wanted him, which was no easy matter. So she did not bare her heart to him. All she said was, 'So that's your question? But I want to hear the good news before I give you the answer.'

Maqbool knew that it would take more to win Malia's heart. 'I know you're dying to hear it,' he said. 'You won't answer my questions until I tell you. I'm sure you won't serve me a whisky either. Boss's orders. But if I clear my bill, surely you won't mind giving me a drink. All right, I'll give you the good news. But first, get me a whisky. And tell me how much I owe the club.'

Maqbool's double Scotch arrived shortly. Checking her books, Malia said, 'Including this drink, you owe the club two thousand three hundred rupees.'

'Two thousand three hundred. Is that all! I assumed I'd run up a much higher bill. Your boss Ratilal and you pestered me so much that I thought it was ten thousand. Here's three thousand. Keep the change. Get a miniskirt. A present from me...'

Maqbool counted the money.

Malia couldn't believe that Maqbool was paying his bill. Where had he got the money? She thought to herself there was no point worrying about all this. He was with her now. She should make good use of the opportunity. 'You're a darling, Maqbool,' she said seductively. 'Thank you for the miniskirt. Now tell me the good news.' She nestled closer to him. Maqbool knew what she wanted. Kisses and lovemaking.

'Of course, that's exactly what I'm here for. I just wanted to check whether you really love me or not. The first bit of good news obviously is that I've cleared my bill. Before I tell you the rest there's something I want to know.'

Bringing her red lips close to Maqbool's, Malia said, 'I love you, darling. Tell me what you want to know.'

'I want some information about Sumita Chaudhuri. Remember her? You introduced us, after which she stood me three whiskies. Pretty and bewitching—she knows how to set a man's senses on fire. I want to know who she really is.'

'Oh, so you want to make love to Sumita Chaudhuri now. She's a juicy one.' Malia sounded irritated. 'Why do you have to chase every woman you see? Let me tell you something. You'll never hit it off with Sumita. She's a smart operator. Anyway, to answer your question, she's Alok Bhatia's girlfriend—his mistress, you could say. But you can't maintain her. She changes her outfit seven times a day, has expensive tastes, drinks the best whisky, and is always on the prowl for money. Our Bhatia is finding it impossible to keep up with her demands. He's more or less bankrupt now.'

'How come? I was under the impression he had a good deal of money as well as his father's property.' Maqbool feigned ignorance.

'He used to, but not any more. He has to maintain not just Sumita Chaudhuri but also his beautiful wife, Suraiya. Besides, he has run up huge losses at the gambling table. He's squandered all his wealth as well as his father's property. I don't think there's much left.'

Breaking off, Malia looked at Maqbool. 'What are you thinking? I'm not making all this up. Alok Bhatia really has no money. It's the truth. I may be sitting behind the bar most of the time, but I know what's going on in every nook and cranny of this club. I can tell you the name of every winner and loser at the gambling table in the next room, and how much each of them has won or lost. Alok Bhatia loses every day. You know he does not get along with his wife. He has to give her money too. They quarrel every day. But why are you asking me all this?'

Maqbool freed himself from Malia's arms. He sipped his whisky and said, 'Don't worry, I won't try to take Sumita Chaudhuri away from Alok. But he's my friend. And it's definitely cause for concern when your friend's girlfriend is so troublesome. I wonder where Alok gets the money to maintain two women with expensive tastes. Who's giving him all this money?'

Malia was silent. Then she said, 'It's occurred to me too. The question is, is Alok Bhatia a miser or a pauper? Mrs Chaudhuri cannot stand misers. They quarrel about money every single day. If I told you their saga it would never end...'

Malia paused for a few moments before continuing. 'Why wouldn't they quarrel, though? Mrs Chaudhuri is a divorcee. She was married to an IAS officer a long time ago, but they separated soon afterwards. I'm told her alimony is a mere three hundred rupees. How can she survive on it? I believe her monthly expenses run to nearly four thousand. Maybe Alok Bhatia has to provide all of it. And now he's lost his job too...'

'Are you saying Alok spends four thousand rupees a month on Sumita Chaudhuri?' Maqbool asked disbelievingly.

Malia locked the door before answering. Then, going up to Maqbool and putting her arms around him, she began her story...

By the time Malia had finished her story a couple of hours later, she was half naked and mad with lust.

It was 9 p.m. Most of Delhi was already asleep. Maqbool Peshwani arrived at Arati's birthday party in quite a drunken state. His legs were unsteady. He had drunk a great deal earlier with Malia. Shouldn't have drunk so much, he told himself. But how could he give up his addiction to beautiful women and whisky? He remembered Arati telling him not to turn up drunk. And not to create a scene. But what was he to do? He had forgotten Arati's warning when he was with Malia.

It was a large, well-lit hall. Arati was standing beneath one of the chandeliers. She was dressed up elaborately for the party, wearing her hair in a new style.

Maqbool went up to her. She looked at him and realized at once that he had had a few drinks. In fact, he was drunk despite her warning. It wouldn't be right to shout at him with so many people around. All she said to him was, 'I'd *told* you not to drink before getting here. Please don't drink any more or create any trouble.'

Maqbool's drunken haze had dissipated as soon as he entered. He perked up and laughed. 'Don't worry,' he said, 'I shall be a good boy...'

There were people around—Alok Bhatia among them. Coming up to Maqbool, he said, 'Where were you all this time, my boy?'

Although Alok was not as handsome as Maqbool, there was a masculinity about him that women were attracted to.

Maqbool was going to answer when Suraiya came up to him. She was beautiful, and needed no colour on her soft pink lips. Her captivating eyes and physical appeal had dimmed the bright illumination of the hall. Her alluring glances drove men mad.

Alok disappeared amidst the crowd as soon as Suraiya appeared. 'You are in good company now,' he said before leaving. 'I have something urgent to discuss with someone here.'

Maqbool wasn't surprised. Malia had already told him of the marital rift between the Bhatias.

Suraiya's perfume was intoxicating. In her sweet voice she said, 'I haven't seen you in ages, Maqbool. Where were you hiding?'

Maqbool smiled. Delhi women said he looked even more handsome when he smiled. 'Where do you suppose?' he answered. 'I was right here.'

But Suraiya wasn't willing to accept defeat so easily. 'Liar,' she said. 'I hear you've got many girlfriends these days.' Maqbool tried to change the subject, telling her, 'Do you know what I think when I see you?'

Women are naturally curious. When it came to their own praise, they grew even keener. 'What were you going to say?' said Suraiya. 'Why did you stop?'

'Today you look like Helen of Troy,' said Maqbool. 'You know what? If I hadn't been engaged to Arati, I would have run away with you tonight. Do you know what the Bible says? Stolen fruit is the sweetest.'

Suraiya smiled. Maqbool knows how to win women's hearts, she told herself. Lowering her voice, she said, 'Don't speak so loudly. Everyone will hear. Arati too.'

Suraiya realized Maqbool was probably flirting with her because he was drunk. Indignantly she said, 'You simply have to stop drinking so much. Women will love you more if you drink less. Anyway, I heard some good news today. Arati said…'

'What good news? What did Arati say?' Maqbool realized Arati had already informed people of his new job.

'Why shouldn't she tell everyone? Good news shouldn't be kept secret. I believe you've been given the responsibility for conducting a confidential investigation in Arindam's department. Congratulations! But don't worry, my lips are sealed. It was a good decision to take the assignment. You're talented. Why should you be without work? I know you won't have time to drink once you start working.'

'You're absolutely right,' Maqbool agreed. 'Do you know what I vow every morning? Today I won't touch alcohol. But as soon as afternoon turns into evening, I forget my promise. People say I don't consume alcohol, that alcohol has consumed me. You know what? I really shall give up drinking now and be a good boy…'

Before Maqbool could finish he saw Ratilal enter. He was talking to Arati. They looked like lovers deep in conversation. A bitter expression appeared on Maqbool's face.

Suraiya stole a glance at Maqbool as he stared at Arati and Ratilal. She smiled, but said nothing. Then, looking at her watch, she said, 'It's almost ten. There's a dinner I have to go to. Good night, Maqbool, see you soon. Work hard, don't drink, be a good boy.'

Maqbool began to mingle with the other guests after Suraiya left. All his friends complained, 'What's the matter with you? We don't see hide or hair of you these days.' Maqbool tried to explain that this wasn't true as he went to the Gymkhana Club or Defence Club every day.

Maqbool felt tipsy again after a few drinks. He decided not to drink any more, but a waiter chose that moment to arrive with a tray of whiskies. Just as he was about to take a sip, Ratilal came up to him.

'So, Mr Casanova, how many have you had today? I heard you had already tanked up at the Defence Club. Cut down, why are you ruining your talent and your life with alcohol?'

Maqbool had never been able to tolerate Ratilal's taunts.

'Never mind me,' he answered. 'How's your smugglers' club doing?'

This was like adding fuel to fire. Rumours swirled about the goings on at the Defence Club, which included not just innocuous lunches and dinners but also arms smuggling and other illicit deals. Government officers were said to be part of the racket. Which was why Defence Club had earned that particular nickname.

Ratilal had not expected this public insult. He was furious. 'I don't know anything about any smugglers' club,' he said. 'The patrons at my establishment are all decent people. It's not meant for drunkards like you.'

'You can't fool me, I know all the dirty secrets of your club. Don't brag about it. Everyone gambles and does drugs there. No lady or gentleman is to be found there, only the degenerates of Delhi. And now you've even started trading in beautiful women,' Maqbool deliberately said in a loud voice. He had long wanted to humiliate Ratilal amidst a roomful of people. Many of the guests gathered around them. They were eager to witness a confrontation.

Ratilal wasn't ready to concede. 'You drink on credit at this so-called smugglers' club,' he retaliated. 'And misbehave with guests. You flirt with every lady there. The doors of the smugglers' club are closed to you from now on. I'll have the doorman boot you out if I see you anywhere near the club…'

Before Ratilal could finish, Maqbool did something dramatic. He threw the whisky in his glass on Ratilal's face. 'To hell with your smugglers' club. Which decent man would want to go there? You'd be in jail if I told the police what goes on there…'

The whole thing happened so quickly that none of the other guests got a chance to intervene.

Arati had been keeping a close watch on Maqbool and Ratilal from a distance. She went up to Maqbool. 'Shame on you, Maqbool, there's a limit to drunken behaviour. I've told you over and over again to control yourself. You have no right to insult one of my guests at my party. Leave at once.'

After a pause Arati continued, 'Thank heavens we didn't get married. All my life I would have regretted marrying a drunkard like you. All you had your eyes on was my money. I don't want to see you ever again. Please go. Don't stand here like a fool. Do not ever come to my house again.'

'I knew you'd misunderstand me, Arati,' Maqbool said in a conciliatory tone. 'Ratilal has poisoned your mind against me. Don't believe a word of what he says. This man will get into trouble. I know it's a great crime nowadays to tell the truth or speak plainly. But I'm not a fraud like Ratilal. I won't get you into trouble. Everything I do is out in the open. Nothing is hidden. You're throwing me out, so I'll go. But you'll soon realize your mistake. Goodbye…'

Maqbool left without waiting for Arati's reaction.

Tears had sprung to Arati's eyes. Ratilal handed her a handkerchief and tried to console her. 'That's a relief,' he said, 'we're free of that drunkard. You've absolutely done the right thing. Thank goodness you found him out for what he is before marrying him. Else your life would have been hell after marriage. You've had to tolerate a great deal of humiliation for the sake of this drunkard.'

Arati was silent. She didn't know what to say.

One of Arati's servants rushed up to Maqbool as he was leaving. 'There's a telephone call for you, sir,' he said.

A telephone call! Who was ringing him at this hour? Maqbool was surprised. Besides, how did the person know he was here?

'Who is it?' asked Maqbool.

'Mrs Saxena, sir. She wants to talk to you.'

Geeta was ringing him. But why?

Maybe she wasn't coming to the party. But she could have told Arati. Why him?

Maqbool went up to the phone. 'Geeta? What is it? Why are you ringing me at this hour?'

'I'm in great trouble, Maqbool,' said Geeta softly. 'Can you come to my house at once? I need you here. Come immediately.'

Maqbool was astonished. What sort of trouble? Why was Geeta calling him instead of her husband? Her voice sounded hoarse. But Maqbool was in no condition to think about it. Before he could answer, Geeta continued, sounding agitated, 'Maqbool, I can't go to Arati's party tonight. I've got a cold. That's why I'm asking you over. Come at once, I'm waiting. I'm alone, there's no one else at home. I don't want anyone to know you're visiting. Don't use the front gate. There's a small gate at the back leading to the lawn. Use that one. Don't be late.'

After giving him instructions, Geeta ended the call without giving Maqbool a chance to speak.

Maqbool was disturbed by Geeta's phone call. She was normally self-composed, not given to anxiety or panic. He could not fathom the reason for her behaviour.

There was no point guessing. Visiting her would reveal all the answers. Maqbool told the servant, 'Mrs Saxena is not coming to the party. Inform Arati madam. Has Suraiya madam left or is she still here?'

The servant told him that Suraiya madam and Alok Bhatia sir had left a long time ago. They had come out of the party together. But after a short conversation outside they had gone their separate ways. Maqbool remembered that Suraiya had told him she had another party to attend. But why hadn't she and her husband gone together? They must have quarrelled again.

Maqbool went out to the road. It had rained earlier. It was still drizzling. He hadn't expected rain tonight.

Geeta Saxena lived in Lodi Estate. Maqbool took a taxi.

It was dark. The streetlights were like fireflies. It was a silent neighbourhood. Entering someone's house in the darkness was no easy matter. He had to find the gate at the back.

When he entered the house it seemed to be deserted. Not a sound to be heard. Arindam wasn't back. He had said he had a lot of work today. He would be late.

Maqbool entered warily. The back door was open. He had no trouble getting in. But where was Geeta? The only sound was of crickets.

Maqbool found a light on in a room at the back. It must be the bedroom. He was hesitant about going in. But it was momentary. An invisible power seemed to draw him inside. Geeta was lying on the bed. Asleep. He was surprised. She had rung him only a short while ago. It was strange that she was asleep fully dressed. She hadn't even taken off her cardigan. Her vanity bag lay open next to her. Maqbool went closer. Why wasn't Geeta waking up? No, she wasn't asleep. Suddenly Maqbool knew she was dead. He realized it was an unnatural death. She had been throttled with a fine silk thread.

Murdered!

Maqbool couldn't imagine that someone had killed Geeta. But he was left in no doubt on seeing her. She was dressed in a Kanjeevaram silk sari and a cardigan. She had either been about to go out, or had just returned.

Maqbool glanced at the clock on the wall. 11.15.

He wondered what he should do. Should he inform the police, or should he ring Arindam? Telling either of them would invite trouble. They were bound to consider him a suspect.

A piece of paper lay next to Geeta's vanity bag. It was a letter to addressed to him, but incomplete. It said, 'I need to meet you, Maqbool. It's because of you that…' Geeta had been murdered before she could complete the letter. The writing pad was lying nearby. Next to it, was a small table lamp. A half-smoked cigarette in the ashtray by its side. The stub of a Gauloises.

Maqbool tried to light a cigarette to calm himself down. But he had no matches. Spotting a lighter next to Geeta's vanity bag, he used it to light his cigarette. Then, almost unknown to himself, he put the lighter in his pocket. He pocketed the unfinished letter too. He'd be in trouble if the police found it.

What now? He shouldn't linger at the scene of the crime. Maqbool was about to leave when he saw a silk handkerchief on the floor. Picking it up, he smelt a strong perfume. It was a familiar scent. The letter 'A' was embroidered in a corner of the handkerchief. Maqbool put the handkerchief in his pocket. There was a glass of water on the bedside table. He drank it. It was 11.30.

Suddenly the telephone rang. Maqbool did not answer. It stopped after a while. Then it rang again.

Maqbool left the house.

The phone was still ringing.

Early the next morning.

Maqbool's mind went back to last night's incident. He went over everything that had happened.

Who had killed Geeta and why? Why had she telephoned him? He had to get to the bottom of this mystery. Then there was the letter Geeta had written him. He pulled it out of his pocket to read it again: 'I need to meet you, Maqbool. It's because of you that…' That was all. Geeta hadn't had the time to finish it. Maybe her assailant had killed her at this point. Perhaps she had anticipated being murdered. That's why she had rung Maqbool.

Did Geeta have any enemies? Or did she have an unpleasant past someone was blackmailing her with? Had the blackmailer killed her? He remembered the phone call as he was leaving. Who was ringing Geeta at 11.30? Was it Arindam or someone else?

Why had Geeta telephoned him? Should he admit Geeta had asked him to meet her? Or should he make up a story for the police? Would the police believe it? He would be in trouble if they didn't, for then he would have to prove someone else had killed Geeta before he reached her house. How would he prove this? Telling the truth would not be wise.

Maqbool realized he had another option. Using someone as an alibi, someone who would confirm having been with Maqbool between eleven and twelve at night. But who could he trust? Arati's servant had told him of Geeta's telephone call at a quarter to eleven. What if the police asked him whether she had called him, and why? He couldn't possibly tell the truth. He simply had to have an alibi for the night. Suddenly Maqbool remembered Sumita Chaudhuri. She might agree to vouch for him if he requested her. He had realized from his conversation with her that she was an intelligent woman. Why not ask her? Of course, Maqbool knew he would have to give her something in return. What was this something? Money? Sex? She had told him, 'I'm willing to help you in every way possible, Maqbool.' Maybe he would have no trouble convincing her.

Where was Sumita Chaudhuri now?

It was 10 a.m. She must be at home. She had given him her address and phone number. Maqbool rang her. The phone rang for a long time before someone answered. 'Hello,' said a woman's voice.

It wasn't Sumita Chaudhuri.

'Is Mrs Chaudhuri in?'

'No, she's gone out. I'm her maid. What do you want?'

'When will she be back? Will she have lunch at home?'

'No.'

'Where can I find her?'

'Try the club. She said she would have lunch there.'

Maqbool decided to go to Defence Club to meet Sumita. But Ratilal had told him he wouldn't be allowed in there any more.

Ratilal must have said this in anger. He couldn't be angry any more. Maqbool wasn't drunk now. He decided to pay a visit to the club and see what happened. Maqbool felt hopeful and took a taxi to the club.

⁘

Mansingh, the gateman, was stationed outside the club. He stopped Maqbool from entering. Ratilal must have given him instructions.

'You cannot enter. Sir has asked me to call the police if you try to force your way in.'

Maqbool smiled contemptuously. He knew Ratilal would never call the police.

'What are you saying, Mansingh? Why am I barred from entering? I was here yesterday too.'

But Mansingh wouldn't yield. 'Boss's orders,' he said.

'I'm an old customer here. Ask Miss Malia, she'll tell you how much money I spend here every day. Your club will lose a lot of money if you turn me away. Don't try to scare me with talk of the police. Your boss dislikes them. He'll be in trouble if the police arrive. They know that senior government officers and businessmen and arms dealers gamble thousands away here every day. There are other illegal activities too. Now, are you letting me in or not?'

But Mansingh stood his ground. 'I know how to stop you,' he declared.

Maqbool stood quietly for a while. What was the way out? He knew there was another entrance. He could slip in through the door next to the office. But what if Ratilal was in there?

Still, Maqbool decided to try. And as luck would have it, Ratilal was indeed there, with Arati.

'Maqbool is so devoted to his drink that he cannot stay away from our club,' Ratilal told Arati.

'And why are you slinking in through the back, Maqbool? Did Mansingh not allow you in at the main gate? Poor fellow.'

Ratilal was taunting him. Maqbool realized he couldn't avoid Ratilal today. What should he do? He decided to apologize.

'I'm sorry, Ratilal, I was drunk last night and behaved very badly. I had no intention of insulting you. But something went wrong and I ended up creating a scene. I am sorry.'

'It wasn't just me you insulted, Maqbool. It was Arati's birthday. You had no business creating a scene on such an occasion.' Ratilal's voice was softening. 'If you must apologize to anyone, it's to Arati.'

'You're absolutely right, Ratilal. I am ashamed about what happened last night, Arati. I had a few drinks before I came to your party. I lost all control. I couldn't think clearly any more.'

Ratilal smiled. 'You can say whatever you like to me, I won't mind. But it's your future I'm thinking of. Stop drinking and womanizing, Maqbool. Don't ruin your life. You were doing some brilliant research, but you've destroyed your career.'

Arati had been silent all this while. 'I've requested you to give up drinking so many times, Maqbool. You didn't listen. Anyway, I'll forget about what happened last night, but I don't want a relationship with you any more. Do you understand what I'm saying?'

Maqbool shook his head. 'No. Explain.'

It was Ratilal who answered on Arati's behalf. 'What Arati is saying can mean only one thing, Maqbool. You're not to be in touch with her any more. Your engagement is over.'

'Yes, Maqbool, Ratilal is right. I'm going to keep an eye on you a while longer. I want to see if there's some change. I'll tell you clearly after that.'

Arati left.

Ratilal smiled and took out a bottle of Black Label from his drawer. He poured two glasses. 'Here. I know you're upset. This will cheer you up. You know what your problem is, Maqbool? You cannot tell your enemies from your friends. Arati was saying last night…anyway, here you are…'

Maqbool took a long sip. 'What was Arati saying?'

'She was saying, Arindam had engaged you with an important project. I was pleased to hear that. I know you have the capacity for hard work. But if you keep drinking you won't be able to do a thing. Arati feels you cannot take on a responsible job. I don't agree with her at all. I told her you've ruined yourself drinking and womanizing. Arindam has done you a favour by giving you this assignment. You know how important it is. I was quite surprised to hear Arati talk about it. Don't worry, though, I won't breathe a word to anyone. I had warned the bosses many times, our security is very weak. We should investigate the people we've engaged to carry out these secret projects. Spies are at work everywhere, both for business and political reasons. There's no lack of traitors. But they paid no attention. On the contrary, I lost my job for plain-speaking. I feel sorry for Arindam. How many scientists of his calibre do we have in our country? I have known him from our days in England. He did some brilliant work in solid physics at Cambridge. That's why the government hired him. But how many things can poor Arindam manage single-handedly? He can't possibly look after both research and investigations. He can't remain inactive either when the secrets are being published in Pakistan. Impossible situation.'

Maqbool listened attentively without responding.

'The government's hiring methods for these crucial departments are extremely old-fashioned. Even if they check on the past of the people they employ, they do not consider the possibility of these people being compromised after joining.'

'You're right, Ratilal,' said Maqbool sipping his drink, 'I agree with you.' He turned towards the gambling room. 'There's a proverb, you know. Lucky at cards, unlucky in love. I've lost Arati after last night's incident. Unlucky in love. Let me see if I can be lucky at cards. What are they playing?'

'The usual, flash and poker. I'm going to play too. Alok is here too. He was badly losing earlier.'

Maqbool poured himself another double.

Ratilal stopped and retraced his steps. He came up to Maqbool and put his hand on his shoulder and said, 'I'm going to say something personal, Maqbool. Please don't mind. I haven't told anyone yet, I'd like to keep it a secret…'

'Something personal!' Maqbool looked at Ratilal in surprise. 'You can tell me, Ratilal, I won't tell anyone.'

'Don't be upset, Maqbool. I love Arati. She likes me. You know that liking must come before love. I realized last night why Arati is sad.'

Maqbool wasn't surprised. 'What did Arati say?' he asked with a smile. 'I've known for a while from her behaviour that her heart is elsewhere. She probably doesn't want me any more.'

'You're right, I've noticed the change in her too. I haven't told her about my feelings yet. I will when the opportunity arises. Arati won't turn me down if I propose to her. I'm thinking of selling the club after marriage and going abroad. I don't enjoy running a business built on alcohol and gambling. What do you think?'

'It's a good idea. You can sell this one and start something better in another country. I'm just hounded by bad luck. Love, research, gambling—I just cannot win anywhere. Let me find out if my luck has turned today.'

They entered the card room together.

Several games were in progress. The room was stuffy. Cigarette smoke hung heavy in the air. Ratilal and Maqbool sat down to play. Maqbool won a hundred rupees on the first deal. He signalled knowingly to Ratilal. Lucky at cards, unlucky in love. After winning nearly two thousand rupees over the next few rounds, Maqbool went to the bar to get a drink. Alok was losing heavily; he was almost ten thousand rupees down. He joined Maqbool at the bar.

'I'm addicted more to whisky than to gambling,' Maqbool told him. 'So I switched to the bar after winning a couple of rounds. How are you? How much have you won?'

'I never win at cards,' answered Alok dryly. 'I'm down ten thousand today.'

'Ten thousand!' Maqbool whistled. 'That's a lot!'

'I have to win it back. It's impossible to borrow money these days. Anyway. I heard you created a scene at Arati's party last night. Everyone's talking about it. What was it all about? I'd left a little earlier.'

'What do I tell you?' said Maqbool. 'These days I can't control my mood after a drink. I did something terrible. Because of which I'm about to lose Arati.'

'You're right. Who can understand women? They're nothing but obstacles in our way. We would have enjoyed life so much more if they didn't stop us all the time.'

'So you're saying it's not right to chase or stick to just one woman? Now give me a cigarette.'

Alok took a cigarette out of his gold case and handed it to Maqbool. An expensive cigarette case, expensive cigarettes too. Gauloises. 'Absolutely. I know what how painful it is to love just one woman. You're lucky there, you're under no pressure, you haven't hitched your wagon anywhere. You're a free bird when it comes to women.' Alok sounded bitter.

'Why are you brooding about women and love, Alok? Let's drink life to the lees.' Maqbool ordered another double Scotch.

'Omar Khayyam may have composed the *Rubaiyat* about love for women,' said Alok, toying with his glass, 'but I have neither the time nor the inclination to listen.'

Maqbool made no attempt to protest. His expression suggested he did not distinguish between women and alcohol. Both led to desire and excitement. He smiled and said, 'You know what Omar Khayyam said?

Some for the Glories of This World; and some
Sigh for the Prophet's Paradise to come;
Ah, take the Cash, and let the Credit go,
Nor heed the rumble of a distant Drum!

'Bird in the hand, brother...'

Blowing a cloud of smoke, Alok said, 'Do you suppose women bother with philosophy? They're so materialistic, they make our lives hell.'

'But what's *your* problem, Alok?' Maqbool tried to console him. 'You have such a lovely wife waiting for you at home, everyone's envious of you. Complaints like these do not suit you.'

'You're a committed bachelor,' Alok laughed sardonically. 'What do you know of marital bliss? You live just to enjoy life. Unmarried people like you will never understand a husband's woes when his wife makes his life miserable.' Taking a long sip of his drink to calm himself down, Alok ordered a fresh round. 'Where was I? Yes, my wife is beautiful and intelligent. And the family falls apart when the wife is too intelligent.'

Maqbool felt curious to know why Alok was saying this. After a pause he said, 'Will you answer a question?'

'What is it?' asked Alok disinterestedly.

'Does Suraiya know of your relationship with Sumita Chaudhuri?'

'Sumita Chaudhuri?' Alok began to laugh loudly. 'Women are at the root of all the distress in life. Yes, Suraiya knows I spend time with Sumita. She neither objects nor tries to stop me. My present troubles all have to do with Sumita. There's only one thing she can talk about—money, money and money. Only a bank manager can make her happy. The further you can stay from such women, the happier and more peaceful your life will be. I'm warning you, Maqbool—stay a bachelor and have fun with women, but never spend your life exclusively with one. Unhappiness is guaranteed. Let me go back to my cards and try to win my money back.'

Maqbool decided to follow him. He had to wait for Sumita Chaudhuri.

~

The card games were on full swing.

Ratilal had won quite a lot. But the game changed course soon afterwards. He had won the last three rounds with ace and king pairs.

The ante was upped for the next three rounds. Despite a running flash versus Alok's queen pair, Ratilal quit the game, allowing Alok to win without asking for a show of cards. Maqbool felt the loss was deliberate. But he had no idea why Ratilal had helped Alok win this large amount. It all seemed very suspicious.

Alok won ten thousand. Ratilal had already won a large amount. The other three players lost a great deal. But Maqbool's thoughts were interrupted as Sumita Chaudhuri entered the club.

He had to speak to her at once. He went up to her.

'Mr Peshwani…Maqbool!' Sumita seemed surprised. She hadn't expected to meet him at this hour.

'I have something important to talk to you about, Sumita,' said Maqbool.

'About what? Is it very important?' Sumita sounded happy.

Throwing a glance at the gamblers, Maqbool said, 'What I have to tell you is both urgent and important. Let's go somewhere else.'

'In that case, go to my flat in Vasant Vihar. 137/1. Here's the key. I'll be there in half an hour. I must first discuss something with Alok.'

Sumita pressed the key into Maqbool's hand. He took a taxi to her flat.

⌐

Maqbool had no trouble finding Sumita Chaudhuri's house in Vasant Vihar. There was a large park next door.

It was a well done-up flat. Maqbool admired Sumita's taste. Malia was right: she was fond of dainty, expensive things. How much did she spend on this flat every month? Maqbool tried to make some calculations in his head. The rent in this part of town was at least three thousand rupees a month. There were additional expenses. Maqbool worked out Sumita's monthly expenditure on her house and herself to be at least seven thousand rupees a month. She was a divorcee, with a small alimony from her ex-husband. It wasn't enough for such a lavish lifestyle. Simple arithmetic suggested that the money must come from Alok Bhatia. Maintaining a mistress was expensive. Alok had to take care of his own household expenses too. If you added it all up, his monthly expenses must run to at least twelve thousand rupees.

That was a lot of money. Maqbool was intimidated by the amount. Alok used to be a government employee with a fixed income of three thousand rupees a month. He had already squandered his inheritance. And to top it all he had been unemployed for the past three months.

Alok had won a large amount of money at cards today. Maybe he had a great deal of winnings from gambling. Or did he lose money more often than not? Probably the latter. It was clear that Ratilal had helped him win today. But why? Maqbool tried to solve the mystery. Suddenly he recalled what Malia had said. That Alok Bhatia was a miser. No, he wasn't a miser, it was just that he didn't have much money any more. Alok had to spend a lot of money on his women. That explained his bitterness. Maybe he had run up a huge debt. He must have lavished a fortune on Suraiya. Now he had to do the same thing for Sumita. It was the lack of money that had robbed Alok of all his ardour.

Maqbool's chain of thought was snapped by Sumita's arrival.

'I didn't think you'd come back so soon just for me,' Maqbool told her.

'Don't you know I dream of handsome men after lunch? I don't like thinking of my women friends at all. I love men. What will you have? Whisky? Campari?' Sumita was smiling provocatively.

'Whisky.'

Sumita poured him one, and a sherry for herself. 'To our love, my darling Maqbool,' she toasted. 'Now tell me what this urgent and secret matter is. I'll do anything you want me to.'

'Seriously?' said Maqbool sceptically.

'You think I'm joking?' Sumita feigned anger. 'I never joke. I know what you're thinking.'

'Are you an astrologer?' Maqbool asked with a smile. 'How do you know what's on my mind?'

'Because I know what all women think about and what all men want. Women worry about how to trap men in a web of love, and men worry about two things…'

'Which are?'

'Money and women,' Sumita answered briefly and looked at Maqbool.

'I think both are important problems,' answered Maqbool, smiling. 'One leads to the other.'

Sumita was silent. Maqbool realized she was thinking of how to respond. But instead of answering, she sat down next to him and put her arms around him. 'Now tell me what *your* problem is,' she said, her voice dripping honey. 'I'm sure you never have to worry about love or women. I know the women of Delhi are mad about you. I must call myself fortunate. I had never expected to have you so close to me.'

'Tell me Sumita, what will you say to a man who has both these problems—money *and* women—at the same time?' Maqbool made no attempt to free himself from Sumita's arms. He felt she was weakening both mentally and physically. But it wasn't time yet to tell her the truth.

'No, I am certain you have no problems,' said Sumita. 'Everyone knows you're a lucky and happy man. This morning I heard at the club you and Arati quarrelled last night. But who can tell from your expression that your engagement has been called off?'

'You're right, women are not a problem in my life. And I've never worried about money.'

'What a fascinating man you are, Maqbool. No one in Delhi can say this with such confidence…' Sumita began to brush Maqbool's lips with hers.

'But I have a bigger problem. That's what I want to talk to you about.'

'It's time for love now, we'll discuss your problem later.' Sumita began to kiss Maqbool. He didn't stop her. 'Mmm, I haven't kissed such soft lips in ages,' she purred.

'Let's talk about my problem now,' Maqbool said some time later. 'It's very important, you could say it's a matter of life and death. Have you ever been in a difficult situation, Sumita?' asked Maqbool, gently extricating himself from Sumita's arms. He knew she was vulnerable now. It was time to tell her the truth and ask for her help.

'I did face a problem with men once,' Sumita said. 'When my husband divorced me, I had no idea how I would survive. I had run up quite a debt. I could have passed the burden on to him, but I chose not to.'

'Has that problem been solved?' asked Maqbool.

'Do you suppose problems about money can be solved so easily? Marrying Deepchand was a big mistake. But then I knew so little about life at the time. I had thought my husband was very rich…'

'But…?'

'After the marriage I realized he had not married me for love. I had married him for his money, and he had married me for a different reason.'

'What reason?' asked Maqbool. He wasn't sure whether he should have asked the question. Maybe Sumita wouldn't answer truthfully, or wonder why he was asking. But Sumita did neither. 'What do you suppose?' she said. 'My husband began using me to further his own career. He introduced me to his senior colleagues, who held the strings to his future. I started going out with them every day. He displayed no interest in ensuring that I came home every night. His career took off all right, but my life crashed.'

'Never mind, my darling, let's have another drink,' said Maqbool.

Sumita gazed at him. Then she said with a smile, 'You drink too much, Maqbool. Cut down.' Pouring him a drink, she asked lovingly, 'Now tell me your problem. I've told you the story of my life, there's nothing more to tell you.'

'No, I want to know more. I don't know why, but ever since I met you I've been longing to know more about your life. Tell me what you think of Alok Bhatia. Maybe I'm not putting it properly. What I want to know is, what sort of man is Alok? The kind who's wealthy, or the kind who's physically and romantically attractive to women?'

'I used to consider Alok a very special man once upon a time. I was interested in him then. I'm not interested in him any more. As you probably know, interest dies when a mystery is unravelled.'

Maqbool pretended not to understand. 'What is it? Has your love for him died?'

'No, Alok can provide me with what I want. Besides, I can't make love to two men. And it's you I need more today...'

'I'm pleased to hear that. Now I know why you're playing love games with me...' Maqbool smiled.

'No, I am not playing love games with you. Because being in love with you is like playing with fire. You're a dangerous man. And I like playing with fire.'

Maqbool couldn't help laughing. 'How did you know I'm a dangerous man?'

Sumita answered after a pause. 'Women consider their future carefully before falling in love. You're the kind of man with whom one has to consider one's future. Why are you interrogating me like the police?'

'What if I told you there's a good reason? I need your help. So I'd like to know how deeply you love me. Women are willing to make sacrifices for a man only when they love him deeply.'

'You're right. What if I told you I do love you deeply? Now tell me what you want from me.' Sumita looked at Maqbool. He really did seem a dangerous man.

'All right, let me tell you about my problem now. Your assumption is right. Indeed I am a dangerous man who also loves playing with fire. Women are drawn like moths to my flame. But then there are a few women who try to put out the flame too. You're one of them. Now listen carefully. I have to use you as an alibi.'

'An alibi?' Sumita was perplexed. She asked Maqbool what the word meant.

'Meaning, you must testify if necessary that I spent an hour with you last night.' Maqbool explained.

Sumita became curious.

'Where were you between 11 p.m. and midnight last night?' Maqbool asked her.

'I was home between 10 and 12 last night,' said Sumita. 'Then I went to Defence Club to meet Alok.'

'What time did you reach the club?' Maqbool asked. There was a trace of excitement in his voice.

'As far as I can remember, about 12.30. Malia said, "You're here very late at night, Mrs Chaudhuri. Mr Bhatia rang for you twice."'

'Excellent. So if anyone asks you, was Maqbool Peshwani with you between 11 and 12 at night, Sumita Chaudhuri, you must say yes, you spent an hour with me. But I'm not telling you now why you must do this…'

Sumita was astonished. 'What's going on, Maqbool? I feel like I'm acting in a crime thriller.'

'You'll have to act in one soon enough. I need someone I can trust to testify that they were with me at that time.'

Sumita stared at him. The whole thing was a mystery to her. Why did Maqbool need an alibi? 'You really are a dangerous man, Maqbool. You wouldn't have asked me otherwise. But why do you need an alibi? Are you trying to protect yourself from something?'

'Exactly. I'll be relieved if you agree.'

'I'll do whatever you want me to,' Sumita sighed. 'If anyone asks I'll tell them you were with me at that time. But on one condition. You have to pay me suitably for this.'

'Very well, what's your condition?'

'You must have lunch with me at Defence Club tomorrow.'

'That's not difficult. I'll definitely have lunch with you tomorrow.'

'Excellent. One more thing, please don't drink so much.'

'There, I give an inch and you take a mile. Giving up drinking is very difficult. It's not the job of women to change men.'

Maqbool prepared to leave. 'Goodbye,' he said with a smile.

'Goodbye, my darling.'

Maqbool could make out from her voice that Sumita suspected him of something.

♪

Maqbool returned home to find a stranger waiting for him. The man's appearance made it clear he was from the police force.

'My name is Govind Narayan,' the man introduced himself. 'I'm a chief inspector with Delhi Police. I'm here to ask you some important questions, Mr Peshwani. Please answer them. Have you listened to the news on the radio this evening? Or read the *Delhi Evening News*?'

Feigning surprise, Maqbool said, 'The news? No, sir, I'm not much of a news animal. Can you tell me what you're talking about?'

'There's been a murder. The wife of a senior officer in the defence ministry, Arindam Saxena. Her name is Geeta Saxena. I'm sure you knew her, Mr Peshwani.' Narayan sounded authoritarian.

Maqbool knew it was best to answer questions from the police as simply as possible. 'What are you saying, Inspector!' he exclaimed. 'Geeta murdered. Impossible, I can't believe it.'

Taking a notebook out of his pocket, Narayan began his questioning. 'We have begun investigations into the murder. We're hoping to get some information from you. You knew Geeta Saxena, didn't you? You used to work as Mr Saxena's assistant. Was that when you met Mrs Saxena?'

Maqbool decided to answer as truthfully as possible without implicating himself.

'Yes, I knew Geeta, Inspector. Arindam took me home many times for lunch and dinner. Geeta and I were close friends. I cannot believe she was murdered. Who killed her? She had no enemy that I knew of.'

'So you did know her. What sort of woman was she?'

Maqbool hesitated, wondering how to answer. Then he said gravely, 'There are two kinds of women in our society, Inspector. One, the news of whose murder will astonish you. And two, the news of whose murder will surprise you but will not be entirely unexpected. Mrs Saxena was a mixture of these two categories. Geeta was quiet, intelligent and not given to impulsive behaviour. But she suffered from the eternal flaw of women, jealousy. I would call it her greatest blemish. She was also very inquisitive.'

Taking a packet of cigarettes from his pocket, Maqbool offered one to Narayan.

'No, thank you, I don't smoke on duty. What else do you know about Mrs Saxena?'

'Usually it's when women are unhappy in their marriages that the possibility of their being murdered or committing murder increases. During marital discord, they like thinking about other men. As far as I know, Geeta did not have an unhappy marriage. There was no reason for her to be unhappy. First, Arindam Saxena loved his wife. And second, he is a brilliant scientist with a bright future. Geeta was highly regarded. I cannot imagine anyone wanting to murder her. It's true that she was curious to the point of being nosy. But then women without curiosity are not lively creatures. I'm sorry, Inspector, but I can think of no good reason for Geeta to be murdered.'

Narayan was listening with close attention. 'It stands to reason what you're saying,' he told Maqbool. 'But solving a murder is not always a matter of cold calculation. We often say this or that murder appears to be without a motive. Do you suppose there's a good reason for every murder that takes place in the city of Delhi? Many murders are committed on the spur of the moment, without a motive. The victim may not even have an enemy. But in this case we have to say Mrs Saxena must have had an enemy. Why else was she murdered? I don't think a beautiful woman from a good family can be murdered without reason.'

'But I can't think of any enemy Geeta might have had. What headway have you made towards solving the murder?'

'Here's a summary of what we have learnt so far. Geeta Saxena was alive till at least 11 p.m. She rang her husband at that time. Arindam Saxena's private secretary took the call as Mr Saxena was in the laboratory. Geeta Saxena was surprised to find the secretary there at 11 p.m. She revealed her annoyance. We have learnt from Mr Saxena that he was developing photographs in the darkroom when his wife rang him. Mrs Saxena asked her husband's secretary to tell him to ring her back at 11.30. When Arindam Saxena returned to his office he found a note from his secretary to that effect. She had left by then. Mr Saxena expressed his surprise to us about this request from his wife. We have not discovered why Mrs Saxena wanted her husband to ring him at 11.30, which he did. When the phone kept ringing without a reply, he got worried and rang his neighbour, Brigadier Arora, to inform him that his wife wasn't answering the phone. He would be obliged if Brigadier Arora could go next door and make sure everything was all right.

It was almost a quarter to twelve when Brigadier Arora went next door. All he could see was a single light in the house. Brigadier Arora rang the bell but no one answered so he went in.

There was no one in the drawing room, the only light came from the bedroom, whose door was open. Brigadier Arora could see Mrs Saxena lying on her bed. At first he suspected nothing, but when she did not respond even after he had called her name several times, he entered the bedroom. He told us that Mrs Saxena's posture suggested to him that she was not asleep but dead. The first thing he did was to ring Arindam Saxena. Mr Saxena went home at once and then called the doctor and the police. The post-mortem says Mrs Saxena was throttled. The doctor's report puts the time of death as somewhere between 10.30 and 12 at night.'

'Sad and tragic,' remarked Maqbool. 'But how am I involved, Inspector?'

Hesitating, Narayan said, 'We only want to ask you a few questions, since you knew Mrs Saxena and met her on occasion. What do you know about her? And is it true that she telephoned you last night as you were about to leave Miss Arati Sharma's party?'

Maqbool realized that the police had learnt about the call from Arati's servant.

'How do I answer your question?' said Maqbool.

'By telling us what you know. We have collected some fingerprints from Mrs Saxena's vanity bag. They will lead us to the culprit.'

By now Maqbool had overcome his shock at being asked about the phone call. He had decided what he was going to say.

'What you have heard is right. Mrs Saxena rang me at a quarter to eleven. She said she had a cold and wouldn't be able to make it to Arati's party. She wanted me to inform Arati. I told the servant to let Arati know.'

'Did you meet Mrs Saxena that night?'

Maqbool was not surprised by the question. He had been expecting it. So he answered with alacrity. Smiling, he said, 'I'm about to tell you something that I hope you will keep a secret, Inspector. Because three or four ladies are involved here. All of them are from well-known families. I don't want them to become the subject of juicy gossip.'

'I can assure you, Mr Peshwani, that no one will come to know what you tell the police. It's not our job to spill secrets. All we're interested in knowing is who killed Geeta Saxena and why.'

'How do I put it? I was a little drunk that night. I wasn't able to control myself. I created a scene at my fiancé Arati Sharma's party, because of which she threw me out. Not just that, she told me to sever all ties with her. In other words, she broke off our engagement. Who wouldn't be heartbroken after this? I went to another lady's house and spent an hour or so with her. I was there from 11 till about 12.'

'What is the name of this lady?' asked Narayan, taking notes.

'Sumita Chaudhuri. She lives at 137/1 Vasant Vihar.'

'Anything more?' asked the inspector.

Maqbool pretended to think.

'I had to walk for a while after leaving Arati's party before I could get a taxi to Vasant Vihar,' he said.

'Are you sure you didn't go to Mr Saxena's house on your way or try to meet Mrs Saxena somewhere?'

'Impossible. There was no question of going to see Geeta at that hour of the night. You said she had left a message for her husband to ring her at 11.30. Either she was not at home till 11.30, or she was at home with someone in whose presence she could not talk on the phone. Who was this guest? And if she did go out, where did she go?'

It was Narayan's turn to ponder. 'You're right. We'd like to know whether Mrs Saxena went out for half an hour, and where. This is what we think happened. Mrs Saxena was throttled to death after she returned. It happened so quickly that she did not even have the time to change out of her sari. She was even wearing her cardigan, which she must have put on to go out. It had rained and the weather was chilly. But the room was warm, which means there was no reason to put on a cardigan indoors. Maybe a thief or an intruder was hiding in her room when she returned. Your theory about Mrs Saxena's having gone out is a plausible one, Mr Peshwani. Where did you go after leaving Mrs Chaudhuri's house?'

'I went back home, and she went to Defence Club. But I was feeling restless at home, so I went to the club. We didn't go together, you know what Delhi society is like, always on the lookout for juicy gossip.'

'Don't worry, Mr Peshwani, what you have told us will stay with us. Preliminary investigations suggest it's a complex case. Catching the culprit will not be easy. We cannot identify a motive. You have helped us a great deal with valuable information. Thank you very much. We'll be in touch again, if necessary.'

Once again Maqbool offered Narayan a cigarette. But instead of accepting it, the inspector took out his cigarette case and handed it to Maqbool. 'Try my special Charminars,' he said. 'Strong but has a wonderful flavour.' After Maqbool had lit a cigarette, the inspector picked up his cigarette case and left.

⌒

Maqbool knew that the police would now descend on Sumita Chaudhuri and grill her about last night. It would be best to warn her. He had not yet told her why he needed her as an alibi.

No one answered when Maqbool rang Sumita, not even her maid. Maqbool began to ponder over his conversation with Narayan. Would the inspector believe his answers? If not, he would be in trouble. He should be careful.

Suddenly, Maqbool remembered the brand of the cigarette Alok had offered him at Defence Club. Gauloises. The same brand he had found in Arati's bedroom. He also recollected the silk handkerchief with the letter 'A' embroidered on it. All these signs pointed to Alok. The perfume on the handkerchief had appeared familiar. Maqbool tried to remember where he had earlier got a whiff of it. Narayan was right. It was a complicated case.

It was nearly evening by the time Inspector Govind Narayan returned to his office. Sub-inspector Siraj Moulik was yawning at his desk. He shot to his feet and saluted when the inspector entered. 'Have the fingerprints found in Mrs Saxena's house been developed?' asked Narayan.

'Yes, sir, we sent everything to the forensic lab. They say they've got a number of prints. One more thing, sir.' Moulik said.

'What is it?'

'We smelt a strong perfume in Mrs Saxena's room, sir. You'd asked me to open the window.'

'Yes, you're right,' said Narayan. 'I smelt the same perfume in Maqbool Peshwani's house today. It's not the kind of smell you can forget easily. We have to find out what perfume Mrs Saxena used.'

'She wasn't wearing any perfume yesterday. Forensics didn't find any traces of perfume on her clothes.'

'In that case…' Narayan paused. 'Send this cigarette case to the lab, Moulik. It has Peswhani's fingerprints. Let them check if there's a match.'

Maqbool telephoned Arati early the next morning. Ratilal had told him last night, 'Forget Arati, Maqbool. I am in love with her. I want to marry her. Don't stop me or come in my way. I'm sure she'll agree to marry me.'

Arati did not seem happy when Maqbool called her. On the contrary, she sounded upset. She seemed to have company in the room. 'Really Maqbool, are you completely out of your mind?' she said. 'Can't you tell that I don't want to have anything to do with you after the scene at my party? My girlfriends are saying my life would have been ruined if I'd married you.

You're ruining your own life too. You could have achieved so much if only you'd wanted.'

'I know, I know. I'm really sorry for what happened. I can explain everything if only you'll give me a few minutes. This won't happen again.'

Arati softened. 'Suraiya and I are going to a ladies' party at the Gymkhana at twelve. Meet me there. But remember to be a good boy. Or it's all over between us.'

'You don't have to say another word. I'll never get drunk and create a scene again. There's something else I have to ask you. If you don't mind.'

'I know what you're going to ask.'

'Ratilal told me last night he loves you. Do you also...'

'Do you have no sense at all?' Arati interrupted angry. 'You're crossing the bounds of civility. You have no right to ask me whom I'm friends with and whom I want to marry. Don't interfere in my private life.'

⸎

Maqbool arrived at the Gymkhana Club at noon. He was dressed in an expensive lounge suit and a matching tie. No one would call him a drunkard today.

Suraiya and Arati had dressed up too. Maqbool admitted to himself that Suraiya looked bewitching. Not that Arati was any less beautiful.

Looking at Suraiya, Maqbool said, 'Both of you look so beautiful that it's hard to tear one's eyes away.'

It was Arati who answered. 'I can't stand you when you behave like an idiot, Maqbool. Are you sure you aren't drunk?'

'Are you mad? Do you think I'm going to repeat the mistake I made that night?' Maqbool tried to placate Arati. He realized she wasn't mollified yet.

'That's why you're looking so handsome today,' Suraiya told Maqbool. 'You look very happy. What's going on? Is there something we should know?'

'What on earth are you saying, Suraiya?' Arati was irked. 'Maqbool's dressed like a buffoon. You may find him handsome, but I don't. I don't like anything about him these days.'

Suraiya smiled. 'In that case, be kind to him,' she said.

Maqbool ignored her taunts. 'But I'm not here to plead for your kindness,' he said, smiling. 'And why should I? I'm no worse than anyone else. I want to give you some good news. I won two thousand rupees at cards at Defence Club yesterday. As they say, lucky at cards, unlucky in love. But I didn't play very long, or else I could have won more.'

'Your accomplishments are increasing, Maqbool. First it was drinking. Now gambling. A truly modern man.' Arati was furious. 'I can't stand either of those habits.'

'Why are you so angry? A piece of news, Suraiya, your husband won ten thousand rupees at cards last night. Ratilal won too.'

Maqbool looked at both of them.

'So Alok is making money gambling,' said Suraiya mockingly. 'Lovely. That's how he lost all his money in the first place.'

For some reason this pleased Maqbool.

'I don't want to discuss gambling. What's the point?' Suraiya tried to evade the subject.

'Whether Alok won at cards or not, I have no interest in money from gambling,' said Arati. Turning to Suraiya, she said, 'You're blaming Alok unnecessarily, Suraiya. He isn't an uncivilized brute like Maqbool. He doesn't create scenes at parties.'

Suraiya gave both of them a frosty look. Glancing at her watch, she said, 'It's one o'clock. I have to be somewhere for lunch. Goodbye, Maqbool. I'll ring you in the evening, Arati. We must go shopping to Connaught Place tomorrow.'

Suraiya left.

'There's a painting exhibition,' Maqbool told Arati. 'Let's take a look…'

'When did you develop an interest in art?' Arati asked in surprise. But her wonder lasted only a moment, because Maqbool tried to take her hand. 'I'm really amazed by your behaviour,' she said angrily. 'Are you trying to flirt with me? What is this madness? Are you drunk?'

'Come on, the day's just begun. How can I be drunk at this hour?'

It wasn't clear whether Arati was pleased by this response, but she showed no enthusiasm about going to the exhibition.

'All right then, let's talk here,' said Maqbool. 'First a couple of gimlets, then lunch…'

Before Arati could answer, they saw Suraiya rushing towards them.

'What's the matter? Why's she in such a state?' said Maqbool.

Suraiya came up to them, panting, with a copy of the *Hindustan Times*.

'Have you read the papers, Arati? Geeta's been murdered.' Suraiya was so worked up that the people around them turned to look.

'Impossible, I don't believe it.' Maqbool feigned surprise.

'Read for yourself. I didn't get the chance to see the papers this morning. It's on the front page. She was throttled.'

Suraiya was trembling. Arati didn't want to believe it either. 'What are you saying, Suraiya! Who did it? When?'

Maqbool tried to quieten them. 'Calm down. Let's have a drink. Then we can talk about the murder…'

'No, I cannot stay here a moment longer. I'm feeling ill. I'm going home.' Suraiya couldn't control her emotions.

'Suraiya is right, Maqbool. I can't stay here either. We're both going home.'

They left. Maqbool wondered about his next step. He ordered a double Scotch. He finished his drink and left the club. After some thought, he took a taxi. 'Vasant Vihar,' he instructed the driver.

Sumita seemed to have been expecting him. 'You'll live a thousand years, Maqbool,' she said. 'I was just telling myself, if only Maqbool were here now…'

'Well, I'm here,' Maqbool cut in. 'Now tell me why you were hoping I would be.'

'I'll tell you. But first, what will you drink?'

'Whisky,' said Maqbool. Sumita went off to get him a drink.

Maqbool looked around Sumita's flat in daylight. It looked luxurious and opulent.

Maqbool was here to find out why Sumita had agreed to give him an alibi. Theirs was not a particularly deep relationship. They had known each other for about twenty-four hours. Yet she had agreed. Why had she, considering the risk involved in lying to the police? Why was a woman who was used to a lavish lifestyle, needed money all the time, suddenly being so altruistic? There had to be a reason. Was Sumita going to blackmail him? It was possible. Maqbool also felt she had a past, which, like all women, she wanted to keep secret. Did she know that details from her past would come out in the open once the police started interrogating her? If she did, she must be giving him what he wanted for a very definite purpose. His thoughts were interrupted as Sumita returned with a whisky for him and a sherry for herself.

'Cheers, darling.'

'Cheers.' Sipping his whisky, Maqbool said, 'Now tell me why you wanted to meet me.'

'Because of this.' Sumita picked up the copy of the *Hindustan Times* lying on the table and showed it to him. 'Read this? The wife of a senior officer in the defence ministry has been murdered. You must have known Geeta Saxena…'

'Of course, I did,' said Maqbool calmly. 'Did you?'

'No, but I heard about her from Alok. Let me tell you something else. Someone came to see me this morning. A very interesting man, who knows you quite well.'

'Really? Who was it?'

Sumita rose from the sofa and drew a chair close to Maqbool. 'He told me a lot,' she said. 'He gave me details about Geeta Saxena's murder. He knows everything about it. More than everything. He asked me some questions too. Not difficult questions, easy ones. Can I ask you something, Maqbool?'

Maqbool realized Sumita was referring to Inspector Govind Narayan. But all he said was, 'Of course. What do you want to ask?'

'Is it true that Geeta Saxena had telephoned you at Arati's party before she was murdered? The post-mortem report says she was killed between 11 and 12. The police asked me whether you were with me at that time.'

'And what did you say?'

'As if you don't know,' Sumita smiled. 'Didn't you tell me what to say?'

'And what did the inspector say when you told him that? Do you think he believed you?'

Sumita laughed. 'Maybe he did. But I don't know whether he was convinced by my answers. He took down my statement and made me sign on it. I didn't object.'

Sumita sat down next to Maqbool and put her arms around him. 'Why are you so worried, darling? There's nothing to fear. I think he believed me.'

'You've done me a tremendous favour, Sumita,' said Maqbool. 'I would have been in great trouble if you hadn't provided an alibi. I think I'm going to be all right.'

'So you can't complain about anything from now on,' said Sumita with a smile. 'See what a good girl I've been? Come on, let's have lunch, I cooked today.'

Sumita insisted that Maqbool join her at the dining table.

After lunch at 3 p.m., Maqbool was relaxing on the sofa with a glass of whisky. Sumita sat down next to him. It was obvious that she wanted to make love.

Putting her arms around him, Sumita began to kiss him. Her intense kisses told Maqbool she was experienced at this game. He sat in silence.

'Why so serious, Maqbool? Are you upset because the police interrogated me?'

Maqbool answered in a low voice, 'No, Sumita, I'm not upset. I have no worries in my life. Mine's a happy existence, there's no room for worry.'

'I agree. What use is worrying? My motto is to take what you get with a smile.'

Smiling, Maqbool freed himself from Sumita's arms and went up to the window. Gazing outside for a few minutes, he returned to Sumita. 'You're absolutely right. There's a big gap between what we want and what we get. We should be happy with whatever comes our way. You know what I think sometimes?'

'What?'

'There are two sides to my character. You could say I have two personalities. By day, a wandering philosopher, by night, a drunkard.'

Sumita began to laugh. 'Everyone thinks of you as a drunkard, but I know you as a philosopher. After all, love is high philosophy. How would we have survived without sex? Another whisky?' Sumita went off to get him a drink without waiting for an answer.

Returning with his glass she said, 'Oh no, you've got lipstick stains. What if Malia or any other girlfriend of yours sees them? They'll refuse to kiss you. Wait, let me wipe them off.'

Sumita wiped off the lipstick stains with her handkerchief.

✧

Inspector Govind Narayan was pondering over Geeta Saxena's murder. The killer was obviously Maqbool Peshwani, but why had he killed her? Was it for money, love or revenge? Geeta's husband Arindam Saxena had confirmed that nothing had been stolen. Therefore it wasn't for money. Did Geeta Saxena have a lover? Was it because of this that Maqbool had killed her?

Narayan's thoughts were interrupted by the ring of the telephone. It was Madhavan Shankar.

Narayan grew alert. Madhavan Shankar was a highly intelligent and demanding boss, besides being the PM's security adviser. He had to be deferential while talking to him.

'Govind, It's Madhavan Shankar. Have you made any progress with Geeta Saxena's murder?'

'We've identified the murderer, sir, but we haven't learnt of his motive yet. We believe it was Maqbool Peshwani, a former research officer in the defence ministry, who killed Geeta Saxena. We have gathered a great deal of evidence. Fingerprints have revealed Peshwani's presence at the Saxenas' residence at the time of the murder. He was there and had spent some time with the victim. We're planning to arrest Peshwani shortly. Once we have him in custody, we will extract a confession.'

Madhavan Shankar was silent for a moment. Then he said, 'So you're saying Maqbool Peshwani is involved in this murder.'

'We have no doubt that he has given us false testimony and provided a fabricated alibi. His behaviour and actions are highly suspicious. He must be arrested soon, or he will destroy the evidence.'

'When do you want to arrest him? The thing is that he is also a suspect in a case involving national security. You're right, his behaviour is extremely suspicious. Therefore...'

Madhavan Shankar paused.

'We're thinking of arresting him tomorrow, sir,' Narayan answered enthusiastically. He was even more certain now of Maqbool's guilt.

'Govind, if you arrest him so soon our investigations will be hampered. What we're investigating him for is far more serious. It won't be right to arrest him now. Wait till our investigations are over before you take him into custody.' Madhavan Narayan ended on a note that suggested he was giving orders.

'But sir, what if he finds a way to...'

'Don't worry about it. The IB case comes before your murder. Follow my orders.'

Narayan was disappointed. 'If you say so, sir...'

'I'm not saying so, Govind, these are my orders. I'll take the responsibility for this.'

꙳

Narayan sat down in a huff after Shankar rang off. He didn't dare flout Shankar's orders. 'Maqbool is not just a murderer, he has deep criminal links,' he told himself. 'The IB wouldn't be involved otherwise.'

Maqbool arrived at Govind Narayan's office at around 5 p.m. Narayan was surprised to see him. What did he want? 'What's the matter, Mr Peshwani?' he asked. 'Why are you here?'

'I have to tell you something important and confidential.' answered Maqbool. 'Look, inspector, anyone implicated in a murder loses his power of reasoning. He complicates the investigation with a mixture of truth and falsehood.'

Narayan looked closely at Maqbool, who betrayed no sign of anxiety or alarm. He spoke calmly. This Maqbool must be made of steel, Narayan told himself. Was he pretending?

'Inspector, I lied to you yesterday. I was not in my senses, I lied to you under the influence of alcohol. Drinking was my passion earlier, it's my profession now. I told you many things that aren't true. This morning I realized I was wrong to have lied. I'm here now to tell you the truth.'

'Remember, Mr Peshwani, anything you say can be used against you. Be careful what you say. Of course, we know a great deal already. We have proof that you tried to hoodwink us. We have found out that you met Geeta Saxena the night she was murdered. The fingerprints found on her vanity bag and the glass of water on her bedside table match yours. Don't try to deny it. If you wish to change your statement, we shall record the revised version. But remember, anything you say is voluntary. We are not trying to extract a statement from you. You may consult your lawyer first. We won't object.'

'Absolutely not, there's no need to consult a lawyer. But first, I have a question. Will you answer it?'

'I can tell you that only after I hear the question.'

'Did you go to Vasant Vihar this morning to question Mrs Sumita Chaudhuri? Did she tell you anything significant?'

'Most certainly I did,' replied Narayan with a smile. 'Mrs Chaudhuri said you were telling the truth, that you were with her between 11 p.m. and midnight on the night Mrs Saxena was murdered.'

'I am sorry as well as embarrassed about this. I had no desire to involve Mrs Chaudhuri in all this, but I don't know what happened to me—I told you a pack of lies after drinking too much.'

'Anyone can make a mistake. We are aware of your fondness for alcohol. Drinking too much can lead to mistakes, but luckily there's still time to correct them. We aren't fools. We suspected you had confused or made up things under the influence of alcohol. I don't want to trouble Mrs Chaudhuri about this.'

'I'm glad to hear that. There's no need to trouble Mrs Chaudhuri. I had requested her for an alibi. She did not know the purpose. I'm sure you know how vulnerable a woman is when she is in love. She did not think twice before telling you I was with her.'

'I'm a police officer. I know the lengths to which a woman can go for the man she loves. We knew right away Mrs Chaudhuri was protecting you.'

'Yes, when she agreed to provide me with an alibi she had no idea that Geeta Saxena had been murdered. She assumed it was for someone else.'

'Please remember you are giving us your statement voluntarily, Mr Peshwani. We are not forcing you.'

'Yes, I'm acknowledging my mistake after thinking everything over. You may take my statement. I will tell the truth this time.'

'Very well, you may proceed.' Narayan began to take notes.

Maqbool began. 'Mrs Geeta Saxena rang me at a quarter to eleven on the night she was murdered, asking me to meet her at once at her residence. I was about to leave Arati Sharma's birthday party. Mrs Saxena told me that she had caught a cold and could not make it to the party.

'It was exactly 11 p.m. when I arrived at Mrs Saxena's house. She had instructed me to enter through the back door. Following her instructions, I entered and went into the drawing room, but she was not there. Hearing my footsteps, she requested me to join her in the bedroom. She was lying in bed, dressed in a Kanjeevaram sari and a cardigan. She said she had a cold.

'We chatted for a while. She asked me to cut down on my drinking. She said alcohol was blunting my talents and would lead to my losing Arati, who did not want to marry a drunkard. I was thirsty. I poured myself a glass of water from the jug on the bedside table. Later she gave me a cigarette from her vanity bag.

'I left after some time. It was about 11.15 p.m.'

Narayan said, 'Thank you for telling the truth this time. We found Mrs Saxena's fingerprints on the glass too. Both of you must have used it. Your statement matches our findings. I have a question to ask you. Didn't you find it unusual that Mrs Saxena was in bed dressed in a Kanjeevaram sari and cardigan?'

Maqbool did not answer straightaway. Then he said with a smile, 'I was in no shape to consider it unusual. As I told you, I was quite inebriated.'

'Thank you once again, Mr Peshwani. We'll be in touch if we need any more information.'

Smiling to himself, Maqbool left.

'You know, Siraj, Maqbool Peshwani isn't smart enough to pull the wool over my eyes,' Narayan told the sub-inspector. 'I'm just waiting for the boss's orders to arrest him.'

Maqbool went directly to the Gymkhana Club from Parliament Street Police Station. Ordering a double Scotch, he said to the barman, 'Ratanlal, some time ago you told me about a nightclub where a lot of gambling goes on, where they play flash and roulette all night and smoke pot as well. Is the club still operational?'

Ratanlal lowered his voice. 'Are you talking of Sweet Sixteen, sir? Don't let anyone hear you speak about it. Yes, it's very much in business.'

'What's the address? Do you know the name of the owner?'

'The owner's name is Dorothy Mendoza, sir. She and her daughter Tania Mendoza run the club. They're both very sharp, but the daughter is more dangerous. Avoid her, sir. If you play cards or roulette, be very careful. There's very little chance of winning.'

'Do you know this Mrs Mendoza?'

'I know Dorothy Mendoza very well, sir. Do you wish to go to her nightclub? I'll ring her at once. You'll be in safe hands with Dorothy. The police are keeping a close eye on the club, sir. The address is 23, Alipore Road. The phone number is 72-3525.'

'Thank you, Ratanlal. I must first call a friend. Oh and I've invited one of my girlfriends here. Can you get me two bottles of champagne?'

'There's nothing money can't buy you in this club, sir. I can get you ten bottles of champagne, not two. We buy foreign liquor and pass it off as Indian.... I have many friends among barmen in different hotels. They supply me with any liquor I need. Don't worry, I'll get your champagne right away and have it chilled.'

Maqbool made a telephone call to Defence Club. Malia answered. 'Hello, my darling.'

'Is Alok there, sweetheart?' asked Maqbool.

'He is. I'll call him.'

Alok Bhatia went up to the telephone.

'Hello, Maqbool? What is it?' He sounded annoyed.

'It's very cold today.'

'Did you call me to give the weather report?'

'Don't be angry. I have something very important to discuss with you.'

'Very well,' Alok calmed down. 'Come to Defence Club in the evening. I'll be here. What time will you come?'

'I could have come right now but I'm meeting a girlfriend. How about around 10 p.m. tonight?'

♪

Maqbool and Sumita were drinking in the Gymkhana lounge. Ratanlal deposited two bottles of champagne on their table.

'What's going on, Maqbool?' asked Sumita. 'Why the champagne suddenly? No one drinks champagne here.'

'If it's free, people here will even drink whale milk, let alone champagne. There's a special reason. The first bottle is to celebrate the help you offered me. And the second is to mark your farewell, or goodbye Madame Butterfly. Call it your severance fee.'

Sumita stared at Maqbool in surprise. Was he drunk? 'What do you mean, goodbye Madame Butterfly? I don't get you, darling. Anyway, all this talk is out of place here in this lounge. Talk of something else.'

'Listen, Sumita, I'm sure you know what calling it quits means. You and I are even now, all our mutual debts have been paid. As for goodbye Madame Butterfly, the meaning couldn't be more obvious.'

'What on earth are you saying, Maqbool? How many drinks have you had?'

'I thought you understood simple statements and preferred it that way. You're in deep trouble. Actually we both are. But I'll be able to come out of it. Not you, though. One more thing. A woman's past is more important than her future. A woman who needs to hide her past can never escape danger. You'll have to be very clever if you want to survive now. More champagne?'

'What's all this?' Sumita sounded annoyed now. 'Why are you talking in riddles? What sort of trouble am I in?'

'Let me explain. It'll make you unhappy though, I'm warning you. Because everything I'll tell you today is the truth, a tragic story. But first, tell me why you pretended to be in love with me. Of course you pretended, because you do not have a heart to fall in love with anyone. It's like stone, cruel and unforgiving. There's no such thing as love in your life, there's no room for it. You're a selfish, cold woman. Money is your only yardstick for relationships. You win men's hearts to extract money from them. I realized the first time you kissed me that you were no amateur. You were highly experienced at this game. Your kisses didn't taste of love. There was a motive behind them.'

Sipping his champagne, Maqbool continued, 'You're mistaken if you think I haven't seen through you. Just like you, I'm no novice either at the game of love, unlike Alok Bhatia. I know very well how to put up a show of love for women like you, who use their sex appeal for financial gain.'

'What the hell are you talking about, Maqbool? And what is this trouble you claim I'm in?'

'I'll tell you. I wasn't entirely sober yet when Inspector Govind Narayan came to my house to interrogate me. I had drunk too much the previous day. I didn't quite remember what I told him in my inebriated condition. I might have told him I was with you between 11 p.m. and midnight. It was some time during that hour that Geeta Saxena was murdered. But I made a fatal mistake. Because in fact, I received a phone call from Geeta at a quarter to eleven and went to her house. My fingerprints were found on her vanity bag and on a glass of water in her bedroom. So the police know that I was not with you but at Geeta's house at that time. Which means the alibi you provided me with was a lie. Do you know the punishment for giving false evidence in a murder case? A life sentence.'

'What is all this you're saying, Maqbool? I don't understand at all. Why have you ruined me?' Sumita began to weep.

'I had no choice. The police suspected me of murdering Geeta or, at least, of being involved in her murder. If I am arrested on these grounds they won't spare you. Both of us will go to jail.' Maqbool sipped his champagne. 'And now the police will investigate your past, to find out who you are, where you came from, what your relationship with Alok is.'

Sumita began to tremble.

'You're a scoundrel, Maqbool,' she hissed. 'Women don't know the dirty character lurking behind that handsome face. All you do is ruin women.'

'Don't speak so loudly,' Maqbool told her, 'everyone will hear. Softly, sweetheart, softly. Now tell me, why did you agree to lie for my sake? Shall I tell you why you provided me with an alibi?'

'What are you trying to say?'

'You agreed because you had no idea I had been to Geeta Saxena's house that night. And you needed an alibi yourself, as much as I did. Isn't that right? Our need was mutual. Your real purpose was to assure the police that you were not alone that night, you were with someone.'

'So?'

'So I'm ready to cut a deal with you, darling. If you want to save yourself, you have to agree to my conditions.'

'What conditions?'

'My conditions are simple. I will help you, but you have to tell me the truth. If not, it's goodbye my love, we may meet again in prison.'

Sumita had turned pale. She took a long sip of champagne. 'And what will I get for telling you the truth?' she asked.

'I will confess to the police that you gave me an alibi on my request. And you did not know the real reason.'

'Will the police spare me if you do?'

'Yes,' answered Maqbool.

'Give me a cigarette.' Sumita held out her hand.

Maqbool handed her a cigarette. Blowing out a mouthful of smoke, Sumita said, 'Very well, here's my story. Alok came to see me at 11.30 that night...'

Maqbool interrupted her. 'No, you have to go much further back. I know you only pretended to be in love with Alok. I want to know why. Was it only for his money? Were you blackmailing him for something?'

Sumita shook her head vehemently. 'Where's the question of blackmailing Alok for money? He has none. He has blown it all up gambling. I'm not denying that I love money. I need it too. Of course, it was only later that I discovered Alok was penniless. But by then, our relationship had deepened.'

'Alok is a scientist, a radar specialist...'

'Maqbool, I have no need of intellectual achievements from men. I need their bodies and their fat bank balances. I'm not interested in clever men. They're not my quarry. But...'

'Yes, when you discovered Alok had no money left you decided to change your target.'

'I did, but I didn't get the chance. Alok stopped me. He refused to let me go. We had a huge row over money a couple of days ago. I no longer wanted to waste my time with him. He asked me for some time, promising that he'd give me twenty-five thousand rupees in a few days.'

'Did he give you any hint of how he would get this money? Didn't you ask him who would give him twenty-five thousand rupees?'

'I didn't believe him at first. Alok had been making similar promises for quite some time. He had never kept them. I did ask him where he'd get this money. He said he had someone in mind.'

'He must have told you who it was.'

Instead of answering, Sumita held out her glass. 'Give me some more champagne.'

Maqbool opened the second bottle and filled her glass. Taking a sip, Sumita said, 'He told me Geeta Saxena would give him twenty-five thousand rupees.'

'Did he say why she would give him that kind of money?'

'No, he didn't. All he said was he would ask her for the money. I know Alok went to Geeta's house that night. He was supposed to take her to Arati's party.'

Sumita seemed to have overcome her initial shock. Maqbool asked her whether Geeta did give Alok the money.

'No. Alok came to my house at 11.30. He said Geeta hadn't given him any money. We fought again. Alok abused both Geeta and me. He told me women were going to be his downfall...'

'Do you know Alok won ten thousand rupees the next day at cards at Defence Club?'

Sumita smiled wanly. 'Ten thousand is nothing. Alok needs a lot more money. He has debts of over five lakh rupees. I told him to go back to his wife because he does not have the means to maintain me...'

Maqbool changed the subject suddenly.

'What do you know about Suraiya, Sumita?'

'I don't waste my time thinking of other people's wives. I'm interested in their husbands. After abusing me roundly, Alok began to cry. I told him to go back to his wife. Shedding tears would serve no purpose. I'd talk to him only if he got me the money. Alok told me he wouldn't go back to his wife. They had broken up because of me. He had quarrelled with his wife at the party. There was no question of going back to her.

'I noticed Alok's appearance. Dishevelled hair, wet clothes, glazed eyes. Why was he looking that way? When you asked me to provide you with an alibi, I began to put two and two together, since he had told me he had been to see Geeta. I didn't know why you were asking me to lie, but I didn't suspect you being connected with Geeta. I assumed you were in some other kind of trouble. But when I read of Geeta's murder in the *Evening News*, I recollected the state Alok was in. Had he murdered Geeta after she refused to give him money? I was afraid. I didn't want to be involved. I realized it would be wise to provide you with an alibi for the time of the murder, since it would be my alibi too. If Alok had killed her, the police were bound to implicate me, his girlfriend.

'The police told me you had been to Geeta Saxena's house at that time. At first I thought it was a trap for me to tell them you hadn't been with me, after all. But I realized the best course of action was to stick to the story. I had come to trust you more than I trust Alok. But now I see I was wrong. You have betrayed me. For all I know, Alok didn't go to Geeta's house at all.'

'How do you know Alok didn't go to her house? He left the party at 10. He must have gone to visit her.'

Sumita didn't have an answer. But she became furious. 'You and Alok are the same,' she screamed, 'both of you have betrayed me. I despise both of you. I never want to see either of you again. You're a very dangerous man.'

Maqbool laughed in response. 'I always thought the word dangerous man applied to me. But didn't you say you loved dangerous men? What happened? You were drawn to my flame, you burnt your wings. You gained nothing. You'd better go back to the person who sent you and tell him your mission has failed.'

Sumita looked at Maqbool uncomprehendingly. But before she could say anything, Maqbool continued, 'Never mind, Sumita. The police, Alok, I—all of us will forget you from this moment on. The champagne was my farewell gift to you. Goodbye.'

Sumita glared at him and ran out of the club.

Maqbool arrived at Defence Club around 10 p.m.

Malia came running up to him. 'I've been waiting for you all evening,' she said to Maqbool.

'Why, Malia?'

'I'll tell you later.'

'Where's Alok, my darling?'

'He's drinking in the next room. He's in a foul mood, I'm not sure why. Didn't he win ten thousand rupees the other night? He's looking for you.' Malia sounded worried.

Maqbool smiled. 'As you know, sweetheart, lucky in cards, unlucky in love. Which is why you won't see Sumita here tonight. Anyway, why worry about all this? Let's have a chat with Alok.'

Maqbool went into the next room. Alok was in a corner drinking. He was with a man and a woman. The man was a stranger, but Maqbool thought he had seen the woman somewhere. He couldn't remember, but she did. 'Hello, prince charming,' she shouted in excitement. 'Remember me? We had a drink together at the Gymkhana the other day. We'll meet again, you said.'

Maqbool remembered her now. 'Hello, ma chérie,' he said, laying on the charm. 'I wasn't expecting to see you here.'

'I asked for you as soon as I came,' she said accusingly. 'The girl at the bar told me no one named Maqbool Peshwani comes to this club.'

Maqbool realized Malia didn't like this woman, which was why she had responded this way. 'Women are so jealous,' he smiled. 'I knew you'd be here. That's why I came to see you. But my darling, I've forgotten your name.'

'You're so sweet, my darling Maqbool,' the woman laughed. 'The reason you don't know my name is that I never told you. You offered me a drink but you didn't ask who I am. I was surprised at your indifference. Anyway, my name is Rina.'

'And who is he?' Maqbool pointed to her companion. 'Is he your boyfriend?'

'Are you mad? Of course he isn't my boyfriend. I don't know him at all. I saw him for the first time as I was entering the club. I didn't know he was here to meet Alok Bhatia. He invited me to have a drink with him.'

Maqbool was about to say something to Rina when he saw Alok looking at them. He went up to Alok and glanced at the other man, who got up and shook his hand. 'My name is Deepchand,' he said. 'I have something important to discuss with Mr Bhatia. So if you don't mind…'

'I have something urgent to discuss with him too,' Maqbool told Deepchand.

Alok was probably a little drunk. 'I don't want to talk to either of you,' he screamed. 'Get out, both of you.'

'There you are,' Deepchand told Maqbool. 'You may leave now…'

Rina intervened to say, 'They have something confidential to discuss, Maqbool. Let them talk while we go to the bar.'

'Allow me to have a chat with Mr Bhatia,' Deepchand echoed Rina.

'I have something to discuss with you too,' Maqbool told Deepchand. 'Let's go into the other room.'

Turning to Rina, he said, 'Wait at the bar, Rina, I'll join you soon.' To Deepchand he said, 'I have some questions to ask you. You can talk to Alok afterwards.'

Deepchand was furious. 'I don't even know you,' he said, 'you can't possibly have anything to talk to me about.'

'You will no longer be so angry once you know who I am.' Maqbool practically pushed him into the next room. There he said, 'Listen carefully, Deepchand. Do not stay here. Take a taxi at once and go home. Else I'll have to call the police.'

'What do you mean?'

'I'm telling you in very simple English. Don't delay another moment if you wish to live. Get away now. I know exactly who you are.'

Deepchand flared up in anger. 'I do not understand a word of what you're saying.'

'Very well, let me make it simple for you. You are a professional blackmailer. You're here to get money out of Alok. Now come clean, are you doing this for yourself or on Sumita Chaudhuri's behalf? Anyway, I don't need an answer. Get out of here.'

'How dare you make these false accusations?' screamed Deepchand. 'I'm no blackmailer. Mr Bhatia owes me money…'

'Look, don't try to pretend. I know who you are. You extract money from people by threatening to expose their scandals. It was Sumita Chaudhuri who told me about you. So don't delay any further, get out of here unless you want to talk to the police.'

Deepchand stood there in surprise, not sure of what to do. But he showed no signs of leaving. So Maqbool said loudly, 'Sumita Chaudhuri has told the police that you routinely blackmail government officials. If you still don't leave I shall tell the police you're trying to blackmail Alok Bhatia.'

'All lies,' protested Deepchand.

'Very well then, I have no choice but to involve the police. Now tell me, are you married to Sumita Chaudhuri? You worked for the government but lost your job on charges of corruption. Then you got your wife involved in blackmail. Don't try to protest. I've seen your photograph in Sumita's house.' Maqbool's voice was rising.

'You've seen my photograph?' Deepchand asked disbelievingly. 'No, I'm not Sumita's husband, I'm a friend of hers.'

'Even better. I was expecting a clear reply from you. But I didn't think you'd confess so quickly. You'd set up a neat blackmailing racket, but you've ruined it with your own mistakes. You need more courage and intelligence. Neither you nor Mrs Chaudhuri are bold enough for this. Luring government officials with women and money is no child's play.'

Instead of protesting, Deepchand asked in a low voice, 'You're saying Sumita's told the police about me, sir. But why?' He sounded frightened.

'Because she's implicated in a murder case. The murder of Geeta Saxena, whose husband, Arindam Saxena, is a senior scientist in the defence ministry. The police say Alok was present at the scene of the crime at that time. Everyone knows Sumita Chaudhuri is Alok's girlfriend. Naturally the police summoned her for an interrogation. Would it be any surprise if they questioned her about you as well? The police know she's involved in blackmail. A woman cannot do this alone, she has to have a male accomplice. The police suspect you of being her partner. Things have gone very far. That's why I'm suggesting you disappear. Leave Delhi—go to Calcutta or Bombay. Don't get deeper into trouble.'

'Scoundrel!' muttered Deepchand before striding towards the door. Turning back, he asked, 'Who are you?'

'Me?' Maqbool laughed. 'I'm your lady business partner's former bed partner.'

✒

'What took you so long?' Alok asked Maqbool.

Maqbool glanced at him covertly. Alok was clearly drunk. Maqbool asked Rina, 'Would you like a gimlet?'

'No, a double whisky, please.'

Maqbool placed the order. 'I have some important things to tell you,' he told Rina.

'Important things? What important things?' Rina pretended not to understand.

'The most important thing for women is love. I want to tell you a beautiful love story…'

'I know you're good with love stories,' Rina smiled. 'But is it a true story?'

'I never make up love stories. It's all from my own life. Ask Malia there. She listens to my stories very day. Then she kisses me. Perfect combination.'

'As for me, I'd rather have kisses before the story.' Rina moved closer. 'I love you, my darling,' she told Maqbool. He realized she wanted to kiss him. This wasn't alcohol, this was the body talking. He needed Rina today. He would have to win her over. So he kissed her. She was clearly an experienced kisser.

'Why do I become so weak when I see you, Maqbool?' said Rina. 'By the way, where did Deepchand, I mean that man, where did he go?'

'You know, Rina, three's a crowd,' smiled Maqbool. 'So he left. "I'm taking your leave, Mr Peshwani," he said. But do you know what he told me before that?'

Rina looked at Maqbool in anticipation.

'Actually, I knew what he was going to tell me. This is what his class of people do. No money of their own, so they try sponge their drinks off other people. First, he tried to blackmail Alok. I came in the way. Then he said you'd asked him to buy you a drink. He had no money. So he asked me to lend him some money. He didn't even have the money to go home. I gave him some to take a bus home. I told him that he can't have a drink with a woman in a club like this without money in your pocket. He left.'

Rina protested. 'What a liar. It was he who invited me for a drink. I never asked him. I was sitting with Alok. Then you came. Believe me, Maqbool…'

'How can I disbelieve you? There's a type of man you'll come across in many of Delhi's clubs and restaurants who cadge their drinks off women.'

'You didn't give him any money, did you?'

'Are you mad? Do you think I'd allow him to buy you drinks with my money?' Maqbool held Rina's hand near his lips. 'What do you do for a living, Rina?'

'Why do you ask?'

'Would you like to make some money tonight?'

Rina sighed. 'Do you suppose it's easy to get a job these days? I'm looking for one. What would you like me to do? I'd like something adventurous.'

'Any assignment I give you will be full of thrills and spills. What if I told you you would have to spend the night with someone? For suitable compensation, of course. Five hundred advance, five hundred when the job is done.' Maqbool looked at Rina eagerly. Her answer would determine his strategy.

Rina wasn't entirely surprised at this proposition. 'You mean sleep with someone? And get paid a thousand rupees?'

'Of course, you'll get your thousand rupees. But no, you don't have to sleep with anyone. It all depends on your intelligence, though. If you're willing, I'll explain.'

'I'm ready. Now give me the details.'

'I'll take Alok to a nightclub a little later. I want to have a confidential discussion with him there. You'll come with me. The nightclub has excellent facilities for roulette and other forms of gambling.'

'This sounds very easy,' Rina answered happily.

Maqbool went up to Alok and had a quiet exchange with him. Then, the three of them set off for Sweet Sixteen.

By the time they reached the nightclub on Alipore Road it was nearly midnight. Alok was seated next to the taxi driver and had fallen asleep. In the back seat, Maqbool whispered the details of the assignment to Rina. 'Don't be frightened. It's going to an exciting night,' he told her.

'You make it sound like I'm about to act in a James Bond film. I've never been so excited,' Rina told him.

'Yes, but remember that this isn't a movie, this is real life. The assignment will be successful only if you can put on a brilliant act, which is not easy.' Maqbool lit a cigarette, 'Alok won ten thousand rupees at cards the other night at Defence Club. He's a compulsive gambler. Tonight, you will be with him at the roulette table.'

'What if he loses?'

'It's all a matter of chance. But Alok needs money desperately, and very quickly. That's what I'm taking him to Sweet Sixteen for. It's up to you and the two owners of the nightclub to ensure that fortune smiles on him tonight. I have already requested Dorothy and Tania Mendoza to help him. Your job is to congratulate Alok if he wins, and console him if he loses. Remember, Rina, a man needs the sympathy of a woman when luck turns against him. As you know, Alok has lost his wife, Suraiya, and his girlfriend, Sumita. You'll have to win his heart tonight with a show of love and affection.'

After a pause, Maqbool continued, 'If Alok is attracted to you, he will ask you to go home with him. Don't refuse. Go with him.'

Rina made to speak, but Maqbool stopped her. 'Don't speak loudly. Alok will hear us. He's sleeping now because he's drunk, but he will soon be awake.'

'You want me to go home with Alok?' asked Rina in astonishment. 'Won't his wife see me?'

'No, she won't. Suraiya and Alok no longer live together. Alok has his own place near the airport. You'll go to his flat with him. I need the address, for starters. You'll have to be very careful.'

Rina listened carefully. 'Am I free once I take him home?'

'No, you real work begins then. You'll have to look for something in his house, Rina. Alok will be too drunk to realize what you're up to. As soon as he falls asleep, you will search the entire flat with a toothcomb.'

'What am I looking for?'

'You have to check for secret documents. You may find some maps and diagrams too. I need those documents.'

'Thank heavens you don't want me to kill anyone. I don't like working with corpses.'

They arrived at Sweet Sixteen. As he got out of the car, Alok said to Maqbool, 'You were flirting with that woman in the back seat. I can't imagine how you do it so easily.'

'What's the name of this club?' Alok asked as they entered.

'Sweet Sixteen,' answered Maqbool. 'You'll like it here, Alok. They have both cards and roulette. You can make a small fortune if luck favours you tonight.'

'I used to play roulette in Soho when I lived in London. I've never played roulette after returning home. But I have very little capital. How can you play roulette with just ten thousand? If only I had some more…'

Alok glanced at Maqbool. He had no trouble interpreting the look. 'Don't worry about money, Alok,' he smiled. 'Remember, money and women are a man's temporary possessions. Both are seductive mirages. Never worry about them.'

'You're right, Maqbool. Women and money are both travellers. They pass through, they never stay.'

Dorothy Mendoza came up to welcome them. 'My friend, the great gambler,' Maqbool introduced Alok. 'He's here to play roulette tonight.'

'Go right through with your friend, Mr Peshwani. It's warming up in there.'

Maqbool glanced at Rina. She went off with Alok into the other room. Maqbool sat down to flirt with Tania.

⌐

An hour later, Alok and Rina left the roulette room to make their way to the bar. Alok looked grim. It was clear he had lost money. Rina was trying to console him.

Before Maqbool could ask, Alok said loudly, 'No Maqbool, your roulette didn't change my luck. I was up twenty thousand, but I lost it all. Do you know how much I am left with? Only twenty rupees…'

'Bad luck,' said Maqbool. 'I hope you'll be on a winning streak the next time.'

'But what can I do with just twenty rupees? What will happen tomorrow?'

'Stop worrying. Tomorrow lies in the future. Let's think about tonight. What do you want to drink? It's on me tonight.' Maqbool ordered two double Scotches.

Alok was not to be consoled so easily. He sounded distressed. His hands were trembling as he picked up his glass.

'I'm going through a very bad patch, Maqbool.'

'We have to discuss something in private now, Alok. Let's get a table. The bar is too public.' Maqbool forced Alok to a table in the corner. Rina stayed back to chat with Dorothy and Tania.

Taking a sip of his drink, Alok said, 'I thought my luck had turned when I won ten thousand at Defence Club and then another ten thousand here. But then I lost it all.'

'I'll lend you some money, Alok. How much do you want? Two thousand? Five? Not that I have a great deal either. But first, there's something confidential I have to talk to you about.'

'Confidential?'

'Yes. Listen. Sumita Chaudhuri has told the police a heap of lies about you and is planning to leave Delhi.'

'What! What are you saying? Sumita's leaving me in the lurch? Run away with whom?'

'I'm your friend, Alok. It's my job to help you, to advise you. Another drink?'

Alok didn't object. Two more double Scotches arrived. 'Where were we?' said Maqbool, taking a long sip of his drink. 'Oh yes, Sumita. Yes, she's planning to get out of here with her friend.'

'I know who the friend is,' shouted Alok. 'That bloody scoundrel Deepchand. He was trying to borrow money from me this afternoon. Threatening me with trouble if I didn't give him money.'

'You're right, Alok, both Sumita and Deepchand are blackmailers. As you know, the police is investigating Geeta's murder. They interrogated Sumita yesterday. She told them you were with Geeta that night. That was when the murder took place.' Maqbool paused to observe Alok's reaction.

'What's all this, Maqbool?'

'The truth, Alok,' Maqbool resumed. 'Geeta rang me at a quarter to eleven that night, asking me to meet her at once at home. The post-mortem report says she was murdered between 10.30 p.m. and midnight.'

'How am I connected to Geeta's murder?' Alok asked agitatedly. 'I know nothing about it.'

'But the police suspect just the opposite. Everyone knows Geeta was supposed to have gone to Arati's cocktail party with you. But you didn't bring her. And when you went to see Sumita with dishevelled hair and wet clothes, you looked like you had just had an argument with someone.'

'That's a lie, Maqbool. I didn't meet Geeta that night.'

'Even if you're telling the truth the police won't believe you. Because Sumita has already given a statement against you. Nor do you have an alibi. Inspector Govind Narayan says he believes Sumita and will present her as a witness. You won't find it easy to escape the charge of murdering Geeta. The police will investigate you, they'll dig into your past, and they'll find more incriminating information that will only make things worse for you.'

'The police are suspecting the wrong person. I didn't kill Geeta. I have nothing to do with her murder.'

'But the police believe Sumita. How will you contradict her? Everyone knows about your relationship with her. Arindam has said you were to have taken her to Arati's party. Sumita told the police you went to get money from Geeta. The two of you had an argument over it. Sumita said you had promised to get her some money from Geeta. Not that I believe her. But the police do. The question is, why is Sumita making all these things up? Is it just to get you into trouble, or is there another reason?'

'Let's have another drink,' said Alok, pointing at his empty glass. The drinks arrived. Taking a sip, he said, 'I don't trust women. Sumita, Suraiya, Geeta—they're all the same. No gratitude.'

'Where did you go that night from the party, Alok?' asked Maqbool. 'Where were you till midnight?'

Alok took his time answering. Then he said, 'I didn't go home directly. I was very annoyed with Geeta. I had no wish to escort her to the party. I walked around the streets for some time. No one was with me. It was drizzling. That was why my clothes were wet when I arrived at Sumita's.'

'Is there any proof? The police won't accept your statement unless you can prove it.'

'It's true that I have no proof. But you're my friend. Surely, you believe me.'

'Does it matter whether I do or not? I'm concerned about the police. Considering Sumita's statement, it will be hard for them to accept yours. It's true though that no one can be accused of being a murderer on mere suspicion. But with the police investigating the case a lot of dirty secrets will be revealed.'

Both of them had had a good deal to drink by now. Alok was beginning to slur his words. Maqbool wondered what to do next. He looked around the nightclub. Where was Rina? She was chatting with Tania. It was time to leave. He had to ensure Alok took Rina home, so that she could search his house.

'Don't worry, Alok,' he said. 'Just come clean with the police. Tell them the truth.'

'But what will I say if they interrogate me?'

'Don't be afraid of the police. No need to be afraid. By the way, I have some good news for you.'

'Good news?' Alok was surprised.

'You'll be happy to hear this. Rina is in love with you. I saw the pain written all over her face when you were coming out of the roulette room after losing. It's true, she has fallen for you. Let her take you home tonight. I don't think you should go by yourself.'

Alok protested. 'There's no need for anyone to take me home.' He was pleased to hear of Rina's feelings for him, but he wanted to stay away from women. 'I think you're wrong about Rina. You were flirting with her. Besides, I am done with women.'

'I'm not wrong at all. Rina does love you. I can tell she wants you. She was saying wonderful things about you in the taxi.'

'Really?' Alok sounded uninterested.

It was almost 2 a.m. Alok could barely walk. His legs were wobbly. Maqbool insisted that Rina go with him in the taxi. Alok protested but he was too drunk to press home his point.

'Don't worry, Maqbool,' Rina said sweetly. 'I'll take Alok home.'

'I'll be relieved if you do. Ring me in the morning. And here's your payment.' Maqbool pressed five hundred rupees into her hand. 'The rest, after the job is done.'

'Thank you, Maqbool. You're very sweet. I do need the money. I'll follow your instructions and ring you by eleven to report.'

It was almost 4 a.m. when Maqbool returned home. There was no point trying to sleep now. Maqbool decided to tell Arati everything. He wrote her a letter.

> Arati, I'm sure you'll be surprised and annoyed to receive this letter. I know you are mad at me. Besides, you have grown fond of Ratilal—perhaps you love him too. I shall not ask you about that. Perhaps you had expected I would reform after getting my new assignment from Arindam. Possibly you are surprised to see there has been no change. I daresay you no longer want me—and obviously do not wish to marry me either. I admit that there has been no change in my nature. I have not been able to give up either drinking or womanizing. However, I do regret my behaviour at your party.
>
> Anyway, let me explain why I'm writing to you. You probably know that the police have been interrogating me about Geeta's murder. Perhaps they suspect me of killing her. You may also know that Geeta rang me as I was leaving your party that night. She said she had a cold and wouldn't be able to make it to the party. However, she wanted me to meet her urgently at her house. I did not know why she was summoning me, but I did go. It was 11 p.m. I entered through the back door, as instructed, and went into the bedroom. I found Geeta on the bed, and it was obvious that she had been murdered. There was a silk thread around her neck.

I was certain the police would implicate me in her murder. At first I thought of calling the police. But I didn't have the courage. Should I call Arindam? I decided not to make anyone suspicious. I left quietly.

I found a silk handkerchief in Geeta's room that night. The letter 'A' was embroidered in a corner. I could also smell some perfume on it. It was a familiar scent. Either Nina Ricci or Opium. Do you know what perfume Geeta used? She was a close friend of yours. Another thing. There was a half-smoked Gauloises in the ashtray next to the bed. As far as I know, Alok smokes Gauloises. You know what I think? I think Alok was hiding somewhere in the flat when I went in. He escaped later. Of course, these are nothing but hunches.

Now let me tell you something else that is significant. I learnt this from Sumita. She suspects Alok of either murdering Geeta or being involved with the murder. When he went to see her that night, the state of his clothes and his behaviour were quite suspicious. Sumita said Alok had an intimate relationship with Geeta. That they were lovers. Geeta used to give money to Alok regularly. According to Sumita, Alok had asked Geeta for twenty-five thousand rupees that night. He had promised to pass the money on to Sumita. Because Sumita is Alok's mistress. He used to pay for her lavish lifestyle. They would fight whenever he was unable to provide money. Alok had told Sumita he was going to get some money from Geeta. Sumita thinks they had an argument over it and Alok killed Geeta in a fit of rage.

By the way, Geeta did not have a cold that night. She had told Arindam that afternoon that if he couldn't go to your party with her, she would go with Alok. She said nothing about a cold. But Alok didn't take her to your party. Where was he that night after he left your party? Alok hasn't been able to give a clear answer. He claims he was wandering around the streets before visiting Sumita after midnight. No one saw him. All he told me was that he fought with Suraiya at your party. Do you believe him? Will the police believe him? I doubt it.

Inspector Govind Narayan interrogated me about the murder two days ago. For some reason, perhaps to save myself, I used Sumita as an alibi. But the police saw through it. They said they had proof that I had been to Geeta's house that night. They had found my fingerprints. Pushed to a corner, I told them another lie. I said I did go to her house, but she was alive when I went, and we had a chat. I left after a few minutes, at about 11.15.

But this was a fatal mistake. I didn't know then that the post-mortem said Geeta had been murdered between 10.30 and midnight. Which meant I could be the murderer too. I haven't yet been able to prove myself innocent. I'm looking desperately for some way to save myself. If I can find some evidence to implicate Alok, I will be saved. After all, he went to her house, according to Sumita's statement.

But I'm torn now over implicating Alok. He's a decent sort, with a good heart, and an able scientist too. He may have squandered his inherited wealth on gambling and women, but that's not enough to prove he murdered Geeta.

I have a request to make of you. Everyone knows Suraiya is a close friend of yours. Can you show this letter to her and ask her whether she knew of Alok and Geeta being lovers? If Suraiya says they were, we may have to accept that Alok killed Geeta for money.

Suraiya may not answer immediately. She will have to think over the implications of her answer. But Alok's fate depends on her response. I will visit you at home tomorrow to discuss this. I'd like Suraiya to be present. I want to tell her something about this. If it is true that Alok and Geeta were lovers, the police have to be informed. You can imagine the outcome.

Maqbool made a copy of the letter. He decided to either post it, or to deliver it by hand. By the time he had finished it was 5 a.m.

⌣

Later that morning.

Maqbool had snatched a few hours of sleep. He wondered when Rina would ring him. Had she followed his instructions? He wasn't sure of her competence. Moreover, he wondered why she had agreed to perform this task for only a thousand rupees. It was not a lot of money. Maybe she had some other reason. Was she really in love with Alok, after all?

As he was eating breakfast, Maqbool saw a letter under his door. It was from Arindam Saxena. There was another piece of paper in the envelope besides the letter. Maqbool began reading the letter.

Dear Maqbool,

I was expecting a letter or a phone call from you. I'm disappointed not to have got one. I'm not in a good frame of mind. I'm unable to concentrate on work after Geeta's death. These days I'm lonely, I try to keep myself busy at the office. You had asked for the names and addresses of all the employees in the department. I am attaching it. Keep it confidential. I hope you find it useful.

My boss, Brij Mohan Iyengar, came to meet me a couple of days ago. He wanted to know about the progress we have made on the investigation. I needn't remind you how crucial this enquiry is. You have to provide a full report soon. I'll add my comments and pass it on to the bosses. Please don't be late in submitting your report.

I heard you made a scene at Arati's party. I'm sorry to hear that. She is a wonderful woman. I'm sure you were to blame. You will regret it if she leaves you. I met her at the Ashoka Hotel yesterday. She told me you're trying to reform. That's good news. Destroy this letter.

Sincerely,
Arindam Saxena

⌁

Maqbool began to plan his next step.

His thoughts were interrupted by the telephone ringing. It was Rina.

'Good morning, Maqbool. I rang twice earlier, you must have been sleeping.'

'Tell me about last night. Did you manage to search the flat? Did you find anything?'

'The answer to your question is both yes and no. I had a lot of trouble with Alok. He was very drunk. I feel bad for him.'

'Tell me everything, Rina.'

'I did what you asked me to. I searched all the rooms…'

'Found anything?'

'I'll tell you when we meet.'

'Where's Alok?'

'He's asleep. When should I meet you?'

'I'm going to the Gymkhana Club. Meet me at the bar at one.'

'Very well, I'll see you there.' Rina's voice held an undertone of excitement.

⟋

Maqbool left for the Gymkhana Club. He posted the letter to Arati on his way.

⟋

At the club he ordered a whisky. It wasn't long before Rina joined him. She was looking very beautiful. 'Get me something strong, darling,' she said. 'I can't talk till I've had a drink. It was a tough night with your friend.'

Maqbool ordered a brandy for Rina. Sipping it, she said, 'You'll be amazed to hear what happened last night, Maqbool. As soon as we left Sweet Sixteen, Alok put his arms around me and began to tell me he loves me. He was clearly saying all that because he was drunk. I was flabbergasted to begin with, then, I began to feel sorry for him. "Where do you want to go?" I asked him.

'"Vasant Vihar," said Alok.'

It was Maqbool's turn to be astonished. 'What are you saying, Rina? He went to Sumita's house and not his own?'

'Yes, I was also surprised to hear him say that he wanted to go to Vasant Vihar,' said Rina. 'You'd told me he lives near the airport. But I didn't ask him any questions. In the taxi he unburdened all his sorrows on me. His marriage had failed, women didn't love him, all of them were trying to cheat him. He was going to his girlfriend's house to ask her why she had betrayed him. He was bankrupt because of the wiles of women. Women are traitors, they were trying to have him arrested by the police.

'I asked him who these women who had betrayed him were. Who was trying to have him arrested by the police? But Alok did not reply. He seemed to be regretting having said these things to me. I tried to sweet-talk him into answering, and soon he relented. He said he wanted to meet Sumita, that she was trying to harm him, and he had some questions for her.

'So both of us went to Sumita's house in Vasant Vihar. I had half expected her not to be at home, but she was in, drinking and playing rummy with Deepchand. Obviously they hadn't been expecting us at that hour of the night. Sumita and Alok began to argue, abusing each other. Deepchand and I stood there silently...'

'I need to know who this Deepchand really is,' Maqbool interrupted Rina. 'Is he Sumita's husband or just a friend?'

'I have no idea whether he's her husband,' Rina answered, 'but I have no doubt that he's a blackmailer. Anyway, Alok came down very hard on Sumita. He warned her that if the police investigate her past they will discover a lot of unsavoury things. That she was doing things that hurt India's interests. But Sumita wouldn't take this lying down. She flung the whisky in her glass on Alok's face. She called him a murderer and said she wanted nothing to do with one. Alok denied killing Geeta Saxena, and accused Sumita of being a blackmailer. He threatened to tell the police the truth about her. Sumita was furious and asked him who had told him she was a blackmailer. He said Maqbool had told him. Sumita said Maqbool was a liar and that he's trying to have Alok arrested by the police.'

'Really?' laughed Maqbool. 'I had no idea I was such a dangerous man.'

'Can you be serious?' Rina said angrily. 'Not that I believe you're dangerous. Anyway, listen to what happened after this. I managed to get Alok out of there. It was 4.30 a.m. We found a taxi with great difficulty and went to Alok's flat in Subrata Mukherjee Colony. I fished the key out of his pocket and unlocked the door. Immediately, Alok passed out on the sofa. Then I began to search for secret documents. But I'm sorry to disappoint you, Maqbool, there was nothing suspicious anywhere. It was a typical bachelor's flat, with very little furniture. Here's the address…'

'Let's have lunch,' said Maqbool. He ordered food, along with a whisky for himself and a Campari for Rina.

'I want to ask you something, Maqbool,' she said. 'Answer only if you want to. I'd like to know the meaning of this cloak-and-dagger mystery. Why do you want Alok's house searched? What are you investigating? What do you need the documents and diagrams for? Frankly, I don't want to play with fire.'

'Don't worry,' Maqbool answered softly. 'You've done your job well. I must thank you. There's just one more task, for which you'll have to go back to Alok after lunch. What's he doing now?'

'Must be sleeping it off. He didn't sleep all night. He's been agitated since last afternoon. He's so exhausted, I doubt he'll be up before five in the evening.'

'All right. You must bring Alok to Defence Club at 10 p.m. tonight. If he refuses, tell him I want to meet him to discuss an urgent matter. Your task is done once you bring him to the club. You will have no further role to play in this mysterious drama. Here's the five hundred I owe you.'

Rina looked disappointed. She hadn't expected her role to end so quickly. 'When will I see you again?' she asked.

'Listen, Rina, everyone says I'm a dangerous man. It's best if you don't meet me again. You'll die like a moth drawn to a flame. It would be wise to avoid me.'

'So I won't see you again? But I love adventure. If you need me again in the future…'

'I'll seek your help if I do, Rina.'

She left.

Maqbool rang Arati from the bar. She said, 'I've received your letter, Maqbool. Come home at 4 p.m. Suraiya will be here too.'

⌣

Maqbool arrived at Arati's house at 4 p.m. Suraiya was dressed in a lovely sari and a matching blouse. Arati was dressed casually, but she was looking pretty.

On his part, Maqbool appeared subdued. He hadn't had a drink since lunch.

'What will you have, Maqbool?' Arati asked lightly. 'The sun hasn't set yet. Too soon for your foreign waters. Tea?'

'Don't worry about me,' Maqbool smiled at her. 'I've given up drinking. I'm trying to reform myself.'

'I'm glad to hear that. I hope you'll be able to concentrate on your work now.' Arati gave him a cup of tea. 'We were very upset to hear of Geeta's murder. Poor Arindam.'

'I still can't believe anyone would want to murder Geeta,' echoed Suraiya.

Maqbool drank his tea in silence. 'I have to leave, Suraiya,' said Arati. 'There's someone I have to meet.'

'You must be going to meet Ratilal,' exclaimed Maqbool.

Arati looked at him in annoyance. 'What's the matter with you? Are you jealous of Ratilal? Where I go and whom I meet is none of your business. I'm an independent woman, not anyone's slave. Let me give you some news. I don't know whether it will please you. Ratilal bought me a diamond engagement ring last night.'

Arati displayed the ring on her finger.

Maqbool smiled sadly at her. 'Heartiest congratulations. Who am I to stand in the way of you marrying the person you please.'

Suraiya congratulated her. 'Wonderful news, Arati.' She turned to Maqbool, 'I feel really sorry for you, Maqbool. You've lost Arati because of your own mistakes. You could have mended your ways much earlier.'

Maqbool did not deny it. 'I know my drinking has done me in.'

Arati looked at both of them before leaving.

Maqbool and Suraiya sat in silence for some time. Suraiya poured some more tea and said, 'Marrying Arati would have changed your life. I hear the police are questioning you about Geeta's murder.'

'Yes. Did you read the letter I wrote Arati? I asked her to show it to you. What do you think of what I wrote?'

Suraiya raised her beautiful eyes to Maqbool. Those alluring eyes could set a man on fire. 'I've read the letter,' she said. 'It's best to tell the truth to the police, Maqbool. Lying can only lead to further trouble.'

'Telling the truth leads to trouble too, Suraiya. The police will arrest Alok if I do. You know I found a half-smoked Gauloises in Geeta's room. And you know who smokes Gauloises. And look, this is the handkerchief that was lying next to Geeta's body. It has "A" embroidered on it. Can you tell me what the perfume on it is?'

Suraiya sniffed the handkerchief. 'It's Nina Ricci,' she said.

'Do you know whether Geeta used Nina Ricci?' asked Maqbool.

'I don't,' answered Suraiya indifferently.

'Thank you for clarifying this. If you don't mind, Suraiya, can I ask whether your marriage with Alok is going well?'

Suraiya's lips curled in contempt. 'It was a big mistake to marry Alok. I hate him. I know him very well now. I've lived with him for two years, after all. I don't know how I would have survived if I didn't have some personal savings. First, there was the gambling, and then there was this business with Geeta and with Sumita.'

Maqbool tried to speak but Suraiya interrupted him. 'Don't compare yourself with him. Everyone knows you drink too much, but you're a good man. You're not addicted to gambling or money. That's why women love you. But the less said about Alok the better.'

'Thank you for your kind words,' smiled Maqbool. 'I'm going to ask you another question, don't be upset. Was Alok having an affair with Geeta?'

'Give me a cigarette, Maqbool,' said Suraiya.

She lit the cigarette and continued, 'Alok is a pauper today. I was once proud that he was my husband but not any more.'

Maqbool pushed his cup towards her for a refill. 'I'm sorry to hear things are strained between the two of you,' he said.

'There's no love between us any more,' said Suraiya. 'Now let me answer some of your questions. Yes, Geeta and Alok were lovers. If you ask me how a sensible woman like Geeta could be Alok's lover, I don't have an answer. I knew he used to meet her in secret. Sumita must have guessed it too. I believe they fought about it often.'

Maqbool pretended to be surprised. 'You knew about Geeta and Alok's affair? Do you know whether Geeta gave Alok money?'

Suraiya smiled sweetly. 'You're Alok's friend. You know he is drawn to money. He didn't hesitate to accept money from Geeta. How else would he fund his drinking, gambling and mistress? Poor Arindam's situation. He was so busy with his research in his laboratory that he had no time to think of his wife. He ignored her. She was lonely.'

Suraiya paused for a few moments before continuing, 'Now put the pieces together. First, a slut like Sumita is Alok's mistress. Of course, I knew it. I objected, but nothing changed. Secondly, as you wrote, Alok asked Geeta for more money the night she was murdered. She refused. They had an argument. He killed her. The theory is plausible. I am convinced by it.'

'I didn't expect you to say these things because Alok is your husband,' said Maqbool. 'You're right, I have to be careful, or I'll be in trouble.'

'What will you do now?'

'I'll meet Inspector Govind Narayan tomorrow and tell him everything.'

Suraiya lit another cigarette. She was clearly disturbed by the conversation. Maqbool felt she was intent on taking revenge on Alok.

'I won't object if you tell the police of your suspicions about Alok,' said Suraiya. 'Do you want to know why? How would any wife accept her husband sleeping around with other women? I cannot stand the idea that Alok keeps a whore like Sumita as his mistress. I want revenge.'

'I wasn't expecting you to back me so strongly, Suraiya,' said Maqbool. 'I couldn't have thought of going to the police without your help.'

Suddenly, Suraiya slid close to Maqbool and put her arms around him. 'I love you, Maqbool,' she purred. 'I'll do whatever you want me to do.'

Maqbool was taken aback, but only momentarily. He realized there was a reason behind Suraiya's sudden declaration. But what was it? Maqbool didn't ask any more questions. All he said before leaving was, 'Thank you for all your help, Suraiya.'

From Arati's house he went directly to Defence Club. Malia came running to him as soon as he entered. 'Hello my darling, how do I look in my new miniskirt?'

She looked sexy, but Maqbool said, 'No, I don't like it at all.'

'Is it the skirt or me you don't like?' Malia pouted. 'Your one-night stand, that Rina, do you know who she really is?'

It was true, Maqbool knew nothing about Rina. He had run into her by chance at Gymkhana Club. When she came up to him to talk, he had assumed she wanted free drinks or perhaps was on the look out for money. He hadn't suspected anything else.

'I didn't imagine someone like Rina would make a fool of you,' said Malia. 'You know women so well, and still you made a fatal mistake. The man with her was Deepchand. Sumita Chaudhuri, Deepchand and Rina have all been hired by my employer Ratilal. They're supposed to lure men and women to Defence Club, for which they get hefty commissions. Of course, Alok Bhatia's case is different. Rina is in love with him. Why was she flirting shamelessly with you then? Why does she want to keep Alok away from you? You must find out. She made up things about Deepchand just to win you over. And you fell into her trap like a fool.'

Maqbool looked at Malia. She had given him vital information. She was not just sexy but intelligent too.

'You've done me a great favour, sweetheart,' Maqbool told Malia. 'I'll keep this in mind. Now listen, I've asked Rina to bring Alok here at 10 p.m. I'll be here too. Tell them to wait for me. I have some important business now. I'll see you later.'

Maqbool rang Arindam. It was 7 p.m. Arindam was usually in his office at this time. He wasn't surprised to hear Maqbool's voice on the phone.

'I knew you'd ring me,' he said. 'Now tell me what progress you've made. Have you found anything?'

'I have,' said Maqbool, 'but I can't tell you on the phone. I need to meet you at once.'

'Very well, come to Gymkhana at eight. Have dinner with me.'

'Excellent idea. I'll be there.'

Maqbool went home to change.

Maqbool made himself a whisky before leaving for Gymkhana Club. Malia had warned him about Rina and Sumita. He should have realized that they were Ratilal's employees.

You cannot size up women, Maqbool, he told himself. Which is why you fall into their trap. But was it he who had fallen into Rina's trap, or Rina into his? He was genuinely surprised by Rina's interest in Alok. More important, though, if she was Ratilal's employee she must have told him by now that Maqbool had asked her to search Alok's flat for secret documents. Although this could also mean Maqbool wanted to get his hands on those documents.

It was hard to say what Ratilal would make of this information. But he would certainly begin to suspect Maqbool...of what, though? And what of Sumita Chaudhuri?

Maqbool pondered his next course of action. First, he had to meet Arindam. He would think about Rina and Sumita later.

Arindam was sitting at the bar when Maqbool arrived at Gymkhana Club. He looked worried. 'Hello Maqbool,' he said. 'I was waiting for you.'

'I'm going to have to tell you some unpleasant truths,' said Maqbool. 'Please don't mind. I didn't want to tell you, but I have no choice.'

'I can take it,' Arindam assured Maqbool. 'You can say anything you want to, I won't mind. But first, what progress have you made on the investigation? The bosses are asking every day whether we have the secret agent in our sights.'

'I'm almost done with the investigation. All that's left is to reel in the big fish. All the criminals will be caught. But I must tell you that we mustn't make a big noise about the findings.'

'I agree with you. It's only a departmental enquiry, and it will stay there.'

'All right then, let me tell you what I've discovered. I'm wondering where to begin.' Maqbool took a long sip of his drink. 'Let's start with Arati's party. As you know, Geeta was to go to the party with Alok Bhatia. But she didn't go—or couldn't go. She told me on the phone that she had a cold, but you knew nothing about a cold.'

'I don't understand what Geeta's cold has to do with your investigation.'

'I'll tell you everything, don't be impatient. Let me finish, after that you can ask all the questions you want. So Alok did not take Geeta to the party. As I was leaving the party at a quarter to eleven, Arati's servant told me Geeta had called for me. Her voice sounded different on the phone. I thought it was someone else, but Geeta told me to meet her at once. She also instructed me not to use the front door but to take the rear entry. I was surprised, but I was too tipsy to pay much attention.'

Arindam lit a cigarette.

'I took a taxi to your house,' Maqbool continued. 'I entered through the back door. No one seemed to be home. There was a light in the bedroom. Geeta was lying in bed. I was surprised to see her this way. Soon, it was obvious she was dead. She had been murdered.'

Arindam looked surprised.

'I couldn't believe it at first,' Maqbool said. 'Who would do this? I looked around. There were no signs of a struggle. Then I found a half-smoked Gauloises in the ashtray. As you know, our friend Alok Bhatia smokes Gauloises.'

'What are you getting at, Maqbool?'

'Hear me out. Later, I learnt that Alok had been to your house too. Before I did. He didn't know I had been there as well, nor that Geeta had asked me to see her. She didn't tell Alok. She was afraid. I suspect—no, I'm certain—she was killed minutes before I went in. In fact, I think the murderer was there when I went. The method was unusual. A silk thread was used to throttle her. Not your usual murderer.'

Arindam took a long drag of his cigarette.

'The question, then: who murdered Geeta? The post-mortem report said the time of death was between 10.30 and midnight. That was when Alok visited your house. He has not been able to account for his activities between 10.30 and midnight. He has no alibi.'

'Right.'

'You were busy with your work, Arindam. You didn't know what was going on at home. You paid no attention to your wife. So she...'

'What are you trying to say?' Arindam interrupted angrily.

'Now we come to the unpleasant truth,' Maqbool told him. 'Alok and Geeta were in love. They had an affair. You were not aware of it. But Alok's wife Suraiya knew. However, she did not want to interfere in your personal life, which was why she kept quiet. Alok had another lover. Or rather, a mistress. Sumita Chaudhuri.'

'No, I don't believe a word of what you're saying,' Arindam shouted.

'You have no choice,' smiled Maqbool. 'I haven't told you the whole thing yet. Now listen to the rest. But first, a question for you. Were you in the habit of taking home secret files from the defence ministry? Did those files have information about arms purchases?'

'Yes,' said Arindam. 'These files would come to me for my comments, and I never had time for them at work. So I used to bring them home. But I kept them very safe, there was no question of misplacing them. Why do you ask?'

'One more question, Arindam. You're a government employee. You have no additional income, do you?'

'No.'

'Alok Bhatia was also a government employee. But he used to gamble, even keep a mistress. He spent seven or eight thousand rupees a month on Sumita alone. Where did he get all this money? You'd be surprised to know that Geeta gave him money regularly.'

'I don't believe it,' Arindam burst out. 'Geeta could never have given Alok so much money. She didn't have it.'

'You're right, Arindam. She couldn't have given Alok any money out of your meagre salary. But I am certain she gave him money. The question then is, where did she get it? Put two and two together, Arindam. Top secret files. Money. Do you understand what I'm trying to say?'

'Are you suggesting Geeta sold the information in those files?'

'Yes, Geeta would pass on the information to Alok. He would sell it. I hope it's clear to you now. She was having an affair with Alok. According to Sumita, that night Geeta refused to give him any money. So he killed her. I have proof that Geeta used to sell the information in your files.'

Maqbool took a lighter out of his pocket. 'This looks like a lighter, but actually it's a spy camera. Here's how it works.' He pressed the lever, and a light came on, followed by the click of a camera.

'I found this lighter in Geeta's vanity bag,' said Maqbool. 'She would use it to take photographs of the documents in your secret files. No one would have found out had she not been murdered.'

'I can't even comprehend what you're saying,' said Arindam

disconsolately. 'My mind has shut down.'

'Don't lose heart. Have a brandy. You'll feel better.' Maqbool ordered two brandies.

'What happens now?' asked Arindam, taking a sip.

'My plan is to put pressure on Alok to extract the truth from him,' said Maqbool. 'He will break down and confess. He's bankrupt, he has no way out.'

'How will you do it?'

'I have a plan. Alok won ten thousand rupees at cards at Defence Club two days ago. He was planning to escape to London from Delhi. So I hatched a plan to ensure he lost all the money he had won. I took him to Sweet Sixteen nightclub, where he lost all his money playing roulette. He couldn't buy a ticket any more. I had to lend him some money just to meet his daily expenses.'

'You're brilliant, Maqbool. I hadn't expected you to carry out such a difficult task so well.'

'You won't have anything to complain about where my work is concerned. I want to prove to Arati I can do things well. I have a request for you. If you were to tell Arati I've done this assignment well, I might get her back.' Maqbool ordered another round of brandies.

'We have to pin Alok down tonight,' he continued. 'Else, he will escape. I will tell the police everything tomorrow. But it would help to get a confession out of Alok tonight. I need to know whom he's been selling the information to. I've invited him for a drink at Defence Club at ten tonight. I will bring him to you at eleven. The two of us will interrogate him together.'

'Brilliant idea. It would be best to work along these lines.'

'I can tell you what will happen next. Naturally, Alok will try to hoodwink us. But as you know, one can't keep up a lie forever. Since he will have to tell one lie to cover another, he will eventually lose track and contradict himself. It won't be difficult after that to get him to confess everything.

'We will tell Alok that we know everything. Once he knows that we know everything he will have no choice but to confess. Then the police will arrest him on charges of murder and present him in court. But we must do all this in complete secret, so that the public does not come to know.'

Arindam was silent for a while. Then he said, 'Yes, we'll extract a confession from Alok tonight. But...'

'But what?'

'We need to think about the whole thing clearly, Maqbool. Don't forget my wife Geeta is involved too, even if she's dead. You're saying she was having an affair with Alok and passed on state secrets to him. I want to hear Alok confess this too. I want to know how deep their relationship was.'

'I don't mind. You can ask Alok a thousand questions in private. I don't have to be present.'

'Excellent, let's proceed accordingly then. I'll interrogate Alok first, then you, okay?'

'Okay,' smiled Maqbool.

'I'll expect the two of you at eleven then. I'll talk to him for half an hour. You can come back at 11.30. I never thought you'd be able to pull this off, Maqbool...'

Maqbool smiled. 'As they say, never say never.'

He left.

⁀

A little later, Arindam decided to meet Madhavan Shankar. He should discuss the whole thing with the bosses. Or else, they would accuse him of negligence.

Madhavan Shankar was pleased to see him. 'I was thinking of you, Arindam,' he said. 'I was going to ring you tomorrow morning to ask for a progress report. Has your dipsomaniac associate made any headway?'

'Don't write off Maqbool Peshwani, sir,' smiled Arindam. 'He's very efficient. I have to acknowledge his intelligence and patience. I thoroughly underestimated him.'

'You're right, Arindam. Maqbool is both clever and resourceful. Now tell me what you've found out.'

'The first thing is that Maqbool claims he didn't murder Geeta. I'm willing to believe him.'

'What did you mean?'

'Maqbool has just given me a verbal report of his investigations. It's clear that he's innocent.'

'Then who killed your wife? Inspector Govind Narayan is sure it was Maqbool.'

'I think it was Alok Bhatia. Maqbool's arguments are irrefutable.'

'The truth is that we had expected Maqbool to make a mistake and give himself away. But now I see he's a sly fox.'

'Yes, we underestimated him. But the logic he presented today leaves me with no choice but to consider Alok guilty of murdering Geeta. Maqbool has given me another piece of bad news.'

'Bad news? What bad news?'

'Alok was having an affair with Geeta. It's a very serious allegation that Maqbool has made, but again, his arguments are flawless. He said I was so busy with work that I neglected my wife, and Alok took advantage of this. Maybe Geeta was seeking a way out of her loneliness. I had no idea of this relationship, however, but apparently Alok's wife Suraiya knew.'

'There's more disturbing news, Mr Shankar. Alok also had a mistress named Sumita Chaudhuri. He used to blackmail Geeta for money and pass it on to Sumita. Geeta and Alok had an argument over money. Geeta was so frightened she rang Maqbool to ask him to come over to our house. By the time he arrived, though, Geeta was dead. Maqbool found a half-smoked Gauloises in the ashtray. Alok smokes Gauloises.'

'Where does Alok say he was that night? Do you know?'

'He's unable to provide an alibi. He told Maqbool he was wandering alone on the streets till midnight.'

Madhavan Shankar paced around the room. 'This is vital information, Arindam,' he said. 'The police have been looking for a motive for the murder. Narayan has not been happy about my interfering with his probe. He wanted to arrest Maqbool. I stopped him. He's convinced Maqbool is the murderer. But if we accept Maqbool's arguments we also have to accept we were wrong about him.'

'There's something else you'll be surprised to hear,' said Arindam. 'Alok Bhatia is our spy. He's been selling defence secrets to foreign governments.'

Madhavan Shankar did not seem surprised. 'Let Maqbool Peshwani present his report. We'll see after that.'

'Maqbool is bringing Alok to my house at eleven tonight,' said Arindam. 'We'll try to get a confession from him. I have to admire Maqbool's courage.'

'Yes, so do I. Don't worry, Arindam, everything will be fine.'

Arindam left.

⌐

Maqbool reached Defence Club at 10 p.m. Rina was drinking a gimlet at the bar. 'I have been waiting for you, Maqbool,' she said excitedly. 'I've brought your quarry here. Happy?'

Maqbool looked at her. Was she employed by Ratilal? Was Malia right? Rina was clearly very fond of Alok. He sat down next to her. 'Why don't you say something?' she complained. 'Alok didn't want to come, he said he was both physically and emotionally exhausted. He's having a drink now. Says he'll play roulette again tonight, that he simply must win some money.'

Maqbool smiled at Rina. 'Don't worry about Alok any more. Your job is done. Alok is my responsibility now.'

Rina paled. 'I can't abandon Alok today,' she said. 'He lost all his money at roulette last night. He's desperate to win it back. I feel very sorry for him.'

Maqbool looked at Rina suspiciously. She was either Ratilal's employee, or she had fallen in love with Alok. 'I'm surprised by your sudden feelings for Alok,' he said in annoyance. 'When did you fall in love with him?'

'My heart isn't made of stone,' Rina retorted. 'Can't you see the state he's in?'

'Let me give you some advice,' Maqbool said sternly. 'It's not a good idea to be so concerned about someone else's husband. It can get you into trouble. Where Alok is concerned, it's best to keep your distance. Don't invite danger.'

Rina wasn't expecting such a response. She was taken aback. 'It's just that I feel sorry for him,' she tried to explain.

'Thank you for your sympathy for Alok. But your job is done. One more thing. Consider it my advice to you. You can't have two masters. Both might let you down.'

'What do you mean?'

'Do you really mean you don't understand? If I have to explain it will mean telling you some unpleasant things. I know who you are. I know what you do for a living. I also know why you agreed to go to Alok's house last night without any objections. I know it wasn't because of the money. Don't act as a double agent, Rina. You'll be in deep trouble.'

Rina was trembling. 'It's time you left,' Maqbool told her.

⌣

Maqbool asked Malia for a double Scotch and a double brandy.

She looked at him in surprise. 'This is a sure-fire way to get drunk,' she said.

'It's the elixir of life,' laughed Maqbool. 'I might get a new lease of life.'

Malia knew it was no use arguing with Maqbool. She brought him his order. Maqbool walked up to Alok with the drinks. 'Drink up,' he said, 'this will refresh both your mind and body.'

Alok looked at Maqbool disbelievingly. 'Double Scotch, double brandy? I'll get drunk in a minute,' he protested.

'No Alok, you're down on your luck today. You need a strong drink to renew yourself. Pour this down the hatch and then listen to me. Consider it advice from a friend. It will help you.'

'What are you trying to say, Maqbool?'

'Your life is in danger, Alok. You have to listen to me if you want to save yourself. Drink up.'

Alok sipped his drink and grimaced. 'It's very strong. All right, what do you want to tell me?'

'You have many reasons to follow my instructions. First, I'm going to give you five thousand rupees tomorrow. I know you need it.'

'Why do you care whether I need money or not?'

'I know you are broke. Now listen, use the money to get out of Delhi. You need to stay away from this dangerous environment. The police have unearthed a great deal of evidence against you. They can easily put you in the dock for Geeta's murder. They're saying you were having an affair with Geeta, that she was your mistress. Your girlfriend Sumita Chaudhuri will support this statement. She has told the police you killed Geeta for not giving you money. How are you going to disprove this? All you can say is you were walking on the streets for two hours. No one will believe you. You don't have an alibi. There's too much evidence against you.'

Alok tried to speak. Maqbool stopped him. 'Don't argue, Alok,' he said. 'Now listen. Arindam will meet us in his house at 11 p.m. He wants to know why Geeta was in love with you, why she helped you with money, why she slept with you. Questions to that effect. You know how to answer him. I'm not going to be part of these discussions.

'There's one more thing. Three months ago, some defence secrets were sold to the Pakistani government. The three of us were sacked because we were under suspicion. But the government could not prove it. Now, some more secrets have been published in Pakistani newspapers a week ago. It can no longer be one of us. The government is trying to find out whether any other employee of the ministry is passing on the secrets. They want to know who the secret agent is. Arindam thinks it was his wife Geeta, using the information in the files he took home. But she would have needed an accomplice to do the actual transaction with a foreign government. Arindam suspects you of being the accomplice. Don't deny the allegation…'

'Me? Why should I sell state secrets to Pakistan?'

'No Alok, you won't go scot-free just by denying it. Arindam won't believe you if you deny murdering Geeta or working as a spy. The wise thing will be to accept the allegations, because there is enough proof. But if you tell Arindam—only Arindam—that you were indeed getting state secrets from Geeta, everything will turn muddy again. Let me explain why I'm asking you to confess. Don't forget the allegations against you are treason and murder. To the government, treason is far worse than murder. Now your job is to try and merge these two allegations. There will be so much confusion that the lines between truth and falsehood will be blurred. You won't be convicted of murder unless the charge of treason is proved. If you say Geeta was supplying you with secrets, you will have to explain whom you sold them to. They will need to prove the identity of the buyer. You'll have to cut a deal with the intelligence department. All they can do is question you until they get proof. They cannot convict you while you are being interrogated. The government will want to know the other Pakistani spies in India. You can delay the investigation by promising to disclose their identities. The government will either put you under surveillance or, at worst, in custody. But if you don't follow my advice, the police will arrest you for murder. Remember, whatever you say tonight will only be to Arindam, not to the police. You can deny everything afterwards.'

Alok could not reply. He was gripped by fear.

'It's no use, Alok,' Maqbool continued. 'After all, none of this is a fairy-tale, it's the truth.'

Alok realized he had no choice but to agree. He finished his drink and said, 'Do you know what I think of you?'

'What?'

'You're the devil incarnate.'

'You're wrong. I'm merely the king of the pack, the ace of spades.'

⌣

They left for Lodi Estate. Maqbool asked the taxi to stop a short distance away from Arindam's house. As they walked along the deserted road,

Maqbool said, 'The fresh air will clear our heads. I have another question for you. What do you think of Rina?'

Alok was surprised. Why was Maqbool asking him about Rina? 'I can't stand any woman these days. They're the reason for man's downfall.' He was slurring his words. 'If only there was a place in the world without women...'

'Do you love Rina?' Maqbool asked. 'You bared your heart to her last night.'

'Really? I must have been drunk. But it's hard not to talk to people either. I don't love Rina, but I like her. Whispering a few sweet nothings in a woman's ear doesn't mean being in love with her.'

Arindam was waiting for them in the drawing room. He noticed Alok was already drunk. 'Have you seen his condition?' he told Maqbool. 'How will I talk to him? Why did you bring him here?'

'Alok gets sober as quickly as he gets drunk,' said Maqbool. 'He'll be fine in ten minutes. No slurring, no confusion.'

'Very well,' said Arindam after some thought.

'I'll be back in some time,' said Maqbool. 'You can finish your questioning meanwhile. Then we'll question him together.'

Maqbool left.

⌒

He went back to Defence Club.

Malia was waiting for him. 'A double Scotch, please,' Maqbool hummed.

She looked at him in surprise. 'Why so happy?'

'I'm thinking of telling you a love story.'

'Will you ever be serious, Maqbool?'

Maqbool couldn't stay very long. The hands of the clock were inching past 11.30. He had to get back to Arindam's house.

'I don't trust you at all, Maqbool,' said Malia.

'You're right, Malia,' laughed Maqbool. 'I don't trust Maqbool Peshwani either. You know something? When I say something seriously, people think I'm joking. And when I'm joking, they think I'm serious. Bye bye Malia...'

⌒

Maqbool was back at Arindam's house a few minutes later.

Arindam looked irritated. 'What's the matter?' said Maqbool. 'What have you found out from Alok?'

'Found out? He's absolutely drunk. He can barely talk.'

Arindam wasn't lying. Alok was lying on a sofa. 'How much has he drunk?' said Arindam. 'I just wasted my time trying to talk to him. It'll be impossible to get anything out of him. Take him away.'

'When I saw him lying there, I thought he was dead. He's alive then.' Maqbool breathed a huge sigh of relief. 'You're right Arindam. Talking to him is impossible tonight. But I need to discuss something with you.'

'What about?'

'Can you give me ten thousand rupees? I've spent a lot of money on the investigations.'

'Ten thousand! Not now, Maqbool. I can manage five.' Arindam counted out five thousand rupees. 'Do you think the police can prove Alok killed Geeta?'

'If Alok is smart he can easily slip out of this. Every criminal case is a battle of wits. There may not be any direct evidence against Alok, but there's a great deal of circumstantial evidence. But then there's circumstantial evidence against me too. Alok's lawyer can easily pin the murder on me. All he has to prove is that there can be some doubt over the identity of the murderer, that someone else had the opportunity too. And therefore the judge will have to exonerate Alok.'

'I marvel at how your mind works, Maqbool,' said Arindam. 'First you proved to me with perfect logic that Alok murdered Geeta. Now you have proven to me that he may go free. Now I can no longer tell whether he's innocent or guilty. He could be either.'

Maqbool smiled. 'There's no doubt Alok killed Geeta, but if the government wants to prove he sold state secrets to Pakistan, they will have to interrogate him to find out where and to whom he sold the documents. And Alok can lead the police to a merry ride there.'

'Take him away, Maqbool,' said Arindam. 'See if you can get any information out of him. A confession will help your investigations.'

'Of course. I'll tell the police if I get something out of him. Inspector Govind Narayan is still convinced that I killed Geeta. We need to establish that it was Alok, and we have to get details about his relationship with her.'

'Exactly.'

'In which case I can tell the inspector that Alok is not only a murderer but also a spy.'

'You think you can do that?' asked Arindam. After some thought, he said, 'Yes, if anyone can, it's you. You have both the courage and the intelligence.'

'Once I've started the investigation,' said Maqbool, 'I have to bring it to a close with all the findings. There's no room for hesitation now.'

'I'm depending on you entirely.'

'Don't worry. I won't leave any stone unturned. We'll identify both the murderer and the spy.'

Maqbool dragged Alok out of Arindam's house. He was still in a stupor as they got into a taxi.

Maqbool took Alok to his flat near the airport. He took the key from Alok's pocket and unlocked the door. As soon as they entered the flat, he made Alok lie down on the sofa. Then he began searching the rooms. Although he had asked Rina to do this, he could no longer trust her after what Malia had told him about her. But Maqbool didn't find anything either. Then he searched Alok's coat pockets. There he found another handkerchief with the letter 'A' embroidered in a corner. It smelt of Nina Ricci perfume. 'A' for Alok, surely. He also found a key and a letter. The paper was familiar, and so was the handwriting. Maqbool was certain Geeta had written her unfinished letter to him on the same kind of paper, and the handwriting was the same too. This one was dated about a week ago. It said, 'take this key back, darling. I dare not keep the key to your flat any more'. There was an address on the letter, although it had been written over. Maqbool deciphered it with great effort. 157/1 Maharani Bagh.

Maqbool put both the letter and the key in his pocket. He began to hum to himself and glanced at Alok. He realized Rina was not as stupid as he had originally thought. Maybe she was reporting his movements to Ratilal.

Suddenly, Maqbool discovered Rina standing at the front door. She had not expected to see Maqbool. 'What are you doing here?' she asked, sounding annoyed.

'I wasn't expecting to see you here, either,' Maqbool told her.

Instead of replying, Rina pointed to Alok, who had passed out on the sofa. 'Are you never going to leave the poor man alone?' she said. 'Let him be. Are you made of stone? I'm afraid of you, Maqbool.'

'You're misunderstand me, Rina. I'm trying to save Alok from danger.'

'What did you put in his drink? I was sure you were up to some mischief. That was why you asked me to leave. What did you put in his drink? Why is he unconscious?'

Maqbool was silent for a while. Then he said, 'Very well, since you asked, I'll tell you everything. Alok and I are in the kind of trouble where the slightest misstep or indiscretion will mean death for both of us. Arindam wanted to know whether Alok and Geeta were having an affair. It's not a question that should be answered. It was to ensure that Alok didn't blurt out anything that I made him drink a cocktail of whisky and brandy. It knocked him out completely. So Arindam couldn't get a confession out of him. Now answer my question, Rina.'

'What question?'

'Are you in love with Alok?'

Rina answered after a pause. 'I don't know what to say. Maybe you're right. Every woman goes through a phase of vulnerability when she needs a companion, a lover. I'm very lonely. I was trying to cling to Alok. But you're coming in the way. Perhaps I'm just infatuated.'

'Is Alok just an infatuation?'

'I am not sure. When you asked me to take care of him at Sweet Sixteen, I felt a fondness for him. You said he hates women. I realized why when we went to Sumita Chaudhuri's house. All the women he has been with so far have exploited him. But I was nervous because of you. You're a very dangerous man. But while I was following your instructions, I fell in love with Alok. How do I go back now?'

'You've got me wrong, Rina. I'm not a dangerous man. I don't want any harm to come to Alok. I'm just trying to get to the truth and save both him and myself.'

'No, whether anyone in Delhi is aware of it or not, I am not sure. But I know for sure that Maqbool Peshwani is a dangerous man. That image of a drunkard and a womanizer is just a fake one you cultivate. You play games with people's lives. That's why I don't trust you.'

'Listen, Rina. Alok will be in trouble if we cannot find Geeta's murderer.'

'No, it's you who will be in trouble, Maqbool. Because it's you whom the police will arrest. You're trying to frame Alok. He doesn't have what it takes to murder someone.'

Maqbool pulled out a bundle of money from his pocket. 'Take this money. I was going to give it to Alok, but you deserve it more. I've told you before, and I'm telling you again, leave Delhi.'

'What about Alok? What if the police arrest him?'

'Don't worry about him,' smiled Maqbool. 'The police won't arrest him. I can promise you that.'

Maqbool left leaving Rina standing in the middle of the room.

⟋

The next day Maqbool woke up at one in the afternoon. He was both physically and mentally exhausted. So he went back to sleep, waking up only in the evening. He decided he had to go out.

Maqbool took some visiting cards out of a drawer. One of them said: Vinod Kohli, Detective Inspector, New Delhi. Maqbool had boxes of such visiting cards. Who knew which of them he might need? He took a taxi to Maharani Bagh. He had no trouble finding No. 157/1. It was a building with several flats. Maqbool went up to the gateman. Without saying a word, he pressed a hundred-rupee note into his hand. 'For you,' he said.

'What do I have to do?' the gateman asked.

'Nothing. You just have to give me some information.' Maqbool flashed his card at him. 'I'm Detective Inspector Vinod Kohli. We're looking for someone. We believe he frequents this place.'

'What is his name?'

'We don't know his name, but we can describe him. He comes here late at night to visit a beautiful woman. Can you give us some information about him? He's a smuggler.'

The gateman was silent for a while. He thought for a while and said, 'I know everyone here. There's just one flat whose owner I do not know. It's occupied by a lady, but she doesn't live here all the time. I don't know her name, but she's very beautiful and wears perfume all the time.'

Maqbool realized he was on the right track. 'Yes, I want to know about her,' he said.

'She comes sometimes late at night. She's usually accompanied by a gentleman. They drive away before sunrise. Are they the people you're looking for?'

'Yes, indeed, I'm looking for them.'

'But they aren't here now. Even if they come, it will be late at night.'

'I want to see where the flat is. I'll be back with a search warrant tomorrow or the day after.' Maqbool spoke with the authority of a policeman.

The gateman was terrified by the idea of the police, but gratified by the tip. He said, 'Go up to the first floor. The last flat on the left. But it's locked. I don't have a key.'

'Don't worry about the key. I just want to see where the flat is.' Maqbool went up to the first floor. He had the key that he had found in Alok's pocket yesterday. He had no trouble entering.

Two rooms in a row, a drawing room and a bedroom. Cosmetics were scattered around the dressing table in the bedroom. Among them were two or three bottles of Nina Ricci. The first drawer was locked. The next one had old newspapers and a bunch of letters. The letters were addressed to Sabina Almeida. All the newspapers were from Pakistan. Yes, they were the editions in which news of India's secret defence projects had been published. Beneath the newspapers Maqbool found a small key. He tried to open the top drawer with the key. It worked. The drawer held copies of top-secret documents of the Indian government. The words 'SECRET' and 'CONFIDENTIAL' were written across all of them. Each of them had notes made by the prime minister and defence minister. There were maps of military airports, including Agra, Tezpur and Kalaikunda, along with details about their runways. Other documents contained details of the surveillance project concerning the F-16s, diagrams of Hindustan Aeronautics offices and naval docks in Bombay. Maqbool stuffed all the documents into his pockets so that the doorman would not see them on him. He also found a red notebook with things written in code.

Maqbool searched the rest of the room, but found nothing of significance. Then he suddenly spotted a TV antenna wire leading into the bathroom. It wasn't connected to a TV. He followed the wire into the bathroom and discovered it was plugged into a wall socket. It was clearly being used to transmit information.

Half an hour had passed already. Maqbool couldn't stay any longer without making the gateman suspicious. He hurried downstairs where he ran into him.

'Did you find anything, sir?' asked the gateman.

Maqbool handed him another hundred-rupee note. He was thrilled at this unexpected income.

'Did you find anything, sir?' he asked again.

'Yes, the man I was looking for does visit this flat.'

'Should I keep an eye on them?'

'Don't worry, my men will be stationed here. Thank you.'

Maqbool left the building and went directly to the Central Telegraph Office to send a telegram. Then he went home and put the maps of the runways into a large envelope. On it he wrote, Ratilal Malkani, Defence Club, New Delhi.

Maqbool took the envelope to Defence Club. He had to meet Malia. He had some good news for her.

The first person he ran into at the club was Arati. She was dressed to kill. 'I'm glad I ran into you, I don't have to call you.'

'Any good news?' Maqbool asked eagerly.

Ratilal was in the next room. Hearing Maqbool, he joined them. Before Arati could answer, he said, 'There's something to celebrate, Maqbool.'

'Celebrate what?'

'We're flying to Bombay tomorrow, Maqbool,' said Arati. 'From there to Paris the day after. We're getting married there. And then our honeymoon too.'

Maqbool was silent. His face didn't reveal any emotion. 'I'm sure you're not delighted,' said Arati.

'Of course not,' protested Maqbool. 'I'm very happy to hear that you are getting married.' Turning to Arati, he said softly, 'I didn't think you'd actually marry Ratilal. But he's a far more suitable husband for you than I would have been.'

'I thought we'd celebrate with champagne,' said Ratilal. 'But I'm very busy today. Lots of arrangements to make for the trip. Goodbye Maqbool, see you again sometime…'

Ratilal left. Going up to Arati, Maqbool said, 'You look lovely. I'm tempted. Anyway, I must say you're getting married in a big hurry. I don't even have the time to get you a present. But I do have something valuable for Ratilal. He'll be very pleased with it. I'm leaving the present with you. Put it in Ratilal's suitcase when you reach Bombay.'

'What is it?' Arati held her hand out eagerly. Maqbool gave her the envelope.

'What's in here? Is it a cheque?'

'No, something more valuable. Ratilal will know how valuable it is as soon as he sees it.'

'Don't worry, I'll put it in his suitcase. He will see it when he unpacks.'

'Goodbye then, Arati, and all the best.'

Maqbool left.

⌁

Maqbool was awakened by the telephone at ten the next morning.

It was Malia from Defence Club. 'Can you come over, Maqbool?' She sounded agitated.

'What's the matter?'

'Rina's been waiting for you since the morning, Maqbool. She has something urgent to tell you. She rang you early in the morning, but there was no reply.' Malia was speaking breathlessly.

'I'll be there in an hour,' said Maqbool. 'Tell Rina to wait.'

Maqbool rang Arindam. 'I have to meet you, Arindam, there's something very important to discuss.'

'Very well, come home after lunch. I won't go back to the office.'

Maqbool reached Defence Club at 12 noon. Rina was sitting in a tiny room, her face pale. She had obviously been through a crisis. She started sobbing as soon as she saw Maqbool. Then, without any preamble, she said, 'Alok died in a car crash last night.'

Maqbool was either unmoved, or he decided not to react. All he said was, 'Alok dead? I'm so sorry. But I had feared something like this would happen.'

'You had feared something like this?' asked Rina. 'What do you mean?'

'Tell me the whole story. I'll explain after that.'

'There was a telephone call for Alok last evening. I don't know who it was, but Alok told me he had to go to Defence Club. There was someone he had to meet urgently. He hadn't had a drink, he was sober. He went to look for a taxi. He was standing on the pavement when a large car swerved off the road at high speed and hit him. He died on the spot. There was no time to take him to the hospital. He's lying in the police morgue now. I don't know what to do.'

'There's nothing for you to do,' Maqbool tried to console Rina. 'Alok met what fate had in store for him.'

'No Maqbool, I loved Alok. I don't know why, but I did. He was helpless, just like me. Why did you kill him to save yourself?'

'You're wrong, Rina. I didn't kill Alok. I'm no less upset than you at his death. But mourning him in public will serve no purpose. I told you to leave Delhi, Rina. Listen to me, you're in danger too.'

'I'm in danger too! Why, Maqbool?'

'Yes, Rina, you are. Alok was killed in a hit and run incident. Do you know why? He knew too much. So he had to be killed. His killers will assume he told you everything. So they might want to kill you too. Leave Delhi at once.'

'I don't understand, Maqbool.'

'There's no need to understand. Just leave the city at once.'

Maqbool left for Arindam's house. He returned home two hours later.

Maqbool sat down to write out his report. He typed out the first line:

TOP SECRET

To
Mr Madhavan Shankar
Director, Intelligence Bureau
New Delhi

Re: Operation Blueprint

Dear Sir

As directed by you, I have completed the investigations for Operation Blueprint. This written report is a follow-up on the oral report I have already given you. It includes a recap of our conversation.

Before my meeting with you yesterday, I met Arindam Saxena and Suraiya separately, once more. From Suraiya I gathered some important information. She enquired whether I had repeated any of the stories about Alok Bhatia that she had told me to Detective Inspector Govind Narayan. My response astonished her. 'What are you saying, Maqbool?' she said in disbelief. She was terrified that I must have babbled a lot of nonsense to the police under the influence of alcohol. She could not believe that I would admit everything to Inspector Narayan. 'What should I do now?' she asked me. 'Why are you worried?' I asked her. 'The police know you have had nothing to do with Alok of late. You are a beautiful woman, with no lack of admirers. And I am here too.'

Suraiya was furious. 'I had assumed you are intelligent, Maqbool,' she said. 'I did not imagine you would repeat my jokes to the police while drunk. You have ruined me.'

When I met you to present my verbal report, you asked whether I had found out who the secret agent was.

'Really, Maqbool, I am envious of you,' you said. 'I'd like to get some tips from you on how to be popular among ladies.' I told you, 'I'm trying to get a patent on how to be a ladies' man, sir.' You said, 'You are able to accomplish any task I set you, no matter how difficult. Inspector Narayan said you have broken the hearts of many beautiful women in the course of this investigation. Tell me all your stories.'

I told you, 'There is some bad news, however. Please inform Inspector Narayan that Alok Bhatia was murdered last night in a hit-and-run case.'

'That is bad news indeed,' you said. 'But will his death hamper your investigation?'

'No,' I said. 'It has made my task easier. I would have more trouble if I had had to deal with Alok. If you now give me complete freedom to conduct this investigation, I shall handover the culprit to you this evening.'

You promptly replied, 'You have complete freedom, Maqbool. All we want to know is the outcome of your investigation. You will get all the help you need from the police and the IB. But the press must not come to know.'

'Don't worry,' I reassured you. 'My investigations are complete. There are only a few loose ends to tie up. I'm relieved that it's over. I have had too many drinks and flirted with many different women in the course of this investigation. Winning a woman's heart is very difficult.'

'You are a fortunate man,' you had laughed. 'Teach me your technique, so that I can try it on my wife. Is there anything else you need?'

'No, sir,' I said. 'But I'll need two plain-clothes policemen.'

'I'll let Narayan know at once,' you said.

After this conversation I went to meet Arindam Saxena at his house. It was almost 1 p.m. He was waiting for me.

'You're most punctual,' he said, smiling. 'Now tell me if you've caught the criminal.'

'Yes, Arindam, I have,' I said. 'My investigation will end once I've got the handcuffs on him.'

'I'm very pleased to hear that. Congratulations. But first, what will you drink? I know your favourite drink is whisky.'

'You're right. I'll have whisky. Because I don't think I'll have the chance to have a drink with you again.'

Arindam poured my drink. 'What do you mean?' he asked in surprise. 'What are you trying to say? This is all very mysterious. Please explain.'

As I sipped my drink, I told him, 'Every play has an opening act and a closing one, Arindam. The prelude and the climax. The climax to our spy drama will be an exciting one. But first, answer my question: why did you kill Alok Bhatia?'

'What are you saying, Maqbool?' Arindam sounded agitated. 'Have you gone mad?'

'Yes, Arindam, the truth is nothing but the ravings of a madman. I suppose you had no choice but to kill Alok. For he was a thorn in your flesh, wasn't he? You may have assumed I'd told the police all the stories I'd been fed about Alok, and that the police would soon arrest him. After which he would have been sentenced to death by a court. But you didn't want to leave it to chance. Alok died last evening, run over by a car. He was killed. Either you or Ratilal rang him before that, telling him there was something urgent you wanted to discuss. Alok believed you. And you ran over him on the deserted road to the airport. You drove your car over him not once but thrice to make sure he did not survive. No one saw you. But my question is, why did you do it?'

'You're crossing all limits, Maqbool,' Arindam shouted. 'Do you know what you're saying?'

All I said was, 'Alok did want to meet you, Arindam. You did not give him the money you promised. He had wanted his due. Instead, you murdered him. You.'

'Great show, Maqbool,' said Arindam, lighting a cigarette. He was staring at me, unsure of how to respond.

'I had feared Alok would meet such a fate,' I said. 'He was a good student, but he was naive. Or he wouldn't have been caught up in a spy ring. Anyway, I wasn't surprised that Alok was killed. You did the job of judge and executioner. No one would make a fuss about his death, everyone would assume he had committed suicide by jumping in front of a car. Still, why did you do it?'

'Why don't you tell me, Maqbool?' Arindam said. 'You seem to already know. Nobody tells these made-up stories better than you.'

'You're right, Arindam. But not all stories I tell are concocted. The principal villain of this drama is you, Arindam, even though everyone, including the police, thinks the greatest devil in town is named Maqbool Peshwani. But I am a novice compared to you. So yes, you killed Alok because he suspected you of murdering your wife. Neither he nor I killed Geeta. Of course, you had assumed Alok wouldn't tell anyone. Not because he was afraid, but because you still owed him money. But when I planted the seeds of doubt in his mind, and he began to fear that the police suspected him of murdering Geeta, he decided to tell them what he knew. He knew a great deal about this ring of spies. If he were to sing, the police would come to know everything.'

'You're a drunkard, Maqbool,' said Arindam. 'I have no wish to listen to your crazy rambling.'

'That's right, Arindam, you mistook me for a drunkard and a womanizer. That was why you did not object to Madhavan Shankar's proposal of engaging me to conduct the investigation. You assumed I'd be incapable of discovering the truth.'

'You're spinning fairy tales,' Arindam said confidently. 'No one will believe that I killed Alok.'

'I agree. I won't be able to prove it either. But I *can* prove you killed Geeta.'

'Oh, really?' screamed Arindam. 'So I'm a professional murderer. Carry on with your story, Maqbool, where does it end?'

'I realized soon after Inspector Narayan began to interrogate me about Geeta's murder just who had killed her. But you did it on the spur of the moment. You hadn't planned it. As a result, you left far too many clues behind. You made too many mistakes. I'll tell you later what the mistakes were. Now, listen carefully. I want to cut a deal with you. Are you ready for one?'

'A deal!' Arindam looked surprised. 'Let me hear your entire story first.'

'It seems to me you won't accept defeat easily,' I said. 'Though I know you have no choice but to agree eventually. Very well then, here's the full story...'

'What do you want in exchange?' Arindam asked me. 'Is it money? A lot of money?'

'Yes, Arindam, a lot of money.'

Lighting another cigarette, Arindam said, 'Why did you stop? Go on with your story.'

'I will,' I told him. 'This spying business began about a year ago. But the planning had started three years earlier, in London. Did you know someone named Sabina Almeida, Arindam? A beautiful femme fatale...'

Arindam paled on hearing the name. He couldn't reply. I continued speaking. 'Yes, I know the name isn't an unfamiliar one. But we know Sabina Almeida by a different name at present. Let me read you a few lines from a letter from my friend at Interpol, Henri Rogers. Here we are.

'Sabina Almeida. Father: Indian; Mother: Iraqi. Her father, Peter Almeida, was posted in Iraq during World War II. He stayed back after the war ended and married a local woman. He was a friend of Nuri Sayeed, a carpet trader who was closely associated with the CIA and the Baghdad Pact. He was arrested in 1958 after Abd al-Karim Qasim seized power in the 14 July revolution. Peter Almeida's daughter Sabina, then fourteen years old and already a striking beauty, entered into a sexual relationship with Qasim's chief intelligence officer Fadeel Abbas. It was with Abbas's help that Sabina and her father escaped to Cairo. The Egyptian president Gamal Abdel Nasser was opposed to Qasim. His supporters in Iraq sent some secret tapes and documents to Egypt with Sabina. From Cairo she travelled to London. It was at this time that senior CIA officers introduced her to Pakistan's intelligence officials. She had no passport then. The Pakistan government agreed to give her a passport, on the condition that she would work for their intelligence department.

'In the late 1970s, four Indian students in England attracted the attention of Pakistan's intelligence officials. They were Arindam Saxena, Alok Bhatia, Ratilal Malkani and Maqbool Peshwani. Alok and you were students of solid physics. Both of you went on to study electronics. Alok, who specialized in radars, was already addicted to gambling. In fact he met Ratilal at a gambling den in Soho.

'Ratilal Malkani was in England to study hotel management. He would gamble at Soho's nightclubs regularly. His father had a great deal of property in the Karachi and Sindh areas of Pakistan. He used to be a businessman in that region before Partition, by virtue of which he also had some money in Pakistani banks. Ratilal was introduced to Sabina Almeida at a nightclub. She promised to help him retrieve his assets in Pakistan. She also introduced him to the Pakistan Intelligence boss Dildar Husain in London. Initially, Ratilal did not know their identities. By the time he found out, it was too late for him to extricate himself. It was decided that he and Sabina would work as spies in India.

'Alok Bhatia was captivated by Sabina's beauty. And then, you fell in love with her too, Arindam, but there was no question of marrying her since you belong to an orthodox family from Uttar Pradesh. Your marriage with Geeta had already been arranged. Therefore Sabina married Alok. But your desire for her did not ebb.

'Alok did not know that his marriage was a farce. For Sabina needed an Indian passport. All of you returned to India after this. I accept the fact that neither you nor Alok joined the ring of spies initially. But both of you did afterwards because of certain circumstances.

'Don't attempt to deny any of this. The Indian government was already aware of the existence of the ring. Besides, Interpol had informed us of Sabina's past. Here in India she introduced herself as Alok's wife, Suraiya Bhatia. We already have enough proof of the fact that Suraiya and Sabina Almeida are the same person.

'Meanwhile, a Pakistani scientist named Ismail Kader got in touch with Maqbool Peshwani, who was a talented student of physics at Bristol University. He was working on lasers and infrared sensors at the university, where Kader was working on heavy water with a view to shoring up his country's nuclear arms research. Kader mentioned the spy ring to Maqbool, who went on to inform a representative of the Indian High Commission in London. They in turn informed the Indian government, enabling us to keep a vigil on Ratilal and Suraiya. Suraiya used her charm to worm secrets out of Indian government officials, which Ratilal would transmit to Pakistan.

'On your return to India you started work at HAL in Bangalore. One day Suraiya turned up and extracted a map and details of research projects at HAL. We learnt from a double agent in Pakistan that the information had been sent there. Our investigations led us to suspect you but there was no proof. Meanwhile, you moved to the defence ministry in Delhi. Alok Bhatia was already working here, but although you were not as bright as him as a student or a researcher, you bagged the senior job. Alok was already working on techniques to track F-16 aircraft. But it still needed a Maqbool Peshwani.

'Maqbool had not been to Pakistan and had no desire to go, either. His friend Ismail Kader had died in the meantime, and he had been unable to provide Pakistani Intelligence with any information that would help them recruit Maqbool. Like the rest of you, Maqbool too joined the R & D department of the defence ministry. Both the research and the spying were going on. But Arindam, the Maqbool Peshwani who came to assist you was not a scientist. You got a fake Maqbool Peshwani. Me.

'On your recommendation Ratilal Malkani was recruited as the administrative officer in your department. Although we knew he was part of the spy ring, we had nothing to pin on him. But the Pakistani spy ring had grown more active. We sent a beautiful and sexy agent to keep track of the activities at Ratilal's Defence Cub. Her name is Malia. She was not a government employee, she was a friend of mine. Ratilal did not suspect her of being an informer. Malia was efficient both at her work and at flirting. We learnt from her that Sumita Chaudhuri and Rina had been hired by Ratilal. I had suspected Sumita immediately, but it took me some time to see through Rina. From Malia we learnt that Pakistan's diplomats did not frequent the club. Why not? We wanted to find out. Apparently it was on instructions from Pakistan. We grew suspicious.

'The spy ring was operating smoothly. Then we learnt from our double agent in Pakistan that a great deal of secret information was being leaked from the defence ministry. It was the double agent who ensured that the news of the space bomb was published in Pakistan's newspapers. Pakistan's Intelligence officials were astonished. They wanted to know how the news had got through to the newspapers.'

There was no reaction from Arindam. 'Now, for the rest of the story,' I told him with a smile.

'Yes, go on,' he said. 'I don't know whether you're the real Maqbool or a fake one, but you can certainly tell a good story. Let me hear your fairy tale.'

I realized he wasn't going to break down easily.

'You stopped passing on information for some time after the news of the space bomb was published. When you were questioned about the leak, you made a strategic move and had three people dismissed from your department on suspicion of spying. You knew that if Ratilal continued working for you, sooner or later your role would be revealed. There were already rumours about the goings-on in Defence Club. It was decided that he would run the spy ring from outside the ministry. You didn't actually suspect me but I was unwanted. Neither you nor your foreign bosses tried to find out my true identity. You took me for a drunkard and womanizer, and when I tried to seduce your secretary Romola you got rid of me. You did not approve of her intimacy with me.

'You had fallen in love with Suraiya. People become spies for different reasons. Some do it for money, some are lured into it by women. Using women to snare men is an age-old practice. In Delhi, you started sleeping with Suraiya. Geeta didn't know at first. Alok knew, but then Suraiya had never really been his wife. He didn't even know of her past or who she really was. By the time he found out you were deeply in love with her. He became insanely jealous when he saw you getting intimate with her every night. You were much inferior to him as a scientist. The job you were holding should have been Alok's by right. All this pushed him to drinking, gambling and women. Suraiya did not object. But Alok needed money to fund his habits. He decided to blackmail you. At first you were so besotted by Suraiya that you did not hesitate to accede to his demands. But when you thought it through you decided to ignore him. Only, you had not expected that this would make things worse for you. Ratilal and you engaged Sumita Chaudhuri to follow him. But here you made another mistake. Sumita began to blackmail Alok. She knew nothing about your spy ring, though. As far as we're concerned she was nothing but a blackmailer.

'So Alok Bhatia's demand for money kept increasing. As a

government employee you were on a fixed salary, with no inheritance. Geeta had some money she had inherited from her father, which she didn't mind giving you at first. But then she began to suspect you. The primary cause was your secretary Romola, who was transferred from Bangalore to Delhi on your recommendation. Her suspicions grew when you did not return home in the evenings, claiming to be hard at work in your laboratory. Moreover, Romola stayed back at the office beyond work hours. She followed your instructions that fateful night. You told her to tell Geeta you were in the laboratory in case she rang you. Romola had no idea that on the pretext of being in the laboratory you were actually making love to Suraiya in her Maharani Bagh flat, which Alok had bought.

'Geeta stopped giving you money. Alok's demands grew. He had no idea who Sumita was. Pakistan would pay you to pass on secrets to Ratilal. Now we adopted a different method to keep an eye on Ratilal. Using Malia as an informer was no longer enough. I needed someone who could keep surveillance on both Ratilal and Suraiya. This someone was Arati.

'Everyone in Delhi assumed she was my fiancé. In fact she is an agent. We pretended to be lovers, but Ratilal actually fell in love with her. Meanwhile Arati became friends with Suraiya. Then, Sumita's ex-husband or boyfriend, whatever he may be, Deepchand joined the cast. He needed money. Alok's capital was exhausted. Sumita threatened to leave Alok and tell every one of his philandering ways unless he gave her more money. Alok had no choice but to increase his demands of you. You refused, but when he threatened to tell Geeta you were sleeping with Suraiya, you got worried. And with the newspapers in Pakistan publishing yet another set of secret information, all of you were instructed to suspend your espionage for some time. The Pakistani government had guessed there was a double agent in their ranks. They instructed Suraiya to return to London.

'As we were getting ready to reel in the culprits, Alok asked you for more money. Indian government officials decided to hoodwink you with the catch-a-spy-with-a-spy strategy, asking you to recruit me. Things moved rapidly after this. You gave an excuse not to accompany Geeta to Arati's party. It hadn't occurred to you that Geeta might want to go with Alok to the party. She had got some inkling of your activities that morning, but no concrete proof. She had discovered a lighter in your pocket. She realized that it was a spy camera. Why did you need a spy camera, she wondered. Then she realized you were taking top-secret files home every day. Maybe you were photographing them. Geeta decided to ask Alok about it. When Alok threatened to disclose the truth about you and Suraiya to Geeta, you realized that not only would your wife kick up a fuss, but your links with the spy ring through Suraiya might also be exposed. Meanwhile, Alok had told Sumita that he and Geeta were lovers, and she would give him money that he would pass on to Sumita. He had said this to make her jealous.

'Alok visited Geeta that night, well before 10 p.m. They told each other many things. Geeta probably showed him the spy camera, while he gave her a handkerchief, Suraiya's Nina Ricci perfume on it, a handkerchief which he said was yours. Geeta was furious on hearing of your relationship with Suraiya and decided not to go to the party. She rang you but you were not available. You were worried when you learnt of her telephone call. Had Alok told her something, then? You went back home. Geeta and you had a row. She showed you the spy camera and accused you of being a spy who was selling government secrets to his lover Suraiya. You had no choice then but to kill her. You throttled her with a silk thread to save yourself. The murder took place at 10.30 p.m.

'Then you had to find ways to protect yourself. First you dressed Geeta in a cardigan, so that it appeared she had just come home. But you were in such a hurry that you forgot some details. You didn't realize that it had been raining, and yet Geeta's cardigan was dry. Then you made Suraiya ring me, pretending to be Geeta and asking me to meet her at once. Suraiya did not ask you why you were telling her to do this. She rang me as Geeta, saying she had a cold so that I did not wonder why she sounded different. But I had a suspicion that it had to be someone who knew I was at the party. Geeta did not know. It could only be Suraiya, who had met me at the party before she left. When Sumita told me that Alok had been to Geeta's house that night, I had no trouble putting the pieces together.

'There were two suspects. Alok and me. Sumita began telling everyone that Alok was Geeta's lover and had killed her over a dispute concerning money. To strengthen the suspicion, I spread the word about his smoking Gauloises. There was also the handkerchief with the letter 'A' embroidered on it. It didn't occur to anyone that 'A' also stands for Arindam. You decided that it was best for Alok to leave the country. You'd be in trouble if he told the truth. You talked it over with Ratilal and arranged for ten thousand rupees for Alok to go abroad. So Alok won that amount playing cards at Defence Club. I was present that evening. It was only afterwards that I worked out why Ratilal had allowed Alok to win.

'Now I had to ensure that Alok could not escape. So I sent him to the Sweet Sixteen nightclub with Rina. He promptly lost the ten thousand he had won the other night, and no longer had the money to buy a ticket. Worried, you went to discuss the situation and my investigations with Madhavan Shankar. He assured you that I was the spy. He did not want you to panic.

'When you couldn't get Alok out of the country, Ratilal and you decided that he had to be killed. But you wanted it done in a way that did not suggest murder. It should look like suicide. When I took Alok to your house that night, I had deliberately made sure he was too drunk to have any meaningful conversation with you. It worked. But you tried to ensure that the police suspected Alok of murdering Geeta by slipping a key in his pocket, along with a letter saying she was returning the key to his flat. The letter was written to suggest it was from Geeta. Since Alok had bought the flat originally, even though Suraiya and you were using it for your trysts, you thought it would implicate him. Especially as the copies of secret documents were kept there.'

✓

Arindam was silent for some time. Then he said, 'All right, maybe you have caught me out. But you won't be able to catch Ratilal and Suraiya. Their planes have taken off by now. Ratilal has left for Paris, and Suraiya has taken a flight as well. They are the bigger culprits…'

I laughed. Then I told him, 'You're mistaken. Their planes have indeed left, but they have not. Top-secret documents have been found in Ratilal's luggage, and he has been arrested as a spy. As for Suraiya, she has been arrested for possession of hashish. Don't forget Arati is my agent. She slipped the documents and the drugs into their bags. As you can understand by now, the scene I created at Arati's party was nothing but an act. Ratilal trusted Arati and proposed to her, which gave her the chance to slip the documents into his bag.

'As for me, you don't know who I really am, Arindam. I am the fake Maqbool Peshwani. The real scientist named Maqbool Peshwani is in his house in Hauz Khas, reading Agatha Christie and solving all the complex problems of physics and mathematics I take to him.'

Arindam was silent for some time. Then he said, 'All right, let's talk about the deal you mentioned. How much do you want?'

'No, Arindam, I don't want money. But let me first hear what you want…'

'Suppose I told you I want to escape.'

'I won't stop you. But you have to go right now. Govind Narayan will be here in a few minutes to arrest you. Where do you want to go?'

'Out of Delhi to begin with. I'll see after that.'

Arindam rushed out and drove away.

I knew he would be frightened on hearing the police was on its way. He drove off at a high speed. But he had no idea of the arrangement I had made. I had asked a truck driver from the sabzi mandi to wait outside. I had had the brake oil drained away from Arindam's car. As soon as Arindam tried to drive out of the gate at top speed, the truck blocked his path. He slammed on the brakes, but they didn't work. Arindam died in a car accident. That's the official version. No one will know the role played by the secret agent. There will be no newspaper reports about the investigation. I gave Arindam the opportunity to escape. What can I do if God decides to intervene?

Before leaving, Arindam had asked me, 'Who are you really?' I didn't tell him that I am.

Yours truly
Byron Ghouse
Agent Double Zero

Copotronic Love

MUHAMMED ZAFAR IQBAL

My dearest friend had fired a gun at me in the corridor of the research centre. Obviously he had wanted to kill me. But for some reason I did not die, and no one except us knew who had shot at me. My left lung was punctured, forcing me to spend three full months in a hospital. My thoughts during this long period had nothing to do with my research. They were centred on human desire, dreams, the inspiration for living and the logic of joy and suffering. Whether it was because of the lonely environment in the hospital or my own illness, I had become utterly depressed and had even considered suicide. That was when my friend came to visit me. He looked gaunt. There were dark circles under his eyes and guilt written all over his face.

'You could have given my name to the police,' that was how he had begun the conversation. 'Thank you for not doing that. But if you believe that this was because of your greatness, which you will now use to lord over me, you are mistaken.'

I looked into his eyes and told him, 'Had I not known the reason you wanted to kill me, I might not have hated you. But now I do hate you.'

He had been perturbed at this. After he left, I had realized that only one of us would survive. Two people cannot exist together with so much hatred between them. The next day I was told that my friend had blown off his skull with a gun. I knew he was emotionally high-strung, but I had not expected this.

∽

After I was released from the hospital I gave up my job as a researcher. I was only twenty-four, and it was at that time that the Pioneer Sub-Structure Model began to be associated with me. It was my brainchild but my dead friend had developed an attraction for it.

It had been difficult to free myself of all ties. I had to face a great deal of cruel, adverse criticism. But I simply could not work up any enthusiasm for life. I had constructed an entire internal universe of ideas, which was where I preferred to immerse myself.

Gradually, the girl who was hired to assist me with my daily tasks also became intolerable. My day-to-day work began to suffer after I fired her. My routine was simple. I used to sleep in late and then paint all day after waking up. At night I used to study philosophy and medieval literature. I met no one. I emptied the letter box once a week and tore up all the letters. I had disconnected the phone. Even the chore of preparing two meals a day and cleaning the house became unbearable. I had to have a helper. I was wondering whether to buy a robot adept at housework. But the very thought of an impassive, mechanical monster wandering about my house, making my morning cup of coffee or ironing my clothes, was distasteful. I wished for the company of a sensitive robot. But robots with emotions had not yet been invented. I decided almost on the spur of the moment to build one myself—according to my specifications.

My life became much simpler after this decision. Most of my attention was concentrated on the blueprint and other details of the robot. Once I began working hard on this project, my chagrin at not having a girl to assist me also dissipated.

Building a robot was not a difficult task. The robot's brain—known as the copotron—could easily be ordered from a firm. But I was not sure what kind of copotron my robot would need. The BF-2 variety was used for household work. Robots used in chemical laboratories had LB-2 type copotrons. The Bivatron in our university was in charge of a robot with an LAF type copotron.

None of these would work for the robot I was about to create, for all of them were replete with different mechanical skills. None of them possessed any sensitivity or what we refer to as emotions. It was true that the mathematically adept BK-21 copotron was being used in robots that composed music, but even though these robots could analyse mathematical patterns to create melodies, they could not feel the music they composed. For only human beings had a monopoly on the mental process known as emotions. I wished to create a robot that would love listening to music, read poetry, smile, or even weep when it was sad. I wanted to experiment whether human emotions like happiness, pain, envy or anger could be created mechanically.

The catalogues did not list a copotron that catered to my needs. One of the firms had however announced that it would soon demonstrate a copotron that could smile. I got in touch with them and found out that by soon they meant another four years. They wrote regretfully that the government was unwilling to sanction the manufacture of robots with emotions, for they had no functional value.

I ordered a local firm to provide me with an ordinary B-1 type copotron. It had four times as many neucaptive cells as other copotrons and nearly half the number of neutrons in human brain. But it possessed no mechanical skills. The director expressed surprise at my choice when handing over the copotron.

I had to work almost as hard as a robot to connect the copotron to different components and create the form of a robot. As I had never built a robot, it took much longer than it should have. Fortunately, I was cut off from all my friends and acquaintances. They would have been inordinately annoyed at my wasting my time on such a childish pursuit.

I was struck by the appearance of the robot when it was ready. It was similar to the gigantic figures from the early days of robots. It had an enormous head and two greenish eyes placed in consonance with the position of the eyes in human beings. Although robots usually had only one eye, I could not help giving my robot a pair of eyes. There was a speaker where the mouth should have been. Because it did not look appealing without a nose, I attached an artificial Grecian nose with screws. Its arms hung on either side of its rectangular body, with thick metallic fingers at their ends. The stiff legs were like pillars, with complex mechanical joints for the knees. The feet were huge and round, so as to give the body balance and stability. I painted toes, muscles, lips, ears, eyebrows and hair on the robot. I have to admit that far from improving its appearance, it resembled a scarecrow.

When I switched on the power, the robot blinked and turned around. A mild hum emerged from its chest. Electric sparks began to dance in its greenish eyes. 'Your name is Prometheus,' I told him.

I hadn't said it with much thought, but there was nothing I could do once the robot nodded in acceptance.

◡

I familiarized Prometheus with my daily activities. He made me breakfast, cleaned the house and occasionally ironed my clothes. I have no hesitation in stating that he behaved entirely like an imbecile. He had no sense of aesthetics. He would iron my trousers horizontally. One day, when he was cleaning the house, he dropped two oil paintings from the wall.

Once I had become well acquainted with Prometheus, I decided to test his intelligence. I asked him some general knowledge questions and recited two lines from the work of a Bengali poet named Jibanananda Das to him:

Sarojini lies here at this spot
I do not know if she lies here

Then I asked him, 'What is your opinion of these two lines?'

'The utterance of an individual with an inconsistent line of thought,' Prometheus replied.

When I showed him a painting of a Polynesian woman by Paul Gauguin; he examined it closely for a long time before saying, 'For some indiscernible reason, all the colours have been irregularly used to paint a figure of a woman of distorted physical structure.'

I found it hard to contain my laughter at this evaluation of Gauguin's art. I laughed uproariously and stopped suddenly to ask him, 'What was I doing?'

'You were laughing.'

'What is laughter?'

'A meaningless physical process.'

'Laugh.'

He emitted a mechanical sound to imitate my laughter.

There were many reasons to be disappointed with Prometheus. But I did not give up hope. I decided to tweak him some to give him the ability to appreciate beauty. I had to study a great deal on the subject to do this. The mathematical analysis of beauty provided material help.

To make Prometheus conscious of beauty, I would have to make arrangements for him to feel happy whenever he was confronted by anything beautiful. It was not possible to directly inject the emotion of happiness into him—but his suffering could be reduced. This meant that he would have to be made to suffer constantly. If excessive electrical pressure could be maintained on the neucaptive cells of the copotron, the robot brain would use all the mechanical means at its disposal to reduce this pressure. This condition could be said to be one of suffering for the copotron. When the electrical pressure dropped, the suffering would be reduced, creating an indirect sensation of happiness. This could be easily achieved by generating a dynamic electromagnetic field in front of the neucaptive cells. But the real difficulty would lie in triggering this electromagnetic field as soon as something beautiful was seen, heard or felt. For this I had to split the cells into different categories. These would be arranged differently under the influence of external stimuli, depending on the kind of stimulus. Whenever anything considered beautiful by mathematical analysis appeared in the robot's field of perception, the electromagnetic field ensured that the suffering of the copotron brain was reduced. In other words, the copotron felt happy. This sensation could be calibrated according to the degree of beauty of the object.

*

I had to work furiously to engineer this change within Prometheus, who had to be kept inactive for a long period while making these modifications. The R-21 robots were skilled at performing this kind of complex operation on the copotron. By the time I had completed my modifications, two months and ten days later, the power of my contact lenses had doubled, while my weight had dropped by four pounds. Of course, I cannot but acknowledge that most of the credit for ensuring that I only lost four pounds belonged to Bula. She was the new girl who was assisting me. The company had sent her when I wrote to them for an assistant during my work on instilling an appreciation of beauty within Prometheus. Like many others, she was working during her holidays to earn some money. She was going to take her Honours examinations in physics next July.

I made enough space as possible in the room to bring Prometheus again to life. I had to wait after pressing the switch—the newly invented radon tubes took as much time as the valves to warm up. Within five minutes, electrical sparks began to play in Prometheus's eyes. He raised an arm and then lowered it hesitantly.

'How are you?' He did not answer my question immediately. This was without precedent. After some time, he said, 'Very well.'

I may have been mistaken, but I thought I detected a tinge of emotion in his words. 'Do you sense any change within you?' I asked.

'No. Why?'

Without answering, I reached out and switched on some music. The melancholic strains of Yehudi Menuhin's violin filled the room. Prometheus staggered as though he had received an electric shock. When I switched the music off he shouted in a stricken tone, 'Don't switch it off, sir.'

'Why? How do you feel when you hear this?'

After a silence, Prometheus muttered, 'It is a harmonious mutual configuration of sound waves of different frequencies. But when I hear it, I feel a strange response within me that makes me want to hear more of it, more of it.'

I realized that it was necessary to acquaint Prometheus with his new condition. I said, 'Prometheus, the obscure physical reaction within you on listening to Yehudi Menuhin playing the violin is known as liking something. You are the only robot in the world who has the ability to like or dislike things.'

Prometheus took a couple of steps forward. A plan to induce expressions of concentration, devotion, et cetera, on his mechanical face flashed across my brain.

'Gradually you will be acquainted with other new feelings and emotions.'

'Such as?'

'Consider this rose.' Opening the window, I showed him the most beautiful rose in the garden.

'Sir!' he screamed, 'I like it.'

'Yes. You are now bound to like beautiful things, but there is no need to scream.' I instructed him to pluck the beautiful rose. He reached out for the rose and turned it round and round in his hands to examine it. I took it from him and shredded it to bits.

A mechanical shriek emerged from Prometheus. I said, 'The emotion you are now experiencing with reference to me is anger. If your anger exceeds preset limits, your copotron will lose its mechanical control over you.'

Prometheus did not speak. He was clearly furious.

'Meaningless acts evoke anger. You liked the rose, I shredded it, so you are angry.'

'I like roses very much,' said Prometheus irrelevantly.

'There is another word for liking something very much. It's called love.'

'I love roses,' muttered Prometheus.

Bula entered at that moment, sweeping back her mass of black hair. 'It's time for your meal, sir,' she said.

'I'll be there in a few minutes.'

'No, sir, right now. The food is getting cold.' She was a little childish, insistent that I eat at once. I did not know how to refuse. In some mysterious way I had come to accept her authority.

I left Prometheus where he was and followed Bula to the dining room. As we were leaving I heard him mutter, 'I love this girl.'

⁓

Prometheus was soon converted to a culturally sensitive robot. His favourite poet was Jean Cocteau. Prometheus's translations of Cocteau's poetry from the original French were being serialized in a literary journal. I had encouraged him to write something original. He was currently involved in writing a book of poetry entitled *A Bunch of Copotronic Doubts*.

Soon he became inclined towards fiction. I saw him run through the works of Gorky and immerse himself in Kafka. He raced through Hemingway, Sartre and Camus.

Bula had taken leave in order to prepare for her examinations. Prometheus had taken over her responsibilities. Although he coaxed me to take a second helping of mutton, just like Bula did, the void she had left could not be easily filled. The girl was beautiful and intelligent, and took tender care of me. It was after Bula's departure that I realized that I had come to love her. These human exuberances had little or no place in my world view, but the more I tried to forget Bula, the more an excessive electrical current asserted itself on my neurons. Therefore my happiness was boundless when Bula arrived one day to inspect the quality of my life under Prometheus's supervision.

'Here you are, Bula!' Although I welcomed her with this laconic greeting, I got to the point swiftly. 'I would have visited you had you not visited me,' I told her. 'In other words, I...' (here I had to clear my throat) '...wish to marry you.'

Bula was taken aback at first. Then she blushed and lowered her eyes. Hesitatingly, I said, 'You can tell me if you have any reservations. I am not a particularly great man, you are aware I am riddled with flaws.'

Bula was no longer shy with me. She gave up addressing me as sir, abandoned her formal way of talking to me, began to use my almost unknown nickname, and eased the way for our relationship so efficiently that I was astonished. I was even more surprised when she informed me that it had been her dream to address me informally by my nickname.

Unable to concentrate on my work after Bula left, I sent for Prometheus. He arrived with an armful of books. Among them were books by Havelock Ellis and Sigmund Freud.

'You said,' Prometheus began sulkily, 'to like something very much is to love it. But these books say something else altogether.' He held out one of Ellis's books. 'It says here love is a sexual attraction between men and women.'

I was nonplussed. I had not considered this problem at all when creating Prometheus. 'I put it that way,' I said, 'because you wouldn't have understood otherwise. You are more advanced than any other robot in the world. You have emotions. And yet you are not complete. You lack a primary feature of living beings—you have no sexuality.'

'Why?' Prometheus was saddened. 'You gave me the ability to like something, to feel sadness too. Why not this?'

I was agitated. 'There's a reason, Prometheus,' I said. 'Living beings have this feature because they must procreate. But what will you do with it? You will never find a female robot who can give birth to a baby robot.'

Prometheus was silent. Putting the books away on the desk, he said, 'In that case, you might as well not have given me this incomplete emotion. Men and women perform certain acts that appear meaningless to me. Finally, I have understood what love between a man and a woman is, but I do not have the capability of experiencing it. I can like, but I cannot love.'

I felt sorry for Prometheus. The eight-feet tall mechanical monster stared at me with his greenish eyes. Then he said in a pleading tone, 'Can you not give me sexuality, sir? Why don't you, just for a day? Let me find out what love is.'

I could not agree to fulfil his wish. Prometheus left, his head bowed.

꜀

Bula and I were married in November. We went on our honeymoon the very next day. Prometheus was in charge of taking care of the house while we were away. To ensure that his power supply was not disrupted by an accident, I added a nuclear-powered battery to his mechanism.

Bula and I wandered about like gypsies. We went to the mountains, to the forests, to the sea. Our honeymoon passed swiftly. There was no longing to return home. I had called Prometheus at home. He had told me that all was well.

After some time, however, I felt an urge to study the sub-structure of quarks. Within twenty-four hours the desire became so irresistible that I cabled Prometheus, asking for a car to be sent to the station. I sent another telegram asking whether the job offer from the university was still open. I wrote to the national library for two dozen books. Far from being surprised, Bula was very happy. No woman can dislike a man for pursuing research-based work with genuine interest. It offers comfort, a pre-planned and secure trajectory of existence, even the possibility of a journey on the road to fame.

We reached home the next day. I handed Bula all responsibility for running the house. I took up the position of researcher at the university. It took six valuable days to get everything organized. I resumed my studies and my research.

One night Prometheus appeared silently in front of me. It irks me if I am disturbed while studying. 'What is it?' I asked with a frown.

'Where can I find the value of zeta-naught in the equation for balancing the residual magnetism created by the electromagnetic field working on copotronic cells?'

I looked at Prometheus in surprise. I hadn't taught him a word of science. But what he was asking for needed knowledge of advanced theoretical and applied physics.

'How did you learn all this?'

'I have been studying since you left.'

'What made you switch from literature?'

Instead of answering, Prometheus lowered his eyes. I helped him find the solution he was looking for. I was secretly pleased—if he studied these things he might be able to assist me.

After this I became completely absorbed in my research. Bula made sure I ate well and slept on time. I spent the rest of my time in the library and the university laboratory. The days passed swiftly.

⤳

'Get rid of this Prometheus of yours,' Bula told me a few days later at the dining table.

'Why?' I was astonished.

'He has written three love letters to me so far.'

My laughter turned to a coughing bout. Prometheus must be reading romantic novels these days. His love letters were charming, and written in a beautiful hand. I would have had reason to be jealous had I not known they were from Prometheus. I knew he could never love a woman, at most, he could like her. Still, I didn't put the incident out of my mind entirely.

A few days later Bula complained that Prometheus had given her a bouquet of roses, held her hand and talked of love for a long time. I was quite surprised. I knew all the secrets of his mechanical parts. I could not understand why he was pretending to be in love.

⌣

We were conducting a new experiment that week. The results were extremely obscure and somewhat mysterious too. I was poring over them. It was late at night. Bula had gone to bed alone, unable to convince me to join her. It was all so complicated and perplexing that I had no sense of the passing of time. Suddenly Bula burst into my room. She had turned blue with terror. Throwing herself into my arms she babbled, 'Prometheus…Prometheus…'

'What is it? What's happened to Prometheus?'

'He's trying to kill me.'

What! I was confounded. Prometheus's workings, the complexity of his circuits, the extent of his thoughts were all my creation. He could never do anything wrong. When I questioned her further, I realized that Prometheus had not tried to kill her, he had attempted to caress her the way a man caresses a woman. I had some misgivings on hearing this. He had long been besotted with Bula because of his attraction to beautiful things. But the way he had been behaving of late was only possible for a human being, not a mechanical monster devoid of biological urges. Taking Bula's hand, I went looking for Prometheus. The light in his room was switched off. He looked at me, startled, when I entered and switched it on. He was holding my Colt revolver, which I had bought in college.

'Prometheus!' I screamed.

'Yes?' He answered coolly.

I wanted to ask several questions at the same time, but I couldn't ask a single one of them. I didn't know why I felt he was going to fire the gun at me, although I knew he was incapable of it.

'Why the revolver?' I asked him.

Prometheus pretended he hadn't heard me. He said, as if to himself, 'I know why you are here. But I really do love Bula.'

I was ready to explode in rage on hearing him say this after everything that had happened. 'You fool!' I thundered. 'What do you know of love?'

'You're mistaken, sir.' Prometheus was not in the least bit perturbed. 'I read about copotrons while you were away. I have performed some operations on my own copotron. I now possess sexuality, just like human beings.'

I was dumbfounded. Bula gripped my hand, shuddering.

'But sir, you were right.' Prometheus emitted a sound similar to a sigh. 'I made a mistake, I did something wrong. I can tell now what love is. I can understand why a man might love a woman so much.' Prometheus switched the gun from one hand to the other, examined the magazine, and then said, 'I love Bula, but I realize no one will ever love me. For all my emotions, I am just a grotesque machine.'

Prometheus's last words sounded like a lamentation. I had no words. 'Why do you have a revolver?' I said. 'Give it to me.'

Again Prometheus pretended not to have heard me. 'I can tell there's no point living,' he said. 'What's the use of an empty existence? What am I worth? A mere machine, some thwarted emotions.' Prometheus gazed at Bula with his greenish eyes.

'Bula! I know my self-sacrifice means nothing to you. But still, remember that a machine fell in love with you and killed himself.' Prometheus pointed the revolver at his right eye. A bullet through his eye would shatter the control tube of the copotron.

'Prometheus…' I tried to stop him.

'Sir! It's the emotion you gave me that has inspired me to die. Do you know what happens to a robot's soul after death, sir?'

It was an old-fashioned revolver. The bang was earth-shattering. Prometheus's head rocked back as the control tube was destroyed. There were several explosions, followed by black smoke and a burning smell. Prometheus stared at us with one eye, his head slumped to one side. His greenish eyes slowly turned cold and lifeless.

Prometheus's dead mechanical body kept standing in the middle of the room. I led Bula out. I could feel her hand trembling uncontrollably in mine.

I felt an emptiness, the kind one feels on losing a loved one. I was surprised. Should one feel grief for a machine?

Horror Stories

Bhuto

SATYAJIT RAY

Nobin had to return disappointed a second time. He hadn't succeeded in persuading Akrur-babu to grant his wish. He had got a taste of Akrur Chowdhury's amazing skill at a performance in Uttarpara. Ventriloquism. Nobin hadn't known what the act was called. Dwijopada had told him. Dwiju's father was a professor who had a huge collection of books on different subjects. Dwiju not only told him what it was called but taught him to spell it too in English. V-E-N-T-R-I-L-O-Q-U-I-S-M. Akrur Chowdhury was alone onstage, but he was conducting a conversation with an invisible person, who seemed to be somewhere on the ceiling. Akrur-babu asked him questions, and the answers descended from above.

'How are you, Haranath?'

'Very well, sir, thank you all.'

'I believe you're involved in music these days.'

'That's right, sir.'

'Classical music?'

'Yes, sir, classical music.'

'Do you sing?'

'No.'

'Do you play any instrument, then?'

'Yes, sir.'

'What instrument? The sitar?'

'No, sir.'

'The sarod?'

'No, sir.'

'What do you play then?'

'The gramophone, sir.'

The hall rang with laughter and applause. Lifting his face to the ceiling to ask the question, Akrur-babu lowered his head to listen to the answer, but it was impossible to tell that he himself was responding to his questions.

Nobin was in a daze. Life would be meaningless until he acquired this ability. Would Akrur Chowdhury accept a student? Nobin had no interest in higher education. It had been three years since he had passed his school examinations, after which he hadn't wanted to go to college. His father was dead, he had been brought up by his uncle, who had a plywood factory that he wanted Nobin to join. But Nobin was inclined towards magic. He had practised and, to an extent, perfected tricks involving sleight of hand, handkerchiefs, rings and balls. But after Akrur Chowdhury's ventriloquism all these seemed like a child's game.

Nobin found out from the organizers of the programme that Akrur-babu lived in Amherst Lane in Calcutta. He took a train to the city the very next day and went directly to the house of the person he had accepted as his guru. But the guru was reluctant.

'What do you do?', was the first question the ventriloquist asked. Nobin felt his heart thumping as he viewed his hero up close. He was about forty-five, with a luxuriant moustache. His thick black hair parted in the middle fell to his shoulders in waves. His eyes were sleepy, although the same eyes gleamed under the spotlights on stage.

Nobin explained what he did.

'Why this sudden fancy?'

Nobin decided to tell the truth. 'I practise a bit of magic, but after watching your performance I have been drawn to ventriloquism.'

Akrur-babu shook his head.

'Ventriloquism isn't for everyone. It requires years and years of devoted learning. No one taught me either. Try it for yourself if you think you have it in you.'

Nobin left that day, but returned to Amherst Lane a week later. All he had done meanwhile was dream of becoming a ventriloquist. This time he would beg and plead if need be.

But it turned out to be even more of a disaster. Akrur-babu more or less threw him out. 'You should have realized the first time that I wasn't going to teach you,' he said. 'Since you haven't, it means you have no brains. Magic is impossible to master without brains—especially this one.'

The first time Nobin had felt dismay. This time he lost his head. To hell with Akrur Chowdhury. Who cared if he didn't teach him, he would teach himself.

He himself didn't know he was capable of such patience and

perseverance. He bought a book on ventriloquism on College Street and began to train himself.

It was a fairly simple affair. Pronouncing the P class of letters—P, F, B, V, M, for instance—meant bringing the lips together, which meant that the movement of the lips could be seen. Words without these letters in them could be pronounced by parting the lips but not moving them. There was also a way out when one of these letters were present in a word being uttered. For instance, 'good morning' could be pronounced 'good norning', moving only the tongue not the lips. The rule was: replace P, F, B, V and M with K, Kh, G, Gh and N or Ng, respectively. So an exchange such as this:

'Good morning, how are you?
'I'm very well, thank you.'
'Very warm today'
'Very'.

would have to be pronounced:

'Good norning, how are you?'
'I'g ghery well, thank you.'
'Ghery warn today.'
'Ghery.'

There were other rules too. The answering voice had to be changed to make it sound different from one's own. This required practice, and Nobin devoted a lot of time to this aspect. When he finally performed for his uncle and a few intimate friends and earned their accolades, he realized that he had more or less mastered ventriloquism.

But it didn't end there.

The era of holding conversations with an invisible person had ended. These days, ventriloquists held a dummy on their laps. The performer inserted his hand into the back of the dummy and made it move its head and its lips. It looked as though the dummy was answering the ventriloquist's questions.

Pleased with his nephew's amazing progress, Nobin's uncle gave him the money to have a dummy made. After a fortnight of deep thought about its appearance, Nobin came up with an unusual idea.

The dummy would look exactly like Akrur Chowdhury. In other words, he would extract his revenge by turning Akrur Chowdhury into a dummy under his control.

Nobin had carefully saved a photograph of Akrur Chowdhury's on a handbill. He showed it to Adinath Pal, the craftsman who would make the dummy. 'I want the same moustache, the same sleepy eyes, the same puffy cheeks.' What a laugh riot it would be when the dummy moves its lips and swivels its head, sitting on Nobin's lap. With luck Akrur Chowdhury would watch the performance some day.

The dummy was ready in a week. It was dressed like Akrur Chowdhury too, in a black bandgalla coat and a dhoti tucked in at the waist.

Nobin persuaded an acquaintance, Shashodhar Bose of Netaji Club, to organize a ventriloquism show for him. His debut was a hit. The dummy had been given a name meanwhile—Bhootnath, Bhuto for short. The audience had thoroughly enjoyed Nobin's conversation with Bhuto. Nobin was a fan of the Mohun Bagan Football Club and Bhuto, of its arch-rival East Bengal. The argument had been so heated that no one had noticed Bhuto saying 'Gohan Gagan' and 'East Gengal' constantly.

After this Nobin began to be invited to many programmes and even on television. He realized that he no longer had to worry about the future—that he had found his means for a livelihood.

⌒

Eventually, one day Nobin did meet Akrur Chowdhury.

He had moved out of Uttarpara three months earlier to rent a house on Mirzapur Street in Calcutta. The landlord, Suresh Mutsuddi, was an amiable man, who held Nobin in high esteem because of his fame. There was great demand amongst impresarios for Nobin now. Success had left a mark on his personality, with a new polish evident in his appearance and conversation.

Maybe Akrur-babu had been present at Nobin's performance at Mahajati Sadan, and had got his address from the organizers. That evening the conversation between Nobin and Bhuto had been on the underground railway.

'Did you know Calcutta is getting a tube rail, Bhuto?'

'Really? I had no idea.'

'What! You live in Calcutta and you haven't heard about the tube rail?'

Bhuto shook his head. 'No, but I've heard about the test tube rail.'

'Test tube rail?'

'Yes. A huge experiment in an enormous laboratory to find out how to dig up the entire city. What else is it but a test tube rail?'

Today, Nobin was writing a new script about power cuts. Power cuts, price rise, crowded buses—Nobin had realized that his audiences were entertained the most when these popular topics of discussion became part of his conversations with Bhuto. He was immersed in writing the lines when there was a knock on the door. When Nobin opened the door, he was disconcerted to find Akrur-babu standing outside.

'May I come in?'

'Of course.'

Nobin ushered in Akrur-babu and offered him his own chair. Akrur-babu didn't sit down. His eyes were on Bhuto. The dummy was perched in one corner on Nobin's desk.

Akrur-babu picked up the dummy and examined its face carefully. Nobin could not protest. It was true that he was feeling ill at ease, but he had certainly not forgotten being humiliated by Akrur-babu.

'So you've turned me into a dummy?'

Akrur-babu sat down.

'Why this desire?'

'You probably know why,' said Nobin. 'I came to you with a lot of expectations, which you shattered. But I will say this—it is your image that has brought me fame today. It's because of this dummy that I am earning a living.'

Akrur-babu had not taken his eyes off Bhuto yet. 'I don't know if you're aware of this,' he said, 'I had a show at Barasat the other day. Do you think it is pleasant to be greeted on stage by taunts of "Look, there's Bhuto!"? I may be helping you earn a living, but what about the fact that I am not able to earn a living because of you? Do you suppose I'm going to quietly accept that?'

It was evening. There was a power cut. Two candles were burning dimly in Nobin's room. In the faint light Nobin saw Akrur-babu's eyes gleaming just as they did on stage. The small man had cast a gigantic, swaying shadow on the wall. Bhootnath was perched on the desk with its sleepy eyes—inert, silent.

'Do you know that ventriloquism is not as far as my magic skills go? From the age of eighteen to thirty-eight, I served as an apprentice to an unknown but extraordinarily powerful magician of our land. Not in

Calcutta, but in an extremely remote spot in the foothills of the Himalayas.'

'Have you performed this magic on stage?'

'I have not. Because it is not meant to be performed on stage. I had promised my guru that I would not use this magic to make money. I have kept my word.'

'I don't understand what you're trying to tell me.'

'I only came to warn you. I have to say I'm pleased by your dedication. Just as I didn't teach you ventriloquism, nobody taught me either. Professional magicians never pass on their real skills to anyone. They never have. Magicians have to carve out their own path—just like you have. But I will not tolerate your impudence when it comes to the appearance you have chosen to give your dummy. That is all I came to tell you.'

Akrur-babu stood up. 'I had black hair and moustache all these years, but they have just begun to turn grey. I see you have anticipated this and given your dummy a few grey hairs already. All right, I shall go now.'

Akrur Chowdhury left.

Nobin closed the door and went up to Bhoothnath. Grey hair. Indeed. There were in fact a couple of grey hairs on Bhoothnath's head and moustache. Nobin had not noticed them earlier. Which was strange, for Bhuto sat on his lap during his act, and he always looked at Bhuto while talking to him. Nobin should certainly have noticed the grey hair earlier.

Anyway, he wasn't going to fret about it. Sometimes things just escaped one's attention—it happened to everyone. He was used to fixing his eyes on Bhuto's face, not on his hair.

Still, the uneasy feeling nagged him.

Nobin used a leather case to carry Bhuto around. The next day, he went to Adinath Pal in Chitpur, dummy in tow. He took Bhuto out of the case and placed him on the floor.

'Look at the grey hair on this dummy's head and in his moustache? Did you put them in?' he asked Adinath.

'What are you saying, sir?' said Adinath Pal in great surprise. 'You never asked for grey hair. I could easily have given you salt and pepper hair if you'd wanted. I have both kinds in stock, it's a matter of the customer's preference.'

'Couldn't a couple of grey hairs have got in by mistake?'

'Mistakes are always possible, sir. But wouldn't you have noticed when I delivered the dummy to you? You know what I think, sir, someone else must have done this without your knowledge.'

That's what it must be. Someone must have done it without telling Nobin.

⸜

Something unusual took place at the Chetla Friends' Club programme.

The proof of Bhuto's popularity was evident from the fact that the organizers saved Nobin's performance for the end. Bhuto and Nobin were engaged in a saucy exchange on power cuts. That was when Nobin observed that Bhuto wasn't following the script all the time. His responses included several difficult English words that Nobin never used. At best, he knew what they meant. This was a completely new experience for Nobin. Not that it did the performance any harm, because the words were used aptly, and the audience was appreciative. Fortunately they had no idea of the extent of Nobin's education.

But Nobin did not care for this unexpected application of English words. He felt that an invisible person was exerting his authority over him. After the performance, Nobin locked his door and placed Bhuto on his desk in front of the table lamp.

Had the mole on his forehead been there before? No, it was recent. Nobin had noticed Akrur-babu's mole for the first time the other day in his room. A tiny mole, it wasn't big enough to catch the eye. It could now be seen on Bhuto's forehead too.

And with it, something else. About a dozen new grey hairs. And dark circles beneath the eyes. There had been no dark circles before.

Nabin rose from his chair and began to pace up and down. He was feeling distinctly uneasy. He was a devotee of magic, but this was troubling him. The magic he believed in was the outcome of tricks performed by humans. As far as Nobin was concerned, the supernatural was not magic. It was something else altogether, something ominous. And there were signs of something ominous in these changes in Bhuto.

And yet, Bhuto appeared to be nothing but a dummy. Besides the sleepy eyes, a faint smile on his lips, and the movement of his head and arms which Nobin controlled, it was as inanimate and lifeless as a doll.

But still there were constant small changes in his appearance. And for some reason Nobin believed that the same changes were taking place in Akrur Chowdhury's appearance as well. He too was greying, there were dark circles beneath his eyes as well.

From the beginning, it had been Nobin's habit to practise his conversational technique with Bhuto.

'It's very humid, isn't it, Bhuto?'

'Yes, ghery hungid.'

'But you're lucky, you don't sweat.'

'I an a dunny, how will I sweat? Ha ha ha ha.'

Today a new question emerged unprompted from Nobin's lips.

'What's going on, Bhuto?'

The answer startled Nobin. 'Karnga, karnga.'

Karma!

It was Nobin who had given the answer as on stage, but without having the intention of saying any such thing. He had been made to say it. By whom? He had an inkling.

♪

That night Nobin ignored his servant Shibu's pleas and skipped dinner. He slept well enough at night, but he did not want to take any chances, so he took a sleeping pill. Around eleven o'clock he felt its effects creeping up on him. His eyes closed as soon as he put down his magazine and switched off the light.

His sleep was interrupted in the middle of the night.

Who had coughed?

Was it him? But he didn't have a sore throat. And yet for a while he had been hearing someone coughing

Nobin switched on the lamp.

Bhootnath was sitting inertly in the same place. But his body was bent forward and his right arm was folded, with the hand touching his chest.

Nobin glanced at his watch. 3.30. He heard the thud of the night guard's stick on the road. A dog was barking in the distance. An owl flew overhead, hooting harshly. Someone next door must have developed a cough. And the wind must have made Bhuto lean forward. Nobin's baseless apprehensions were completely out of place in this well-populated part of Calcutta's Mirzapur Street in the twentieth century.

Nobin switched off the lamp and soon fell asleep.

♪

The next day, Nobin had his first taste of failure at the annual programme of the Finley Recreation Club.

It was an elaborate programme in an enormous auditorium. As usual, his was the last item of the evening. Modern songs, elocution, Rabindrasangeet, a Kathak recital, and finally, Nobin's ventriloquism. He had done everything necessary to take care of his voice that morning. It was critical to keep his throat clear, for ventriloquism needed minute vocal control. He had checked that his voice was fine before going on stage. Even his first question to Bhuto had come out clearly. But disaster struck when Bhuto had to reply.

The answer would not reach the audience because suddenly he had lost his voice. But only when it came to playing Bhuto's role, for during his own questions his voice was clear.

'Louder please,' someone shouted from the back of the hall. Those in front were more polite, and did not boo, but Nobin knew they could not hear a word of Bhuto's answers.

After trying for a few minutes more, Nobin apologized and left the stage. This was the first time he had had such an embarrassing experience.

He did not accept his fees for the evening's performance. He couldn't possibly have accepted any money. But surely this terrifying situation could not last forever. Nobin was confident that things would soon return to normal.

It was the month of August. Stiflingly hot. And then this incident happened. By the time Nobin got home, it was 11 p.m. He felt ill. For the first time he was slightly mad with Bhuto, though he knew Bhuto was nothing but a dummy that he controlled. Bhuto's shortcoming was his shortcoming.

Nobin placed Bhuto at his usual place on the desk and opened the southern window. It was a Saturday and there would be a power cut, which meant the fan wouldn't work until midnight. There wasn't much of a breeze blowing, but some fresh air was welcome. He lit a candle. He froze at what he was seeing. There were beads of perspiration on Bhuto's forehead. Moreover, Bhuto's cheeks were no longer glowing, his skin had turned pale, and eyes red.

Nobin decided to inspect the dummy closely. He was determined to find out the many surprises and horrors that awaited him. But he couldn't take more than a couple of steps towards Bhuto. Something stopped him in his tracks.

Bhuto's chest was rising and falling gently under his coat.

Bhuto was breathing.

Was the dummy breathing? Yes, of course, it was. On this silent night, undisturbed by the sounds of traffic, two people could be heard breathing in Nobin's room.

A strangled cry emerged from Nobin's throat, possibly out of a combination of extreme terror and shock.

'Bhuto!'

And at once a disembodied scream flung Nobin backwards towards his bed.

'Not Bhuto! I am Akrur Chowdhury!'

Nobin was fully aware he had not said these words. It was the voice of the dummy. By some extraordinary magic Akrur Chowdhury had given it the power to speak. Nobin had wanted Akrur Chowdhury to be a dummy under his control. He had not wanted this. He couldn't possibly remain in the same room with this living dummy now. He would immediately…

But something happened.

All this while there had been the sound of two people breathing—had one of them stopped breathing?

Yes, exactly.

Bhuto wasn't breathing any more. There was no perspiration on the forehead. The eyes were no longer red. The dark circles beneath them had disappeared.

Bhuto's head could not be made to turn any more, his lips could not be made to move. The mechanism had jammed. Could the head be made to turn if Nobin applied a little more pressure?

When he did that Bhuto's head came apart from the body and fell on the desk.

᠅

The next morning Nobin met his landlord Suresh Mutsuddi on the stairs. 'What's this, you haven't shown me your magic act yet,' the landlord complained. 'Ventiklogium or whatever you call it.'

'I'm done with it,' said Nobin. 'I'm moving on to other kinds of magic now. I'll certainly perform for you since you're interested. But why do you ask suddenly?'

'I read in the papers that someone from your tribe has died. Akrur Chowdhury.'

'Really?' Nobin hadn't read the papers yet. 'What did he die of?'

'A heart attack,' said Suresh-babu. 'That's what 70 per cent of the people die of these days.'

Nobin knew that if he enquired, he would be told that the time of death was exactly ten past twelve at night.

The Moon is Back

ADRISH BARDHAN

The first report was published almost two years ago. Russia had fired powerful missiles at the moon. Not just one but several in succession. The missiles had caused explosions on the dark side of the moon, the one never seen from the earth. Several rockets and radio telescopes had sent back valuable data about them.

The second news item was published a year and eight months ago. It appeared in an insignificant corner of the newspaper, evading most people's eyes. But not mine because day and night I was engaged in this complex international research programme in a remote area of Mysore on whether we could send a pair of moons to the sky over Earth, just like Deimos and Phobos, the twin moons of Mars. So the news attracted my attention.

During the last solar eclipse, a strange phenomenon had been observed. The moon had arrived nine seconds later than the appointed time. The news was not sensational enough to have lasted in people's memory. Initially there was a heated debate over this in the scientific community of the West. We were all so caught up in our research work that we forgot about the incident.

Exactly a year later, on 1 October, a letter arrived from the British Lunar Society.

Dear Dr Dutta,

You must have noted the anomalous events of the solar eclipse last year. You are required to be in London to participate in an urgent discussion on the subject. Please do not delay your visit. Remember that the Earth is hurtling towards grave danger with every passing second. May I request you to keep the contents of this letter confidential and arrive in London before 9 October?

Yours sincerely,
Dr Percival

Percival was my assistant during my stint as the secretary of the Lunar Society in London. I was aware of the fact that he was not given to anxiety attacks without good reason. So I had postponed my research for a few days to fly to London.

⌒

There wasn't room for a fly in the crowded convention hall of 23/9 Shaftesbury Avenue near Covent Garden. The door was closed at the predetermined hour. Dr Percival took the stage.

Ladies and gentlemen,

I have invited all the members of the society to convey some extremely alarming news. I am pleased to see that practically all the members are present here. Before I make my statement, I have a request. The shattering news that you will hear today is completely secret. Therefore, please do not discuss it with anyone—not even your wife or husband. We are maintaining a high degree of caution in order to keep the public from panicking. Those who consider themselves unable to fulfil this request may leave the hall now.

Percival stopped. He scanned the countless faces, covered by hair both black and grey, running his eyes all the way to the back of the hall. But there was no sign of agitation amongst the motionless figures.

Taking a deep breath, Percival continued:

Thank you. My statement is a brief one. I trust all of you recollect the solar eclipse of 7 August last year. There was consternation in scientific facts over the observation that the moon had arrived nine seconds late for the eclipse.

Having delved into the records, the scientists decided to wait another year for more readings. They postponed discussions till after the eclipse of 17 July this year.

The observations have put it beyond dispute that this time the moon was delayed not by nine but seventeen seconds.

They have also determined the reason for the delay, and their conclusion appears so accurate that there is no room for doubt.

Some unknown force has pushed the moon out of the orbit along which it has been circling the Earth since its birth into a different trajectory.

As you know, the average distance between the Earth and the moon is 238,857 miles. By midnight on 17 July, the moon was 35,357 miles closer to the Earth.

Calculations show that the moon is covering approximately 800 miles every 24 hours in its journey towards the earth. And the closer it gets, the more the distance it covers every 24 hours.

Tonight at midnight, the moon will be 203,500 miles away from the Earth. And it will be another 850 miles closer by midnight tomorrow.

Following closed-door consultations with various international organizations we have decided not to announce these developments to the public at the moment.

Tonight is a full moon night in October. Scientists will see significant differences in the appearance of the moon, although these changes will not be discernible to the common man.

But the next full moon, in November, will see the moon appear even larger, for it will be 30,000 miles closer to Earth by then. It will not be possible to keep things hidden from the people thereafter.

At this point a man with a head of white hair jumped to his feet to ask, 'Have you not been able to work out why the moon has suddenly changed its trajectory from an orbit it has followed for 4.5 billion years?'

Percival was caught in a quandary. 'Look, there are several theories that can explain this mystery. But...'

'I can explain,' I stood up and announced gravely.

Countless surprised eyes were trained on me. A murmur spread from one end of the hall to the other. Someone shouted from the back row, 'We want to hear who is responsible for this cataclysm—is it nature or is it the Earth?'

I paused for a breath. 'What if I said it's the Earth?'

'The Earth!'

'Yes, the Earth. None of you could have forgotten the findings of our lunar research.'

I briefly described how several explosions had been engineered on the side of the moon that's shrouded in mystery.

'What does that prove?' asked the white-haired gentleman belligerently.

'In South America, an enormous 10,000-tonne rock is balanced on another one in such an extraordinary way that even a tap of a finger could send it rolling off. Is there any proof that the balance of the moon hanging in space has also not been destroyed in the same way? The side of the moon on which the explosions were engineered was the side from which the moon was more or less forced out of its orbit—towards the Earth.'

'I believe Dr Dutta's hypothesis is correct.' The speaker was Sir Herbert Jones, president of the British Astronomical Society. Lifting his deep voice above the murmurs, he said, 'As you know, the principle behind satellites dictates that the moon must return to the Earth one day. But there was no difference of opinion over the fact that this is not going to happen in less than ten million years. We humans have accelerated this process in the course of our quest for knowledge.' A sad smile spread across Sir Herbert's dignified face.

The white-haired gentleman asked devoutly, 'I get it, but what will be the outcome? If the moon does crash on the surface of the Earth, our planet will either be split into two by the impact, or be ejected from its orbit. Isn't that so?'

'That may not happen. Does the impact of a cherry on an orange harm the orange? The moon is nothing but a cherry in comparison with the dimensions of the Earth. But yes, there may be floods and tempests—all the signs of an apocalypse. Then again, nothing may happen.

'About a hundred years ago Roche had formulated a theory. As soon as the moon arrives within a certain distance of the Earth, the force of gravity will act on it to break it into pieces. As a result, the moon will create something very similar to Saturn's Rings around the Earth. It will be visible every night like the giant tail of a comet.'

I had to stand up again since no one was asking the most important question. 'But what if that does not happen? Have we calculated the date when the moon is likely to crash on the Earth?'

An uneasy silence descended on the room. The very air seemed to be throbbing with anxiety. Countless questioning eyes were trained on Percival.

He wasn't perturbed at all. With a steady hand he wiped his glasses and said, 'The moon, our nearest neighbour, is scheduled to fall on the surface of the Earth around 8.40 p.m. GMT on 4 May next year.'

∿

I will not bother with a detailed explanation of how the seven intervening months passed. Rumours began to fly in November. In December, the

United Nations announced the imminent catastrophe. Many underground steel vaults had been constructed during World War II. Thousands of underground chambers modelled on them began to be constructed around the world. But the public were terrified about the impending doom. If 4 May was the last day, what was the point of living according to the tenets of religion and the hypocritical rules of society? Social structures broke down, and revolutions broke out. Amidst this worldwide anarchy, the moon grew bigger and bigger. Its gentle glow gave way to a dazzling, blinding glare. Furious storms and destructive tides began as nature extracted its incredible cruel revenge.

Finally the moment came—8.40 p.m. GMT 4 May. The Earth had already been devastated. Black clouds hung low in the air. An unbearable sultriness made it difficult to breathe. A devastating cyclone sprang up. My laboratory was located on one side of a hill. But the violence of the storm suggested that a heartless nature was intent on plucking out the entire hill and tossing it away.

Then the fury of the storm abated as suddenly as it had begun. I don't know how long I had been sitting there overwhelmed. The warning bells of the apocalypse had numbed my senses and made me unaware of the microseconds and nanoseconds.

All of a sudden the air in the room seemed to explode. Something seemed to have burst within the laboratory…in silence the windowpanes shattered into pieces…. I did not hear the glass shatter nor the rustle of the papers on the desk being blown away through the window…

I began to gasp for breath. My lungs seemed ready to collapse for lack of oxygen. It took me less than a moment to understand what had happened. The Earth had lost its atmosphere. And so the air in the room had escaped, breaking the windowpanes with its force. And in the absence of air, there was nothing to carry the sound of the glass breaking.

I stood up with great effort, my legs trembling uncontrollably, my eyes radiating the boundless fear of death. With whatever little oxygen was left in my lungs, I dragged my half-conscious body to the door of the adjoining room. I entered a specially prepared, oxygen-filled chamber and locked the door behind me. I used my remaining strength to seal the gap below the door before slumping unconscious to the floor.

When I regained consciousness, the unbearable silence around me was like nothing I had ever experienced. I unsealed the door slightly—but no, the air in the chamber was not rushing out. I hesitated for a few moments before gathering my courage and flinging open the door.

Yes, the atmosphere was back on the Earth. The air was not as pure as before, it held a whiff of sulphur, but still it was air. I filled my lungs with it. I glanced at my watch. It was 9.30.

The scheduled time for the collision was 8.40. So I had not died. The Earth had not been smashed into smithereens flying off into space. The third planet in the solar system had survived by some miracle.

I was ecstatic. I rushed to open the front door. I was transfixed by the scene that lay before me. I heard the gentle lapping of waves. Before my eyes was a gigantic sheet of water, staring at me out of the darkness. My laboratory was 2,000 feet above sea level and 300 miles from the coast. But some magic had brought the ocean almost to my doorstep. Even the tallest trees on the horizon were submerged. And the water was rising constantly. Another 500 feet at most—if it did not stop before that, everything around me would vanish into the watery grave of the advancing ocean.

I have written this account by candlelight. I do not know why I have. Perhaps as an acknowledgement of the supreme failure of science and of the irresistible will of the maker of the universe. After the floods have receded, perhaps all those who have taken shelter in the countless underground chambers around the world would be witnesses to the dreadful fate of the Earth. I am writing this tale for their benefit. The pace at which the black water is rising makes it clear I do not have long to live.

If someone in the near future wishes to know what happened to the moon, let me tell them. The moon has returned to Mother Earth. It has taken shelter beneath an ocean somewhere—and these vast waters signify the celebration of this homecoming. Like a spring, the deep waters absorbed the violent impact of the moon falling diagonally into the ocean. But, overflowing as a result of this enormous object falling into the seas, the rising columns of water have probably claimed the entire planet.

Saradindu and This Body

GOBINDOLAL BANDYOPADHYAY

Saradindu won't return. He hasn't come back to see me ever since he left. I also know that I will not get my old life back even for a fleeting moment.

The place where I have been put now is not remotely pleasant for other people. It is unfit for normal, healthy people to live in. It's a tiny, darkness-infested coop. The only window is high up on the wall, near the ceiling, and barred. The solitary door is made of steel. It is locked and no light or air can pass through it. I am imprisoned within these four walls.

That door will open very soon to let in two or perhaps three people. Their grave expressions will not slip for even a moment. There will be no hint of a welcome from me amidst an air of uncertainty. For these determinedly grim individuals have been visiting me almost every day. They interrogate me about my reasons for deliberately creating fissures in my own personality.

I fume with impotent fury and venomous agony at times, the blood pounding uncontrollably in my head. I take deep breaths to calm myself. For the answers to their questions are not unknown to me.

Unfettered, overactive imagination. Introspection. A change of course from thwarted emotions. And so much more.

Saradindu—I wasn't like this before. Through the crystal-clear glass of my memory I can now see the past clearly. I got married far too early, while still a student. I had only just passed my ISC examinations. It was on my teenage wife's request that I enrolled at the Medical College, following her advice to move to the college hostel in Calcutta to study. Even before I could make Sharmistha my beloved, I was victim to the pain of separation that tore me apart.

So many evenings ended with the bleakness of the night. How my thoughts of Sharmistha swirled from a distance of two and fifty miles. How many times did I tell myself, let me go and meet her. But I did not dare flout my father's orders. I did not have the confidence to ignore my wife's request.

It's just as well that Sharmistha has died. I learnt to hate her. I still do.

My youth was dying a slow death under the unstoppable deluge of time. Sharmistha took such a long time to die. I was a well-known psychologist by then. Living under the restraints of principles and ethics, I was forced to let my life flow along a predefined channel. But I was like a wounded soldier, surviving somehow, withdrawing deep within myself.

Sharmistha took far too long to die. If it had been a little earlier I might have had the time to savour a new freedom. My life might have taken a different turn. How could I claim that I would not have experienced all over again the elation of blood flowing in my veins?

I did not charge any fees to patients who came only for advice at a specified hour on Saturday afternoons. It was during this period that Sharmistha had died in a car crash. I did not see patients for money on Saturdays.

I believe that psychologists have to keep their minds clear before they attempt to solve other people's problems. Which was why I had immersed myself in work after Sharmistha's death so I could bury the grief of losing her.

It was in the middle of my time of mourning that Saradindu had arrived one day. A fine-looking man, lithe and tall, with a head of unkempt hair. He was dressed in pyjamas and shirt with the sleeves rolled up.

My new patient entered the chamber hesitantly. He stopped abruptly after taking a few steps and looked around suspiciously.

I didn't find his presence pleasant. With my eyes I indicated the chair opposite mine.

There was no one but Saradindu and me in the chamber.

Finally, he began to talk calmly and smoothly, 'I wouldn't have had this opportunity if your receptionist Mrs Gupta hadn't made the arrangements. I've heard that your fame as a…'

He stopped midway, deliberately.

I replied modestly, 'I don't know if I have all the qualities you've heard of. As a matter of fact I'm a human being, just like you.'

'Oh yes!' Smashing his fist lightly on the desk, he said with an air of agreement, 'You're absolutely right.'

Saradindu wasn't wrong. There were some similarities in our appearances, but I was slightly older than he was. My hair had thinned, and I was balding at the back. I probably did not have the courage to follow my whims, as he seemed to.

'You haven't told me your name yet,' I said.

'Saradindu Sanyal,' he answered, leaning back in his chair. 'You must call me Saradindu. I've heard a lot about your achievements already from Mrs Gupta. You have solved many people's problems.'

'Not exactly,' I said. 'Everyone should solve their own problems. My task is to help understand the real problem.'

'What a clever man! I do the dirty work and you receive a fee.'

The mockery in Saradindu's voice was palpable. But I was not the least bit upset. 'I don't accept fees at this time on this day of the week,' I replied calmly. 'I'm sure the receptionist has told you as much. Do you think you've ever been deceived by anyone, Saradindu?'

Saradindu frowned at me without replying.

'I probably won't be able to help you unless you answer my question,' I said with urgency in my voice.

'You won't be able to help me even if you try,' Saradindu said helplessly. 'No one can. I have realized my problem only too well.'

'Why can't we discuss it?'

'I'm afraid, doctor. If this force within me cannot be stopped, I might do something wrong.'

'What do you mean by wrong?' I was curious.

Saradindu curled his fingers like a beast and cracked his knuckles with great force. Drawing a deep breath, he said, 'I wish I could tear someone apart with these hands.'

'Everyone experiences this kind of desire to some extent, Saradindu. It isn't right to consider yourself abnormal because of it. By the way, have you ever assaulted anyone?'

'No, not yet. But...'

'Go on, don't stop.'

'I've become drawn to other people's things. I steal them. But it would be unfair to say it's out of need. I'm compelled by some irresistible force.'

'What sort of things do you steal?'

'Things that pretty women like. She was very beautiful too.'

I asked Saradindu whether he ever thought about his own state of mind while actually committing the thefts. I knew that the nature of the objects stolen sometimes held a clue to the reasons for stealing. But Saradindu changed the subject instead of answering my question. 'I'm not worried about this, doctor.'

'Do you accept that theft is the first step on the downward journey?'

'I do it out of compulsion,' said Saradindu. 'You know what, doctor? I've had to withstand two massive blows.'

'Blows!'

'Yes. Related to the heart.'

Saradindu stood up suddenly. In a calm voice he said, 'Since you don't accept fees on Saturday I'd better not waste your time. If I can come to terms with myself this will be my last visit. Goodbye.'

He left through the swing door without giving me a chance to respond.

Manjusree Gupta, my receptionist, came in a little later.

Manjusree was an intelligent young woman. She'd been working for me for about a year. She was about twenty-two or twenty-three.

A polite, well-behaved woman, she never gave in to uncontrolled displays of emotion. Her kohl-darkened eyes were grave, their depths holding a strange attraction.

'Miss Ghosh Chowdhury has requested you to visit her at home tomorrow morning, doctor.' Manjusree's voice was gentle.

'Did she ring?'

She nodded.

'Very well, I'll go.'

As she was about to leave, I said, 'Are there any other patients, Mrs Gupta?'

'Yes sir, two.'

'Serious cases?'

'One of them is schizophrenic…'

'I have a splitting headache, that last patient talked so much…' I cut her off, rubbing my temples.

I didn't finish what I was saying. Deliberately.

'Why blame the head?' Manjusree chided me, smiling. 'Let me get you an aspirin.' She went out.

Manjusree was an unusual receptionist. She kept a close watch on me. Sometimes I really enjoyed this. Despite being a trained nurse, she had absolutely no vanity about herself.

'Doctor.'

Her voice returned me to the present. I looked at her. She was waiting with two aspirins and a glass of water. I took the medicines as instructed by her and gave her the empty glass back.

'I'm thinking of leaving a little early today, doctor,' said Manjusree.

'Why?' I asked.

A little embarrassed, she answered, 'We haven't planned anything. So we didn't invite you. Mrinal and my…'

'Wedding anniversary,' I said. 'Of course. How quickly a year has gone by…'

My mind began to wander.

'No, just six months,' said Manjusree. 'It may seem strange to you, but then six months is not a short time.'

I laughed suddenly. Not in my head, but loudly. It sounded discordant, even to my own ears. I stopped and proclaimed wisely, 'You're right. How many happy couples are there in the world anyway.'

I had thought Saradindu wouldn't come back. But he appeared in my chamber again on that special day of the week.

His clothes were dishevelled, his hair rumpled. A duffel bag hung from his shoulder.

He put the bag on my desk and sat down heavily in his chair.

'What's the matter?' I asked. 'How are you?'

'Terrible,' he replied. 'I'm all but finished.'

'What do you mean!' It was my turn to be surprised.

Saradindu was petrified. His limbs seemed frozen. 'Open the bag, doctor. Take out everything.'

I was curious so I opened the bag. A heap of saris and blouses piled up on the desk.

'What are you going to do with all this?' I asked him.

Saradindu sat up in his chair. Agitatedly he said, 'I feel poison in my veins, doctor. Some strange frenzy is eating through my brain like a worm. I've begun stealing things again.'

I was not surprised. But my eyes grew alert and my brow creased.

Saradindu rested his elbows on the arm of the chair and cupped his chin in his palm. His voice wavering with doubt and exhaustion, he asked, 'Will I never get well, doctor?'

Smiling at him reassuringly, I said, 'Why not? Control yourself, Saradindu. You'll never find peace by alienating yourself. You need self-control. Don't bring ruin upon yourself to forget your pain.'

Suddenly Saradindu clutched my arm and said in a wheedling tone, 'That's what I'm here for, doctor. The addresses of the houses I stole all these from are all in that bag. Please have them sent back. I give you my word that I will never steal again.'

I agreed even though I knew it wouldn't be easy. It would be extremely irksome to answer the questions that I was going to be confronted by in the course of returning these stolen things. Which was why I stuffed everything back in the duffel bag and put the bag away in the steel almirah in my chamber.

But Manjusree caught me out. She discovered the bag and its contents one day.

The next morning she asked me directly, 'I saw a duffel bag in the almirah, Dr Mukherjee. I saw the things in it. What's going on? Why are these things here?'

I explained everything to her in detail, but without mentioning Saradindu by name. Laughing, she said, 'I've never heard of such a funny theft.'

'You might find it funny,' I told her seriously, 'but I am sure this patient is afflicted by mental conflicts. I do feel bad for him.'

⏜

Saradindu had followed my instructions exactly. He did not indulge his impulse to steal.

Two weeks later, I was busy at work. As I was about to ring the bell to indicate to Manjusree that she should send the next patient in, Saradindu barged in like an embodiment of chaos.

Throwing himself into the chair opposite mine, he held out a wad of ten-rupee notes. 'I don't need advice today, make arrangements for my treatment.'

'Is this my fee?' I asked.

Saradindu nodded. 'Fifty rupees, isn't it?'

'Yes, you should have paid in advance and made an appointment with Manjusree, Saradindu.'

'There was no time. Anyway, I'll pay it where I have to.' Returning the money to his pocket, Saradindu said, 'I've bought a pair of binoculars, doctor. I am deeply attracted to beautiful married women. All the pretty wives around my third floor balcony…'

'I realize your wife was beautiful too,' I interrupted him. 'But why must you nurture the pain of losing her even now?'

'The agony is unbearable, doctor. Yesterday afternoon I sat on the park bench opposite your chamber looking at your Manjusree through my binoculars. She was drinking a cup of tea and scribbling in her notebook. You have to admit she's pretty.'

'Manjusree is married,' I told him a serious voice. 'Her husband is the cashier in a merchant office. They are a happy couple. I'd prefer it if you didn't cast your eyes on her.'

'I want her, doctor,' said Saradindu calmly.

'Saradindu!' I shouted at him.

He wasn't the least bit upset. Nonchalantly he said, 'I didn't say anything wrong. I've fallen deeply in love with Manjusree.'

'There are plenty of other women. Pick one of them, marry her and try to be happy.'

'What if I wrote to her about how I feel?'

'I'll have no choice but to go to the police.'

'I understand, doctor, I understand everything.' Saradindu rose to his feet. 'You don't want to cure me. You want to enjoy my predicament. Fine, you don't have to treat me. Here's your fee.'

He threw down five ten-rupee notes on the table and left.

I was seething with rage. My first instinct was to inform the police and close Saradindu's case. I even dialled the police headquarter number, and someone answered. But I didn't say anything. Instead, I decide to meet Saradindu once more before taking a decision.

I was certain he would be back.

‿

Two days later I found a letter addressed to Manjusree in the office letterbox. She had never received a letter here. In a fit of curiosity I opened the envelope and extracted a sheet of blue notepaper. A love letter from Saradindu to Manjusree.

My forehead creased with worry, while my lips curled in hateful contempt. I shredded the letter and the envelope to pieces.

There was another letter three days later.

From Saradindu, to Manjusree. The same thing.

I didn't tell Manjusree.

The Moving Shadow

After this there was a letter every day.

I read them, tore them up, and burnt with pure rage and hatred for Saradindu.

Saradindu appeared on Saturday afternoon. The last patient had just left. I was thinking of leaving as well when he parted the swing doors and entered.

'How are you, Saradindu?' I said. 'You must have taken a decision by now about all that we have discussed.'

Saradindu came up to me. Instead of taking a seat, he kept standing. 'Yes, I see a ray of light,' he said. 'You won't have any more complaints from me, Dr Mukherjee.'

My brow furrowed. 'I don't quite understand, Saradindu.'

'Once I've taken responsibility for Manjusree you'll see me a changed man,' he said, 'my mental illness will be gone.'

'There's still time to correct your mistakes, Saradindu...'

'I didn't come to you for advice, doctor,' he interrupted me. 'I sent her letters every day but she hasn't replied to a single one. I can see that she's willing. Send for her...'

A fire of determination burnt in Saradindu's voice as he issued his order.

I felt hopeless. 'That's impossible,' I stammered. 'Breaking a home to...'

'Perhaps. I'm quite strong physically. As you know, to the victor the spoils.' Softening his tone as much as possible, Saradindu said, 'I want to live, doctor, I want to live. There's no meaning in destroying myself bit by bit.'

Suddenly he pressed the bell on my desk. A wave of sound rose in the air. I couldn't stop him.

Manjusree entered a few moments later.

'Yes, doctor?' Manjusree asked.

'Come closer.'

Manjusree didn't demur.

Saradindu went up to her, stopping only when he was face to face with her.

'Manju!'

Manju looked askance.

Suddenly clutching her hand, Saradindu said, 'What pleasure do you get from tormenting me this way, Manju?'

Freeing her hand with a jerk, Manjusree stared at him, protesting vehemently. 'What on earth are you saying?'

'I'm not saying anything wrong, believe me. I want you as my own. Fill the emptiness in my life, Manju.'

'Have you gone mad?' Manjusree made to leave.

Grabbing the end of her sari, Saradindu said harshly, 'So you dare turn down my plea for your love?'

'Yes, I abhor the idea of talking to a madman. Let me go, let me go at once.'

A violent desperation took hold of Saradindu at that moment. His face turning grotesque with anger, he squeezed Manjusree's throat with both his hands.

'What...what are you doing?' A strangled cry escaped Manjusree's swollen lips.

'I'm doing what's right. After all these years of agony of not having anyone, I'm not going to tolerate rejection now. I'm dead anyway, why should you live happily?'

Struggling for air, Manjusree uttered just one word, 'Doctor...'

A flash of astonishment ran though me. Manjusree was not addressing Saradindu, she was addressing me. Why me?

'Dr Mukherjee, you're killing...' Manjusree ran out of words.

I seemed to find myself finally. Letting go of Manjusree, I looked around the chamber. No, there was no one else.

I glanced at the carpeted floor.

Manjusree's dead body lay at my feet.

So I was not a spectator, I was an actor. Why would I have played Saradindu's role if our illnesses weren't identical?

Saradindu didn't come today.

Foreshadowed

BHABANI MUKHOPADHYAY

The phone rang again. Hemanga quickly rose to his feet to take the call.

'Why do you jump up whenever the phone rings? Where's the rush?'

Throwing a probing look at Madhobi, he went out to take the call. But Madhobi kept sitting, quiet and unmoving. Only her lips were slightly parted as she tried to follow the conversation with great concentration, even though it was impossible to hear what the other person was saying.

Returning to his seat, Hemanga lit a cigarette and said, 'That was the clocksmith. He's saying it's the weekend tomorrow and day after, and then Eid. He can't fix the clock till Tuesday.'

Hemanga was a well-built man, something of a misfit in an ordinary Bengali family. His hair was thinning in front but his flowing locks at the back caught the eye.

His eyes seemed to be blazing when he turned to Madhobi.

'You don't look like a Hastings Street attorney, you know,' Madhobi told him. 'You're more like a mounted policeman. Or like their horses— perfectly capable of raring up on your hind legs, provided trouble erupts, of course.'

Hemanga looked at her in surprise. How strange her demeanour, how peculiar her conversation. No one would imagine that she was head over heels in love.

'But you simply won't tell me why you're so restless whenever the phone rings,' Hemanga said harshly. 'You seem to be waiting to hear from someone, Madhobi. What's going on?'

'Don't be silly.'

After a moment of silence, Hemanga continued brusquely, 'There must be a reason, you can't fool me. I insist you tell me.'

Madhobi kept sitting, pressing her fingertips to her temples. Then she said softly, 'I didn't tell you earlier—I wasn't sure what you'd think, you might think I've gone mad, but the dream—ohhh…'

'What dream?' asked Hemanga, his voice steady.

Madhobi held her pose for some time. Then, fixing her gaze on the table, she said, as though speaking to herself, 'It sounds almost preposterous. Early this morning I dreamt that Nilu was sitting by my bed. I asked him, "Where did you come from at this hour, Nilu?" He said, "I'm dead, didibhai. I died at midnight." I was heartbroken. Maybe it's nothing but my imagination, a mere dream, but I can't help thinking I saw him clearly, he was sitting in front of me just as you are now. I turned around to see you sleeping soundly.' After a pause Madhobi continued, 'Nilu also said that I would find out this morning that it's true, there would be a trunk-call from Delhi to say my younger brother had died.'

Hemanga looked at her. He was speechless—what was Madhobi talking about, what was the matter with her? He reassured her, 'All right, but it's almost ten now, there's been no phone call. And suppose...', Hemanga hesitated for a moment, 'Nilu has been ill for a while, I know you are very close to him but you must accept the truth, you've been warned that this could happen a long time now. If this tragic incident has indeed occurred...'

Madhobi gazed at the table and said, 'You're right, but there was something else that Nilu said in the dream. You know what he said...' Madhobi looked directly at Hemanga before saying clearly, 'Nilu warned me that I too would be dead after midnight tonight...'

'What do you mean, after midnight tonight?' exclaimed Hemanga. 'What nonsense! How many times have I told you to stop reading those absurd ghost and detective stories? You never listen.'

Madhobi's voice was low but sharp. 'No, I will die too,' she shrieked. 'It's just a matter of a few hours now.' She cast a fearful look at the clock before bursting into tears.

For a moment Hemanga felt a wave of sympathy, he wanted to touch her and comfort her. But instead, he took a cigarette case out of his pocket and flipped it open. Then he said, softening, 'Look, I don't know if you're imagining all this, but even if you're not, it's still a dream. And if it's a dream it's only a bad dream. There's no point worrying about a bad dream, you must forget it, learn to forget it. What's the use of brooding over it?'

Still in a trance, Madhobi said, 'Nilu said that I will know that he is telling the truth when the news reaches me. That his warning was in fact true.

'What nonsense,' said Hemanga, 'nothing will be proven. You knew your brother was seriously ill, he had been suffering for a long time. You're an educated woman, Madhobi, surely you know siblings sometimes communicate this way. It's called telepathy, you get to know what's happening elsewhere.'

Moving away from the window, Hemanga put his hand gently on Madhobi's head. He tried to console her, 'Think about it carefully, Madhobi. How can we believe this ghostly message in our Bright Street house in the year 1955? It's easier to walk with your head on the floor and feet pointing to the ceiling. Such things do not happen. And besides, Nilu loves you too much to frighten you this way. Come on now, on your feet, get your work done, enjoy life. Do you hear me?'

Hemanga noticed that Madhobi was trembling. He gripped her shoulders to give her some strength, some courage. He was finally ready to believe that the story about the dream was not a figment of her imagination. A few moments ago, he had thought Madhobi was putting on an act to confound him.

Madhobi pulled herself together and said, 'Very well, maybe you're right. I'm the one who's confusing things. Perhaps the dream was just a symptom of a psychological problem.'

The phone rang again a little later.

Madhobi buried her face in her hands. Hemanga rushed to answer the phone. It was some time before he came back. Madhobi looked at him and asked, 'That was from Delhi, wasn't it? So Nilu is gone.'

Hemanga nodded. He was absolutely quiet now. All the things he had been laughing at all this while had been proven to be cruelly true.

Hemanga was dumbstruck with horror. Still he tried to mumble something comforting about telepathy.

He decided not to go to work and spend the day with Madhobi. But she objected vehemently. Eventually she said, 'I might find some peace if I'm by myself, I'll feel better that way, let me be alone for some time.'

Before leaving Hemanga said gravely, 'Honestly, I feel awful about making fun of you. I shouldn't have said what I said about the phone call.'

'So what, it doesn't matter, these things happen,' said Madhobi coldly.

She rushed to the phone as soon she heard Hemanga's car driving away. She broke down in tears the moment someone answered her call. 'What's the matter?' the voice asked tenderly. 'You have to tell me.'

Madhobi managed to tell the whole story somehow as she choked on her tears. She stopped in between because she was hurt by the response to what she was saying. But she added some details of the dream that she had not told Hemanga.

'When Nilu was sitting on my bed, Pratul, I asked him, what's the point of warning me if what will happen is inevitable? Is there any way to be safe, I asked him. Nilu said, "There's no such thing as no, there's certainly an escape route. If you're very careful you can avoid your destiny. You might save your life that way." But then he looked at me miserably and said, "But Madhu the way you're obsessed with Pratul, I doubt you'll get a reprieve so easily."'

Madhobi fell silent, listening attentively to what the voice on the other side was telling her. Then she said faintly, 'I can tell there's no escape this time, Pratul, if a half of the dream has come true the other half is bound to come true as well. No one can save me. Pratul, our...'

Pratul said, 'Nonsense, what rubbish is all this. Please be strong my darling, this is no time to let yourself be so weak.'

'No Pratul, it's not entirely nonsense,' Madhobi said fiercely. 'I noticed this morning that he has become very suspicious, he's been saying nasty things. I ignored them. He even suggested that I was eagerly waiting for a phone call from a lover. What will he say next?'

'Oh my God, is that what's been going on?'

'Yes, which is why I believe what Nilu said can't be dismissed.'

'But Madhobi,' said Pratul, 'assume Nilu's right, but the whole thing is still implausible. Let's say Hemanga comes to know about us. Are you saying he will kill you?'

'I don't know what he will do or not do. All I know is that I'm afraid, terribly afraid. Let's not meet today. It's best not to meet till the danger has passed. Nilu's prophecy may not be fulfilled if we don't meet today. You can call it self-sacrifice. Nilu had said, you might not be able to control yourself considering the state you're in. I'm not coming over today then...'

After a long argument, Pratul finally agreed. 'But promise me, Madhobi, that you won't worry about this any more. You won't even think of it. I'll ring you after midnight.'

'Okay, do that, Pratul, ring me after midnight, but before a quarter past twelve. I'll know then that the danger has passed and you'll also know everything is all right.'

'But...' Pratul was about to ask a question.

'There's nothing to worry about,' said Madhobi quickly, 'he's dead to the world as soon as he goes to bed. He sleeps that way every night, and moreover today's Saturday, he'll go to the club, you can imagine, he'll barely be in his senses. Ring me immediately after midnight. You'd better be the one to ring. If he's awake, I'll say it's a wrong number.'

Dinner was long over. Hemanga had gone to bed a while ago. Madhobi was sitting quietly in front of the dressing table, looking at herself in the mirror. It had taken a lot of effort to send Hemanga to bed. He had refused steadfastly before relenting, 'You'd better go to bed too, no need to sew tonight, you've been upset all day, you need the rest,' he said.

Madhobi hadn't responded.

Hemanga had asked her again, 'Are you sure you're all right?'

He had gone to bed knowing that there were tears in her eyes. Finally Madhobi was beginning to feel some relief. Nothing had happened after all, midnight was not far away, what could harm her now? Just because the first half of the dream had come true, it didn't mean the second half had to as well. Maybe she would fly to Delhi tomorrow if she felt well. She couldn't very well erase all thoughts of Nilu from her mind. Going up to the window, she drew the curtains. There was a tiny garden just below. With many seasonal flowers blooming, it looked like an indistinct carpet in the dim light.

So near and yet so far. If only she could fly out through the window, if only she had wings, how wonderful that would have been. Madhobi would have ignored Hemanga's scowl and flown away, merging into the clouds on the distant horizon.

But what were all these mad thoughts? Why did she need wings? If there was indeed a falling out she always had the front door, and the wide road beyond it.

Madhobi was feeling much better now, so much so that she began to laugh in her head at her own wild thoughts.

Amidst the silence she heard an unfamiliar sound, exquisite in its resonance. At first Madhobi could not identify it. Then she remembered that these were the sounds the clock on the staircase wall made before it started ringing. Then the hours began to ring—one, two, three…

Madhobi listened closely. It stopped after twelve. Still she waited. She wanted to be sure that it was past twelve.

She sat for a long time, resting her forehead on the back of her palm. She had passed the evil hour and entered a new life, she had escaped a crisis. The danger is over, she told herself repeatedly.

Wearing a triumphant expression, she tiptoed to Hemanga's side of the bed before moving away to the telephone and sat down in front of it, so that she could answer as soon as it rang. In her head she counted the minutes—one, two, all the way to seven, eight. She couldn't wait any longer. Picking up the receiver stealthily, she gave Pratul Lahiri's number to the operator in a trembling voice.

'Hello,' came the response after a long time.

'What's the matter with you?' complained Madhobi. 'It's long past midnight, past twelve-fifteen too. Why haven't you called?'

'What! It can't possibly by a quarter past twelve yet, it's just a quarter to, your clock must be running fast.'

Suddenly there was a rustle behind Madhobi. Startled, she looked around fearfully to discover Hemanga standing there in silence, wearing rubber slippers. His eyes were distraught.

'Oh, you've been eavesdropping,' said an agitated Madhobi.

Flinging the receiver away, Madhobi stormed out of the room. Hemanga followed her, she could hear his footsteps. Madhobi went directly to the window, her body shaking with fear. She climbed onto the windowsill and launched herself into space.

'Madhobi! Madhobi!' Hemanga screamed. But her body was sprawled on the seasonal flowers even before he could reach the window.

In the distance, the clock in the police station rang twelve.

Acknowledgements

Grateful acknowledgement is made to the following copyright holders for permission to reprint copyrighted material in this volume.

'Parashar Barma Makes a Bid' by Premendra Mitra. Reprinted by permission of Mrinmoy Mitra.

'The Moving Shadow' by Swapan Kumar. Reprinted by permission of Dev Sahitya Kutir Pvt. Ltd.

'The Secret Agent' by Vikramaditya. Reprinted by permission of Dey's Publishing.

'Copotronic Love' by Muhammed Zafar Iqbal. Reprinted by permission of Prof Dr Zafar Iqbal.

'Bhuto' by Satyajit Ray. Reprinted by permission of Sandip Ray.

'The Moon is Back' by Adrish Bardhan. Reprinted by permission of Patra Bharati.

'Saradindu and This Body' by Gobindolal Bandyopadhyay. Reprinted by permission of Patra Bharati.

While every effort has been made to trace copyright holders and obtain permission, this has not been possible in all cases; any omissions brought to our attention will be remedied in future editions of this book.

Notes on the Contributors

Premendra Mitra (1904–1988) was a novelist, short story writer, poet, scriptwriter and film director of the 'Kallol' era in Bengali literature. He also wrote thrillers, fairy tales, ghost stories and science fiction, and was associated with the journal *Kalikalam*. Born in Varanasi and brought up in Uttar Pradesh, he later lived in Dhaka and Calcutta. He created the beloved children's book character, Ghanada. He was awarded the Sahitya Akademi Award, the Rabindra Puraskar and the Padma Shri, among many other honours.

Swapan Kumar (1927–2001) was an Indian Bengali writer, doctor and astrologer. Born as Samarendra Nath Pandey, he wrote fiction under the pen name of Swapan Kumar. He created the popular detective character Dipak Chatterjee and wrote hundreds of works of pulp detective fiction. He also wrote books on astrology under the pseudonym 'Jyotishi Sribhrigu' and several medical books under the name of 'Dr S. N. Pandey'.

Vikramaditya (1924–1995) was the pen name of Ashok Gupta, who wrote a number of thrillers using this pseudonym. His novels feature spies, double agents, killers, state intrigue and figures from 'high society'. He started his career as a journalist and later joined the Indian Foreign Service. His last posting before retirement was at the Indian embassy in Paris.

Muhammed Zafar Iqbal is one of the pioneers of science fiction in Bengali literature. A physicist by profession, he also wrote several non-fiction books on physics and mathematics. His first story, 'Copotronic Bhalobasha', was published in a local weekly magazine, *Bichitra* while he was still in university. He has written more than a hundred fictional works and his autobiography *Rongin Choshma* was published in 2007. He has been honoured with the Bangla Academy Literary Award (2004) and the National ICT Award in 2017.

Satyajit Ray (1921–1992) was born in Calcutta, and educated in the city and later at Visva-Bharati in Santiniketan. He worked at an advertising firm, and started illustrating books and designing covers. He made his first film, *Pather Panchali*, in 1955, which won several international prizes, including at the Cannes Festival. It is the first part of Ray's famed Apu trilogy. He was also a well-known writer, and created the popular characters Feluda and Professor Shonku. He revived *Sandesh*, a magazine that had been founded by his grandfather. In 1992, he won an honorary Oscar, and was awarded the Bharat Ratna.

Adrish Bardhan is one of the most notable names among West Bengal's sci-fi writers. Under the pen name of Akash Sen, Bardhan was the editor of *Ashchorjo*, the first Bengali science fiction magazine. Later, Bardhan was the editor of the magazine *Fantastic*.

Gobindolal Bandyopadhyay was a prolific writer and editor of pulp fiction. He launched *Gobindalal Bandyopadhyay's Mystery Magazine* in 1953, modelled on western publications like *Alfred Hitchcock's Mystery Magazine* and *Ellery Queen's Mystery Magazine*. Bandyopadhyay wrote under a number of pseudonyms, including Samudra Gupta, S. Madanmohan, Ranjan Roy and Anupama Sen.

Bhabani Mukhopadhyay (1909–1991) was a government employee by profession, who wrote a number of novels and was also a prolific translator into Bengali. He also wrote several biographies of Indian and international writers.